Do You Know Who I Am?

L.R. Thomas

PublishAmerica
Baltimore

First printing

At the specific preference of the author, PublishAmerica allowed this work to remain exactly as the author intended, verbatim, without editorial input.

ISBN: 1-4241-5809-5
PUBLISHED BY PUBLISHAMERICA, LLLP
www.publishamerica.com
Baltimore

Printed in the United States of America

THIS NOVEL IS DEDICATED TO:

Nigel and John who were my guardian angels in Canada.

Mystyn, my daughter, and Randall who helped me begin over again.

Perry and Amber, my adopted step brother and niece, who brought me such laughter and joy and made me realize life is so worth living.

And I can never forget Michael and Colt, my sons.

I also thank so many other people who touched my life. You are all the greatest!

Prologue

The bats were fluttering and swooping, doing fly-bys at everyone who had gathered for the presentation in the conference room, curiously concentrating on Mr. Johnson. The men shouted and ducked, half of them crawling under the table, a couple of them standing and actually chasing after the flying rodents. One of them was waving Anderton's presentation manual around at them, vainly trying to swat them down as though they were mosquitos. Anderton was going nuts over that, mumbling to himself, biting his fingers, off in a corner watching the spectacle unfold.

"What's going on?" asked Wayne, the maintenance man, entering into the pandemonium. Wayne who had been handsomely rewarded with his own box of Krispy Kremes to go along with their employee prank, had asked to be in the area. "Jesus! Bats! Hang on!" Wayne started muttering to himself and brandishing his…

"Oh shit…!" whispered Shelby Jacobs as she peered through the vent, connecting the rooms from her perch on the ladder in the room next door.

Welding torch!

Wayne had been nearby re-soldering plumbing fixtures and apparently brought it with him for additional drama to their prank. Charles and Shelby crouched near the grate, pulling back sharply when Wayne took a swipe a smidge too close for comfort. Then Wayne jumped on the mahogany conference table, kicking more of the manuals aside, chasing after the bats, flames showering around him everywhere as he waved the torch.

"Be careful with that thing!" someone shouted at him.

"BURN THE BASTARDS! Watch you don't roast off Johnson's wig if a bat lands on him again! We've got a 2:30 tee time!"

"Someone close the door! Don't let them out of here!"

"You get up and close the door! I don't want them to bite me, they could be rabid!"

"PUSSIES! All of you a bunch of pussies."

"It touched me! Don't call me a pussy until it touches you!"

"If you're so brave, go close the door!"

"I'll get the door closed, dammit. JOHNSON, go close the door!"

Wayne caught up to one of the bats who'd landed directly on a sprinkler head. He didn't even hesitate. He turned the torch on him full force, shouting, "FRY, FUCKER!" The bat fluttered away, trailing a shower of sparks. Wayne couldn't see that the bat had escaped through the combustion of his torch. Then the sprinkler exploded with water, sending a wet shower everywhere.

Charles and Shelby nearly peed in their pants, laughing so hard, while everyone in the board room scampered again. Anderton took flight, scurrying around the table to collect his manuals, "My presentation! My manuals, all that work!"

"Anderson, you drip, fuck the papers, grab the DOUGHNUTS!"

"They're just doughnuts!" he hissed.

"Aw, shit, the stress has made the poor boy flip out. He's irrational. Johnson! Grab the doughnuts!"

"I'll get soaked!"

"I'll let you stop and change before tee time. Dammit, I want another cream filled!"

"What happened to the bats? Where are the bats?"

"What about my presentation?"

"One of them touched me! I felt it! It touched me!"

A ball of flame fell fluttering onto the center of the table, accompanied by, "Back to hell, you furry little beasts!"

Chapter 1

Shelby Jacobs was sitting at the bar in Caesar's Palace in Las Vegas. It was simply another vacation; she visited regularly. No, scratch that, she was not on vacation this time. She was actually on a business trip, in from San Francisco. And she was waiting to meet one of the Online Dating men she had arranged to have a drink with here at the bar.

She called over her favorite bartender, buddy, and pal, Vince, ordered her drink, then took off in desperate need for the ladies' room.

The ladies' room was blocked off with yellow cones and a closed sign. She could go to another one, but the nearest one was a bit of a hike and she *really* had to go. She was nearing the stage of having to cross her legs because she'd sat there way too long having fun. Not to mention, her feet were still a little sore from those shoes she'd worn earlier in the day for that business meeting thing.

She had to pee. Now. To heck with it. She pushed the door open, hoping she could sneak in without anyone noticing. No such luck. There was a guy right inside the door and he barked at her that the ladies' room was closed.

Shelby turned around and looked at the men's room door. Business was a bit slow tonight, and she didn't see anyone coming out. She checked around to see if anyone was heading toward it. No one. Her feet hurt. A shiver went up her spine, making the pressure against her bladder even more pronounced.

Shelby went for it.

She pushed the door open and peeked in to make sure she didn't catch some old rich guy at the urinal. No one. She walked in and entered the first stall. At the precise moment the door latched and she started to unzip her pants, a crackling sound emanated from outside her stall door then a man's voice saying, "Security."

How in the *heck* did he get here so quickly? Were there cameras on the floor everywhere? Did the eye in the sky really sic security on her that fast? Small wonder she felt safe in this place. Safe unless she decided to take a pee in the men's room. Darn!

She ignored him. She barely got her pants down in time, that's how badly she had to go. And she heard him again just as the peeing started. "Miss, you can't come in here, it's the men's room."

Honestly. This was so embarrassing. God, he was standing right outside the stall door listening to her tinkle.

"You have to leave right now, Ma'am," him warning her again.

She was a 'Ma'am' now, that's how she knew this was serious.

Did this gonzo really think she'd stop mid-stream and leave? Couldn't he hear the urgency of her flow? This was no minor little tinkle, this was massive. She muttered an 'ok' as she finished up to try and stall him. Shelby zipped up and hung her head when she came out of the stall. Offered a mumbled, "sorry". She headed to the sink.

When she put her hands under the faucet, the guard grabbed her elbow. "You have to go right now, Ma'am."

"I'm going, I'm going, but I have to wash my hands. That'd be gross…"

"Ma'am…"

"The ladies' room was closed!" she cut him off. "You know how big this place is, I…"

"You cannot come in the men's room, Ma'am," he said forcefully while he tugged on her arm. Clearly, she was not charming him at all. He hustled her out the door and said something into the walkie-talkie on his shoulder.

Outside the door, she picked up her pace to try and get away from him, but he steered her along, up the stairs and toward the front doors, escorting her out.

"You're kidding, right?" Shelby asked him.

"Miss, I'm going to ask you to leave."

Well, at least she was back to Miss again. "But, but…"

He opened the door for her. Fine. She could use some fresh air anyhow. She walked out the doors and shivered. *Great, she'd probably have to pee again as soon as she went back inside.* She jumped down the steps, ignored the soreness when her sandals rubbed against the raw spots on her feet, followed the sidewalk and went in the next set of doors by the lobby.

When she hopped back up to the bar, Vince handed her a fresh drink. "Have fun?" He smirked.

"Dude, I just got kicked out of here."

"I know."

"You know? What do you mean you know?"

"I was watching you and I knew you were gonna bolt into the men's room."

"YOU called security on me? God! That was embarrassing! He listened to me tinkle!"

He shrugged, obviously pleased with himself. "Just a little excitement. Kept you away from the tables for a couple minutes, didn't it?"

"Yeah…"

"There you go, I saved you money. You should thank me."

Shelby sipped on her drink and looked across the bar. She did kind of have to laugh, just thinking about what just happened. A smile played across her face as she took in the scenery.

SportsCenter was playing on the TV behind the black marble, sunken bar slightly off the main casino floor and the barstools were comfy. The piano man, Billy, tapped away behind her, echoing everything from glory-days jazz to modern pop to help fill the air.

People rested their weary feet on plush, black carpet while soft, warm, golden light held the mood, keeping it dark enough to make everyone look better than they did, yet still bright enough to stay awake in case they were moved to drop a few Franklins into the hungry corporate machine that sponsored all this debauchery.

There were a couple of glitter-eyed hookers around; braless, flawless, and overall painted and puffed in all the right places. A few guys in suits looking to impress; neatly pressed, alcohol-aided de-stressed, but still overall uptight and pinched in all the wrong areas. There were some vacationing couples; somewhat dazzled, leaning into frazzled, but overall happy and romantic in this big, new, flashy environment. A group of overgrown frat boys who just knew they were SO money, thinking they were slick, wagging their personal parts, but mostly just partying and living like all heck during their Spring Break. And several random scattered oddballs, which she openly acknowledged to be one of.

She waved Vince over again. After all, he owed her after his little ladies' room stunt.

"What's up, sweetheart?" he asked ever so innocently.

"Look," Sheby answered, "will you do me a favor and make a couple of lemon drops up nice? Give one to him." She motioned in the direction of an alone guy who looked kinda cute and happened to be her Online Dating date. She recognized him from his picture he had sent her.

Vince smirked, helped her out in his own weird way by addressing the guy as he grabbed a couple glasses. "She's buying you a shot. You know she's pushing her fanny, right?"

Shelby laughed. It was a running joke between she and Vince.

The guy just looked confused, but he smiled and asked, "Pushing her fanny?"

Vince elaborated. "She's a hooker, she's trying to pick you up," he explained and started making the drinks. There was no doubt he intended to keep his ears and eyes on the exchange that was about to happen, though, since he had opened the door to this game for her.

The poor guy still looked confused. "You're a hooker? You're trying to pick me up? But I thought from the dating site…"

She smiled, interrupting, "No. I'm really not. I just want to be mistaken for one so Vince tries to help me out."

"You *want* to be mistaken for a hooker?" he asked with a smile.

He was definitely cute. Shelby hadn't even noticed he was this cute when she decided to open the door to conversation. She had intended to duck out quickly if she didn't like his looks. Demurely, "I wouldn't actually DO it, you know, follow through. I just think it'd be a compliment to have a guy be willing to pay money to have sex with me. To be able to earn money for sex because you're so good at it." She became flustered suddenly and worried she that was talking too much. "It's ah, um, look, it's just a dumb joke we have, that's all."

"Ok," he said as Vince put the drinks in front of them.

Vince didn't charge her. Vince never charged her. He was a good guy from Jersey she had befriended and she always paid and then some, in the end, with money, that is. She had her newly blossoming business reputation in the corporate financial world to protect, after all.

The cute guy was deciding about whether or not to play along. Suddenly he looked back to her and scratched the corner of his mouth. Then he asked, "If you were a hooker, what would you charge?"

Game on.

She picked up her drink, swirled it around, licked her lips. "You mean what's the going rate around here? Is that what you're trying to figure out?"

"No, not exactly. Well, yeah, sort of. Why? Would you be the average rate?"

"Well, I think average is about a grand, so…"

"Hold up! A *grand*? You're telling me that these chicks here make a grand every time? For *what*?"

Shelby shrugged. "I don't know, I could be wrong, but I've talked to some guys who blew it off because it was too expensive. They start at one price but work like strippers or something." He didn't nod or agree, so she continued. "They'll start something for one price, and then say, 'Do you want me to do this or that, cause it'll cost you more money' and by then most of the guys naturally want them to keep going, so the price keeps going up."

"A thousand bucks? Bullshit."

"I'm serious. Ask one of them."

"Ask one of them?" He looked around. "How am I supposed to do that?"

"There's a few in here. They'll come talk to you sooner or later."

He scanned the room. "They're gonna come and talk to me? Why?"

Laughing, she answered him. "Because you're a guy and you're alone. Or, well, you were. I might be screwing it up for you by talking to you. Stop talking to me and they'll come over pretty quickly."

He leaned in closer in her direction. "Nah, I'd rather talk to you."

Picking up the shot, she nodded at his. "Listen, let's do these. You ever do one before?"

He hadn't, so she explained how. "You take a lick of the sugar, then a gulp. Don't try to down the whole thing. Vince made 'em up nice for us. You ready?"

He smiled then did the lick and drink thing.

Shelby licked and gulped. "You like it?" she asked.

He licked and drank again, then he turned and stared at her, grinning wickedly. "So, if you were a hooker, and your prices were different for each guy, how much would you charge *me*?"

Oh God. There it was. Flirting, flattering, and funny. All of it, all in one line. Shelby was impressed.

Suddenly Vince leaned against the bar between them. He motioned over his shoulder. "Check out the guy over there. He's wearing slippers."

She glanced across the bar. Nothing too outrageous. Just some guy, age anywhere from a really beaten, alcoholic 45 years old to a normal-life mid-60s range. Grey hair, sort of like a lion's mane, framed his face. Big glasses, looked pretty clueless and drunk. But otherwise, nothing spectacular, except for the slippers that weren't in her line of vision.

"Check out the bar, he's emptying his pockets," Vince instructed.

The guy was pulling two decks of cards out and fumbling with them. Already in front of him and on display were: A small round mirror. A large shaving brush. A 10" model of what she presumed was the Titanic. And lastly, but certainly not least, the biggest penis ring she'd ever seen in her life. Not that she'd ever really seen any, other than in porno mags.

Now, come on. She had to get up early tomorrow. She just did a shot, had this really cute, and also apparently charming guy from Online Dating, talking to her, and across the bar they had a dude wearing slippers and displaying the Titanic and a penis ring. Did she really have to leave all this pretty soon for boring sleep?

This was her second night of a business trip in Las Vegas. She'd arrived yesterday and actually managed to pull the reins last night. Got herself to bed before sunrise, woke up on time, got dressed and wore pants and real shoes which made her feet bleed, hauled herself to this convention where she didn't know anyone, avoided the blackjack tables, signed in, wore a nametag, smiled politely and made small talk. And on top of all that, she then managed to sit still, listen intently and even take notes on this ridiculously dry stuff that was of very minimal importance to the inner tickings of her normal day job in San Fran.

She only had to still get through tomorrow and then she was free. The midnight hour had just rolled around and her favorite bartender, Vince, was now on duty. So this should be a piece of cake. Just pick her ass up, excuse herself from cute guy, go to bed, do her thing for work tomorrow. Then, tomorrow night, she'd be free to drink and flirt and play all she wanted.

But, right then, the cute Online Dating guy got up and closed the gap of the empty seat between them. His eyes were big and a little heavy lidded. He smiled, saying, "Well, we *gotta* find out what's up with that dude."

Vince cocked an eyebrow at her.

Shelby sipped her drink. Decision time. The question wasn't whether or not she wanted to sit at this bar any longer. Sit here and flirt with this dark-eyed, crooked smiling, vein-showing, probably girlfriend-having, sexy kind of a guy. Suck up free drinks from Vince, find out about that massive penis-ring on the other side of the bar, maybe shoot a few more dice before the night was over. Yeah, oh yeah she wanted to do that.

The question was: Should she do that. Of course she *could* do it. But *should* she? *Would* she? Good responsible girl? Or fun, bad girl? Which would make her happier? Because that was what it was all about—happiness—right?

So right now it was one lemon drop drink, one dice table trip, two vodka sodas, and one bartender change later smoking a Marlboro Red, drinking a beer and flashing smiles almost constantly. They'd huddled together with Vince, writing a note to the guy in slippers across the bar.

"Vince, what's the number here?" Sheby asked him.

"Are you gonna have that freak call me?" he asked.

She nodded, "Yeah, you can be my pimp for the night."

"I am every night, sweetheart," Vince winked and gave her the number.

"Well, you're doing a generally shitty job, then."

The cute guy mocked offended. "What about me?"

Vince nodded to him, "Twenty percent. Whatever you give her, my cut is twenty."

"I still don't know what she charges," he shrugged.

Folding up the napkin, she handed it to Vince and he delivered it across the bar. Within one more sip of her vodka soda, the slipper guy called Vince back over and asked him where the note came from. He immediately padded over.

He was drunk, she could tell right away. He sat down next to the cute guy instead of next to her. She checked him out again, the cute guy, and wondered if he was getting drunk or not.

"Good evening, you fine kids," the slippered man greeted them with arresting enthusiasm. He stuck out a large hand and said, "I'm Vegas Vic and I just can't tell you how marvelously pleased your little note made me!"

He was gay.

Shelby shook his hand, he gripped hers really hard, like one business tycoon trying to prove his strength to another one. Then he dragged his eyes up and down her guy before holding his hand out to him. She couldn't see his eyes behind his thick lenses, but she could see the frames moving up and down, the lenses changing as they caught different reflections of light in their vertical path.

Definitely gay.

"And what's your name, young man?"

"Robert," her guy answered, politely shaking his hand. *So now he had a name.*

She watched as Vegas Vic's shake was conspicuously different from the one he gave her. Not a harsh one-pump job. It was darn near a caress. Ok, so, he was extremely gay. And possibly horny. Not that she could blame the guy. Robert's hand was nice.

"Why are you called Vegas Vic?" Shelby asked to interrupt, just as Vince strolled up and leaned against the bar, definitely intent on watching what was happening.

"Why am I called Vegas Vic? Now that is a long story. What's your name, young lady?"

"It's on the note," she reminded him.

"Stella," he read aloud.

"Oh Jesus," Vince sighed, shaking his head at her.

Robert noticed, Vegas Vic didn't. "Stella. Is that really your name?"

Robert swung his attention to me, too. Vince answered for me. "Yeah, her name is Stella and she's a hooker, too. I get twenty percent."

Vic brightened at this, saying, "You know, you look like a Stella. I'm a male prostitute myself."

Vince cracked up and wandered off to wait on some other people.

She decided to steal Robert's line from earlier. "So what would you charge me for a night of your services, and what would I get for that money?"

"Oh, Stella, sweetie," he answered while looking directly at Robert and putting his hand on his knee. "He's my clientele, not you."

She freaking knew it! "I'm out," she announced, standing up.

Robert turned and grabbed hold of her wrist. "Don't go, come on, really." His hand felt warm, strong, but not forceful.

"I'm just going to the ladies' room, that's all, I'll be right back."

"Promise?" he asked, lowering his chin and looking up at me with puppy eyes. Yeah, he was working it. Maybe it was working on her.

Smiling, "I promise. I might gamble a little bit, but I won't be long." Shelby leaned down and spoke softly in his ear. "Promise you won't take off with Vic here? Remember what I told you about how those prices go up. He might seem like a bargain now, but…"

"I'll be right here," he said loudly.

"Listen," she whispered. "My name's not Stella."

She started to back off, but he still had her wrist. He pulled her back and closer into him. "And you're not a hooker." He blinked, then met my eyes. "Almost a shame. I'd pay the thousand."

Shelby laughed. "Robert, baby, you wouldn't have to."

Washing her hands, she peered into the mirror above the sink, searching for some glimmer of what he thought he saw. She did have nice hair, a thick, flaxen mane, all the way to her butt. The eyes were nice, sort of cool, bright blue-green and big. But weren't everyone's eyes nice? She had good teeth, clear skin, and Nordic features from her German ancestry, but so what. She still didn't get it. And certainly her body was nothing to get excited about. She did have big boobs and long legs, but as far as she was concerned, she was too tall and too slender.

A short while later, she returned from the ladies' room, minus incident, thank goodness, and whispered to Vince, "What's going on over there?"

"Oh, you gotta get back over there, the guy's a total nut."

"My cute guy?"

"No, no, Slippers."

"Vegas Vic," she corrected him.

"Yeah. He has a clone."

"Stop."

"I'm telling you, you gotta hear this guy," he answered then grabbed her drink and walked it to the other side of the bar for her.

As she sat down, Vegas Vic greeted her. "Stella's back," he announced with unbridled glee. He reminded me of Charles Nelson Reilly. Only older. Hairier. Gayer. And with props.

Robert turned and gave her a smile. That was all the encouragement she needed. She pulled her chair closer to his. Close enough so that she could feel the presence of his body, get the slightest aura of his heat. She wondered if it would have the same tingly effect on her if she hadn't done that shot. Probably not. Who cares.

"Robert, is Stella here your girlfriend?" Vic asked him.

She waited to hear this answer. "No, we just met, but she seems really cool," he replied.

"Do you have a girlfriend?" Vic prodded.

Robert nodded slowly. "Yeah, sort of. She was here earlier. She got pissed at me and left though."

She freaking knew it!

"Where did she go?"

"I don't know, she and my sister left. I don't know what I did to piss them off."

"Well. That's a shame," Vic consoled.

"Yeah, well, it's ok, I'm having a good time anyhow…"

"No, no, I mean it's a shame about you and Stella here. You really do make a fabulous couple."

Maybe he decided to stop hitting on her man.

"Stella, that is just a fabulous name," Vic continued. "Now tell me, are you married, Stella?"

And there it was. "Nope," she answered cheerfully. Lots of single chicks had a problem with that question, but it really didn't bother her. Come on, she was only twenty-three, no big hurry, right?

Cocking his head to the side, Vic asked, "Why not?"

And there THAT was. That question really did bother her. Shelby never understood what people expected someone to respond to that. Honestly. So she did her best. "Because that would take the spontaneity out of dating," she answered even more cheerfully.

Vic seemed pleased with that answer. Eyeing Robert again, he said, "Well it looks like you two are having fun. And it was so wonderful of you two, I mean, this note." He picked up the napkin and waved it around. "It's all just so tremendous, it made my night and now I get to talk to you two. Let's do a shot to celebrate."

She and Robert nodded in agreement, so Vic called over Vince and placed the order. Once they had their drinks, Vic raised his glass to them. "What shall we drink to?"

"You bought, you toast," she answered.

He looked flummoxed, shook his head and said, "Oh no, I defer."

"Alright," she raised her shot, "to Vic's fur."

They drank their shots and before she could thank him, Vic asked her, "Stella, how much do you sleep?"

Confused, she answered him anyhow. "Um, about four or five hours a night."

"Robert? You?"

"More than that, that's for sure. Probably seven or eight hours."

"Now, you see, I've never slept. I have never once slept in my life. That's how I stay ahead of my clone."

Robert nudged her but didn't look away from Vic. Vince, on the other side of the bar, but obviously listening, snorted loudly and continued mixing drinks.

"I see," Shelby replied, then sat back and listened awhile. At one point she asked about the Titanic model. Vic informed them that it was most definitely not the Titanic, but the Andrea Doria. He built it himself, not from a model, and he was certain it was actually seaworthy.

That set him off on a tangent talking about the rest of his props. When he got to the penis ring, which all kidding aside, had to be about 5 inches in diameter, his words were, "Of course, this is extremely tight on me," as he reached out and placed his hand on Robert's knee again. *Maybe he was still hitting on her man.*

The piano man behind them started tapping out "Take Five" and she knew it was for her. So she got up and slid a few bills in his jar and thanked him, made chit chat for a couple of minutes. When she turned around to go back, she discovered a gorgeous whore in a fur jacket in her seat right next to Robert.

Sighing, she returned to the bar, stood on the other side of the whore and ordered another drink. She was talking to Robert, he was listening, Vic was still fumbling with his collection of things.

As Vince slid her drink in front of her, Robert made an effort and introduced the whore. "This is Diamond," he said.

She moved her head up and down politely while the whore gave her the dumb-fucker look. Everyone knows that look. She wasn't sure yet if she should give her a nasty look to make her leave, or if she should back off and let her have him. Or if she should be nice to her in case she was interested in a three-some. She held out her hand. "Nice to meet you," she said. "I'm Diamond."

"Diamond?" she took her hand, almost feeling slimy for touching it. "Nice to meet you. Are you going to sit here awhile and talk to him?" she motioned to Robert.

"A little bit," she replied and swept her eyes up and down slowly. Coyly.

Shelby did her shot and simply announced, "Ok then. I'm going to gamble." She turned and left, heading for one of the exits, aiming for one of the other hotels on the strip and a casino.

She refused to compete for a guy's attention. If he wanted her, he wanted her. Period.

Or maybe it was because she didn't really care that much. She'd never invested much in retaining a man. Never had a boyfriend, never even really had been on a date. Which was not to say she'd never invested in *getting* a man, she simply didn't want to hold on to them. Luckily, the feeling seemed quite reciprocal.

So what was the point in competing for something she had no intention of even keeping?

She picked a $25 minimum table. The shoe was pretty low, so she figured she'd warm up and let it play out and start on a clean one. There were two other people at it, but the first base chair was open so she slid into it, threw down her money and card. She shouldn't use a player card in this situation, but screw it. She'd always wanted to stay at Bellagio, see how the ultra-rich lived. And the only way she'd ever be able to afford it is if she worked up some sort of player rating.

She settled back, settled in, and played a few hands. Even though it was useless, she kept a count just to warm up. Keeping track of the numbers within a deck was highly frowned upon in the gambling industry. But, she had this natural gift of photographic memory, when she chose to apply it, and what was wrong with applying it to win some money? She didn't do it all the time, just sometimes when it seemed to kick in all by itself around anything with numbers; it was hard to control. That challenge thing. Yeah, right. Shelby smiled.

Ten minutes later, "Oh, you are kidding me!" Shelby said out loud after losing because of an elusive ten card and looked up. She was shocked for an instant. She had vaguely noticed another dealer come on, but was so wrapped up in the game, she didn't really greet him or even look up at him. Obviously she hadn't, because she would have taken note.

It was the dealer's turn to smirk, and he did. "That was a good one, huh?"

His gaze lingered on her a couple seconds longer than it should, and she attempted to match him. She'd checked out his face when she first looked up, seeing his high cut cheekbones, really dark, short hair. But now she became momentarily engrossed, almost lost, in his dark, hypnotic eyes.

Shelby remembered to breathe and it set her straight again. She blinked and looked down at the table, suddenly aware of how inappropriate that was. She became even more rattled at the thought at what he was potentially thinking when he gazed back at her.

"Are you always this lucky?" she asked him.

He cocked a brow. "Don't know, this is my first time." Sweeping the cards off the felt and putting them in the discard deck, he glanced over at her again.

"Get out. This is your first day dealing? And you're at the Bellagio?"

"Nah, huh-uh. I mean, like, it's my first day dealing this game. 21." He pulled the cards out of the shoe and she noticed that his hands did move more slowly and deliberately than most dealers.

"Well, you're doing a good job. For them. Not helping me much." She didn't want to sound like she was whining, so she made sure to say it jokingly. "Let's see if you have good luck if you're playing this side of the table. This one's for you."

She had the count at +13 and checked out her hand. Or rather, the hand she was playing for him. He slid her an ace, finished the table, then came back around and painted her with a jack. *Now finally the elusive ten showed up. Where the hell was it last hand when she desperately needed it.* As he paid her, she slid the chips back to his side of the table. "That's yours. I guess you are lucky."

"You don't gotta do that, I don't deserve all that," he said as he collected the discards. His hands seemed to move a bit more rapidly this time. They were nice hands.

"Yeah, I want to, it's cool. You earned it."

Shifting his weight, he nodded his head once, tapped his hand in front of her and pointed briefly. Then said, "Thank you, really, thanks."

"You're welcome. Now let's see if we can get some luck for the rest of us on this side, too."

"Yeah," he winked at her again, "you deserve some luck, too."

"No one deserves luck," was her comeback. "But I'll try and earn it anyhow."

Lowering his head and smiling, he started dealing and said, "Alright, c'mon now, let's go. Good cards for my cutie on the end here." Sliding the cards in front of her, his tongue settled onto the corner of his mouth. "Yo, how's that, huh? You like those? Not bad, huh?"

Looking down she saw two face cards. "Yeah, I'll take that. Thank you." Shelby swept the table quickly with her eyes and did the math in her head.

The guy next to her took a card, then held with an 18. The dealer flipped his hole and he had 17. "There you go," the dealer said as he paid them off, "start of a hot streak for the players on this table." Licking his lips, he winked at her yet again.

One cosmopolitan, two shoes, several wisecracks, a couple of leering glances, and many hands later (won or lost on luck alone), the dealer got tapped out.

Clearing his hands for the cameras above, he stepped closer to her before walking away. "Hey, thanks again for that hand. Really. You come see me on the dice table sometime, ok?"

She smiled. "I might do that."

"Serious, we'll have fun, I'm better at that."

"Ok," Shelby answered.

"'Ok. I work swing most o' the time. I'll be on tomorrow at that time."

"They didn't trust you on the blackjack tables during the busy hours?"

He laughed. "No, they didn't, they didn't. Good move, huh?" He glanced at her hand, indicated the ring on her finger. "You gonna bring your husband with you?"

"Don't have one of those," she answered, wagging her ring finger and explaining, "Just evening out the tan lines today."

"So you ain't married, huh?"

"Nope."

"How come?"

"Why would I want to wreck a perfectly good sex life?"

"I'm Antonio," he said and blinked slowly, impossibly long eyelashes sweeping hypnotically up and down over those deep brown eyes. They were softer when he opened them again, and stared straight into her eyes, saying, "Come see me again." Then he walked away.

Shelby watched him go, amused by his walk. He carried one hand against his stomach, head up and shoulders a little slouched. He didn't walk so much as stride. Long, loping steps with just the slightest hitch in his gait. Unusually tall for an Hispanic male, very handsome. Kinda like a Latin lover with class. Hmmm…

She already had a mental note logged into her brain cells to come play dice with him sometime.

Hopefully soon.

Shelby admitted it. She felt a little proud of herself right now. She'd hustled some dough, hustled some conversation, hustled the spark of sexual tension out of that hot dealer.

Sometimes, she was convinced she could charm a rattlesnake.

There really was no other explanation for it. She wasn't a crazy girl, nor a gorgeous whore. Since she understood and recognized what she didn't have, at least as far as she was concerned, intelligence definitely created a hindrance when it came to good looking hunks, all she could figure out was that what she did have was charm.

Yet, while she might be charming, more often, she fell under the spell of others.

Like Las Vegas. Like alone guy, cutie, Robert. Like that dealer.

She didn't mind. She liked it. Thrill her, charm her, seduce her. She'd try to do the same for somebody else. Make life worth living. Be upbeat. Yes!

Walking through the row of shops to the exit, she remembered that she and her sisters were due for their monthly get together in a little over a week. At Tiffany's, she entered and walked straight to the back room to pick her up something sparkly. It was tradition for her. If she played and won at the Bellagio, she had to get something from Tiffany. Since she rarely wore jewelry, she usually bought stuff for everybody else.

And the front room? Forget it. The front room was the really sparkly stuff. Where the whales shopped. Diamonds, pearls, and platinum. Shelby took her mom in there once and went right to the back room: silver trinkets and other gifts. She offered to buy her the standard silver Tiffany bracelet. Her mom didn't like it so much. On the way out, her mom looked inside a case in the front room and pointed to a charm bracelet she liked. It was $75,000. "Keep on walking," she'd told her.

She picked out a dangly necklace for each sister. They only wore silver, so it worked out nice for her. She'd drop all this leftover money into the fund for the next trip.

Chapter 2

Serina Jacobs never intended to live the life of a starving artist. She never intended to be a starving *anything*. For that matter she didn't intend to be a *dead* artist either, death being a well-known byproduct of starvation, but as things had turned out, she was, at this turning point in her life, an artist who was not selling very many of her paintings. Nor could she be certain that, like other painters, her work would start selling like proverbial hot cakes after her death, which of course in normal circumstances wouldn't have mattered anyway. Then again nobody would have considered Serina a normal female under *any* circumstances, though just about everybody, or at least the few people that knew her, recognized she was a woman who had reached a point where something had to give.

So with palatable anticipation and growling, gastrointestinal yearning she awoke on a bright San Anselmo, California morning, because that Friday night, for the first time since her last show many moons ago, she would eat relatively solid food: various cheeses, deli meats, assorted cold vegetables with ranch style dip, sumptuous pastries, chips. Hardly a square meal—but to her at this point in her artistic career it was certainly something to look forward to.

When Serina remembered the show she quickly swung her long, curvy legs out of bed and reached for the telephone on the night stand, but the cradle was empty.

"Darn it," she said out loud. She scratched herself in an unladylike fashion under her arms and scanned the one-room apartment, trying to recollect events from the previous evening. There was only one empty wine bottle, a half-dozen soda cans, no stray men's undies, no cigarette butts smashed into plates of cold spaghetti, no red wine stains on the curtains. From all appearances, it had been just another lonely night, but her memory was fuzzy, and the phone was nowhere to be seen.

One way Serina could put last night together would be to check what was in the CD player. She opened it up. "Ah ha!" she said. She remembered stalking around her apartment with a flat bristle brush full of hansa yellow in one hand, a bottle of merlot in the other, singing "better get a day job" alternated with "rather have some sex" to the tune of "New York, New York", while she alternately dabbed at the autumn foliage of a serene, pastoral landscape that was slowly turning into a psychedelic mess.

This revelation did not lead directly to the location of the phone. If it were her car keys that were lost, the first place Serina would have looked was the refrigerator. Never, not once, did she leave her car keys in the refrigerator. Still, she would always check the fridge first, leaning back, holding the door open, surveying the shelves. It was usually a couple of minutes of standing in front of the fridge before she could remember exactly what she was even looking for, at which time she would shake her head and shut the door as if to say, what the hell am I doing looking for my car keys in the refrigerator?

As she placed the CD back in its case it occurred to her that perhaps if the phone were her car keys, they *just might* be in the refrigerator. Just then, as if the phone we're looking for *Serina* instead of the other way around, she heard a muffled ring. She stopped, listened. It sounded like someone was strangling a turkey in the refrigerator—no…it was coming from the freezer! She opened the freezer door and there it was, the only thing in there, nice and frosty, next to the ice trays. She reached in, grabbed it, hastily pressing the "talk" button. But the phone, having spent the night in the freezer, was cold, icy—it immediately slipped out of her hands onto the linoleum floor and skidded under the fridge. She could hear the caller—it was the owner of the California Heritage Art Gallery— the only gallery that showed the paintings of Serina Jacobs—Rex Wilcox.

"Hello? Serina? Are you there? Serina? Serina!" She fell onto her hands and knees and stabbed her hand under the refrigerator, only to knock the phone further into the assorted clumps of thick, oozing grime that tended to collect under appliances.

"Serina!" yelled Wilcox. "I know you're there! What the hell are you doing? Say something for God's sake!"

"Coming!" she yelled as she lay down and stretched her arm full length, coaxing the phone this way and that through the muck until she could get a grip on it. Finally she yanked it from its scuzzy hiding place, slicing the back of her hand on the metal cooling unit in the process.

"Oh! Oh my God! Oh you son of a so and so!" Serina howled as she lifted the phone up to her ear.

"Well good morning and screw you, too!" shouted Rex Wilcox.

"Wilcox! Jesus, Wilcox!" Serina shouted back into the frozen phone. "I'm bleeding!" She stumbled over to the sink, switching the phone to her good hand while holding her injured hand in front of her as if it were diseased, the three inch cut on the back of her hand welling up with blood, then quickly oozing out into several directions.

"Well that certainly doesn't surprise *me*," said Wilcox in his typically flippant tone. "Just exactly who are you wrestling with in that little love nest of yours? That skinny little art gigolo, Stefan, I presume?"

Serina watched in irrational horror as the blood formed into droplets and slid off the back of her hand into the sink. "Wilcox—I'm seriously bleeding here. I've got a major cut here, Wilcox—major blood flowing out. Help!"

"Well…put a Band-Aid on it, you helpless female!"

Serina imagined Wilcox, sitting in his silk kimono and slippers, probably fondling his balls in the warm Northern California morning sun on his deck in Mill Valley—if of course the fog hadn't set in over night. It was often hard to tell if the fog was in from Serina's apartment in San Anselmo outskirts, which was protected from the coastal climate by the tall ridges of Mt. Tamalpais.

Even in her weakened state due to her shock of observing all the blood coming out of her hand, Serina could hear Wilcox take a noisy slurp of steamed milk off the top of his latte.

"Band Aid?" she whimpered. "I don't have any Band-Aids! Jesus! Hold on a second, Wilcox—I have to *do* something here." She looked frantically around the kitchenette for something that would stem the bleeding. It was just a scratch, really, but enough of a scratch to create a scary crimson watercolor in the bottom of her white porcelain sink.

All the rags were covered with dried oil paint and evaporated turpentine—not the kind of thing you would want to apply to an open wound. Seeing nothing of use in the kitchen, Serina ran to the bathroom and ripped off what remained of her last roll of toilet paper and pressed it to the back of her hand. By the time she got back to the kitchen and picked up the phone, which had nicely managed to warm to room temperature, the toilet paper stuck to the back of her hand had soaked through. Those horrible blood droplets were forming once again.

"Well?" said Wilcox, opening his kimono and exposing his hairy belly to the sun. "Are you going to live?"

"Jeez, Wilcox—I don't know," Serina answered, watching the blood continue to flow. "It's still coming…it looks like this TP isn't gonna do it. I can't believe it!" She took long, fast strides back to the bathroom, trying not to let the blood from her outstretched hand drip onto the floor while holding the phone with her good hand.

"Ok, Serina…" said Wilcox impatiently. "So you've got a little cut. I really don't have all day to play Florence Nightengale…you know I have to get the gallery ready for an opening tonight."

"An opening?" she asked, searching her bathroom cabinets for something that might substitute for a Band-Aid. "Tonight?" she asked again as she spied a box of Lightdays Panty Liners in the back of the cabinet under the bathroom sink. "Ah—here we go," she mumbled. "Hold on a minute, Wilcox—I wanna hear about this opening." Serina put the phone down with a clunk on the linoleum floor as she grabbed the box of panty liners. "Hmmm—about time somebody put these to good use," she voiced out loud to herself, never using such things and wondering who the heck gave them to her in the first place as she tore open the box then fished one out with her good hand, ripped off the adhesive back and affixed the absorbent panty liner to her cut. "Ok," she said, picking up the phone. "I found some panty liners. I think we're ok now. Tell me about this opening you're having, Rex."

"Panty liners?" said Wilcox, shocked. "You're putting a feminine hygiene product on your *hand*? God, Serina—you are gross!"

She smiled and rolled her eyes. This was exactly the type of thing she would expect Rex Wilcox to find offensive. And, even though Wilcox took every opportunity to exploit Serina's weakness for men, she took pains to circumnavigate the personal, sexual preferences of Rex Wilcox.

"Ok—what about this opening? Are you phasing me out now, or what?" Serina asked, who in all the excitement concerning her cut hand had completely forgotten it was *her* opening that was scheduled for this evening.

Wilcox, on the other hand, was not surprised that Serina forgot. First of all, his client had been producing paintings so slowly that it had been almost six months before he had enough new work to warrant another show. And, since Wilcox was the only gallery owner in town—make that all of Northern California—that would include new paintings by unknown artists alongside well-known California "masters", particularly if they captured at least some of the spirit of the turn-of-the-century California impressionist movement, Serina had little outlet for her work. So the shows were few and far between.

Most artists would have been watching the calendar like a hawk for the next show, Serina included, but the episode with the phone and the subsequent cut on her hand was disorienting. She cradled the phone between her chin and shoulder while she pressed the pinkening panty liner against her injured hand.

"Well, Serina," said Wilcox, feeling coy, "I don't think you're going to want to miss this one. I have personal confirmation from Michelle Morgan's secretary that Ms. Morgan herself plans to be there."

"Michelle Morgan—film producer Michelle Morgan? Art collector Michelle Morgan?" she asked, standing up. Things were definitely looking up. Maybe she'd be interested in some of her work.

"That's the one—looking for some California landscapes to put in that fancy new studio she built in those cow pastures up north." Wilcox smiled and opened his kimono up a little further as the sun began to warm his little condo deck. There was no fog this morning.

"Landscapes! Darn, Wilcox—did you tell her about me?" she asked.

"Well this particular show features a very bewitching female painter—just out of the Oakland school. Quite talented.

"Oh—sorry, Serina. There's a call coming in on the other line. Call me back though, will you please? I don't think I can make it through the day without knowing exactly how you became so mortally injured. Bye now!" Wilcox hung up, grinning.

She put the phone down—relieved. She had more pressing issues. First, she had an urgent need to shower and cleanse her sticky body, except her hand, of course, and second, she was starving. She hadn't had a bite of anything, many liquid swallows, but no bites, since a paltry bagel & cream cheese brunch the day before. A quick bathroom makeover, breakfast—then she could stop and think. Something about Wilcox's opening sounded fishy. What was up with that?

After a long, delightful pick me up in the shower, Serina focused on finding sustenance. It was already going on 1:00 in the afternoon. The choices were depressing: a few sorry dill pickles floating at the bottom of the jar, a drawer full of mustard, ketchup, sugar and nondairy creamer packets, a couple of bottles of merlot, and a lone can of tuna. She checked her wallet to see if she could at least afford a donut and a cup of coffee at the corner Quik n' Easy—but it was empty. Like the refrigerator, the cupboards, the medicine cabinet, the gas tank of her antique Saab, and her rapidly sinking heart—empty. It was at the very moment that she cracked into the can of tuna with her can opener and got a full whiff of the "chicken of the sea" that she once again remembered: it was her own gosh darn opening! And Michelle Morgan was coming to buy her paintings—not the paintings of just any bewitching young thing—her paintings—the paintings of young, bewitching Serina Jacobs!

She better email her sisters to remind them of the 'big event'.

Chapter 3

After coming to the realization that her paintings were being featured in a show at the California Heritage Gallery that night only a few hours away, and that Michelle Morgan, a film producer of some worldwide note who had just completed building a gargantuan movie studio in the pristine valleys of Northern Marin County, was going to be there, Serina became excited. And angry. How could she let that simpering fag, Rex Wilcox, nicknamed in high school "Rex Wil*suck*cox", yank her chain like that?

She finished her dry tuna and dialed Wilcox, who sounded as if he was waiting for the call. "You're an asshole!" she hissed. "I know you know that but I just wanted to make it official—you're a triple grade-A prime asshole."

"Ah, yes—that's one of the distinct privileges I have as a businessman in the art world. Helpless femme fatales like you get to call me names. So you finally figured it out, eh?" Wilcox laughed out loud, his belly jiggling in the midmorning Mill Valley sun as she continued to curse on the other end of the line. "But I am curious, Serina. I mean, you're not normally *this* retarded!" laughed Wilcox. So I figure the cut on your hand must really have you…*upset!* What in the world has been going on over there this morning?"

"Are you kidding me about Michelle Morgan?" she asked, getting seriously pissed.

"I am not kidding you about Michelle Morgan. She is honestly interested in having some local Marin County landscapes showing in her new…whatever it is…compound! It's just so unfortunate that you didn't get out there to paint those beautiful valleys *before* she ruined them with all those hideous buildings!" It truly pained Rex Wilcox to have the raw materials of his livelihood sullied by commercialism, although at the same time he was thrilled about the prospect of actually being allowed inside the hallowed compound where such films as

"Battle Planet" and "Wizards of The Cosmos" had been made. The men he met who worked there, most of them Hollywood transplants, were so handsome and cosmopolitan!

"Well…Ok. That's great I guess—maybe she'll like something—a little California scene in the men's room, perhaps," said Serina, sounding deflated, but then who wouldn't after a single can of dry tuna for breakfast.

"Oh lighten up, Serina—please! You'll never get anywhere with that attitude of yours! Now, before you cut yourself *on purpose*, please tell me what the hell was going on there this morning!" Wilcox, although he had not made any money off of Serina for quite some time, believed that, despite her low-self image as an artist, she had great potential; more than that because she was one of those few painters who actually had talent. Her composition skills were solid, and her sense of color, according to a few of his patrons, was "trippy". Since she had never set foot in an art school, much less an art class (except one), she was always struggling with "technique", not realizing she had her own special technique. The one art class she took in college she referred to as her "bong hit class". Ironically the spacey, impressionist landscape she painted of Boulder Creek was praised by the chain-smoking professor, Mr. Dudley, earning Serina an "A" in painting—although it was also clear that Dudley expected some kind of sexual recompense from the young, tall, slender, blonde-haired student. It was her first and last art class.

"Wilcox—what do *you* think was going on this morning?" asked Serina, baiting, thinking payback.

"All I know is that it took seven rings for you to answer the phone," answered Wilcox in his high pitched 'I'm really concerned voice'. "Either you were "en flagrante" with some lonely male you managed to talk into taking you home, or you're so hung over you couldn't find your way to the phone."

"Ok, so I couldn't find the goddamn phone. I was looking all over for it, too—I wanted to call you about tonight's show, check the menu…you know? Then I heard it ringing but it took me forever to figure out where it was," she explained.

"Where was it?" asked Wilcox.

"In the freezer of all places!"

Wilcox scratched his head at this point. "The freezer?" Wilcox asked after a long pause.

"Yup—frozen solid but still working. So when I picked it up it was slippery as hell and I dropped it under the fridge. That's how I cut my hand." Serina held her hand out and surveyed the now soaked-through panty liner. Time for a fresh one.

"All right, Serina, work with me on this. How in the world did your phone end up in the freezer? Did Stefan call last night?"

And then it all came flooding back. She had been waltzing around her canvas of "Summer Grass on White's Hill" with her bottle and brush, singing along to Pavarotti's duet with Liza Minnelli "New York, New York", when Stefan, her ex-husband, had rudely interrupted her reverie.

"Serina—I can't come over tonight," Stefan had told her. "I've met somebody." Serina was somewhat surprised that Stefan would even bother to call. Normally he just didn't show up when he broke a date. What really pissed her off was that he had to tell her that he was screwing someone else that night.

Serina had placed the phone next to the speaker so Stefan could clearly hear the loud jamming of "New York, New York", and sang at the top of her lungs and along with the melody inserting the phrase, "Gotta get a blow job!" She could hear Stefan trying to explain his promiscuity, even with the phone sitting on the shelf next to the speaker. She had picked up the phone—Stefan was expecting a response. And so it went. Serina wanted to do something equally vitriolic—some comeback that would transcend whatever words he might come up with. So she put the phone in the freezer and slammed the door shut. And that was the end of that conversation.

"So you put the phone in the freezer!" laughed Wilcox. "Ice him down, eh? Cool him off? Good Lord, woman, you are, at the very least, a creative femme fatale."

"Wilcox—that's the most encouraging thing I've heard in the past six months. I'll see you tonight."

She hung up the phone, took a long look at "Summer Grass on White's Hill", contemplated whether to work, go back to bed, or take a bike ride. The empty bottle of merlot on the kitchen table explained why her head was a bit touchy. A bike ride would at least clean her out enough to face her important evening. Besides, the sun was shining, the sky was blue and the heat of the first fogless day in summer hadn't yet settled into the Central Marin watershed. A bike ride would do just fine.

Serina was a woman driven to excess. When she ate, she consumed as much of everything available without getting sick. When she drank, she had the unendearing habit to drink until she passed out. And when she went for a bike ride, she would not head home until she was already thoroughly exhausted, even though the home trip was mostly downhill, and mountain bike coasting down a bumpy trail was in many ways more exhausting as pumping pedals up.

But, she was not really an outdoors-woman, though in college she occasionally enjoyed the thrill of hooking angry brown trout in pristine Rocky Mountain streams. These days she didn't have the means to travel to such places, or the funds that would enable her to own the necessary equipment.

She did, however, own a mountain bike, and in Marin County, California, that was almost as good as owning a BMW. Almost daily Serina would take her old bike onto the fire roads and trails of the municipal water district. From her long-term rented room in a local, small, family owned hotel, she could be on a dirt road leading up to Phoenix Lake in less than ten minutes and ride until the ache in her muscles drowned out the cacophony of imagined melodies, rhythms, conversations, and lurid sex fantasies that would begin with her first waking moment of the day.

Almost without fail, the rhythm of Serina's pedaling over the first mile or so would recall—or replay—the dream she had the previous night. These dreams increasingly involved men—guys, actually—that she hadn't talked to or seen in a few years. These were dreams of her very first boyfriends—vivid memories of the smell of John Donahue's fully muscular developed hairy 15-year chest and the hint of what was below the pants waistline—offered freely, eagerly, aggressively—when they laid on the eucalyptus leaves behind the baseball diamond during their school's open house. John Donahue had been a fast reader of some racy sex novels secretly lifted from his parents. She remembered the night that John wanted to try out a new technique.

"Uh—Serina. How would you like to try a blow job?" They had been making out on Scotty Matthew's bed, just down the street from John's house. Scotty was in the kitchen with Serina's best friend drinking those wine mixed drinks and rolling Colombian joints—making out was not on their minds—but for Serina and John it was as common as after-school sports, study hall, and baby-sitting. John frequently visited Serina while she was baby-sitting, where they would roll around on the living-room carpet for hours, John making his exit before the unsuspecting parents returned home. That night, in Scotty Matthew's bedroom, John was feeling adventurous.

"Uh—yeah…!" said Serina. And then, "Are you sure"?

"I think so—I think it's supposed to feel real good. I read about it in one of my books."

It wasn't until Serina was in her twenties that she realized John Donahue *was* fast. And, although he could be rather greasy, slovenly, sweaty and overweight, she would always regret the day she broke up with him to pursue the more attractive sports jocks that congregated around the high school cafeteria. They were not, as Serina soon discovered, offering special lessons. They just took what they wanted, instead of making it fun and playing for awhile.

Anyway, John Donahue undid his pants, slid down his briefs and released his young hard-on. What happened next became Serina's favorite story to share among her pals. "Get this," she would say. "You won't believe it…I actually blew air on his pecker!" Apparently Serina took the phrase quite literally, and, there on Scotty Matthew's bed, she actually *did* blow on John Donahue's stiff wiener. Of course John explained to her that "blow job" was a figure of speech, and informed her that he believed she was supposed to be sucking—not blowing—which she ultimately did with such youthful enthusiasm that John woke up the next morning with a welt the size of a grape on his very young penis.

Serina did not dream of John nearly as much as she did of Harlin Radner, even though he had never explored the pleasures of oral sex with her, had never touched her breasts or ventured between her legs—except for later, only a couple of years ago and Harlin decided that he wanted to, if only once. As a favor, almost. A mercy fuck. In high school, Serina preferred the tough, tattooed motorcycling types that smoked PCP instead of using Ecstasy, pushed her around, laughed when they barfed and passed out in her parents' yard.

Before leaving on the bike ride, she had scotch-taped a fresh panty liner on her refrigerator wound, which throbbed almost pleasurably as her breathing quickened and she got into her rhythm, starting now to approach the earthen dam at the north end of the narrow, green reservoir. As the sun warmed the dust and manzanita bordering on the fire road, she could detect the aroma of vanilla, a sign that late summer had officially arrived and hot, dry days in the watershed were soon to come.

She hardly noticed when the lake came into view. As Serina pedaled up the dirt fire road toward the lake, she recalled yet another dream of Harlin Radner, this time of their experiences together as childhood playmates. They would play make-believe with old puppets she'd found in her parent's attic. Serina had named hers Charlie and Harlin's was Langley. While most of the boys played kickball and the girls swung round on the monkey bars (which the boys called "the underwear show"), or played four-square, Harlin and Serina would spend their first-grade recesses with Langley and Charlie, completely oblivious to their classmates' noisy ruckus. Langley and Charlie, as it turned out, had important matters to discuss, although Serina could not recall exactly what they were.

As she dismounted and filled her water bottle at an artesian well next to the fire road that circled the lake, she could picture Harlin Radner with his little Langley puppet, standing on the blacktop with the rugged slopes of Mt. Tamalpais in the background, under a deep blue, northern California sky.

Further down the fire road at the Five Points junction, she recalled the many high-school afternoons she spent with Harlin Radner on green, grassy slopes speckled with the springtime bloom of lupine, poppies and purple aster near Alpine Dam, Serina practicing some of the new songs she had written and Harlin with a bottle of wine and some weed. There on the hillside they sang every song over and over and over again until the chill of the foggy evening breeze sent them down the winding road, with Harlin behind the wheel of his forest green, 3 year old, 2 seater sports cars his parents bought for him, driving back into Fairfax and the Ross Valley.

Serina knew then that they were not in love. Nothing about Harlin—his bony, ungraceful frame, the angular cheekbones and jaw, his wild, straggly dark hair that he was constantly pushing off his face—even the jet black, bottomless pupils, surrounded by a brilliant almond shape of white—even that did not give Serina that weak, yearning sensation that accompanied her frequent crushes on guys. And, of course, Harlin was taken—he always had a younger girlfriend who was usually either expelled, had dropped out, or worked after school in a fast food place and didn't seem to care all that much about spending time with Harlin. Harlin didn't talk about his girlfriends with Serina. No way; he never would.

So why was Harlin Radner continually crashing her dreamscape? She had only spoken with him twice, briefly, in the last two years. Yet he continued to appear in her dreams—always remote, unattainable, yet with the unspoken strength that Serina felt she needed so desperately to somehow to get hold of in her life right now. She crested the final curve of Fish Gulch Road, her heart pounding in her ears, sweat stinging her eyes, her breathing ragged from booze and dreaded cigarettes she desperately craved to quit, and a panty liner soaked and brown with sweat, dust and blood, when she once again had that overwhelming urge to find him. If she could see him, just once in the flesh, she could sleep in peace for a change and gather that courage in her life to continue as an artist. She was convinced of it. Harlin was her lucky charm.

Had she known how meeting Harlin again would indeed change her life, she might have continued to ride on up to Bolinas Ridge, down the other side and straight into the Pacific Ocean right then and there. Instead, she turned north towards Bon Tempe, then back down Shaver Grade to Phoenix Lake and finally to her apartment on San Anselmo Avenue, to nap, shower again, and prepare for her night of relative fame and sumptuous dining at the California Heritage Art Gallery.

Chapter 4

After Shelby Jacobs arrived at the San Francisco International Airport, she picked up her Jeep from long term parking and headed straight home. When she got there, she pulled open the inner screen door to the alcove, and a bat flew into her face. That's right. A real live, flying *bat* attacked her. She was absolutely certain it was a bat because it was furry and little as it flapped in her face with its little wings.

She promptly freaked out. While screaming, it scuttled down to her chest, and she screamed louder. It hovered a couple of seconds, then flew against the screen door she was still holding open. It occurred to her not to close the door, because if she did, the bat would be trapped in there and one step closer to the inner door leading into her home. So she did the sensible thing and screamed some more. She just figured the bat had screwed up sonar or something because he kept flapping and hitting the screen. Finally with her voice getting a bit hoarse from all the screaming, she decided to kick at it to help the bat along, and it spiraled down and out from the door. She checked herself, making sure there were no scratches, and hastily opened the inner door and rushed inside. Geez!

Late that morning at her office, she buckled down and concentrated on focusing on her job again. Work itself was never hard. In fact, she really enjoyed work—it allowed her to focus on things that made perfect sense and most of the time she didn't even have to think about it. She was a natural whiz in her profession and highly sought after by the top ten corporations. Not that she really cared; she just did what came natural to her.

Two workdays, part of today and all of tomorrow, one lawn-cutting on her tiny strip of land this evening, no alcohol, the necessary phone calls to family members and friends, one night out, meaning tonight, with same said friends, uncountable thoughts of Robert and Antonio (the ones about Antonio were pretty dirty and she didn't even *know* the man), and Friday would finally roll around tomorrow. What was wrong with her; this restless mood of hers? She'd only just returned and couldn't wait to leave again; totally unnormal for her.

Good and caught up at work even though she arrived late, she spent the afternoon reading news and screwing around reading Salon Online, covering all the serious stuff. Afterwards, she read Cary Tandry's advice column. She liked Cary. He was funny without being nasty or demeaning, and seemed to give fairly sensible advice.

She had to be feeling particularly vulnerable. Or left out. Or weird. Because after reading about 15 letters about relationship problems, she finally clicked the link and started an e-mail of her own to him.

"Cary—here's the thing, I'm twenty-three years old and never had a boyfriend. I don't really mind, I don't think I yearn for one or anything. I only find it mildly disturbing because I'm starting to wonder if there's something wrong with me."

She halted suddenly getting a disturbing vision of a couple of young interns reading her e-mail instead of Cary. Then them going out and talking about it to their other friends, laughing at her and her insecure pathos. Then one of them emailing back and screwing around with her. Signing her up for a bunch of spam email for Viagra and weight loss products.

Screw it. Give the interns something to laugh at.

"I've had plenty of sex, but no one ever likes me. I think I'm reasonably intelligent. And I think I'm reasonably nice. I'm ok in the attractive department, but come ON, Cary. I've seen ugly people hooked up before. Is there anything you can tell by this letter that would project some severe deficiency to you?"

"I realize we aren't supposed to validate ourselves solely on other people's opinions of us. I hate to be so needy, but I'm hoping maybe you'll write back and either:

tell me I'm normal and just unlucky thus far, or,

be able to see the major flaw that drives people away and point it out to me so that I may begin finding a way to correct it. "

The phone rang, kinda shocking her, she'd been that intense during the composition of this email. It was her one of her triplet sisters, Serina.

"3Jacobs."

"Hey, 1Jacobs. What's up?" Serina was 1Jacobs since she was the elder sister by thirty minutes. Sherri was the middle child; 2Jacobs, and Shelby the 'baby' of the "Three" clan, which she hated, but what the hey. No way to change the fate of the timing of her birth. "I've been waiting for you to call." She minimized the email window.

"You should have called me," Serina chastised her.

"I forgot your number since you changed it. I guess I forgot to write it down."

"3Jacobs," she sighed, "how can you not remember my phone number? Numbers are what you *do*. And what about that memory thing of yours? Did it take a hike?"

"Yeah, I *know*. That's the point, I have tons of numbers in my face all the time, so I don't remember them unless I remind myself *these* numbers I have to remember. You know how hard I worked at *not* remembering everything."

"Yeah, Yeah, I know. And you don't want to work at remembering my number? Nice."

"Stop, I *knew* you'd call me."

"What*ever*. I need a vacation from my poverty level."

"Hey, Serina, let me call you right back. The dreaded 'dread' is due in my office any second. Besides, I have an idea about a vacation for the three of us."

"Seriously?" she asked. "Yeah, but forget it. I don't have the bucks for a vacation.

"Yep, seriously. Wait until you hear my plan. Talk to you shortly." She quickly hung up.

She pulled the mail screen back up, re-read the message, then x'd out of it, feeling even more needy and foolish for having written it. She couldn't actually send it. It'd be playing with fire somehow. Better *not* to think about why she didn't have something she craved. Besides, it wasn't even witty or interesting enough for him to bother printing. Nor was it worthy of answering based on content.

And she didn't really want anyone. Wasn't really lonely. She was just alone.

By choice.

She quickly trashed the message, checked the time and clicked offline. Pulled up a spreadsheet riddled with indecipherable and meaningless formulas. It was nearly time for the visit.

Like clockwork, he appeared. Fidgeting with his tie, clearing his throat, and actually looking down at the border of carpet where her office started. Hesitantly, he stepped in, saying, "Uh, good afternoon, Ms. Jacob."

"Jacob*s*," she corrected him.

"Uh, yes."

He watched her fingers, probably checking to see if she hit the alt/tab to change windows. Her hands remained folded in front of the keyboard.

Brightly, "What's up Gary?"

A clearing of the throat, "Uh…"

He'd prefer it if she called him by his last name, prefaced with the obligatory and respectful 'Mister'. Not gonna happen.

He took a few brisk steps, peered at her screen. Blushed.

She laughed. Not only because he just had to take a peek at the screen, but because she knew he was so confused with what he saw he wouldn't dare ask what she was working on. His ego wouldn't allow that.

Gary Anderton, the new manager here at The Company. He was tiptoeing around her, presumably because he'd been forewarned about the special circumstances governing her employment here. Basically, when she got hired, she made an agreement that she'd work for less pay on the condition that she'd be allotted ample time off—without pay. It worked out fine for her. She didn't have the ego hangup that drove some people to seek higher salaries, nor did she have the necessity for a higher salary. She got compensated fairly for the work she performed; the service she provided, if you will.

But all the money in the world couldn't buy time, so she preferred to use hers judiciously. She completed her work and she did it extremely well, and then she played.

She played a lot.

It was all fine before Gary Anderton arrived here. It still was fine, but she knew he sniffed around her because he couldn't quite comprehend how she wrangled such a liberal deal. Probably because he didn't have the good sense to recognize a deal when he saw one. It wasn't traditional, so it didn't fit neatly into his game plan.

Also, he probably was having a hell of a time trying to figure out if he was really her boss or not.

He held "team" meetings. He didn't make the big bucks. He was just a lackey for the guys who did. The perfect middle manager. Ultimately, he wasn't responsible for anything. How could he be when he didn't make any decisions or do anything. Simply an overgrown babysitter in a rumpled suit.

He ate all natural peanut butter and tofu hot dogs. No one liked Gary much. All in all, though, he was a good manager to have around if you had to have one around. He didn't interfere too much with anyone's job. This was a good thing.

She liked sticking it to him. "Jeez, Gary. What? Did you think I had porn up on the computer or something?"

"Oh, er, no…"

"I never download porn during the work day, only just before it's almost time to go home." She couldn't tell if it was merely the word 'porn' that made him fidget, or if it was because he was taking the thought further and actually trying to picture *her* surfing porn, or maybe even a step further and trying to picture what sort of porn she'd look at. No. He wasn't that imaginative. It had to be the mere mention of the word porn.

"Uh, Ms. Jacob…"

"Jacob*s*."

"It's against company policy for you to use the internet for ah, entertainment purposes. We could ah, check your files at any time…"

"Jeez, Gary. You can't check my computer. I have highly confidential material on here that you're not authorized for. Hasn't anyone told you that?"

Blushing again. (Hee hee!) "Uhm, considering the complicated rules governing your equipment, you should be especially careful so that you don't get a virus."

She laughed. "Who'd a thought, huh?"

"Excuse me?"

"I mean, about viruses. We thought we finally found a way to have sex without transmitting diseases, perfectly safe from behind a monitor and keyboard, and it turns out you can *still* get viruses from it even through a fiber optic wire."

"Ahh…mmhmm." He checked his watch, turned crisply and walked out the door.

As he was leaving, she called out after him. "That'd be a good slogan for Norton. 'A condom for your computer. Don't have cyber-sex without installing it first.'"

So she called her sister, Serina, back.

"What's up, 1Jacobs?"

"I got nothing except this art gallery thing tonight."

"That sounds good. Anyone you know showing their work?"

"Yeah, me."

"1Jacobs, why didn't you tell me? You want I should come?"

"I emailed you and nah, maybe next time when I'm a success."

"Don't be so insecure. And I didn't get your email. You have my right address?"

"You know I am, insecure, I mean. Send me an email so I get it right."

"Yeah, why is that exactly? And, yeah, I'll send you one."

"I don't know. We can't all be as strong as you."

She just snorted.

"I'm serious," Serina continued. "I'm not like you, I worry what people think."

"So do I!"

This time Serina snorted. "Bullshit!"

"I care what some people think. Sometimes. I just do what I want anyhow, though."

"Yeah, but you don't worry like I do," she shrugged on her end of the line. "Maybe because in the creative world, you gotta deal with so much rejection."

"Yeah, you're terrified of being rejected. Maybe you should seriously consider another career."

"I know. Maybe after this, I will. But I'm scared."

"Yeah, I know that…"

Serina gulped then asked, "So tell me about the trip to Vegas!"

Shelby told her, leaving out a few details. Then they hit a lull, so she asked, "So what are we doing for our monthly thing?"

"I don't know.

"You wanna go somewhere? That vacation getaway you want so badly?"

"3Jacobs, you know I can't afford it! Shit, I'm living in a hovel!"

"We should go to Vegas," Sheby interrrupted. Sherri'd love it!

"Aren't you listening to me? I can't afford to go, even if I sell ten paintings tonight, which is highly unlikely…."

"All the more reason," she interrupted again. "It'll be a whole celebration-fest kind of thing to turn our lives around. Com'on. My treat, 1Jacobs. You know I can afford it. I can afford to pay for Sherri, too, if I have to. Please?"

Serina paused before speaking. 3Jacobs' treat? Wow. How could she say no? "Ok."

"You'll seriously go?" she asked her.

"Yeah, what the hell. We'll have a good time and partyyyy…!!!"

"Yes!"

She purposely did not wish Serina luck for tonight since that would assure bad luck.

So she booked the Vegas vacation for all three of them and emailed Serina the info. Then she booked an immediate flight back to Vegas for herself, leaving in a few hours. Crazy, yes. But she had to go back. She could mow her strip another night; see her friends another night. Her work was a breeze, so no problems there. Something about Antonio had sparked an interest. She couldn't get him out of her mind. Time to take a risk, see where it went.

Chapter 5

Serina needed a new maxi-pad. She also needed a hair trim, high-powered body wash, manicure (dried oils under fingernails required professional attention, especially pthalo blue), a clean, pressed shirt and at least one pair of jeans without a hole in her private region. It was 6:30 PM—only a half hour before her art gallery opening at the California Heritage Gallery.

After her phone conversation with her sister, Shelby, not being able to reach her sister, Sherri, for her second dose of positive mental reinforcements, she'd taken a quick shower, threw on some two-day old jeans and a clean, black Tee-shirt that read "Antone's—Home of The Blues" over an illustration of a Fender Stratocaster (the official guitar of Austin, Texas). The back of the shirt listed over 100 blues artists that had played the famous club, but the patrons of the California Heritage Gallery would not see the back of the T-shirt tonight—a black trench coat effectively covered the shirt, most of her paint-stained jeans, and the hole in her private region.

"I'm gonna sell some paintings tonight, boss," Serina told the owner of the Kwik n' Easy a short while later, not bothering to take off the headphones of her Walkman. A dose of Brother Ray Charles, "Don't You Know", along with a couple of shots of merlot, would give her just the proper amount of hip swagger she would need to get through the evening. The inside pocket of her coat now held a small bottle of merlot, which she bought on credit from the Jamaican owner of the Kwik and Easy convenience store that was located just around the corner from the gallery.

"You better sell lots!" shouted the owner wanting to make certain Serina heard him. "You got big bill to pay! I tink I come wid you—your customers can pay me direct!"

"Don't worry, boss. You're at the top of my list, I promise," she told him, gently patting the brown paper bag in the inside pocket of her trench coat, not hearing but figuring that's what the owner said.

"Why you wearing maxi pad on your hand?" The store owner shouted, pointing at Jacobs's hand. "Maxi pad for woman's panty, not for hand!"

Serina removed the headphones. "If you'll loan me some gauze and surgical tape I would be more than happy to lose the maxi-pad."

"Gauze and tape? You tink dis is a hospital? Hell wid dat. Go get a Band-Aid!" He shouted, pointing down the aisle.

She went and grabbed a box, removed the maxi-pad and covered the coagulated cut with a couple of Band-Aids.

"You want to make money with art, you should do like this," the owner said, pointing at a collection of paintings on black velvet: Elvis and a '57 Chevy, a tiger skulking through a bamboo forest, Jesus in white robes floating on golden clouds—the usual fare.

"Right," said Serina, turning to leave.

"I know where you live!" shouted the owner as Serina walked out the door.

The California Heritage Gallery stood between Roberto's Plumbing and the Dragon's Breath Karate studio on a block of connected shops facing the main drag through town. The gallery was really just a well-lit, spacious white room, with four walls, and several free-standing white walls, each of which held numerous 18" x 24" paintings, depending on the size of the frames. Tonight the gallery was set up with 75 of Serina Jacob's small oils, most of them framed in simple light pine by Rex Wilcox. Wilcox generally framed Serina's work in the alley behind the shop, as long as the sun was shining and there was enough room between the plumber's trucks that usually packed the alley. Wilcox had no problem being amongst the plumbers in their greasy coveralls, thinking about their sweaty bodies underneath.

The opening was well under way by the time Serina made her appearance, a couple of swigs of merlot warming her empty belly and Brother Ray wailing "It shoulda' been me/with that real fine chick/it shoulda' been me/gettin' my natural kicks" in her headphones. Rex Wilcox had cornered two short and wide silver-haired ladies near the entrance to the gallery, keeping one eye on the street for his erstwhile painter and praying under his breath that she would show. Finally, Serina appeared in the doorway.

"Well," announced Wilcox, raising his arms in a 'gimme a hug' gesture. "It appears the guest of honor has……"

Serina, thinking about the fresh merlot on her breath, stopped short of the doorway and slowly removed her headphones, held her open hands out and said, "My toilet is leaking."

The silver-haired ladies looked quizzically at Wilcox, who dropped his arms and grinned. This was an ongoing joke between them. "Oh—I think you want to go next door, to the plumbing shop."

Serina scuffled off to the alley and the back entrance to the gallery. This way she could skulk around the food table for a few minutes, cram a few mini-quiche's into her hungry face, and quickly down a glass of cabernet before mingling with the patrons, most of whom would not recognize her anyway. She had only managed a couple of mini-quiches and cheese squares before someone did recognize her.

"Hungry, Serina?"

It was her ex-husband, Stefan, on the arm of one of his gay friends, who Serina vaguely remembered was called Bushy, or Boozy, or something like that.

"You remember my friend, Billie?" Stefan cooed, nuzzling into his friend. Billie was a hippie in layers and layers of thin, brightly colored clothing, including a long wizard robe with shiny stars. He wore rose colored granny glasses underneath a floppy velvet cap. He might have been blond, possibly overweight, but underneath the get-up, he appeared mostly shapeless: an amorphous mass of patchouli-scented blubber. He giggled and placed his arm around Stefan, kissing his forehead.

Serina felt as though she were about to retch. Not that she objected to gay men—like any warm-blooded American hetero, she liked to watch, although hadn't had the fortune of being involved in a frisky three-way, but this was her ex-husband, for chrissake, and he had gone to the other side. It stung! Talk about feeling inadequate—even if Stefan's dishonest, manipulative, hot-tempered, knee-jerk personality made her squirm, there was at least some reward in knowing that his sexual needs were satisfied. Serina poured herself half a glass of Chardonney and looked past the nuzzling couple to the crowd on the floor.

"Well gentlemen, I think I must be mingling!" she said with a wise-ass smile. Stefan grabbed her belt buckle and held on with his other arm around Billie's waist.

"But you will be joining us later, won't you Serina? Billie and I have something we'd like to show you." Billie giggled.

Ecstasy without a doubt, thought Serina. The guys were on the wet drug—perhaps her time for a frisky three-way had finally come?

"Well all right!" said Serina with enthusiasm. "As Chauncey the Gardener used to say, 'I like to watch!' But now I must be greeting my public. I'm sure you understand."

"Of course," said Stefan, winking. "We'll see you later."

God he was confusing, thought Serina. She had never met anyone so out-and-out sexual—he just loved to fuck and suck, and would do it with anyone at any time if he was in the mood. It was the "anyone" part that Serina simply couldn't live with, because he would often hook up with a sex partner for weeks on end and simply disappear out of her life, only to show up at her door again one day and expect to be taken in like a lost puppy. Plus it was just plain socially awkward to know that the fry cook at Hilda's Coffee Shop had been riding your husband like an Appaloosa just before she cooked your eggs, or that the bartender would pour you a free double as "payment", or worst of all, knowing that the guy in the flower shop had your husband's crotch on his breath. Better not to be married to *that*, Serina finally decided.

The gallery was surprisingly busy, considering that Serina Jacobs was not a well-known artist by any stretch of the imagination—her work had never been shown outside of the Bay Area, and then in only a handful of public places for various contests, benefits and so forth. The California Heritage Gallery was in fact the only professional venue that carried her work. Yet Serina did have a bit of a local reputation: her work was eminently affordable by almost anyone who wanted a small, original, oil painting of local scenes. It was this, plus her attention to the nearby landscape, the majority of her work centered on scenes around the reservoirs in the watershed below Mt. Tamalpais, that attracted the locals, including the film producer, with a known fetish for collecting art, Michelle Morgan, who had already seen some of her work and was indeed very interested.

She scanned the crowd, eagerly searching for Morgan. She noticed that many of the patrons were already owners of Serina Jacobs originals: there was Ellen something-or-other, a tired, dowdy third-generation Marinite who claimed to have "grown-up" on the Yolanda Trail and had bought several of the mountain scenes she had painted from that vantage point. And there was the tall, thin, investment banker from the country club who had bought one of Serina's larger paintings and hung it in the reception area of his small office in Larkspur

Landing, and who couldn't help raving about her uncanny knack for painting "realistic" water reflections. What was the secret, the gangly investor wondered. "I just paint what I see," she would invariably say. And there was the born-again, mousy divorcee who had used her sob-story of her debilitating liver disease to get a bargain price on another of Serina's larger works, only to go out and spend twice the amount on an elaborate gold-leaf frame. She was the one who spread the notion that Serina Jacob's color schemes were "trippy", although Serina could not remember if she had ever painted under the influence of psychedelics; possible, but doubtful. There were Ben and Kathy Rosen, who had bought a medium-sized oil of Lake Lagunitas to hang in the cabin of their 50 foot sailboat on a round-the-world family cruise. And a dozen or so others that Serina could identify not by their names, but by the paintings she had done and they now owned. But no sign of Michelle Morgan.

There were also some people that Serina did not recognize, and one fellow in particular caught her eye. He looked as if he had just stepped out of a Bond film where he might have played the role of some big bumbling Eastern European thug: black turtleneck, black sport coat, herringbone slacks, mesh Italian loafers with no socks, closely cropped goatee, slicked-back blonde hair tied into a short ponytail, tinted glasses on a hawkish nose—a misdirected attempt at soave. That, combined with his sheer height and girth, made him hardly the stereotypical art patron. She kept her eye on him as he exchanged greetings with the customers in the crowd. Then the investment banker emerged, took Serina by the arm and dragged her before a medium-sized oil of Bon Tempe reservoir, next to where the Bond character stood scribbling notes onto the show guide.

"Jacobs, you've done it again, by golly," said the investment banker, his voice almost Gomer Pyle-like with enthusiasm. "That water looks so good I feel like I could dive in and take a swim!"

"Ok!" Serina laughed, having taken many an illegal moonlight skinny-dip in that very spot, and having never once been caught. "Watch out for those park rangers, though."

"Rangers?" questioned the banker, scrutinizing the painting more closely "I don't see any rangers!" She rolled her eyes when the banker turned around and laughed. "Ha, thought you had me going there, didn't you? But really, Serina, this water is something else." And then, turning to the big spy-looking guy. "You can see what I mean—doesn't the water look…really real?"

The man was alternately staring at the painting, then back to Serina and the banker. "Rangers?" he said. "What do you mean, Rangers?" His voice was low and his accent Transylvania thick.

Well, heck. He was Eastern European!

"Oh," laughed the banker. "I was only kidding—you see there are Park Rangers in the water district that will fine you if they catch you swimming in the reservoirs."

"Rangers are people?" asked the big man in his thick accent, scratching his goatee.

"Yes, of course. They drive around…" the banker began.

"There are no people in this picture," interrupted the big spy, clearly getting irritated.

"Right," said the banker. "I was talking about the water in the picture."

"There is no water in the picture either!" growled the man, shoving the banker out of the way as he approached the painting. "There is paint! Only paint!" he shouted, roughly tapping the canvas with his beefy index finger.

The banker back stood back aghast, nodding his head. "Right," he repeated. Then, "I think I need a glass of wine, Ms. Jacobs," at which point he backed his way through the crowd towards the hors d'oeuvre table.

Serina watched him go, then turned to where the upset thug was rubbing his hand over the painting. She put her hand on his shoulder. The thug quickly turned and straightened up.

"Just paint," she said, pointing to the painting. "Nothing more."

"Yes—but it is not smooth," said the man, still seemingly bothered by the painting. "Some places there is too much paint!"

"Well, yes. That's the way it's supposed to be," she answered.

"Oh," said the thug, looking disparagingly at Serina in her torn jeans, tee-shirt and trench coat. "And what do you know? You are just a homeless looking for free food, no?"

She smiled and held out her hand "I'm Serina Jacobs, the artist." But the thug's attention had shifted elsewhere, looking over her shoulder.

"Well, Karl," came the voice of Michelle Morgan from behind. "How are you enjoying your adventure into the world of fine art?"

"It is not good," said Karl. "The paintings are not smooth. In some places there is too much paint, in others not enough."

"Oh really?" said Morgan, half laughing. "Perhaps we should take a belt sander to them, no?" Then, addressing Serina, "Sorry, couldn't help but overhear your conversation with Karl. Just kidding, of course, Ms. Jacobs. We like to humor Karl now and then." Morgan shook hands with the painter. "Michelle Morgan. I expect you heard I was coming—I'd like to see what we can do to get a few of these paintings into some of our studio offices up on the ranch. How many you got here? 75 or so? Well, we'll have a look—maybe we can take a few off your hands."

But Serina had not heard a word, for there with an arm around Michelle's waist, glowing like a harvest moon, was Hadlin Radner. She actually physically pinched herself. Was this another one of those dreams with Harlin in it, where Harlin spreads his bright wings over her dark thoughts and lifts her into the light? Or smothers her in a blanket of warm, soft skin? Part of her hoped that it was just another dream, and that she would wake up to life as usual without any major emotional challenges to contend with. But another part of her saw only Harlin, the real Harlin, standing there grinning like a first-grader who had just gotten 100% on his spelling test—grinning and looking down at her with shining eyes and a face like a sparkling gold nugget.

"I can't believe it!" he finally said in a burst. "It's you! Still got your Charlie puppet?" He was a bursting bubble of pure joy—a lithe thoroughbred, frisking about in a fresh green field—exactly as Serina remembered him, not one ounce of his brilliant spirit dimmed by the passage of the past few years. She thought she might cry, pass out, or both. But instead, her attention snapped back to the question he had just asked.

"I might," said Serina, smiling broadly in response to his light bulb visage. "Course he hasn't had anyone to talk to for—oh jeez—how long has it been? 10 years? 11?"

"Tahoe," he answered, reaching out and touching her hand. "I think that was the last time I saw you."

Serina's mind went reeling back to only a couple of years ago, to the one night where Harlin, almost out of sympathy, decided that he should consummate his long friendship with this self-destructing femme fatale called Serina. She had been high on speed and copious quantities of wine, playing her acoustic guitar and singing a smattering of original songs to a small crowd after hours at a local restaurant. Harlin pulled a chair up not 3 feet in front of her and had sat transfixed by her music for almost an hour. They shared some more speed and he drove them back to the mountain A-frame home he shared with three pals, led her up to his bed in the loft and gently explained that she would have to be on top—some kind of lower back condition—but after a few minutes Serina selfishly rolled him back into the missionary position she was accustomed to, and quickly finished. He had insisted it was very nice, but the next morning she awoke alone, feeling guilty for not being more sensitive to her longtime friend's desires, and drove back to her parent's home in the Bay Area. It was years since she had seen him and she still felt the guilt as if they had been together yesterday.

"Tahoe?" she lied, not wanting to encourage what she figured would be a disappointing memory for Harlin.

He smiled, knowing she remembered, but was too polite to press.

"Well…it was a long time ago, that's for sure!

Michelle Morgan had been patiently observing the conversation between her fiancé and this tall, a bit unkempt, but rather haunting, stunningly beautiful artist. "Well," she said finally. "It appears you and Ms. Jacobs have some catching up to do. I'll get myself a glass of wine and see what Karl has found out about these paintings." The crowd parted as Morgan and Karl headed for the hors d'oeuvre table, keeping their distance from the famous film producer and her aura of superiority.

"Oh, Serina," Harlin said, smiling and squeezing her hand. "I think I've missed you."

She smiled and squeezed back. "Well, I guess I've missed you, too…. except that you're always crashing my dreams—so it's not as if you disappeared from the face of the planet or anything."

"Crashing your dreams?" he pulled himself closer, half whispering. "Whaddya mean by that? I'm in your dreams? Get outta here!"

"No, I'm serious!" said Serina softly. "You make an uninvited appearance in my dreams about once a week! Usually with some lowlife speed freak female biker lurking somewhere in the background."

Harlin laughed out loud. "Ha!" Then, again in a half whisper, gesturing to where Michelle Morgan stood with Karl and Rex Wilcox at the hors d'oeuvre table. "Well, as you can see, my taste in women has become…more refined, shall we put it?"

Serina leaned close and whispered back, "A little short for you, isn't she?" Harlin always did prefer the taller females; smelly, but tall.

Harlin pulled back—Serina wondered whether she had misjudged him. The Harlin she remembered wasn't particularly sensitive to cruel slurs. But this wasn't the cause—he suddenly was smiling even more broadly than before, if that were possible.

"I sense the presence of merlot!" he announced, sniffing the air. "And I think merlot's calling me outside to partake!" at which point he took Serina's clammy hand and led her past the art patrons into the fog-cooled night air.

Rex Wilcox had no particular affinity for Michelle Morgan. He did not find her attractive and was turned-off by her aloof demeanor. And even though her bodyguard, Karl, was definitely a rock-hard hunk of pure Aryan power, the whole bodyguard thing was just too cold to get into. Rex did, however, have a strong affinity for many of the characters in Morgan's films, especially the daffy limp-wristed British robot in "Space Vampires" and the clumsy, pimply high-school nerd in "Cruising Main Street". He wondered, as he approached Morgan and Karl at the hors d' oeuvre table, how such a stiff, detached little woman could have come up with such endearing, *cute* characters.

"I'm so pleased you could make it to our little show!" cooed Wilcox. And then, grandly gesturing with his silk kimono-clad arms to the paintings surrounding them: "Don't you just adore the way Serina has captured the *love* in our local landscape?"

Michelle Morgan didn't have any problem with gays, even borderline flamers like Rex Wilcox. Many of her best art directors, film editors, cameramen, sales executives—employees across the board—were openly gay. And, having spent most of her adult life in the Bay Area, Morgan had gotten to the point were "gayness" just didn't register with her anymore—it was a non-issue, and had nothing to do with the fundamental value a person brought to a transaction.

Karl had a different view. While rugged anal sex between strong, muscular men was certainly an honored tradition dating back to the ancient Greeks, Karl did not like men who acted like women. Without a doubt he had a very strict definition of what he considered to be proper male behavior, (and female behavior, for that matter) and felt that acting like a "sissy" was a conscious and willful attempt to break the rules. Wilcox, in Karl's mind, was a classic example of a social troublemaker that simply needed some good old fashioned discipline, an opinion Karl displayed in his steely expression.

"Love?" hissed Karl, incredulous. "What are you talking about? There is no love in those paintings!"

"But of course there is!" cried Wilcox. "Look at the warmth of the light, the tenderness of the shadows, the softness of the billowing clouds, and then name one contemporary Northern California plain-air painter that displays such obvious affection for his or her natural subject!"

"Well," interrupted Morgan. "Jacobs certainly captures the character of the area, but I wouldn't say she's in the same league as say, Chatham—at least not price wise, that's for sure." Morgan laughed. Jacobs would have to sell her entire catalogue of small oils ten times over to equal the cost of one Russell Chatham original, even the rather underdeveloped oils Chatham had painted back in the Seventies.

"This one here is not too bad," said Morgan, approaching a medium size oil of Bon Tempe Reservoir on a cloudy, autumn afternoon. A northern California autumn—not trees of red and yellow but a few purple clouds reflected in the still water, the shadows of isolated oaks stark against the tawny grass on the hillsides. "I think it would look good in the lobby of the employee gym, don't you, Karl?"

"It is paint. Nothing more. A trifle, no?" Karl said, dripping with condescension.

"A trifle?" snickered Morgan. "At $1000 dollars I would hardly call it a trifle!"

"$1000-Hmmpf!" Karl spat on the floor, almost getting Wilcox's Japanese slippers. "It is paint—how much paint is worth $1000? You would need to fill this entire room with paint! Ha Ha!"

"You've got a point there, Karl," mused Morgan, pulling on her streaked, coarse hair. "And I'm sure you would agree that it would be a privilege for any artist to hang a painting in the gym of a famous film studio. I was chatting with Sylvester Stallone on the recumbent just the other day. Think of the exposure!"

Wilcox could scarcely believe what he was hearing. After all, wasn't Morgan herself an artist of sorts? Could she not remember her struggle to become an established filmmaker? Wilcox felt a strong urge to step outside for a cigarette—maybe even a pull off Serina's ever-present bottle of merlot.

"On the other hand, Karl, painting is this woman's livelihood. We can't expect her to give away her work, can we? How would she eat?" asked Morgan, feigning sincerity.

Karl sneered and shook his head. "It is not really work—this is no way to make a living."

"Well," said Morgan "you know how I like to support the local artists. And we do need something for the gym—I say we give a couple hundred bucks for it, don't you think, Karl?"

"Couple hundred bucks you could have tune-up on *all* the limos," muttered Karl.

"Excuse me..." blurted Wilcox, unable to contain his disgust with this conversation any longer. "But the gold leaf frame alone is worth $300. I spent $300 out of my own pocket to frame it!"

"You did?" asked Morgan, surprised, arms crossed in front of her ample bosom. "Why would you do that? I'm not sure I even *want* the frame! Does that mean I get $300 off?"

"Ahhhh," sighed Wilcox, smoothly slipping back into the art sales mode he knew so well. The frame was often an issue and Wilcox always had an answer for it, approaching the painting on the wall and doing his Vanna White thing with his hands. "The frame is as much a part of the total painting as the paint, the canvas, and the vision of the artist. It is the total package that has caught your eye, including the frame."

"$300 for the frame alone? Well—you're the expert on the framing angle, Mr. Wilcox. So say we throw in another $200 for the painting?" said Morgan.

Wilcox was not new to the art business, and one of the professional traits he had learned early on was the appropriate expression of snobbery when prospective buyers questioned the value of a painting.

"This particular piece is priced at $1000. If you look around you may find paintings that fit more comfortably in your budget," Wilcox replied.

Karl bristled. How dare the little faggot take that tone! I'll wrap his stinking artwork around his neck! But Morgan was tuned into Karl's temper and quickly stepped in.

"I'll give you $600 hundred bucks for it. Oh...and look around, Mr. Wilcox. The crowd appears to be thinning out. I don't see anybody else expressing an interest in this painting. I've got $600 on the table right now—you can snatch it up or wait and take your chances."

Wilcox fidgeted. Serina Jacobs was not a well-known artist—she was a starving artist. Literally. And here was Morgan—a multigazillionaire—bargaining for a piece of art like she was at a Turkish bazaar. And, even though a couple of many smaller oils in the $300 range had sold at the show, and some of the larger works were put "on hold" (which could always change and often did—a mildly buzzed art patron is generally more willing to write a check for a piece at the opening show than a sober art patron is the next day), a $600 sale would put the whole event in the black and make a dent in a few of Serina's debts as well. Even though Serina would no doubt be pissy and indignant about the whole thing, Wilcox decided to go ahead with it.

"Can we step into the back room for a moment?" suggested Wilcox to Morgan. "I suspect we can work something out."

Michelle Morgan had the air of a woman who had just had frisky, athletic sex with a 21-year old Olympic gymnast as she strode out of the California Heritage Gallery to where Karl stood by the open door of his black BMW limo, the Serina Jacobs painting wrapped in brown paper under her arm.

"Good work, Karl, as always," Morgan said as she slipped into the back seat beside her bleary-eyed, grinning, somewhat lit fiance, Harlin Radner.

"Danke, sir," smiled Karl, pulling the black BMW limo onto the quiet streets of San Anselmo. Eventually, the limo turned onto Sir Francis Drake Boulevard, down the Ross Valley towards the Bay, past the Marin Art and Garden Center where Serina Jacobs first showed her work and now had a few pieces in the rental gallery. It wasn't until they reached the giant iron sculpture of a nude lady sunbathing in front of the Bon Aire shopping center that Harlin Radner broke his slightly drunken reverie.

"Did I tell you that I went to school with Serina Jacobs?" he said softly, turning to Morgan.

"School? I thought you said you skipped college. Got into motocross or something silly thing like that," replied Morgan, who had set up a flagon of Glenlivet, a glass of ice, and a standard ashtray size dish of cocaine on the fold-down tray between them. In the dish sat a small silver spoon that had been custom-built for Morgan's nostril. Morgan snorted a spoonful, took a long draw off the Glenlivet, then refilled her glass. "Ahhh," growled Morgan in a very unfeminine fashion. "When I get a head full of whiskey and cocaine, I feel like I want a gorilla up the ass!"

Karl swerved slightly at the thought. Harlin cringed, not so much from the crassness of the comment, but from the thought of having to probe Michelle Morgan's anus. But Morgan never broached the subject of sex with Harlin. Except for rare occasions when Harlin mounted Morgan in his half-sleep so he could remember how to get off, Harlin didn't think of Morgan as a sexual being, period. A social partner? Yes. A movie maker mover and shaker beyond his wildest dreams? Definitely! But a lover? Hardly. And he suspected Morgan felt the same about him. Especially since he did not remotely resemble a gorilla.

"Not college," explained Harlin, trying to steer the subject away from bestiality. "I went to grammar school *and* high school with Serina Jacobs. We used to play puppets on the playground during recess." Harlin grinned, felt warm all over thinking about the cute little Langley and Charlie puppets.

Ever play with Jacobs's meat puppet?" Morgan laughed and quaffed her drink.

Harlin sighed. Why talk to this female pig about his childhood sweetheart, and what tender memories it raised? Probably not a good idea. Harlin turned to watch the moonlit fog pouring across the Bay into Berkeley as they headed north on 101.

Chapter 6

When she entered one of the Bellagio gambling rooms, she saw him almost immediately. He was bent over paying out a winning roll, his tongue set on the corner of his mouth. It was a fairly busy table, three people on his side, but the spot on the curve right next to him was open.

Taking a deep breath, calming the bubbling in her veins, she straightened her posture and walked over. She timed it so she could drop her money and card between rolls. His eyes followed the cash up to her hand, flickered for a second when they arrived at her chest, then finally landed on her face. His face broke into a grin and he nodded as he passed the money to his boxman, obviously reading the name on her card, Shelby Jacobs, before handing it off.

"There's my girl," he smiled. "Good to see you, amiga."

She returned his smile, happy he remembered her. "Very good to see you, Antonio."

"You live here or somethin?"

"No, why?"

He slid her some black chips and she did a double take, attempting to remain as controlled as possible. Suddenly realizing she was at a $100 minimum craps table, she felt like kicking herself. She'd been so excited, she hadn't even checked.

He must have noticed her glance because he leaned closer and lowered his voice. He slid his lashes up and down in a slow blink, met her gaze with a pacific look in his eyes, holding her there in wordless confidence. "Place the six n' eight, he's hittin 'em."

Shelby tossed him a couple black chips and he winked at her. "I don't usually play that way, but if you say so…"

"I know you; pass line, full odds, come bets. Relax, chica, I'll take care o' you, it's cool, it's cool."

The guy rolled an eight and Antonio winked again as he slid her the winnings, then started chatting again. "Nah, I just thought, you know, you live here or somethin cause I just saw you recently."

"You remember me, huh?" Her stomach quickened with that thought, the carbonated blood pumped to her head. "You remember my losing, then my winning for you."

"Huh uh," he shook his head as he paid off another eight. "It's your smile."

Liar. What a total fucking liar. He was working her.

And it was working on her. Cute. What a fool she was.

She always told herself about these dealers, the bartenders, even Vince; they were here to make money. And the more people they could get to come back and spend more money in the casinos, the more they were gonna make. It was all about time and tips and charm and oh so cunning.

Vince was hands down the best bartender she'd ever seen. He could take seven orders, fill them, cash them, and made it look like nothing. He was fast and efficient. He also knew exactly how to grease people and keep them coming back. Those drinks were set up before you even sat down. He'd stand and talk to you and act interested. And he could adjust on a dime. He'd talk to her and say 'shit' every third word, but be a perfect gentleman with an eighty year old couple and talk about their golf game.

Same with these dealers. They counted and shuffled and added and paid with the best of them. But the best of them could also read a person in a heartbeat and knew exactly how to treat them. They knew if they should back off and leave them alone, or if they should give them extra attention. And they made it look effortless. They made it look fun. But bottom line was the almighty dollar. They were in it for the money.

So as nice as they were to her, as often as they called her sweetie and struck up conversations, there was still a little wall, a little border that made her step back and wonder how real it really was. Most of the time, she figured they liked her. Just cause they were working didn't necessarily negate the possibility that they might really like her.

But she'd be willing to gamble pretty heavily that if she was broke, the curtain would get pulled back and *poof*, just like vapor, a lot of the attention would be gone.

But even though she mentally knew that, it still worked. Go figure.

So as Antonio here told her he remembered her smile, she couldn't help but think, *liar.* But, she still grinned and felt a rush when he winked, and part of her believed that actual magic was at work here instead of it just being a cheap trick worthy of a whore.

She did have a nice smile. She flossed every day.

She acted casual. When he slid another chip her way from a six hitting, she nodded and told him to press it up.

"Good girl," he commented. "Smart move. So you don't live here? You live close, LA?"

"No, a bit further north."

"Yeah? I'm from New York. So what're you doin out here again so soon? You come out here for business or somethin?"

"No, just fun."

"Gonna take this down now a little, alright?" he asked, sliding her winnings from another six. He licked his lips and shifted his weight. "Fun huh? Yeah, you havin' fun right now?"

She picked up the black chips and flipped them through her fingers before setting them back on the rail. "Yeah, this is a little fun."

"What's fun? Winnin money? Or talkin to me?"

Cocky. Very cocky of him. She liked it. She answered by smiling.

"So you stayin here?" he asked.

"Here? Bellagio? No, huh uh. Caesars."

"You like it there? What do they got that we don't?"

"They're nice to me." As she said that, the roller sevened out. The stickman tapped out, meaning he was going to move over and deal in Antonio's spot. Up several hundred bucks, she was still playing way over her head. She was just too faint hearted to have to take five hundred bucks of odds on an eight or six if it was rolled next.

Especially with Antonio gone.

So she picked up her chips and winked at him. Tossing one onto the felt, she said, "Thanks for the place bets, those worked well."

"You leaving already?" he asked as the stickman moved around behind him and tapped his shoulder. "Back to Caesars, huh?"

She nodded. "Yeah, time to go."

"Thanks," he told her, dropping the chip into the toke box. The other dealers also nodded at her. "Come back tomorrow, 'k? Give us a fair shake to treat you good at the Bellagio here, alright?"

"Ahh, I don't know. You can try. They're pretty good to me over there, though."

"Yeah? Maybe I should come see what they do over there? Check out the competition?"

"I'll show you around anytime you want."

The stickman took his spot, so he stepped closer to her, leaning a shoulder dangerously close. He stared into her eyes. "I'd like to, you know, check it out, but I work till three tonight."

She had to break his gaze, so she glanced down and took a step back, speaking softly. "I'm sure I'll be around, craps tables or bars. Come over if you'd like," she replied, then quickly turned and walked away.

Do you even freaking believe that? She thought he was hot before, but when he stood next to her and looked her dead in the eye, he was positively electric. And that was beyond flirting, that was outright *bold* what he did.

Back in her room, she checked the time. 2:20. *He wasn't going to show up. Why would he show up? She never even told him where to show up, so even if he did, he might not find her.* She grabbed a few condoms. She *should just NOT even take these. If she didn't take these, there was no chance that she'd use them, right? Play it cool. They would be a shitty reminder when he didn't even show up and she'd have to put them back.* But of course she took them with her.

She was still just bubbling thinking about him standing close to her and being so coy and blunt at the same time. "I work till three."

He must be a hound. Just a total fucking hound. Sure, she put off the vibe to him. No way she couldn't have. And she *was* working it, too. So of course he totally sensed that she dug him. But now she knew that he knew that she dug him. And now she was pretty sure he dug her. Or that he was just a total hound.

Those eyes of his. Holy shit, those eyes! It sounded stupid to judge someone so much by the look in their eyes. People could fake it. This was Vegas man, people bluffed all the time. There was that saying; the eyes are the windows to the soul. And she believed that, but only so far.

But his eyes took it to another level, a rare level. She'd never had anyone make such strong eye contact with her. Frankly, if he wasn't likeable, it'd be offputting. Or even challenging. It was a little challenging, first to meet his gaze, then to look away. But wasn't confrontational, rather much more the opposite.

Inviting.

She dropped some cash into the safe and grabbed a fresh pack of smokes dirty habit, but one she and her sisters for some reason had never shaken completely—oh, they could quit for a day or two, but then light one or two up in one given night, then quit again for a day or two—kinda like closet smokers, she supposed—maybe that meant something, and headed back downstairs.

Vince set her up with a drink before she sat down. Asking, "You get lucky?"

"Not yet, but maybe."

"Huh? You were gone a long time, couldn't have been too bad."

"I went next door for awhile."

"Blackjack?"

"Hot craps dealer."

"Oh yeah? He treat you right?"

"Hopefully. I'll let you know tomorrow," she winked at him.

"Where's he at?" He scoped the casino.

"Still working right now. He said he'd come over here when he was done. I doubt he will, though."

Looking past her, he said confidently, "He'll show up. What's he look like?"

"Uhm, he's hot. Dark hair, dark eyes, Latin, tall."

Still looking past me, Vince said, "He's here."

"Huh?"

"There's a guy coming this way, he was looking around and he saw you and he's coming over—right about…now."

She turned around, and there he was.

"Yo," he told her as he slid into a seat next to her.

"Hi. That was quick."

"Yeah, I asked for an early out an' got it, it's not all that busy there tonight."

"What can I get you, buddy?" Vince asked him.

"Uh, Bud's fine, an' one for her, too, man," answered Antonio.

Vince winked at her as Antonio pulled out a few bills and handed him the cash.

He swallowed some beer and looked around. "So this is Caesars, not bad, man, not bad. So you like it here, huh?"

She moved her head up and down and checked him out for the first time away from the dice table. He was nervous, she could tell. She'd noticed before that he was always in some kind of motion. Taming him would be like pinning down mercury.

It was actually quite charming. She couldn't figure out why he'd be nervous around her, so she took it as a compliment. Maybe she could get him to relax. "It's very cool of you to come over here. I'd think you'd want to get done with work and just get off the strip."

"Nah, it's cool, you know, it's cool. It's nice to grab a beer an' chill out a little bit."

"But you've never come over here before?"

"Oh, uh, yeah, I been in here a few times, not too much, though. When I first came out here, I walked around in here once or twice."

"Where do you like to hang out?"

He shrugged. "Not too many of the big casinos, you know, more off the strip little joints. I like some of 'em, though. Hard Rock, that's cool, I go there sometimes."

"I love the Hard Rock. It's where I go when I can't take the bubble-gum music anymore."

"Yeah," he grinned, "I hear you. I'm like that, too. I hardly even notice it anymore at work, though."

"Good thing, cause this place is full of shitty music. Hey, you want a shot or something? It sounds better with a buzz on."

"Yeah I'll do a shot," he agreed.

"Vince, line 'em up, baby," she told him.

"What do you want, lemon drops?" Vince askd.

"Ask him. I'll do whatever he wants."

Wickedly grinning, Antonio said one word, "Cuervo."

She amended that. "One Cuervo for him, lemon drop for me."

Vince laughed and started pouring.

"Won't do the tequila, huh?" Antonio asked.

"I can't stand it. It makes me mean."

"I can't picture you being mean," he teased and swigged at his beer. Meanwhile, Vince cracked up at that comment. "So you know him?" Antonio asked, indicating Vince.

"Yeah, sort of."

"Yo man, what's your name? Vince?"

Dropping off her shot, and setting up Antonio's to pour, Vince held out his hand. "Yeah, I'm Vince."

"Antonio," he said as they shook hands.

The handshake amused her, they both held hard, that guy thing. Vince looked Antonio dead in the eye, almost challenging him, no hint of a smile. Antonio took it in stride, didn't back down or seem the least bit annoyed.

"So you know her?"

Vince answered him, "Yeah. I know her."

"You think she can be mean?"

"I don't know, I've never seen her drink tequila," he answered, pouring the shot. "You need lime and salt?"

"Nah, I'm good, thanks." He turned his attention back to Shelby. "Ready for all this?"

"Always," she answered.

He barely grimaced when he shot his. She gulped a few times to get hers down, caught him watching her as she licked the sugar from the glass. He swallowed hard.

Behind her, she heard a voice, "Good evening, Stella!"

"Oh, shit," Shelby muttered and turned around. There he was, Vegas Vic padding up the stairs in his slippers, glasses and furry face, ready to sit down and join us.

Vince didn't even hesitate. "Keep on moving, buddy," he said, pointing away from the bar. "Don't even fucking think about it."

Vic stutter-stepped once, did an about face, and wordlessly headed back down the stairs. Once out on the casino floor, he shouted, "He's more handsome than Robert, Stella."

"Stella?" Antonio asked.

"Never mind, really," she replied.

"Robert?" he then asked, nudging her.

"Don't worry about it, it's nothing."

"Oh, I ain't worried 'bout it, you know, since I'm more handsome anyhow," he grinned.

Vince cut in, "That guy's a fucking freak. He still owes me thirty bucks."

Antonio seemed content to blow it off. "Thanks for the shot."

"Thanks for the drink," Shelby answered.

"Thanks for having me over here."

"Thanks for meeting me over here."

"So how come you let me come over here and hang out with you?" he asked.

"I don't know. How come you came over?"

He laughed and avoided. "You givin me a hard time?"

"Not really. Just fuckin' with you a little bit."

"I see that. How come?"

"Because you take it well, and you're really cute when you're a little flustered."

He cocked a brow and smiled, directed his gaze directly on Shelby for the first time since sitting. "Oh, flustered is it? You think I'm flustered?"

"I think you're a little nervous, yeah."

"But you think I'm cute, too."

"Oh come on, you know you are."

"I wanna know what you think," he teased.

"I just told you that."

On the other side of the bar, Vince threw down his bar rag and grabbed his smokes. "I'm going on break," he announced to everyone.

As he walks away, Antonio watched him, then commented, "I don't think your friend likes me much."

"Don't worry about him, he just looks out for me, that's all."

"I think he likes you a little, that's what I think."

"Yeah? I'd rather know what you think of me."

"I came over here, didn't I?" his cocky response.

"I thought you wanted to see Caesars," she challenged.

"I've already seen Caesars," he answered. "I wanted to see you."

"Oh. Thanks. Here I am."

"Yeah, I see that. Now who's all flustered?"

"I'm not flustered," she laughed. *She totally was.*

"Yeah, ok. Well, there you are. Here I am."

"Yep," Shelby nodded.

"So, you ready for all this?" he repeated from earlier.

"Always."

They both took long slugs off their drinks. She smiled and he did the same. She absorbed, taking sidelong glances at him and trying to note, log and detail every nuance of him.

Antonio wore all black; black shoes, black pants, black T-shirt. It fit his coloring well. A tiny flash of gold around the back of his neck, but not a thick chain. The front tucked under his shirt, so it wasn't really ghetto. Not as nervous as when he sat down; either the Cuervo took the edge off, or he was getting more comfortable with her. But still that constant, fluid motion. His forearm sinewy, every tendon moving when his fingers, his hand. His shirt hugged him a little tight in the sleeves, not in an exaggerated *'International Male'* kind of way, but that vein, that one glorious vein that traveled up the front of his biceps, peeked out and protruded.

But even more appealing than all that was the crooked grin on his face. It wasn't smug. Smug would piss her off. It seemed genuine, almost sort of sweet. Almost sort of surprised.

Interrupting her secret thoughts, he asked, "Ready to gamble?"

"Always"

"Alright, c'mon, then." He finished off his beer, and grabbed her hand. "Let's do it. I wanna see just how lucky you are."

Over an hour later, she was literally jumping up and down. They really did have it going on tonight, and he looked pretty damn impressed, too. She was convinced it had to be his luck driving all this good fortune, which only made her feel even luckier to be with him.

They cashed out and sat back down at Vince's bar. Antonio ordered drinks and a couple shots of Cuervo with a wry grin. Shelby didn't argue cause she was liking this. All of it. She wasn't sure if it just felt good to be out with Antonio because he was so contagiously fun, or if she just really liked winning that much money, since she liked to keep her winnings under $5,000. a day to avoid coming under scrutiny, or if it was the drinks. But she also didn't really care.

Shelby relaxed, suddenly not feeling like she was in over my head, wasting time on one thing when she should be doing another. Looking over at him as he raised his beer and drank some, all those niggling little insecurities seemed to vanish.

Vaporize.

It had to be his dark, good looks and crooked smile. His slightly slurred speech patterns, the way he moved—all that energy trying to escape. He was witty and sly, bold and shy. He was so easily masculine. He was magic. Pure and simple. God did she have it bad.

And yes, he made her feel special.

He nudged her. "How you doin'?"

"I'm doing just fine," Shelby answered. "How about you? You've seen Caesars, won a little money. Now you see why I like it here?"

"I can see they like you here, man. The dealers, waitresses, you know, they all know you. Even the machines like you."

"They're just doing their job, being nice, that's all."

"Nah, I think it's you. You're cool, you're nice to them, you deserve to be treated well. Lots o' people are dicks, you know?"

"Yeah, well, everyone deserves to be treated nice until they act like a dick."

"You come here a lot? How come I never seen you before?"

"I don't go to Bellagio too much, I guess."

He laughed, "Cause we ain't nice to you like they are here?"

"Sorta," she smiled. "See, they're nice to me here cause I've earned it, and in return they earn my loyalty. I don't think anyone deserves anything. But I'll take whatever I've earned. Which is why I can't figure out why you're hanging out and being so nice to me."

"Yeah? You don't think you deserve that? Wait, I mean, *earned* that?"

"Not really. But I like it anyhow."

"Maybe I just wanna. I mean, I didn't do nothin to earn hanging out with you."

"Yeah, I think Bellagio sent *you* over here as a customer relations thing is all."

"Yeah, I'm a spy. Tell you what," he nudged her again. Then he turned and peered directly at her. His eyes flashed serious for a second, then softened as he said, "I haven't seen everything here yet. I'd kinda like to see what the rooms are like."

"Oh…well! Ooh, ok, um, well.."

"Nah, I'm sorry. I haven't earned that, I know. I didn't mean…"

"No, it's ok, it's cool, I um, you just surprised me."

"Well, to be honest then, I did mean…"

"Oh, I know what you meant. I just mean, that well…"

"It's ok, really, forget it. Forget it, you know, I'm sorry, I shouldn't have…"

"No no no," she interrupted. "You should have."

"Oh. Well, you know, you showed me around. How 'bout I show you around?"

"Um," Shelby hesitated, weighing how much she trusted him against potential for danger. "Ok."

"Yeah?" He sounded surprised.

"Yeah. I mean, if you want.

At that moment, Diamond the gorgeous whore who wound up with Robert the last time Shelby was in town, took a seat behind Antonio and winked at her as she pulled her chair closer to his.

Pulling a bill from the pile of cash in front of her on the bar, Shelby held it up and said to her, "I'll give you a hundred dollars to go away immediately."

Reaching over, she plucked the bill from her hand, replying, "Not exactly how a lion would handle it, honey, but whatever you want." And she sauntered away.

Chapter 7

Serina Jacobs wove through the dense fog on the old, Panoramic Highway along the Pacific coast in her worn out Saab, empty wine bottles and scotch bottles clattering on every turn. Anyone within earshot might have thought the engine was falling out, the wheels were falling off, or perhaps the entire vehicle was disassembling. But at 3 AM on this particular night the Panoramic Highway was deserted. Besides, the fog was so thick that, as the locals said: "you couldn't see your hand in front of your face." Nobody in their right mind would have taken the coast road that night; the route over Mt. Tam would be an infinitely more reasonable route—at least the redwoods, eucalyptus and roadside manzanita would provide some reference point. On the Panoramic, there were only steep embankments on one side and sheer cliffs on the other with the rocky shoreline of the Pacific Ocean below.

She was feeling kinda happy, kinda sad after her art show. Serina pulled over at a turn out point to open a new bottle of merlot. Was this the second bottle or the third, she couldn't recall. But, who cares. The old Saab was still running. She'd shifted the car into neutral, though the parking brake had not been engaged. The road declined slightly toward the cliff's edge and the car started rolling very slowly, but Serina didn't notice. She was having difficulties getting that next bottle of merlot open. Finally, in an act of true frustration, she placed all her weight on her feet, one foot still situated on the accelerator, in her effort to remove the cork from the bottle of wine.

The Saab squealed to the cliff's edge and launched itself a couple of hundred feet into the fog in a graceful arc above the Pacific. By sheer luck, or rather stupidity, Serina's driver door flew open and she fell out, landing in the dark, cold water of the Pacific Ocean before the Saab went crashing into the cliff and erupting into a ball of flame. Fiery pieces of her trusty mount then tumbled and leaped into the ocean, landing in the water in a hiss of steam, barely missing her when she emerged, gasping for oxygen.

Over an hour later, having clawed her way up the cliff side after washing ashore, very crusty, salty wet, shivering from the cold, pissed as all heck which was providing the adrenalin to sober her up and walk after such a shocking ordeal, Serina headed down the Panoramic Highway toward Stinson Beach in the thickening fog.

The Pacific coast immediately north of San Francisco is not as populated as one might expect, given it's proximity to a major metropolitan area. However the Marin Headlands and Mt. Tamalpais pose a significant barrier between Mill Valley at the head of the Richardson Bay and Muir Beach, Stinson Beach, Bolinas and other points along the Pt. Reyes Peninsula. This was country Serina knew intimately, having hiked and biked over the mountain from San Anselmo to the beach on hundreds of occasions over the course of her life. On many of those occasions Serina, sometimes with one of her sisters, a girlfriend or a boyfriend, and once with Harlin Radner, would illegally sleep in some of the dense thickets, hollowed out redwoods, rocky overhangs and otherwise concealed areas of the mountain and coast. It was a particularly dense thicket along a freshwater stream that fed the Bolinas Lagoon. Tonight, or rather this morning, the wind, many times, blew her perilously close to the cliff's edge as she aimed for a resting area as she felt more and more weary.

The fog was becoming a lighter shade of gray in the east. She walked a half mile up the small stream that led to the thicket she was searching for, but it was still pitch dark on the ground, causing her to stumble occasionally on the slick stones. Finally, she found it as the sky became lighter by several additional shades. The thicket was dense and cool, almost a solid canopy of small leaves and branches, with a compact open area next to the stream. As the birds began to announce the coming dawn, Serina lay down in the dark thicket, the shock and exhaustion finally overtaking her.

Chapter 8

After a short trip to eat some food at another casino, Shelby and Antonio were back at Vince's bar. They barely were seated when another couple arrived, taking the seats right next to them. They were all decked out, best of everything, but it came together in a rather austere way. The woman glanced at them disdainfully, dragging her eyes up and down the two of them then turning back to her husband. She said something to him, Shelby couldn't hear what, but he then also checked them out. Antonio seemed to be aware of it, because he moved closer to Shelby and his grin faded.

The closeness caused her to smell him, and it pulled her attention back to him. Reaching up, he brushed the hair off her shoulder and locked her in a smoldering look for a couple seconds. Shelby was about ready to fall completely into him, willing to let him overwhelm her.

Then the guy next to them suddenly spoke. "Good evening," he said, and there was no doubt he was talking to them.

So she looked over and nodded at him with a half-smile. "Hi, how are you?"

"We are doing quite well," he answered.

"Glad to hear it," Antonio added in an attempt to be friendly.

"Are you out here on vacation?" the woman asked.

"Oh, um, I am, yeah. He lives here," said Shelby, pointing to Antonio.

"Are you staying here?"

"Yeah, I am."

"Really?" She said it in a manner that if it were written on a page Shelby'd actually be able to see the disbelief and disdain dripping off it. "Hmm. We always stay here. We stay in a suite, they're just wonderful. You should try that sometime. It's expensive, but if you could afford it, it would be worth it." She sniffed and shook her wrist. It was weighed down with a fantastic, sparkling, diamond bracelet.

Shelby could see Vince roll his eyes behind the bar.

"It looks like you got some sun today," she continued.

"Oh yeah, we finally had a warm day out here."

"We were outside, they gave us a cabana at the pool, wasn't that nice of them? But I tried to stay out of the sun. Besides, he," she waved to her man next to her, "was busy playing in the high roller area so I figured I'd go out shopping."

She scrunched her nose at Shelby, making what Shelby could only assume was a face that she thought was cute.

"Then I went to the salon here. Have you been in there, yet?"

Shelby shook her head, "Nope, haven't checked it out."

"You should go," she said, shaking the bracelet on her wrist. "I bet they could do something with that hair of yours."

She looked past her and at Antonio, giving him a wink. "That's a very nice bracelet," Shelby commented to change the subject.

"Tiffany's at the Bellagio," she answered obviously very proud of the expensive purchase. "My wonderful husband here just bought it for me today."

"That's great. Good for you," Shelby answered politely.

"I deserve it," she laughed.

Her husband grinned and glanced at Antonio. "Fine women should possess fine things. I'm just lucky to be the one keeping her in the diamonds she deserves." He laughed.

Antonio leaned close and whispered in Shelby's ear. "Hear that, huh? Bet that was one hell of a blow job she gave to get that. Wonder if he jacked up his Porsche on the sidewalk as she finished him off."

Choking back a laugh, she elbowed him lightly.

The guy, her husband, continued, "So are you winning anything?"

"Oh, doing ok. No diamonds from Tiffany, but having fun," she replied, hoping he'd pay attention to his wife and let her fall back into Antonio in a more romantic pose.

"Well that's nice," he said. "It doesn't look like that's your style anyway."

"No, I guess not. Not really down with the bling bling," answered Shelby. But he appeared confused, so Shelby restated it in terms he would understand. "Don't really like a lot of jewelry."

"I see that. Why is that exactly?"

She moved her head back and forth slowly. "Don't know to be honest; just don't really care for it."

"But you have a very attractive tattoo. Isn't that like jewelry?"

"Yeah, well, sort of. I guess you're right," she answered, hoping he'd give it up.

But he didn't. Instead, he stared directly at Shelby, briefly at her face, then allowed his gaze to wander down and linger for a time on her boobs.

Shelby knew they looked good in this shirt.

He lingerd too long, though.

So Shelby turned her body slightly toward Antonio. She knew he noticed all this, because he was staring at the guy, not a hint of humor in his expression. His jaw clenched when he decided to speak. "Yeah, you know, beautiful as she is, she don't need anything to show off. Her beauty says it all."

Not believing he just said that, Shelby glanced up at him and he gave her a wink. Not breaking his gaze into her eyes, he lightly traced his thumb over her shoulder, down across her back, causing a tiny shiver up her spine. Then he lazily rested his hand against her back, warm, but subtle. He leaned over and kissed Shelby on the temple. So very sweet and hot all at once. She just wanted to climb all over him right there.

But the guy was relentless. He kept at it. "So what is it you don't like about jewelry, exactly?" he persisted. "I see you wear a ring at least."

He was beginning to annoy Shelby. The wife's sitting upright, with her board up her ass posture, looking smug and proper and classy and oh-so bottled blonde. She dripped of money but there was obviously something missing because she was not satisfied with her diamonds. She was satisfied with *showing off* her diamonds. Shelby almost felt sorry for the pathetic, pampered little priss. Because her husband next to her, he was not leaning into her the way Antonio leaned into Shelby. Instead he was looking right past her and at Shelby's boobs.

And even more aggravating, they were distracting Shelby from Antonio. From the heat of his body only inches from hers, from the feel of his warm hand on her back, from his dark eyes and crooked grin.

Thinking about him, she softened up, deciding she was being too touchy. But then she glanced back over at them, and the woman was blatantly checking out Antonio. She was staring right past Shelby, diamond clad arm perched beneath her chin, and her eyes locked directly on Antonio. She even licked her lips!

So Shelby decided to tell him exactly what she didn't like about jewelry. "Well, I don't wear gold, because it's pretty ghetto. And I don't wear diamonds because the slave labor and civil war in Sierra Leone is tragic and I can't bear the thought of people living in hell and dying in bloodbaths just so I can exploit them and have a high-priced piece of shiny fossilized coal to wear."

Antonio quickly covered his mouth to hide a smirk just as she began to get a guilty pang. Maybe she was too harsh. Maybe they really didn't mean to act snotty and put them down and she just insulted them for no reason. Maybe she was simply an insecure bitch.

The lady spoke up again. "Yes, well, I don't know about that, but I do think it's nice when people know their limits and are content within those limits. You know, instead of wanting more; things they know they can't have. That would be a horrible feeling."

Ok. So. They were definitely snotty, skinny, arrogant bitches. No question about it.

Her husband laughed really loud. "Luckily we don't have that problem," he said. "But it's true. Most people are suited for what they have anyhow. Their tastes suit them perfectly. Like you two," he continued. "So I take it you two aren't married then?"

"No," Shelby answered. "We'd like to get married, but his wife is against the idea."

Temple visibly throbbing, Antonio waved Vince over, "Couple shots right here," he ordered and turned to Shelby. "What do you want?"

"Cuervo," she answered.

"You two want a shot or something?" he offered to the couple.

"Tequila?" the guy asked. "I think we can do better than that." He ordered a bottle of their best champagne from Vince, who proceeded to finish pouring their shots first, then started filling a bucket with ice for the other couple. "See, that's how Vegas has changed," the guy announced.

"Oh my, yes," his wife agreed as she clicked open a gold cigarette case, probably Cartier, and lit up a long, skinny cigarette. Probably a Virginia Slims. "It used to be a different breed out here. Champagne, tuxedoes and cocktail dresses all the time. It's different now, though."

Her husband signed the tab as she inhaled and raked her eyes over Antonio again, fixating momentarily on his arm, his hand on Shelby's back. Antonio nudged into Shelby, nodding at their shots.

They raised them and downed them. The burn was instant, a path of liquid lightning going straight from Shelby's throat to her gut. She had to concentrate hard to not gag or cough. Sucking in a breath, she looked over at Antonio who had one eye squinted shut as he dragged off his smoke. Grinning, he rubbed his hand up and down her back, asking, "You alright?"

The husband distracted her again.

He commented, "See, smooth," as he swirled his champagne around in the glass. Locking eyes with Antonio, he continued, "When you can afford the finer things in life, you acquire the taste for them. People are like diamonds in that way. Some of them are just rough, need to be polished up a bit. But some will always be rough and uneven, while some are coal and will always remain just coal."

He was staring at Antonio when he made that lovely statement, and Shelby knew Antonio was not about to break the eye-fuck. She could only imagine how intimidating his glare could be, so Shelby watched the guy. Before long, he chuckled and sipped his champagne.

Pussy.

So Shelby turned back to Antonio, still staring at the guy, but with a look of passive calm. The only indication of his mood she detected was his clenched jaw. Shelby chose to kiss him right there at that tension point. He might be a little drunk right now, and he might be dumb enough to be hanging out with her, but it didn't take Freud to figure out when you're being insulted. It really pisses her off. She'd seen it before at the tables. She'd seen how some of these rich bastards just loved giving the dealers a hard time. Antonio probably put up with that type of insult every day at work, and now he had to deal with it here when all he was trying to do was have some fun. And worst of all, more than likely it was all her fault since she was a white, blond chick.

If he was somewhere else, this wouldn't have happened. Or even if he was here with someone else, not lightbulb blonde Shelby, it wouldn't have happened. She was the impetus causing his ego to get fucked with. Yeah, he's got to be grateful he met her right about now.

"Sorry," she whispered to him.

"Ain't your fault," he mumbled, then turned to whisper in her ear. "Sorta funny, in fact. They are insulting us and hitting on us at the same time, right?"

His breath and voice sent a delighted chill down her back, and the actual words struck her as really funny. "Yeah," Shelby answered. "That's pretty much it."

He whispered again, "Thought so. Just makin' sure."

Next thing she heard was the couple next to them saying goodnight. He scooped up the ice bucket and she rose fluidly and glided away next to him.

Antonio asked Shelby, "Ready to have some fun?"

"Always."

"Good." He stood up.

Grabbing her hand, he pulled Shelby along as he followed the couple over to the elevator bay. She followed him easily, certain he was up to something.

They were standing only a foot away from the other couple, Antonio close behind Shelby, waiting for a bell to ding and the doors to open and take them up. She wondered briefly what the hell he was doing since her room wasn't in this tower, basically wanting to just stay the hell away from them anyhow. The thought passed quickly while her gaze wandered around, admiring the dark green reflective walls, the gilded elevator doors. Frank Sinatra crooned all around and Shelby grinned at that.

Antonio's hands rested on her shoulders, tingling her hot skin, making it sear where the cool air couldn't reach. He leaned down and started sucking on her neck. Shelby leaned into it with a grin and a giggle, shyly eyeing the other couple then looking back down. He was breathing hotly in her ear, sending spikes of pleasure through her whole body, warming her even more.

Shelby's head tilted back reflexively and he started to mumble some words. "Beautiful," she heard as his teeth razed against her lobe and worked it back and forth a few times. One hand kept massaging her shoulder, moving lower, stroking up and down her naked arm as the other moved to the front of her neck. He slid it up and down her throat, lightly across the top of her chest.

She urgently wanted to moan as the tingles from his hands and mouth worked through her entire body. Slightly drunk, getting rubbed and kissed, feeling oh so relaxed. But Shelby remembered where she was and decided to open her eyes, glancing into the reflective walls again. She can see their reflection, darkened, but vivid and crisp, staring back at her. She was stretched out in front of him, his hand roaming up and down her arm that had dropped to her side. His naked shoulders were hunched into her, his mouth buried against her neck. Him with streamlined edges, straight and angular. Shelby with slender curves, and breasts lush and rounded.

She could see him look up, still kissing her neck, but eyes meeting hers in the reflection. One of them in the reflection is dark, the other light and seeming to sparkle. Shelby felt they looked stunning together.

Then she noticed his hand, still lightly stroking across the top of her chest, and underneath it, her breasts rising and falling in tune to her already heavy breathing. Shelby could actually see her nipples, darkening and hard, poking at the thin cotton material of her shirt.

Out of the very corner of her vision, she spotted the other couple, he in a crisp suit, her in a black silk knee-length dress. Her shoulders were bare, too, and her man stood behind her, his hand possessively on her waist. They were so neat, so squeaky clean. So thin-lipped and fake blonde, tight and groomed and proper.

And they were watching her every move, her every gesture.

Demurely, suddenly feeling so very trashy, Shelby glanced down and bit her lower lip.

She caught Antonio's glance again and attempted to take a step away, beginning to raise her arms to cover her full chest as she slouched down. His hands quickly grasped her wrists and brought them back down to her sides, and he whispered one word in her ear, "Don't."

His chest pressed into her back. It made her straighten up and pushed her breasts up and out again. Shelby's cheeks burned hot as her stomach tightened, but his hands slid up and down her arms, soothing her as he whispered again. "You're fucking gorgeous, baby," he said and licked again slowly up and down on her neck.

A tiny ding sounded and the golden doors of the elevator opened up. He tugged on her hand as he moved from behind her, walking into the car behind the other couple. He waited for them to press a button marked PH, then he reached over and hit a few more, a lot more, acting like his hand slipped. Antonio pulled Shelby close to him again and claimed her mouth before the door even closed. She felt his tongue slip out and a sudden pulse surged through her. Remembering where she was, she pulled back, trying to stay cool and discourage him.

He moved right back in, urging her with his mouth, his hand squeezing her hand. His other hand skimmed over her shoulder again, sparking her hot skin in the cool air. Her eyes closed as his jaw opened wide and he laid into her mouth and tongued her deeply. He turned her around, dizzying her head as her body lurched with the sudden upward movement of the elevator.

She looped her fingers around his belt on each side to steady herself. His hands grazed over her neck and shoulders again while he turned her more, gently pushing Shelby back against the cool mirrored glass wall. The coolness was an enjoyable shock contrasting her fevered skin. He still tongued her, just the right hint of teeth, and she gave in to it. Screw it, why not make out in an elevator, she figured, surrendering to his demanding strokes.

Antonio's hand on her shoulder started rubbing and he moved from her mouth back to her ear. He whispered in Spanish, then English, rolling the words off his tongue. "You're my girl, do this for me," he told her. He pushed at the thin strap of her tank top, moving it off her shoulder, still leaning close against her, shielding her, pressing her into the chilly green reflective wall. He whispered instructions for her to relax while his hand worked the strap lower down her arm.

Shelby shrugged into him, tucking her head down and bashfully curling up, arm rising to cover herself. His hand caught her wrist and pulled it back down, placing it against his side. The edge of her shirt pulled against the top of her breast, strap pulled taut across her biceps. She felt him kissing her, breathing in her mouth, her ear, his hand possessively stroking her naked shoulder.

The elevator stopped at the first meaningless number Antonio had punched. No one was waiting to get on, and Shelby faintly hoped he'd drag her out and end this, or that the other couple would get off, just take another elevator. But, no. Everyone remained stationery.

She realized she was breathing hard, fully turned on from his attentions, the heat from her skin deepening and mixing with the liquor throughout her body. The elevator door closed again, no luck at being alone. He pushed the strap lower, all the way to her elbow. Then his fingers stroked across her collarbone, all the while he continued kissing her; sucking on her tongue, biting her lips.

His fingers danced lower, nails teasing under the line of tight fabric, rubbing back and forth, pulling down. Antonio tugged at it and slid it over her breast, rolling it all the way down as Shelby shivered in response.

He shifted his weight and moved slightly to the side, leaving her completely exposed. She could feel it, the cool air hitting her without the protection of his body, his fingers whispering over her naked nipple, hard and sensitive to his touch. It felt so tingling good, but she became suddenly hyper aware. Inside, she was thrumming with excitement and dying of embarrassment, half naked for the whole world to see.

Still in Spanish, he whispered to her again, "Touch me," he commanded. Swallowing hard, she reached down, blindly following his lead. Thinking, it won't be so bad if it's him, too. Shelby inhaled at his neck, taking in the spiced musk he was wearing, the deep note of him under it. She stroked at his thigh, found nothing there. Smoothing her hand higher, she discovered his erection pressing against the fly of his pants. She stroked firmly a few times, biting on her own lower lip. Shelby stole a glance at Antonio's face. He was not watching her. Instead, he was leering over at *him.* His hand cupped her breast, his thumb stroked lightly over her nipple.

Too late. It had gone too far to push him away, to try and stop him. To stop this. The damage had been done anyhow. Her eyes darted to the mirrored wall in front of them and she caught another reflection—him pressed close to her but standing to the side, her shirt completely off her shoulder, large, round tit fully exposed, dark nipple hard, his hand proudly setting it off.

Shelby couldn't help but feel hot and completely turned on. Oh God, it looked so sexy, him possessing her and smugly showing her off while she rubbed up against him. But her eyes flitted over and landed on them, the other couple, the proper, frosty ones. They were standing stiff, trying not to look but unable to stop looking—she was stealing disgusted glances, still longing on Antonio though, and he was outright gaping through upraised eyes as his fists squeezed around the ice bucket in his effort to remain controlled, prim and proper.

And Antonio was wickedly watching him. Antonio was watching *him* watch Shelby. Her face blushed hard and hot. She buried her face in Antonio's neck and shoulder, finding safety there, hiding her shame and her lust. But he moved, exposing her again. He bent down to kiss her neck, and *oh fuck, no, don't do that,* raced through her mind and she shivered. But he continued, leaning lower and running his tongue across the swell of her breast, then went lower yet. His tongue grazed across her hard, exposed nipple. Involuntarily, Shelby's mouth dropped open and she sucked in a deep breath, squeezing her eyes shut and turning to the mirrors to escape when it sent a mild volt through her body.

His teeth lightly rubbed between them, and she fought off a moan, strangled it in her throat, not allowing that embarrassment. Then his lips were circling it, tightly, tighter, drawing it in. And then he sucked. Hard. The sensation shot straight to her crotch—rocking her against her will.

Sucking in a breath, she forced her eyes open as the elevator crawled to another halt. Praying they'd leave, she squirmed unconsciously as Antonio sucked deep once more. Shelby watched them, just standing there, the woman's bracelet sparkling in the golden lights, both of them stiff and unyielding. They were not going to leave. They were staying because they were enjoying this erotic spectacle. They were enjoying the free turn on show, but more than her body, more than Antonio working on it, she sensed they reveled in watching her struggle. They were stealing glances to see how far she'd go, how much she could manage to fight off the sexual excitement. How this was killing her, because they knew Shelby was totally turned on. They knew she couldn't fight him off, because she really didn't want to.

Of course, they would never admit their heightened involvement either. Antonio knew that, too. They'd finally leave at some point, and Antonio and Shelby would haunt them. They'd talk down about us, never admitting to each other, or even themselves, how much they loved watching it all. Fuck them. Fuck them, their bracelet, and their champagne, she thought as the elevator doors closed again and Antonio took another drag on her, pulling her deep, shooting the sensation right to her throbbing crotch.

Shelby wanted to shift her legs but she fought it off, trying to give up, give in as little as possible. Her body was pulsing though, burning with heat, her own juices dripping and seeping through her panties. Almost like a mind reader, Antonio snaked a hand up her thigh. Shelby swallowed hard, silently begging him not to do it, knowing how ripe and hot she already was. His hand moved higher though, so she squeezed her thighs together to shut him out and she silently begged him to stop as the elevator lurched up.

He rose up and answered her, indicating it was ok, telling her to give in, that he would let go, too. Shelby noticed Antonio eye them briefly, then looked back at her. "Unzip my pants, take me out," he instructed in a coarse whisper. He kissed her neck as she reached for his belt and swiftly undid it. He helped her get his pants open and she reached in for him immediately. The skin on his shaft was hot to the touch, hard, twitching in her hand already. She couldn't stop it. It was out of control. She was long gone, obviously so was he. Then Antonio reached under her skirt with both hands and clamped them around her panties. His fists worked against her lower stomach as he used all his strength to tear them open. And then, oh dear sweet Jesus, the guy, the other guy, actually dropped the ice bucket and bottle onto the floor.

She couldn't bear it. That final indignity. She was certain it would kill her on the spot if she came. Worse, Shelby knew she was going to. She was one big, raw, excited nerve now. Antonio's breathing shallow in her ear, dying for her, making her higher. And Shelby, her head spinning, her whole body rushing and flushed and she was itching, throbbing, dripping wet. As soon as he touched her there, she was going to come. She would shudder and blush, and they'd know exactly what was happening. She wouldn't be able to hide it, the pleasure and humiliation all at once. She tried to figure out how she let this go so far, so fucking fast, so much want and lust and yes, Goddamn NEED for it now.

Antonio dipped down slightly, and she buried her face in his shoulder and raised her leg around his waist. Still holding his cock, she felt him twitch again as she lined him up, started to guide him into her. Then she released him and held on to his neck. He wrapped his arms around her waist.

Swift, strong, he shoved up and back, slamming Shelby into the glass wall, lifting her off her feet, and entering deeply into her. They both gasped and she began to die.

Shelby exploded immediately, came so hard it nearly hurt. Pleasure and heat bolted through her. Her face tucked into his neck, his down in hers. Her legs clamped tightly around his waist. Her back arched. He powered into her a few more times. Shelby shuddered intensely, suddenly coming harder. Waves thundered through her. She choked back a scream. Antonio dug his fingers into her sides as he squeezed her. She spasmed again, blood rushing hard. He shoved once more, sending another shock through her. He grunted, loud, right next to her ear. He went stone stiff in her arms. Gripping him tight, she felt him coming inside her, hot, wet spurts. He shuddered violently, right along with the volts running through Shelby.

Slowing, aftershocks still going through her, him still deep inside, she started to breathe again. Shelby heard a hollow, distant ding as the elevator lurched to a stop. Antonio panted against her neck, his grip around her loosening, his stance slumping. Swimming back to coherence, still shivering, she eased her grip on him, too, and looked up to see the elevator doors open, the couple walking away. There was another guy on the landing, gaping in at what he saw. He just stood there, staring at Shelby, not daring to get on.

Furry faced and slipper footed, he gapped and sounded amazed with his one hushed word, "Stella."

Then the doors push closed.

"Ooh, shit," said Antonio, catching his breath. "That was a good one, huh?" Then he started to laugh, still holding her up.

"You're such an asshole," she told him. He laughed harder, slouching into her, shaking her with it. "Such a fucking asshole," she repeated and laughed with him.

"Suits my taste," he said in a mock voice, laughing again while she slid down off of him, giggling, too, legs weak and quivering. "White people," he said simply, as if that explained it all, and shaking his head.

Shelby shifted as he reached between her legs and wiped at the stickiness on her thighs with her torn underwear, his hand gentle and smooth. Wordlessly, she watched as he quickly wiped himself off with them and then zipped back up. As she felt the elevator slowing, she reached down and straightened her skirt, pulling her shirt back up and arranging the shoulder strap. "Asshole," said Shelby. "I can't go back and sit at the bar in just this short skirt."

"C'mon, I got an idea," he told her and grabbed her hand, pulling her along again, this time out of the elevator. She flashed the peace sign and winked to the camera as they exited.

Antonio smirked and winked at her as he wove through the casino, past rows and tables of slots and out into the white marble hallway. They walked up a long line of shops, and she wondered what he was up to now, but just wandered along next to him, happy to have her boobs tucked back in her shirt.

When they reached a sundry shop, he ducked inside, pulling her along after him, looking around. He weaved through the clothes racks until he got to a rack with underwear on it. Shelby watched as he gave it the once over, then cracked another wide smile as he plucked a pair up and waved 'em at her. They were white with sequined dice on the front, and they read "Viva Las Vegas" across the ass.

"Oh Jesus," she sighed when he flipped them on the counter and pulled out a couple bills, asking for a box. The clerk looked at him oddly as he asked if they had changing rooms and pointed them out to him. Still just following his lead, she allowed him to push her into the room. He flipped the panties out of the box and handed them to her.

"Christ, Antonio, if this is your taste or you think this is my taste, then I am one trashy chick," said Shelby, pulling them on. Would he like the conservative side of her personality, you know, her normal every day life one, the *non* sex starved one?

"Hey, Viva, baby, Viva Las Fuckin Vegas. Ain't diamonds from Tiffany's, but it's somethin sparkly," he said and slapped her ass with a wink. Then he pulled her sticky ripped ones out of his pocket, dropped them in the box, and pulled her out, striding out the door and dragging Shelby back to the front bar again.

Once there, he waved Vince over and said, "Yo, man, know those two who ordered champagne? They charge it to their room?"

Vince nodded.

"Any chance we could get their name and room number off that receipt?"

Vince went over to his drawer and pulled out the receipt, then walked back over to them. He waved it around a second and said, "I really can't give you information like that, man, wouldn't be right." He waved the receipt again until it "slipped" out of his hand and floated onto the bar. "Shit, could you hand me that?" he asked Antonio.

Grinning, Antonio picked it up and read as he handed it back. "Thanks, I owe you one," he said, then quickly pulled her away again and headed back to the store.

Confidently, he strutted up to the counter. "Yo," he said to the clerk. "Yeah, we uh, we just bought this, and we don't wanna carry it around. Can you like, um, have this sent up to our room?"

Shelby's eyes opened wider and she choked back a laugh as he reeled off their name and room number to the clerk. Then he pulled her along again, back toward the casino, she following willingly.

Chapter 9

Deadly car accidents consistently commanded front page placement in the Marin Independent Journal, which was neither "independent" nor was it much of a journal. On the contrary, the IJ (aka the Independent Urinal) was owned by a giant media conglomerate—and as such followed the reporting philosophy of its nationwide model. That is, if the story didn't fit in 2-columns on a single page, it was too complicated.

The story of Serina Jacobs's fatal accident was perfect front page fodder: a simple story of a drunken artist driving her car off a cliff into the Pacific Ocean, the only remaining evidence being an array of broken wine and scotch bottles strewn down the length of the bank from the road to the ocean, CD's ranging from jazz, classical, and rock such as the The Beatles Anthology, Eurythmics and Pink Floyd scattered amongst the cans, Serina had all the windows open during the drive that night, and of course, shattered glass and pieces of the old Saab among the boulders on the shore. The paper assumed that Jacobs, who was most likely already dead by the time the car reached the ocean, they noted that she must not have been wearing a seat belt, had quickly been washed out to sea where her body was no doubt consumed by the great white sharks that prowled the Northern California coastline between their breeding grounds in the Farallon Islands, the Golden Gate and the Point Reyes peninsula. The reporter also conjectured that the accident had happened at least two days before it was discovered, and as such, the sharks had plenty of time to discover and consume their prey.

Rex Wilcox, although shocked and dismayed when he read about his client's death in the not-so Independent Journal, fortunately Serina Jacobs was not Wilcox's *only* client, was not surprised that it took two days to discover that Jacobs had driven her Saab into the Pacific. Given Jacobs's typical social calendar, Wilcox was surprised that it didn't take weeks for someone to notice that she was missing. Of course, she did have sisters, but they seemed to lead very independent lives, or so he had always gathered since he'd never met them.

"What a loser," Wilcox voiced aloud sadly as he read the article in his kimono on his Mill Valley deck, gently warming his saggy nutsack in the late morning sun that filtered through the redwoods. His affection for Serina Jacobs was not like the affection he had for men or other women. Had Wilcox had a chance to be a father, he imagined that what he felt for Serina might be what he would feel for a wayward daughter: unconditional love coupled with aching disappointment and regret, particularly at his own inability to mold Serina Jacobs's talent into a productive life. What was almost worse, Wilcox thought, was that there were so few people he now needed to inform of Jacobs's death, and fewer still who gave a darn. Other than Serina's sisters, Shelby and Sherri. He'd never met them, but he got the impression they had at least a caring relationship, just didn't see each other that often. Surprisingly, one of the people Wilcox put in the "don't call, doesn't give a care" category called him at the very moment he was closing his kimono and preparing to fix himself another cup of coffee: Michelle Morgan.

"I see in the IJ here that your artist bought the farm on the Panoramic the other night."

Actually it was Harlin Radner who pointed the article out to Michelle. She had just returned from an early-morning horseback ride on the fire roads that crisscrossed the grassy ridges and stands of stately redwoods above the film studio. Harlin had settled into a teak rocker on the sunny porch of Morgan's offices where a male servant served him cappuccino, chocolate croissant and the not-so Independent Journal. "Marin Artist Becomes Shark Bait off Panoramic Highway", read the headline.

"Shit!" Harlin had muttered to himself as he read the first few sentences. "Serina, you silly loser." Part way through the article, after he read about the "veritable liquor store" that had been strewn along the path of the hurtling Saab, he had put the paper down on his knees and stared out across the morning shadows as they crept off the golden hills and into the wooded lushness, thinking about the times he and Serina had sat in silence years ago observing similar scenes—almost always in some chemically altered state. Why was it that the booze and chemicals became completely unimportant to him as he grew older—an entertaining side show at times, but never center stage—whereas it appeared that such substances controlled the life of Serina Jacobs and eventually drove her right into the Pacific Ocean. He smiled—better living through chemistry had held such *promise*!

Harlin briefly thought that, perhaps, had he reunited with Jacobs earlier, he might have prevented this tragedy, steered her back onto the right path, dragged her lazy ass into a 28-day program, hooked her up with other chronic substance abusers so they could talk about how totally fucked-up they were all day long, then go back to their lonely apartments and struggle with their private miseries. Or perhaps Jacobs was too far gone—and that cleaning up at this point might have had a disastrous effect. Moot point now, he thought. Moot fucking point. But damn, until now, realizing there never would be another opportunity to talk to her, to see her gorgeous, angelic face, he was surprised to discover he'd actually had some pretty strong, dormant feelings for her. Damn!

"Michelle!" he had shouted from the porch when he completed reading the one column front page article on Serina's demise. "Have you read the Urinal this morning?" Morgan emerged from her office in silk pajamas and purple velvet robe, exquisitely embroidered with images of characters from her science fiction films. He held up the front page while she looked over his shoulder.

"Serina Jacobs…didn't we just buy one of her paintings?" Morgan mused, rubbing one hand over her short, cropped hair.

"Yup" said Harlin. "She was my old grammar school girlfriend, remember? The one who gave me the necklace made of macaroni with the bone on the end."

"Right," said Morgan, taking the paper from his hands as she read the article. "This is interesting," she said after a moment. "I think we paid something like $400 for that oil. Bet it's worth $1400 now. Maybe more."

"I never knew the poor girl was such a drunk…," muttered Harlin.

"Still peanuts I know," said Morgan, mostly to herself, dropping the paper in Harlin's lap. "But over time her work may be worth something, you never know. Hmm. This is interesting."

"Do you remember the name of her agent—the fag that runs that little gallery in San Anselmo? We were just there for that show," Morgan asked.

"It's too bad, just too damn bad," Harlin said, not listening to Morgan. "Real artists are treated like shit in this country, you know. People like you make gazillions with these silly science fiction movies and the real artists—the one's who are actually trying to create some real culture in our society—they drink themselves silly and drive into the fucking Pacific. Ridiculous." He shook his head.

"Karl would know," said Morgan, and strode back into her office.

Harlin sat there, staring across the golden hills, now in full sunlight, and into the deep blue sky beyond the highest ridges, wondering why he had an overwhelming desire to shed tears for his old friend, Serina.

And so it was that the first call Rex Wilcox received regarding the death of Serina Jacobs, almost immediately after he had read the news and was preparing his second cup of coffee on a sunny, fog-cooled, Mill Valley, Indian summer morning, was from Michelle Morgan. Morgan considered having Karl make the inquiry but thought better of it after telling him about the accident and sensing the immediate disdain Karl had for Rex Wilcox, Serina Jacobs and the art world in general. "It is just paint," Karl said. "Paint is cheap, practically worthless." Fortunately, Michelle Morgan didn't see it that way, as Wilcox would soon find out.

"How many of Jacobs's paintings do you have?" Morgan asked Wilcox, who was now pacing over the thick, white shag rug of his pseudo oriental-style living room with nervousness, his white cat unsuccessfully trying to rub up against his bare ankles.

"Well I don't really know, to tell you the truth, Ms. Morgan. I just this moment found out about the poor woman's unfortunate accident! Oh it's just so sad!"

Morgan, not wanting to witness an embarrassing gay emotional outburst, kept it short. "Wilcox I know you're probably upset. Just do me one little favor. Don't sell anything. I'll call you again in a few days. Hopefully you'll have had a chance to collect the inventory and we can look it over. Chances are I'll want all of it. Ok?"

Wilcox hadn't meant to sound emotional. After all, it was just his natural way of communicating and it certainly was sad. Wouldn't everybody who read about Serina Jacobs being chewed to pieces by hungry great white sharks think it was *sad*? But now Wilcox did have a surge of emotion—or almost pure exhilaration. How many of Jacobs's paintings did he have? 75? 100? And now that Jacobs was dead, what would they be worth? Certainly more than if Jacobs were alive. Even if they were merely double the normal price that could mean some significant money! Then another thought came to him—he felt as if he had dipped his balls in a bucket of ice water.

"Well, Ms. Morgan. I'm not sure that these paintings are mine to sell, or not sell as the case may be! Certainly these are part of Serina…I mean Ms. Jacobs's estate. I suspect it will be up to the court to determine what to do with them."

"Don't worry about *that,* Wilcox," Morgan quickly snapped back. "I can fix that. Just don't sell anything until you hear from me, understood?"

Wilcox did not respond well to this kind of pressure, even if it was a movie mogul trying to make a deal with him. "Well I have to notify the family…" he said.

"We can backdate the check, make it look like I purchased the paintings before Jacobs bought the farm. Listen, Wilcox—there's a lot of money in this for you. A lot of money. We can do the deal today if you want. Where are the paintings? At the gallery?"

Well isn't she the eager beaver, thought Wilcox. Then, to Morgan: "Like I said, Ms. Morgan, I'm not entirely sure where they all are, and I can't say I'm entirely comfortable 'doing a deal' as you say, since the paintings are not really my property." Of course Wilcox was itching to "do a deal". The right "deal".

"Believe me, Wilcox, I will make it worth your while," said Morgan, deadly earnest. "And nobody will have any reason to think that this isn't just a normal transaction. You'll have to trust me—I know how to do this and I have a number of ways we can work it. And you'll have absolutely no exposure."

Wilcox was now standing on his porch, overlooking the streets and shops of Mill Valley bustling with tie-dye twenty-somethings sipping lattes and skateboarding at The Depot while rich matrons bought expensive lingerie and clever, overpriced toys for their high-strung offspring. Easy money. Everybody deserves a little easy money from time to time. Was this his chance to cash in? His head, which had been tingling, now started to throb. He pushed the cat away with his foot—practically kicked the poor little pussy—and instinctively reached for his balls with his free hand, which reminded him of a little tune he often sang to himself: "When I get a little nervous/When I get a little scared/I reach for my balls/I reach for my balls." Then as he vigorously squeezed his scrotal sack, he said to Morgan. "Meet me at the Gallery in an hour, Ms. Morgan. I think we can probably work something out."

Chapter 10

After spending almost all her time exclusively with Antonio this Vegas trip, Shelby had to fly back to San Francisco in the morning. Tonight was their official first *date.* At the moment, she was good and lit up from the wine she'd consumed while gambling, and people were buzzing everywhere. Machines clanked, heels clicked on the marble floor, Sinatra crooned all around, interrupted only by the bark of stickmen and cheers from winners. Snippets of other people's conversations floated around her; everyone painted, everyone sparkling. Everyone appeared to be excited and flushed. Happy.

Antonio halted at a bar, "Yo, if we get a bottle here it's gonna be expensive, but we don't have to stop again."

"Get it here," she agreed with him.

"You sure, cause we could…"

"Get the bottle. Now. Get two."

He placed the order and she handed him some cash for it. He started to protest, but when the bartender returned, he gave in and took care of it.

"I don't want change," she told him.

He gulped visibly, grabbed the bottles and began pulling her along again. Outside, the night was still warm, darkness had settled in comfortably, and beyond the fountains all the lights twinkled away.

They both stood speechless, watching the water pumping out of the fountains, waiting for a cab to pull up. When it did, she slid in, him after her, both of them sitting straight, a good foot of seemingly empty space between them sparkling with energy. Shelby didn't even look over at him. Not once, the whole way.

The ride was disorientatingly fast, yet painfully slow.

When they turned off the strip, all the lights, gamblers, hookers, dice, cards, and comics left behind, her throat tightened. By the time they pulled up to his apartment building, she had no idea where she was, and mixed with the heady buzz and overpowering desire already consuming her, a new twist grabbed hold of her

Nervousness.

Shift in your seat, full blown anxiety, hand wringing, fidgety fussy nervous.

She grasped his hand to get out of the car, and when he grabbed the back of her neck as they walked along, she nearly jumped out of her own skin.

He guided her up a couple of stairs, into an elevator that took them up, steered her down a hallway, handed her the bottles as he fumbled with the keys, opened the door as he flicked on the lights. Chewing her lip, she forced her feet to move forward, through the door.

She wasn't scared. It wasn't quite that paralyzing "Oh shit. What had she done? He could rape/murder/beat/hurt her" heart-pounding terror thing. Rather it was that dry-mouthed "Oh shit. What if this sucks. What if she sucked? What if he *hurt* her" heart-fluttering insecurity thing.

He sensed it. Taking the bottles from her arms, he motioned his head for her to follow him. He lead her to the kitchen. Opened the fridge and put one of the bottles in, then started rummaging through drawers, she presumed, for a wine opener. Shelby drank him in, feeling foolish for watching him so intently, then forced herself to look around.

It was nice. It was really nice.

Shelby wasn't exactly shocked. Well, he did have a nice car, right? And he was a dealer at Bellagio, and the dealers there had to do pretty well, but that wasn't it either. His place was clean. Everything seemed in order, but not in an impeccable way. He lived there. But there were no dirty dishes, the floor was clean, all the counters and cupboards were polished. It was all new, from the appliances to the floor. His schedule was posted on the fridge with a Bellagio magnet. He was supposed to work the past few nights until four. Neat people didn't generally rearrange their schedules.

That struck a chord in her. All day, she wished she could learn more about him somehow. This was like hitting a home run. This was all his. It was the ultimate resource for research. Paydirt.

"Fuck," he said and headed out into another room. She followed into the living room. Huge television, black leather, stuffed couch and matching chair. Soft, slate grey, plush carpet, just vacuumed; she could see the telltale lines from where the sweeper ran. Nice stereo, oodles of CDs lined up near it. Speakers all around the room. And he was behind a bar. He had a freaking bar in his living room.

Shelby *knew* she liked him for good reason.

"Finally," he uttered when he produced a corker. Sheepish, he explained, "I don't drink much wine usually."

"Me neither," she responded. "I'm impressed you have one of those things."

"Me, too," he laughed and started on the bottle.

"This is really nice," she felt compelled to comment.

"What?"

"Your place here, where you live. This is—great."

"You like it, huh? Yo, pick out some tunes, anything you want."

Shelby scanned the CD's; they were alphabetized, and he had all sorts of good stuff. She chose Pavarotti duets and put it on as he poured out the wine. Handing her a glass, he asked, "You a big classical fan?"

"Once upon a time," she answered. "I'll catch the duets now and then, but I'm not chronic."

"Yeah, me, too. I like the mix of classical with rock. I hope this stuff is ok," he commented about the wine and took a sip.

She tested it. "Works for me," she told him. "I can't believe how nice this place is."

"Yeah, ain't Caesars, but check this out," he said and moved to the other side of the room, pulled open floor length drapes and opened a large sliding glass door.

Shelby followed him out onto a balcony. "Wow," she said.

"Not bad, huh? Not bad."

Directly below was a lighted, sparkling blue pool, a few other structures and shorter buildings. And beyond that, reaching into the mountains on the horizon, all she could see was more sparkling lights of the city that overwhelmed the desert. Above the mountains and overhead, the sky sparkled back with stars. It looked as though someone took a handful of jewels and tossed them all over the place.

Leaning against the railing, he nudged her, saying, "Breathe, senorita, breathe."

"Working on it," she answered.

"Yo, I bought this place cause o' the view," he said as he gazed out across the panorama.

"The rest of it's not bad either."

"Yeah, I got lucky to find it, but the view, that's what did it, you know? Like, I never had nothin like this back home." His one hand bounced up and down on the railing next to her arm as he shifted his weight to move a smidge closer to Shelby. He sniffed, glanced down at the pool, then back over the sparkling lights. Saying, "Like, first time I came out here, it felt really different from home, but not all freaky flaky like LA. You ever been to LA?" He nodded with a grin and continued. "Then you know what I mean, west coast thing I guess, you know. And like, it's nice there and all, but I'm just more, I don't know, it's different in the east…"

"You're very east coast," she agreed with him. He looked over questioningly so she nudged him. "In a good way," she explained. "I mean that in a good way. You have more energy."

"You mean I'm hyper," he laughed.

"No. No, it's not that. It's just yes, I know what you mean about the difference between east and west coast in this country, that's all. I like the east coast, but I also appreciate the west coast."

He grinned and looked back down. Got his hand to stop bouncing and extended his index finger and lightly moved it back and forth across her forearm a couple of times.

He still seemed weighted, like he was saying something and she had veered him off course and he wasn't sure he wanted to go there again. So she prodded him. "So you love the view of Vegas. Or did you think it'd be romantic and would help you score more?"

Grinning, "Nah, it ain't that. It was just for me, you know?" He sniffed again, shuffled his feet. "Like, it was crazy out here. Everything was so bright, know what I mean? An' it wasn't like a whole other world than home, it was just, I don't know, better somehow. My first time here, I went up and checked out the view from the Rio, you ever been up there? Yeah, you see the whole city, not just the strip, but the whole city. An' nothin 'bout it looked ground down or beat. It didn't look like a grind. Cause everyone was out there partyin an' shit. They weren't all dragged down. They weren't locked into this life. It's like people decide to come here, you know? They ain't just here cause they was born here and got nowhere else to go. I don't know, I ain't makin any sense, huh?"

"Yes, you are," she answered.

"I am? Huh. So like, I think that's why I decided to move here, you know, cause it all looked different. Like nothin would be ordinary or somethin. Like I wouldn't get bored. So that's why I got this view. It ain't the strip, but it was all bright. I didn't see it during the day when I looked at the place, but I could picture it. So I came back the next night an' checked it out, it was just like I'd imagined it. So I got the place."

"I like that," said Shelby. "So you come out here and check out the view and it amps you up."

"Nah," Antonio answered, shaking his head. "That's the thing. I stopped comin out here. This is the first I been out here in awhile."

"How come?"

"Cause I was out here one night, and it hit me. Just hit me, you know. It ain't any different down there. All those lights, they first seemed like all this excitement, all this, I don't know, somethin. Then this one night, I finally got it. All them lights, they're just people. And they ain't all that excitin or different. They just get up in the morning and grind it out. Same as everybody else. Day after day, go to work, go whatever. Even the ones on vacation and shit, this is just a temporary break for them. And then I seen that I had my light on, and I figured that someone else, someone with a higher view was probably lookin down on my light. But they wasn't even seein *my* light, you know? It was just one little part of the whole view. Nothin different 'bout it, just blurred in with all the others, just addin to the whole picture, but not really even doin that. Cause if I'd shut off my light, no one would notice, you know. It wouldn't really affect the view at all. It'd still be the same.

"That's when I got it. It hit me really hard. I'd become part of the grind. I hadn't meant to, you know, it just happened. Just happened. And I wasn't all that special, and this place wasn't all that exciting no more. It's just the same old shit, over and over. Everyone out there. So I stopped comin out here and lookin at it. Too fuckin depressing. Too ordinary."

Holy shit! Shelby didn't know what to say. She wanted to reach out to him. She wanted to make it better, but didn't know how. It was the juxtaposition of him that got to her. All that outward strength, the hard coiled muscles, the cockiness and swagger. But what he just said and the murkiness in his gaze counterpointed all that. It made him more human.

He was right. He was just like everyone else. He was fragile.

And yet, he wasn't like everyone else. He was nothing like anyone else.

Was his happiness an act the past couple of nights? No, she didn't think so. He was proving her philosophy. About people who could push through the mundane or depressing. Fight their way back up to still see the lights sparkle sometimes.

And it didn't make him weaker because he showed her his chinks. It made him stronger.

"You're not ordinary," she said thickly.

His index finger stroked across her arm again as he looked over at her. "Can I tell you somethin? Tonight? Right now. This view looks really good again."

He moved closer to her and she jerked, breath catching in her throat. Slowly, he placed an arm around her waist. "We can go. Like, if you don't like it here, we can go, I didn't mean to scare you."

"No, I want to be here. I like it here. I'm just nervous, I don't know why. It shouldn't be, so…whatever."

"I know. I kept givin you a hard time though, you know, I don't want you to think you gotta do anything."

"Oh, I want to," she said quickly.

"You do?"

"You don't?" asked Shelby.

"Oh, I do."

Gently, he dipped his head, and she stretched up and into him. He brushed his lips across hers, taking his time working up to a kiss. It was soft and tentative and reassuring. When his tongue finally peeked out, she was tingling all over. Stopping, he leaned his forehead against hers. Gravelly voiced, he asked, "Wanna go inside?"

She allowed him to lead her in, his hand rustling through her hair to rest on the back of her neck again as he lead the way. He stopped to grab the bottle of wine, guided her through the living room and down a hallway. "That the bathroom?" she asked.

"Yeah, go ahead," he told her. "I'll be right back there," he pointed to the room at the end of the hall.

His bedroom, it sinks in as she ducked in and fumbled around for a light switch. Clicking it on, she closed the door, exhaling deeply and trying to clear her head. What the FUCK was wrong with her? Why was she so nervous? It's not like she was a virgin and this was her first time. But that was how she felt. It felt like prom night. Suddenly, it hit her.

She really was on a date. Twenty-three years old and her first official date. Wow!

If that wasn't pretty sad. Twenty-three years old, and she'd never been on a date, never had a boyfriend, never had anyone interested in her for longer than one night. Oh, she'd had guys dying for her before. Horny guys momentarily swept up by her charm. She called it the tequila effect. Better known as 'awwfuck disease'. They were smitten with her that one night, the next day they'd wake up and think, "Awwfuck. What the fuck did I do?"

But this guy had been there with her for three days running. Never experienced anything like that before. Worse, She'd never cared before. Before, she could always take them or leave them, but not him. She wanted him, bad. Never before had she been so aware of her body. Aware in the sense that she could actually feel it. Feel it humming for him, in her stomach. In her crotch—throbbing. And even worse yet, in her chest. Shelby swore she could actually physically feel it in her heart. No doubt he'd invaded her mind. More than wanting him, she also liked him.

And Shelby believed she might even love him. What else could be so overpowering? Lust was lust, and that was going on in spades. But it was—More.

Stranger still, either he was really jerking her around for some bizarre sport, or he was sincere and he really liked Shelby. He sure wanted her—bad.

She had to stop thinking about it. It was time to let go and just trust it. That was the only choice. Trust herself. Trust him.

Opening her eyes, she checked out her surroundings. Just like the kitchen, it was immaculate. Black and white checks, which was a little disorientating. But it was spotless. Clean tile, and clean towels hung on the racks. Peeking into the shower, no soap scum anywhere. Everything was neat and orderly; his soap, shampoo, everything. There was a speaker on the wall and she turned the dial; music from the living room came floating through. That cracked her up. She peed, hoping it would relieve some of the throbbing. It didn't.

Talk about a font of information, though. Shelby couldn't help but peek behind the mirror. Nothing extraordinary. Razor, shaving cream, cologne, toothpaste, toothbrush, aspirin, bandaids, no floss—bad—floss was mandatory in her mind.

A big box of condoms. Unopened. She smirked, but that also pulled her back to some form of reality.

She marched back to his bedroom, determined. Shoes off, he was sitting cross legged on the bed, but hopped up when she entered. The music played in here, too. Another good-sized room, another big TV, sliding door mirrored closets. Thank goodness the bed wasn't at an angle to look into the mirror; parallel instead of perpendicular.

The main lights were off, just a neon beer sign in one window, a pretty cool illuminated wall clock, a big fish tank, and a string of white Christmas lights going around the perimeter of his ceiling provided soft, warm, romantic lighting.

It was obvious the Christmas lights were strung for the purpose of mood lighting. And it worked. So very bachelor. *So* very grown-up stoner. So very *player.*

There was another window open, slight rush of air audible, moonlight and city lights seeping in, but it wasn't cold. Same thick, grey carpet as the living room, big, black bedspread on a huge king sized bed. She gulped.

"Pour yourself more wine," he said and nonchalantly brushed past her, into the bathroom himself, she presumed.

Shelby gulped again, set the glass back down and climbed onto the bed, kicking off her sandals. When he returned, he stopped in the doorway saying, "I been dyin to see that."

"What?"

"You. In my bed."

"Come here," she instructed.

Climbing up slowly, he lingered and placed a kiss on her knee, then stretched out to meet her face to face. On their sides, heads propped on hands, he reached over for a kiss.

"Valdez," Shelby stopped him, "I have to tell you something. I looked in your medicine chest," she admitted.

He smiled. "'K," he said.

"I'm sorry, I know I shouldn't have, I just…"

"It's cool," he said. "I'd look in yours."

"You would?"

"Fuck yeah, everyone snoops around at first," he said and rubbed his own stomach. "I'll give you carte blanche, look anywhere you want."

Grinning, she replied, "I might do that. Later."

"Yeah, I was hopin it'd be later," he answered and tried to move in again.

"Here's the thing," she continued, putting him off. "When I looked, it reminded me of something. You have a big box of condoms in there." She checked for his reaction. Not much of one. "Well, last night, when we, you know…"

"In the elevator," he prompted, smiling a lazy, oh so innocent smile.

"Yeah, we didn't use one," she reminded him. "And we should. I mean, don't worry, don't get freaked."

"I'm not," he answered.

"Good, cause you don't have to worry, I'm good and healthy. I know I am, and I'm taken care of. I won't get pregnant or anything, not that I'd hold you responsible if I did, of course." She suddenly realized she was babbling, and thankfully he stopped her.

"I'm not worried," he told her.

"Well, I don't want to insult you either, it's just, you're really freaking hot, and…"

"You don't have anything to worry about," he said and took her hand in his, stroking her fingers. "I'll wear one if you want, but I had to get tested just a few months ago."

"You did?" She didn't want to pry. What was she thinking? Yeah, she did.

"I'm a boxer," he explained with a shrug. "Gotta get tested all the time, 'fore I get in the ring for an official fight."

"Oh."

"So I'm careful, too. Then I just had to get tested again."

"You did?"

"Yeah, well, I didn't have to, but I got this," dropping her hand, he lifted up his shirt and exposed a pink, raised scar stretching across his ribcage. "So while I was there, an' bleeding and all at the hospital, I made sure, just cause, well, you know…Mindy, my ex-girlfriend, an' all the guys she's been with, an' all, an', well…Don't hurt to keep gettin checked."

Reaching out, Shelby ran her fingers along the new scar, "What's it from?" she asked him.

"Make you a deal. I'll tell you later when you're going through my closets."

"Ok," she agreed and started to lean in to him.

"So you want me to get one?"

"Huh?"

"You want me wear a condom anyhow?"

"You trust me?" she asked.

"Always," he answered, sounding very sincere.

"Then I trust you."

Knowing better. Looking into his huge, dark eyes, serious but soft, inviting her to get closer.

"'K," he said. "I'm gonna kiss you now."

And he did.

The grey early morning light of pre-dawn filtered through the window to wake her up. Blinking her eyes, she didn't even have to sit up to realize she was still drunk.

Not drunk on wine, drunk on him.

She was so comfy. It was very tempting to like slither down and slide next to him, breathe the same air as he breathed for awhile.

But there was such a thing as overkill. There was such a thing as sobering up.

It was better to go like this and have it all stay good in her memory, have a couple of "what ifs" lingering instead of staying and having him sober up, break the spell and start flopping around his bed in discontent, waiting for her to leave. Worse, have him wake up and be grouchy at her.

Not that she thought he would do that. She didn't think he'd be like that. But right now, she wasn't willing to take that gamble. Besides, she needed to catch that flight home.

Stopping in the bathroom, she put on her bra and fixed the sweater. Grabbed a few aspirin from the medicine cabinet, hastily taking them with water. As she walked down the hall towards the front door to leave, she noticed how sore she was. Her arms and shoulders were achy and tired, and her legs were absolutely raw. Similar to the deep-burn sore from a heavy workout, concentrated mostly in her upper thighs. Upper, inner thighs. Even her stomach pulled when she reached in the freezer for ice.

The pain felt great! When she got into the cab, her cell phone rang.

Chapter 11

The fog was beginning to dissipate and the thicket began to brighten. Serina moved carefully, slowly, awakening into the third day after the car accident, unbeknownst to her. Tiny shapes of birds flitted through the canopy of delicate branches that grew closely around her hideout, their twittering becoming more infrequent. Fleetingly, she thought about her adolescent days, when she had fancied herself as an amateur naturalist, religiously learning the names of the local flora and fauna and once or twice actually catching a small chickadee or junco with her bare hands out of the feeder near her parent's kitchen window.

But during those youthful years, her interest was chasing boys, or at least she thought it was. She was feeling kind of groggy, foggy in the mind, odd, disjointed memories. During these pursuits, she never scored with the boys she really wanted and almost always ultimately settled for anyone who was horny enough to have her. Vince Piccione, a short, heavy-set, large chested, ruddy Italian boy with braces, with whom Serina performed a famous "panty pull-aside" penetration on top of the washing machine in the laundry room of a Belvedere estate (of course, he did the penetrating), came to mind. Vince threw up her 4 vodka Collins in the laundry room sink immediately following the experience.

Sam Gray came to mind as well: an attractive though somewhat mousy high school senior, slender frame, though, who apparently decided to fuck as many girls at their graduation party as he possibly could. She'd been selected during the band's break time for a quick ten minute romp in the sack. It all happened so fast that she was inclined to apologize, but later decided it was not necessary when she heard that one of her friends had a similar experience with Sam Gray only a few minutes before.

Inevitably Serina's reminiscences led her to think about Harlin—his sparkling, deep brown eyes and shiny, black hair, his broad smile of perfectly shaped white teeth against those soft lips, lips she had the pleasure of experiencing, albeit briefly, during their reunion at the California Heritage Gallery. As the sound of the birds faded and sleep began to claim her again in the shady thicket by the quiet stream, Serina's thoughts of Harlin morphed into a dream drama where they stood beneath an arbor of exploding purple hibiscus, similar to the thicket where she slept. Outside the arbor were tables of fresh fruit, vegetables of all shapes and colors, baskets of unshucked almonds and walnuts—an outdoor food market of sorts—owned by Harlin.

In the dream, he is eager to attend to the customers standing at his many stalls, but Serina cannot let him go, although he is wary of his wife, who is lurking somewhere behind the market. He knows because he can hear the greasy lout revving her Harley. They must hurry. Serina and Harlin are embracing and she feels she is melting into him. As she closes her eyes to revel in his scent, she suddenly realizes he is gone. The customers have gone, too; the stalls are empty leaving nothing but bare tables, and the evening has become chilly and damp. As Serina surveys the quiet market, she spies a piece of paper, perhaps a folded note, taped to the entrance gate. She opens the note, recognizing Harlin's handwriting. "We must meet again—I sense you are feeling la la la la la la la la la…" and Serina hears the song he is referring to, a syrupy Motown ballad that had always caused her to change the channel when she was listening to the car stereo with her sisters, waiting for their mother while she shopped for groceries: "la la la la la la la la la…I love you."

Naturally when she awoke once more, she had the song in her head, and the but the dream was fading and she couldn't grasp onto its remnants. The coastal fog had moved back in for the evening, causing moisture to collect in the branches of the thicket, which was now dripping slowly onto the old, crusty, down sleeping bag she'd found in this little hideaway. She wiggled out of the bag, still fully clothed, and took a long swig off a water bottle she'd found somewhere. Now, as night was falling, she sensed it was time to travel. To exactly where she was, she was not entirely sure—somewhere between Stinson and San Anselmo, away from civilization, that much was certain. She remembered a grove of first growth redwoods near the Kent Reservoir, where the ancient trees had huge hollowed-out bases from centuries-old forest fires that would provide excellent shelter.

But why did she want to remain sheltered and hidden? The reason eluded her. For that matter, she wasn't exactly certain who she even was. And who was this Harlin in her dreams? She recalled that name; Harlin. Hmmm.

She set off upstream, thinking of herself as just another ghost haunting the cool, foggy autumn evening.

Rex Wilcox was dreaming of soft, furry sheep when his doorbell rang at 4 AM in the foggy, damp pre-dawn of Mill Valley. The closest Wilcox had ever gotten to a sheep was when he and a friend purchased a blowup sheep at a sex shop on the corner of Kearny and Pacific, back in the heyday of gay bathhouses when gism flowed freely through the streets of San Francisco. Wilcox' friend, a chain-smoking cowboy from Dallas, had become strangely ill after the experience with the blowup sheep in the bathhouse—said he "caught a cold and just couldn't shake it". By the time he wasted away many of Rex' friends seemed to be coming down with every bug that came through town. Wilcox's memory of the onset of the deadly AIDS epidemic, though it loosely coincided with the blowup sheep experience, didn't mess up his current dream of the soft, curly-haired creatures.

After hearing the doorbell in his dream for quite awhile, it occurred to Wilcox that the sound was not the gentle tinkle of his sheep's bells ringing with the rhythm of their love. "Jesus," he muttered to himself once he had opened his eyes and realized someone was at his door at 4AM. He switched on the light, stumbled out of bed, pulled on his kimono and started for the door when suddenly he stopped. "Oh my God—what if it's the cops?" he whispered out loud to himself. "What if they found out about Morgan and the paintings? Holy shit!" Wilcox paused and, as he had done since he was a child in stressful situations, he reached into his kimono and grabbed his balls, squeezing just hard enough to force concentration. And, while the doorbell continued to ring, Wilcox imagined himself cuffed and taken away by the police as Jacobs's sister, or her mother, or even Stefan and one of his patchouli-scented gay friends. "God forbid, this must be a dream," Wilcox continued to speak to himself out loud.

"Or perhaps I am sleepwalking," he muttered aloud which caused him to think of a fraternity brother of his from his days at UC Berkeley who was famous for his nocturnal sleepwalking adventures. Once JT, as they called him, had found his way up onto the roof of the old building, dragging his sleeping bag up the ladder and through the trap door, where he promptly put the sleeping bag over his head and, approaching a pair of collegiate lovers who had decided to spend the evening on the mattress the coed fraternity had situated on the roof for such occasions, began to shout, "stop shooting that ray gun at me, stop shooting that ray gun at me." It took the young naked couple some doing to awaken JT, remove the sleeping bag, and gently coax him back down the ladder to his bedroom.

Meanwhile, the doorbell kept ringing and Wilcox had determined that indeed this was no dream. Step one, he decided, was to discreetly determine who was at the door without revealing the fact that he was awake. So he loosened his grip on his swollen testicles, got down on all fours, quietly crawled across the shag carpet to the window near the door, and slowly peeked out to see a hooded figure pacing back and forth. Suddenly the figure stopped and, having detected some movement near the window, was now crouching down to investigate. Wilcox ducked.

"Wilcox?" the whispered voice came from outside. "Wilcox it's me, Jacobs."

Jacobs, thought Wilcox. How could it be Jacobs? Jacobs was dead, launched her rusted out Saab over a cliff in a drunken stupor and became shark bait.

"Wilcox I know you're in there in your stinking little kimono, crouched on that stinking shag rug and most likely clutching your nuts in terror."

Jesus, thought Wilcox quickly. Who else on the planet knew about his ball-squeezing habit? After his father had severely remonstrated him when he was just the tender age of six in front of the entire little league team for having one hand in his pants while playing center field he thought that he had successfully limited his nut clutching episodes to private venues. But perhaps there had been a few tense moments with Serina present where he had attempted a few surreptitious squeezes. "Oh My God!" Wilcox whispered aloud. Did I have my hand in my pants when I was negotiating the sale of the late Serina Jacobs's portfolio of oils to Michelle Morgan?

"Wilcox! Take your free hand and open the goddamn door!" whispered the figure at the window.

It sounded like Jacobs—and by now Rex Wilcox simply had to know if he was still a public scrotum scratcher, and if anyone would know it would be Serina Jacobs. So he stood up, undid the latch, and opened the door just a crack, and there peering in was what looked to be the ghost of Serina Jacobs, whisps of long blond hair escaping out from the hood of her jacket. But there she was; the late Serina Jacobs, clearly alive, looking exceptionally healthy. So Rex Wilcox, one hand still firmly gripping his shriveled sack, slowly opened the door and let the dead woman in. And as soon as she finished crossing the threshold, he grabbed a heavy, marble statue from the table in the entry way, and calmly clobbered the young woman over the head with it. She immediately fell into an unconscious heap at his feet.

PART 2

Chapter 12

Jacobs was still unconscious and or asleep on the sofa in Rex Wilcox's living room when the afternoon fog began to blow back over the Marin headlands into Mill Valley. After awakening around noon, Wilcox phoned one of his on-again, off-again boyfriends, "Poofy" McFadden, plastic surgeon, Dr. McFadden, who worked in his oh so private doctor's office in San Francisco. Poofy was to come to Wilcox's home that afternoon to discuss the "remake" of Serina Jacobs—into what, he didn't know yet—but Wilcox had confidence that if anyone could bring Serina back to life as a completely different person, it was Poofy McFadden.

Wilcox was still in his kimono when his part-time lover appeared at his door, looking like a Scottish fisherman, his thinning, red hair pushed back from his freckled forehead, his thick forearms covered in red fuzz, his characteristic red fu-man-chu mustache curled up under a smile of his perfectly white teeth, and his fifty-four year old blue eyes still sparkling.

"Rex, honey, it's been a hell of a long time! Look at you—you've lost weight!" grinned Poofy as the two embraced and gave each other a light kiss on the lips, McFadden having to bend over considerably to reach Wilcox's face.

"Don't 'honey' me, you shameless slut!" Wilcox said, a broad smile on his pudgy face. "I know how you wealthy doctors are! Different queen every night!"

"Oh, but only if I have a special patient, honey. The barter system is alive and well I'll have you know!" laughed Poofy, surveying Wilcox's apartment with an approving eye. Wilcox had excellent taste in interior design, and the interesting combination of Scandinavian and Japanese elements gave the place a light, airy feel.

"Well, dear, I don't know if I can muster enough hard-ons to barter my way through *this* particular project," said Wilcox, turning in his kimono with a flourish to where Serina Jacobs lay sleeping, under a Mexican serape on the futon sofa. "Where, pray tell, are the tools of your trade, you old Poofster?"

"Oh, after what you explained on the phone, I have all that in my van. Have to diagnose my patient before I can prescribe the treatment, yes? So let's have a look at her," whispered Poofy conspiratorially as he moved toward the sofa. He carefully drew back the serape and revealed Serina Jacobs's perfectly shaped frame minus most of her clothes that Rex had chosen to remove.

"Good God, Rex! This is a fine specimen of a woman!" gasped Poofy.

"Well what did you expect? Didn't I tell you on the phone she was quite beautiful for a female?" said Wilcox under his breath.

"Yes, yes of course. Actually…" said Poofy almost tracing his hand over Jacobs's fine ass "she might be a beautiful man, if she had a sex change operation."

Just then Jacobs awoke with a start, very disorientated after such a hard knock on the head. "Jesus! Wilcox, what the hell is going on here?" she shouted as she quickly covered herself with the serape, pulling herself into a ball on the futon, as far away from his examiner as possible. "Who the hell is this?"" she asked, pointing at the bigheaded man with the red fu-man-chu mustache.

"Serina just calm down. This is Poofy, my friend, a doctor who is going to turn you into a new woman…or man!" Wilcox tried to explain in his most soothing tone. "Serina, you're supposed to be dead. I'm getting ready to sell your paintings for a lot of money because you're a dead painter now, don't you understand?"

Jacobs took a long, hard look at Poofy, then back to Wilcox, then back at Poofy, then back to Wilcox, both of them with shit-eating grins, and grimaced. Shit! She'd forgotten that Wilcox had never met her. Shelby knew all about Wilcox from Serina when they would get together. They used to laugh about Wilcox's ball scratching habits.

That made her remember when she arrived home last night in San Francisco from her Vegas trip. At least she thought it was last night. Listening to her voice mail messages. Several people, including Wilcox, telling her Serina had died in a car crash. They had all read it in the papers. God, was it really true? Sherri had left an urgent message on her cell phone, telling her she was on her way to Vegas early for their get together vacation, so she hadn't even heard about Serina yet. She'd tried to reach Sherri but they never did connect and she didn't just want to leave a voice mail message. This was something she wanted to tell Sherri face to face. And she didn't really feel like Serina was dead. So Shelby had decided to check with Rex; make sure Serina was really gone. But weren't triplets supposed to feel something when something bad happened to one of them? She didn't feel anything. She felt perfectly normal other than this throbbing headache when that fool hit her over the head. The balls, or rather, scratched balls of the gay nut!

Unexpectedly, tears slowly began to pour from her eyes, forming a delicate stream down her pale cheeks. Serina. She glared at Wilcox and this Poofy. "I'm Shelby Jacobs, one of Serina's triplet sisters. I was so upset when I found out what happened to her, I wasn't thinking straight. I came straight over here because I know you were one of the last people who saw her alive. I wanted to talk to you; *needed* to talk to you." She gulped in some air in an attempt to calm herself.

Chapter 13

She'd gone from Caesar's to Ballagio's, wanting to check out the scenery there when she was confronted by a drop dead gorgeous Hispanic guy who walked up to her, smiled at her in a playful manner, immediately flirting with her with his very sexy eyes.

"Hi, beautiful. I was hoping you'd pay me a surprise visit and spirit me up to your hotel room away from all this."

Wow! This guy wasn't shy. Ok, she'd play, but no harm in playing a little hard to get. "Here's the thing, I'm not alone," she shot back at him, adding a hint of shyness in her voice.

"Yo, you got a man?"

"No," she laughed. "I'm here with a sister, and she's upstairs, sleeping. I can't go up there and wake her up." Sherri had not made an arrival yet, wasn't even sure exactly when everybody was supposed to show up, but she figured it was a good thing to let this guy think someone was here who would come looking for her if something happened. Better safe than sorry. She wondered, too, when her other sister would make her appearance from San Anselmo. Where was everybody? She must have the right date for their Vegas trip since there was a reservation for their suite when she checked in. She closed her eyes for a second. It was so confusing. She lived in San Fran, didn't she? Serina was the one who lived in San Anselmo, right? Then why had she been in the San Anselmo region only this morning? She shook her head slightly. What was wrong with her?

"Oh. Well, you know, how 'bout I show you around this time?"

"Um," she hesitated, weighing how much she trusted him against a potential for danger. "Ok."

"Yeah?" He sounded surprised.

"Yeah. I mean, if you want."

He nodded. "You ready to go?"

"Yeah," she nodded in return. "Always."

Then she grabbed her smokes, finished her drink and when she stood up, he took her hand and pulled her along next to him. She hoped she didn't just make a dumb choice. Hands woven together, his thumb rubbed the top of her hand as he pushed through the big glass doors out into the night. No, she definitely thought she made a good choice.

When he dropped her hand to reach in his pocket for the valet ticket, she shivered in the cool night air, reflexively crossing her arms to keep warm. Handing the ticket to the valet, he slid his arm across her shoulders and drew her up against him. Pressed close, she could tell he was warm through the T-shirt, and she snuggled up as close as she dared, but resisted putting her arms around his waist. She was pretty sure she made the right choice.

Dipping his head, he placed his other arm around her waist and grazed his lips across her mouth. Without thinking, she tilted her face to meet his and he went for it, tentative at first, just a soft, light kiss, but she closed her eyes and gently responded. Then he took another kiss just like that first soft one, then another. Wow, this guy moved fast. He shifted and moved the other way, kissing the other side of her mouth, still keeping his touch light, but before backing away from that one, he slipped the smallest flick of his tongue. He backed off and hovered for a second, then he moved back in and really laid one on her.

His arms enclosed her, pulling her tight against his body. He went hard and deep, working her upper lip, lower lip, then slipping in some tongue, making her blood sing. She kissed back because suddenly she can't get enough; head dizzy, legs weak, she held of his sides and now was tugging at his waist, sliding her arms further around his back so she could press up against him. God, he was spectacular, kissing and biting and sucking and licking all at once, his rough shadow of stubble scraping against her skin in contrast to the glide of his tongue on her teeth, her lips, her tongue. And his taste, oh my, his taste. Naturally salty, and tangy from the booze, and bitter from the smokes and he was kissing and biting and sucking and licking all at once. She backed off and broke the connection before she started melting right on the sidewalk in front of everyone. He caught her bottom lip between his teeth as she pulled back. Now she was certain she made the right choice even if things were moving very fast. She had a right to take risks, right?

His eyes fluttered open, heavy lidded now, impossibly long lashes, moving up slowly, and he cracked a grin, snuck in one more kiss, tossed her a lingering look before backing off a little.

"Huh. Hmm," is all he said, still watching her. His eyes gleamed, no mistaking what emotions they were conveying right about now.

"Mm. Mmmhmm," was all she said in return.

The valet pulled up and Antonio said, "This is us." He handed the valet some bills.

"Thanks, Antonio. Have a great evening," the valet said to him.

Antionio, at least she knew his name. She checked out the car, a liquid black, Jaguar 2-seater convertible. "This is your car?"

"Yeah, you don't like it? You did before"

"Are you kidding me? This car rocks!" Before? What was he talking about?

"Think so?" He gallantly opened the door.

"Oh, you know it does," she teased back as she slid into the cushioned seat.

"I know it does, I was just wondering what you think." He walked around and got in the other side, cocked a brow and said, "So you like it, huh?"

"Dude, I drive a Jeep, ok? I mean, I love my Jeep. I wouldn't trade it, not even for this. But this is way cool. This is like, ultimate luxury right here. It's more comfy than my bed." The seat was like sitting on a buttery leather cloud, the inside all black with soft glowing digital green lights. When he pulled forward, she didn't even feel the faux cobblestone road beneath them. The car just absorbed the bumps as though we were riding on a cushion of air.

"Kinda cold out tonight," he commented. "C'mere and keep me warm."

Without giving it a second thought, she slid over next to him. He clicked something on his steering wheel and the radio came on, playing the Dixie Chicks REALLY loud, so he clicked it down a few notches while she resisted kissing him again just for that. Then he rested his arm around her shoulders again, pulling her against him.

"You wanna listen to somethin else?" he asked.

"No, this is good, really good. So, do you like living here, in Vegas?"

"Yeah, it's cool, I guess. I been here awhile now, six years, so it's not all that exciting, you know? Like, when I first moved out here it was all new." He pulled onto the strip with its glittering lights and constant motion and beckoning signs and promises of riches and dreams come true. "Now, though, I dunno, it's sorta 'been there, done that'."

"So you're bored?"

"Yeah, and no. I like it. I fuckin hated winters, man. I like boxing, there's always good fights goin on out here. I even got to fight out here."

"You're a boxer?"

Nodding as he steered, "Uh huh. I thought I told you already."

"I don't remember. You've had a fight out here? Championship?"

"Fuck no," he laughed. "No, I ain't all that. It was an undercard though," he said, a little proud.

"No shit. That is really cool. What weight class?"

"Super middle."

"Like Roy Jones Jr.?"

"Nah, he's a light heavyweight. You know 'bout boxing?"

"I know a little. Not a lot. I know there's a lot of weight classes. Even more organizations. I watch a little."

"You know Roy Jones?" he asked.

"He's always on HBO. Anyhow, I'm just saying. It's very cool. That's exciting."

"Yeah, it was cool. I mean, I like it here, it's just not as exciting as it was at first, that's all."

"You need some stranger reminding you about the excitement," she replied.

He laughed a little, shrugged, "Maybe. I don't know. Maybe, cause right now it's just all part of the routine."

"Because you've done everything?"

"Yeah." He stopped at a red light and kissed her again.

It was great. It lightened her up brighter than any neon sign in sight. She opened her eyes during the kiss and saw him looking back at her, watching her reactions, then she closed them again, trusting he'd do the same. Reaching over, she slid her hand across his chest, kissing him back hard, then moved her hand down to his stomach, rubbing across it a few times, then sliding her and down lower yet.

Between his legs.

Breaking the kiss, she asked him, "Have you done this before?" Then she bit his neck.

Cars behind them honked. Oops, the light had turned green. She glanced at his face, watched him snap out of it and remember where he was, get the car in motion again.

Around them, Frusciante set down a few of his legendary slow bended blue notes, and it causes the devil in her to come out and she went for it. She rubbed him harder, feeling him rise beneath the fly of his pants. She traced the line of his jugular with her tongue, licking along his jawline as she fumbled with his belt. He was wordless next to her, staring straight out at the road, but he liked it. He loved it, she was sure. He was strung tight as piano-wire, white-knuckled around the steering wheel, breath coming shorter already.

She managed to get his belt un-hitched by the next stoplight, and he turned to kiss her mouth again, really hard and deep, plenty of tongue, much hotter, full-court-press kissing. He started making noises into her mouth as she fiddled with the zipper. They were short "mm"s and "ahhh"s until she got the zipper all way down and reached inside, over his boxers, beneath his jeans. He growled, a libidinous guttural sound, long, drawn out and stuttering.

The light turned green, so she instructed him to drive. Licking his lips, he hit the pedal and they moved forward as Anthony Keidis unleashed a high-pitched wail. Dipping under his boxers, she grabbed hold of him; he was hard as could be already, and he lurched. Satisfied, she asked him again, "You ever done this before?"

Breathing hard, chest rising and falling exaggeratedly, he stuttered, concentrating on the road. "Uh, huh-uh. No."

She debated about a half-second before deciding he earned this. He made her feel spectacular in such a short period of time, so, well, reciprocity and all.

She released him to dig into her pocket and pulled out the little square. Quickly, she ripped it open with her teeth, spitting the little piece of foily paper on the floor with a decidedly unsexy "pfoot" sound as Flea plucked away pizzicato on his bass. She took the condom out and tossed the wrapper onto the floorboard. Antonio didn't seem to mind the littering.

At another the red light, she took hold of him, stroked lightly while he was still bare-skinned and asked, "You ready for this?"

He nodded quickly, visibly sucked in a breath, met her gaze. "Always."

She got him covered, then held him firmly and waited a few seconds.

The light switched green, Smith hit a downbeat, she leaned over, Antonio hit the gas, and she took him in her mouth.

"Oooh. Shiiit! Yesss," he hissed above her and lurched again.

The seat was back far enough so she wasn't squished against the steering wheel too bad, plus the seat was soft and comfy. He was obviously loving this, fully hard and responding already. So she went at him the best she knew how.

She figured if she was gonna give it, she'd give it good. She moved in time with the music, letting its rhythm set hers.

He stroked his hand across her back, tangling his hand in her hair. His legs shifted, the car slowed and they glided to a stop again. She went at him really good then, wanting him to keep making those noises. And he did. He continued encouraging her with yesses and moans, slightly grinding his hips back into the seat further, then up into her, nearly squirming. Considerately, he brushed the hair from her face, gathered it in his free hand and said, "Your hair, uuhhhh, it's fuckin gorgeous, UUUHHH!"

She loved hearing that, so as he hit the gas and they were in motion again, she took him in really deep. Thumping bass lines pulse around them, he writhed beneath her, groaned really loud, "Mierda, that's great. Oooh, shit, uh, you're killing me…ooh shit, si, si, YEAH!"

She had to back off a little before she started to choke, so she licked, added some tongue. When she did, he mumbled in Spanish and picked his hips up pretty high. That turned her on so much, she began sucking, picking up the pace again.

They were still moving, he was still "ahhhhhh"ing, the lights kept twinkling around them, and she went at it harder and faster.

He panted above her, becoming even hotter in her mouth, and she could feel their steady movement picking up smooth speed. He was close, really close when his hand tightened in her hair and he pressed up into her even harder. So she took him as deep as she could tolerate, as hard as she could, all the way, and clutched at his thigh with her other hand.

Above her, "Ahh…Ohhh…Shiiiiiit!" He jerked, hissed some more, and she stayed on him as he came. Easing up, still working him for every last bit, every aftershock, she swore she felt the car pulling, swerving to one side. He was still moaning, "Oooh, shiiiit."

Just as she pulled off him, the car jacked violently over a bump. CA-CHUNK! A big one. Head still in his lap, she couldn't see, but it felt bad.

THUD! Then him: "Ahh, shit!" His thigh beneath her hand moved quickly. Slowing, turning, the car jerked again. A loud screech of the tires, a horrible, teeth-jarring metallic scraping sound—*SCRIIIITCH *—

Then him: "AW, SHIT!"

They slammed to a stop.

Raising up, she looked around. "Oooh, shit." They were on the sidewalk. The fucking walkway in front of the Riviera. The Crazy Girls statue was to her right and behind them.

He hit it. He hit the Crazy Girls statue. She smirked inwardly. Possibly outwardly. He jumped the curb, went on the sidewalk and nailed one of the most famous and luckiest statues on the strip. The Crazy Girls.

Good.

Good for her. Good for him. Good for her for making him do that. Good for him for liking it so much he did that.

"OH, SHIT!" he said again and looked around.

Luckily, miraculously, no one was really close. He didn't hit anyone, the statue looked pretty much ok. He couldn't have been going that fast.

"What the fuck? What the fuck did I do?" he asked.

She scanned the area. Oh, there were a few people around. It was never empty, was it? It just couldn't be completely desolate. Well. What were they gonna do? They weren't that close. They noticed though that everyone stared at them with their mouths wide open at the black Jaguar on the sidewalk.

"Go," she told him.

"Go? I should go?"

"Do you want to explain this to the cops?"

He threw the car back in gear and hit the gas, checked the traffic, then pulled out onto the street, letting the car thump back down over the curb. Turned down the first side street, and kept going.

A couple of blocks later, still fighting off the smirk, she said, "I am really so sorry."

"Nah, don't be, it's cool," he replied, but his jaw clenched, his eyes were steely hard. He reached down and peeled off the used condom, carelessly tossing it out the window.

"Dude, you hit that thing, didn't you? That's what I heard, right?"

"Yeah, I fuckin hit it."

"You wanna see if the car's ok?"

He pulled into a 7-11, tucked in, zipped up, and got out. Walked around to the passenger side of the car and checked it out closely. His jaw clenched again, and she swore she could see a throb in his temple. Bending down, he inspected the side of the car, then stood up and sighed.

She was getting a little worried, concerned he would go off on her pretty good now. It was partly her fault since clumsiness and bad luck did kind of follow her when it came to shit like this.

This was a CAR, a very nice car that just got scratched up cause of her being stupid.

Antonio's jaw clenched again, now he glanced in the window at her. "Oooh, shit," he laughed.

She got out of the car to check it out herself. Her heart sank. There were two large gashes in the door that extend to long scrapes all the way to the back end of the car. "Antonio, I'm so sorry. I don't…, I don't know what to say. This is all my fault."

He reached for her hand and pulled her next to him. "Yo, 'salright, serious. Don't feel bad."

"Your car, your beautiful car. This is…I'm so sorry. I'll pay for it, I'll…"

"Yo, relax, baby," he wrapped his arm around her shoulders again. "It was worth it, you know. Wasn't your fault, I just sorta got, like, distracted."

"But that was my fault, I shouldn't have done…THAT."

"Yeah, well, THAT was great. I'm glad you did that."

"Was it something new?"

Hugging her close, he laughed again. "That was definitely new. That was…intense, is what that was."

"So you're not pissed off at me?"

"Fuck no! I'm a little jacked at myself. I guess I closed my eyes or somethin. I don't know, I just sorta got, well, you know, it was *intense*."

"I'm still really sorry."

"C'mere," he said and leaned down to kiss her.

She pulled back just a bit, but he swooped in anyhow, held her tight, gave her a pretty good one. Convinced her he was not pissed at her at all. His hands started roving up and down her back and he got more into it.

Gently, she backed him off as she scanned the sky. The dark wasn't as inky thick anymore, stars were fading out. "I really ought to get back to the hotel," she told him.

"Huh? You don't wanna come home with me no more?"

"No, I want to, I just don't think I should. It's really late, and I should be there when my sister gets up."

His eyes became slits. "You're sister ain't really another guy, is she? Just so you don't hurt my feelings? It's 'k, just tell me now, I'll try and understand."

"No, she's a girl, I told you. I don't have a man like that. It's just my sisters and I planned this Vegas vacation for the three of us to get together, do a 'girl' thing, you know?"

"Yo, I see what's up here. You make me fuck up my car, you know, then cause you don't like the sneak preview, you're skippin out before the movie, even though you played the movie before."

"You're fucking with me, aren't you?"

"Yeah, little bit."

"I am really so sorry about the car, I will pay for it, I will."

"Stop it, I was fuckin with you, it's cool," he said and hugged her tighter again, taking another soft kiss. "You sure you wanna go back?"

"I know I don't want to go back, but I really should."

Another kiss, a little longer one, one that made her knees start to weaken again.

Softly, he said, "Cause I really liked that preview. We should make another whole movie."

The sky above lightened even more, dawn was fast approaching. It *had* made her pretty hot, hearing him moan and groan and come so easily. But she sucked up her resolve. "I'd love it, I know I would, I just don't know if I want to get back in a car with you driving again."

"Ooooh, that's harsh," he grinned.

She really wanted to climb right inside his T-shirt and feel his bare skin against hers. Kiss him all over, taste the curve of every muscle. But— "I should go," she said instead.

"I just feel bad, you know, like," he nuzzled her ear, whispered. "I got everything, what about you? I'd like to do something for you. I wanna thank you."

"You're welcome. I had a good time, really."

"Yeah?"

"Yeah," she reassured him. "Very good. Did you have a good time?"

"I had a fuckin great time, you kiddin me?"

"Then I really should go."

"'K, I'll take you back, if you trust me to, that is."

"Thank you."

"Can I have another kiss?" he asked.

She gave him a good one, full tongue, hint of teeth. He was a rare one—just as good at getting kissed, easing back and accepting it as he was at giving kisses, moving in and working her.

"Mmmmm," he sighed when she pulled away and climbed back into the car. He then slid in on his side and turned the ignition over, shutting the stereo off. "C'mere," he motioned for her to slide next to him again, so she did.

Cuddling into his side, she was struck by that. He still wanted her close to him.

All the lights on the strip were still on, but in the fading darkness they didn't seem as bright. Pulling up in front of Caesars, he released her. "Want me park it and walk you in?" he offered.

"No, I'm fine, thanks though."

"So, um, what're you doing tonight? Later? I gotta work again, but, I don't know, can I call you or something since we seem to have something good goin here?"

"You want to see me again?" This was all so quick, but, yeah, that sounded great.

He kissed her as his answer, so she gave him her suite number, opened the door and climbed out. As she shut the door, she gave him a long look. He sat perfectly still, no leg shaking, no head nodding, no snapping of his fingers. He just leaned back in his seat, gazing at her, completely at ease. Calm. His dark eyes met hers and even in the growing daylight and with a fading buzz, they still seemed brilliant.

"Thanks," he grinned, but his eyes looked melancholy, "you know, for everything."

"Drive safe," she responded and closed the door.

Not so much the walk of shame; rather the walk of pride when she wound through the hallways to get upstairs.

Although, she couldn't wait to brush her teeth.

Sherri was there and woke up shortly after she entered the suite, came into the living room and lit a smoke. "What time is it?" she asked groggily.

"A little after six," she answered, lighting her own smoke

"And you're up already?"

"Sort of."

"You went out real late, didn't you?"

"Yeah, for awhile."

"You have a good time?"

"Well, yeah. It was interesting."

"What'd you do?"

"I gambled a little, won a little bit. Gave a really hot dice dealer a highway hummer, made him crash his car a little."

Crushing out her cigarette, she said, "I'm going back to sleep. You can tell me about this at the pool."

Fair enough.

Three hours of sleep, four hours at the pool where she did 78 laps in the pool and got tons of sun, two hours of serious blackjacking where she managed to lose $800., two more hours of blackjacking where she cleared $1200., and several celebration drinks later, she asked Sherri, "Want to have some dinner?"

She sighed. "Alright, you pick where."

"Morton's?"

"No, not in the mood for all that, answered Sherri."

"Ok, how about Battista's."

"No, I don't really want Italian. I'm sort of in the mood to just hang out here. We have those free tickets anyhow."

So that night they go to the dinner show at Caesars. Caesars Magical Empire, they called it. 2Jacobs was pretty smashed. While they were getting dressed, she bitched a little. "Dinner? What the fuck are we supposed to do at dinner?"

"It's all the wine we can drink," she reminded her, knowing that would win her over.

"Oh, ok, then we'll go. I hate magic, are they gonna do magic? Sherri asked."

"I assume so, considering the name and all."

"Magic sucks, it freaks me out."

"Dude, magic is cool. The world needs more magic."

"It's not real. It's just tricks to make us feel stupid."

"No, you've got it all wrong. You're not supposed to feel stupid just because you don't know how they did it. Just be impressed and roll with it. So what if it's sleight of hand? It's still pretty cool that they have that skill. I like magic."

"But it's not real, that's what I'm saying. You don't believe in real magic," said Sherri.

"Yes I do. I followed the Dead for five years, 2Jacobs. I believe in a lot."

"Oh. What are we doing there again? You know, you're acting more like Serina than Shelby. What's up with that?"

"Having dinner. What's up is we're having dinner. Come on, let's get going."

"I hate dinner. I don't want to go. Magic freaks me out," Sherri reminded her.

"It's all the free wine we can drink."

"Ok, I'll go. Just let me smoke a cigarette, put on some lipstick, curl my hair, pick out some shoes and then I'll be ready."

It was a nice show. Outside, they had a wizard-looking dude doing close-up sleight of hand magic like David Blaine. She was impressed, 2Jacobs was amazed. "I really LIKE that," she said. "Where's the wine?"

"Inside, they'll have it inside."

Inside, they walked down a dark hallway that freaked her out and she grabbed onto her. "I don't like this, this is why magic sucks." She calmed down once they were seated in their dining chamber and she poured a glass of wine. She sipped and passed the glass to her as she caught the waiter. "I can't drink this, she'll drink this. Can I have a glass of beer?"

She drank 2Jacobs's wine, she drank her own wine, she asked for more wine. By the time dinner was over, she was on the same alcoholic level as Sherri was. They were escorted out of the dining chamber and led to a dark area with a bar, a huge fire pit and rooms around it. In the rooms they had more magic displays. There were wizards walking around doing tricks for people, and there was a fortune teller.

"We HAVE to do that," said 2Jacobs, dragging her to the fortune teller. "Do you believe in this?"

"Um, no not really. I believe in free will over fate. I don't think it can hurt, though."

"Yeah, well, I believe in it," said Sherri.

She didn't bother telling her that even more than believing in free will, she believed that the chick sitting there was a pure entertainer, not a psychic. The girl was cute all dolled up in sparkly jewels and an outfit that looked like she blinked her way out of *I Dream of Jeannie* re-runs.

"You first," she told 2Jacobs as they sat down. "Want me to leave?"

"No, you can stay," Sherri answered, then turned to the girl. "What do I do?"

"Well, first you ask me three questions that you're wondering about. Then I'll have you draw the cards, and I'll read them for you and answer your questions."

"Wait," she interrupted. "What's your name?"

"Mine? Sabina."

That threw her. Was it a stage name or not? She presumed it was since even Dell operators, shoot, most computer users, used stage names these days.

Sherri had her questions all ready to roll. Impatient, she blurted them out. "Will I get married? Will I have children? Will I live a long time?"

Sabina had Sherri pick out some cards, and then she laid them out. She tuned out on the answers when a particularly handsome wizard appeared in her line of vision. She watched him cross the room and do a card trick for another couple. After he finished and walked down a corridor, she shifted her attention back to Sherri's reading.

"You should be very happy, and your family will all live long prosperous lives," she said.

She checked out the cards, knowing nothing about the Tarot deck, so no clue if Sabina was actually reading what was on the cards, or if she just answered Sherri any way she wanted, fake or true.

Sherri was all into it, though. She hunched forward, hooked on every word and listening intently. "So the guy I'm with now is the one I'll marry, then?"

"Yes, that's what I see for you."

"And that's the right thing to do?"

Sabina stumbled briefly with that question. "That's all I can read in the cards."

Very skillful reply.

When 2Jacobs finished, she seemed rather pleased. "That was really cool," she said. "You should go now."

"Alright," They switched chairs. "Lay it on me, Sabina."

"First, give me your name, date of birth, and time of birth. Since you are twins—oh, no, sorry, triplets, time of birth you know, *the hour and minute* you were born, is very important. Then after that, ask me anything special you want to know."

She told her the exact hour and minute she, the 3rd triplet, was born. "Um. Ok, will I hit the Megabucks jackpot while I'm out here?"

She smiled at her. "I don't think I have to read your cards to answer that one, but good luck anyway."

While she was pulling out cards, she prodded again. "Anything else?"

"Will I ever meet Vin Diesel?"

"Who?"

Sherri chimed in, "She loves him, he's an actor."

Astonished, she asked, "You don't know who he is? Well, do yourself a favor and find out, ok?"

"He's really cute, huh?" She arranged the cards and peered down at them. "Well, here's what I see with your *exact time* of birth. You're a natural leader, people like to follow you. And I see a great deal of strength here, the kind to overcome or obtain nearly anything."

She paused and she suddenly wished she had listened to what she said to Sherri more closely. Where was she pulling this from? She assumed she'd just tell them what they wanted to hear, use the clues from our questions to go on. "Sabina," she interrupted. "How long have you been doing this?"

She blushed. "Only a couple of months. That's what takes me awhile. I have to think about what the cards mean sometimes."

"So you did study how to read a tarot deck?"

"Mmm hmm," she nodded, then continued. "I see an awful lot of wealth here." She looked up at her, beaming. "Maybe you will hit the Megabucks jackpot!"

"Do you see Vin Diesel in there?"

She shook her head. "No, I don't see anyone."

"Excuse me?"

"I see you working hard, and…focused. But I don't see any loves."

"Wait a minute," she interrupted, shaken. "You don't see anyone in there for me? Ever?"

"No, I don't. You're very…brave. I see that."

"Oh come on, you have to see someone, some man. Someone loves me, right? I love someone?"

"Nothing like that."

Well. Jeez! Honestly. Granted, her memory had been a bit foggy in recent days. Parts of her life were kinda missing, truth be told. Like she wasn't really who she was, but didn't really know who she was, kinda confusing. Was this supposed to bother her? Did she even want a boyfriend, someone chaining her down, holding her still and smothering her? Marriage and a picket fence and children and dogs or any of that. Or did she want to roam and party and flirt and live free?

But come *on* man. This chick was actually telling her that no one *ever* would love her.

Like never, ever! Shit! That sounded like doom, like very, very lonely!

"Well, thanks," was all she could say and tossed the money down on the table. She turned to Sherri for some support, to tell her how whacked the chick was, something to negate those depressing words, that depressing future.

"Dude, she nailed you," she said instead. "She's really good, don't you think?"

They walked around and checked out the magic acts in the other rooms, then went back upstairs to the casino.

"What do you want to do?" she asked Sherri.

"I'm sort of tired," was her response.

"You want to just hang around here? Or you want to go up to sleep?"

"I was actually thinking of sleep."

Sure, she can sleep easy. She was just told she was going to have a grand long life with loved ones and happiness surrounding her, while she'd been told she was going to live a prosperous but shallow existence with no one even knowing she existed, was even alive.

"Alright, you want me to walk you upstairs?" she offered.

"Yeah. Well, were you going to go to sleep?"

"I don't know. It's still early."

"But if we go to sleep now, we can get some good sleep, get up early for the pool, be ready to rock in the morning."

"Yeah, ok, I'll go up," sensing Sherri didn't want to be alone.

But once up in the room, the message light on the phone was blinking. Her heart skipped, thrumming in hope Antonio had called. Sherri picked up the phone and pressed the button, holding the receiver to her ear. "Ahh, it's Don," she tells her. Don was Sherri's boyfriend, kind of a jerk, if you asked her.

She gave her some privacy and went to the bathroom, brushed her teeth. *Dumbass. He'd never call.* Hollow-hearted, she brushed her hair and concentrated on pushing aside visions of his crooked grin as well as avoiding her own reflection.

"Hey, you got a message on here, too," 2Jacobs yelled in to her. "Antonioooooo," she taunted. "He said he was on break, and he'd get off at two tonight. He'll meet you at the same place as last night. You want me to save this message so you can listen to it?"

"Of course."

"You going to meet him?"

"Of course."

"You like this guy, don't you?"

"Of course."

"No, I mean, you really like him, don't you?"

"He's really fun."

"Sounds like he likes you," she said.

"Huh, yeah. He just knows he has a good chance of getting lucky with me."

"No, I don't think so."

"You've never even met him."

"Nevertheless. He sounded nice on the phone."

"Yeah, well, according to that tarot-card reader, no one will ever really like me," she reminded 2Jacobs.

"Oh, fuck her. The bead-wearing bitch."

"So how's Don?" she asked to change the subject.

"He's fine. He misses me."

"Of course. How's work for him?" Her memory about Don was really vague, other than the jerk part. How come, she wondered. Wasn't Sherri close like a sister is supposed to be? Shouldn't she know everything there was to know about her triplet's fiancé? Kinda weird.

"He says it's good. He just wants me to come down there soon. So what are you going to do?"

"Do you care if I go out for awhile?"

"Nope."

"What time does that clock say?"

"Um, it's almost two now. You excited?"

She shrugged noncommittally.

She had to be excited. Her entire body hummed with adrenalin, rushing into her head. But more than that, she began throwing clothes around, trying to find something she'd look good in.

Sherri made an attempt to calm her down. "You look fine," she assured her." Shelby was acting kinda bizarre on this Vegas vacation. Forgetfullness. She totally forgot to bring any clothes; her purse even. How weird was that? Good thing she always packed way too much. And now, acting like a school girl over some guy. Way not Shelby's normal personality.

"I don't want to look fine, I want to look HOT."

"Oooh, he has you ALL tied up."

"Alright, fuck off, ok?"

Sherri held up a tight cami shirt and skirt. "How about these?" she asked. "It's white, so your tan will look good, and the shirt is tight so it should make your boobs look good."

"I don't wear skirts, ever. Why are you even showing me a skirt?"

"In case you want to try and look hot!" answered Sherri.

"Let me try it on," she told her.

She quickly changed in the bathroom. Sucked in her stomach as she looked in the mirror. Her boobs did look amazing in it. But her ass, it looked horrible. She checked with 2Jacobs. "Don't lie to me," she instructed.

"Shelby," she blinked. "Go like that! Go exactly like that!"

"But what about my ass? My ass looks really REALLY fat."

"No, it doesn't. That's silly, you're slender like I am. Besides, he won't be looking at that."

"Do I look too sleazy?"

"Actually, no. I mean, you look strange to me, because I'm not used to seeing you like that. But you look good. You look like, like…"

"What?"

"A girl. You look like a girl in the skirt. It looks nice. Feminine, helpless, it suits you."

"It's not too short?"

"Hell no, I wear shorter than that to work," Sherri told her.

"I'm changing."

"NO! You're going to be late, you have to go."

"You just want to go to sleep, don't you? You're getting rid of me."

"Yeah, but you do look good."

"Goodnight, 2Jacobs."

"I'm waking you up to go to the pool at eight," she reminded her.

She grabbed a fresh pack of smokes, a couple of bills from their mutual stash sprawled out on their sitting room table and headed downstairs.

Chapter 14

Shelby, dressed in a sleek, short, fitted cotton dress (Rex Wilcox just happened to have the dress in his closet in case one of his friends needed it) that accentuated her new deep Las Vegas tan and the pale fuzz on her arms, was seated in the bar drinking beer and scotch, waiting for ball scratching Rex to return from the men's room and for Poofy McFadden, who was joining them from San Francisco, to arrive. The three were at the restaurant to discuss what to do about triplet Shelby and how to sell at phenomenal profit the Serina Jacobs paintings. As she sat their impatiently, she noticed the maitre d' hand a cordless phone to another patron. Of course, God, sometimes her brain was so slow. She'd call Sherri who had to be in Vegas by now for their planned vacation. Shit, 2Jacobs didn't even know about Serina's demise. And Shelby sure as hell wasn't interested in any plastic surgery, or was she? Maybe her nose, her mouth? Her ass sure could use some tightening. Imagine, at twenty-three, ass firming surgery already. Anyway, sensible Sherri'd know what to do. She requested a phone and called Sherri's cell number

"Sherri here," came the muffled voice over the other line.

"2Jacobs, it's me. I need your help. Serina was killed in a car accident and the art gallery owner who commissioned her pictures kinda took me hostage." She had to pause for a minute. All thoughts of breaking the news of Serina's demise to Sherri gently flew out the window. She needed help and she needed help right this second. Besides, she still couldn't take in the reality that Serina was really gone. It seemed like only baseless words to her still.

"What? Who is this?" Serina asked, sitting up in her bed.

"What do you mean, who is this? How many sisters do you have with a triplet sister named Serina?" Shelby asked.

"Shelby?"

"Yeah, Shelby! What's the deal with you?" Why was she acting weird? She didn't have time for this!

"Shelby, are you downstairs at Vince's bar? Do you need me to come down?"

"No, I'm not downstairs in the bar. I'm in Mill Valley north of San Francisco."

"What're you talking about, Jacobs? How can you be north of San Francisco when I just saw you in our suite here at Caesars not thirty minutes ago!"

"Sherri, what the hell is wrong with you! Are you dreaming? I've been stuck with this gay, scrotom scratching gallery owner north of San Fran for almost two days. Our sister had a fatal car crash. She died which is why I'm came to visit this nut in the first place!"

"3Jacobs, I'm not joking you! This is my second night in our suite and you've been here with me. We even laid out by the pool almost all day today. Right now, you're down with that hot male friend of yours."

That caught her attention. What hot male friend? "Hot male?" she asked.

"Yeah, you know, Anthony. Oh, excuse me," 2Jacobs added a touch of sarcasm, "Antonioooo…"

She was sure her heart stopped right then and there. Then, it started pumping again. Only one explanation. "2Jacobs, this person you think is me looks just like me?"

"Well, yeah…oh, no."

They both said it at the same time, "Serina!"

"Shit!" Shelby added. "Don't you move. I'm on my way. I may have to rent a plane, but I'm on my way!" she informed Sherri.

Shelby looked out the window to where a black BMW had parked next to Rex's silver convertible. Poofy McFadden had arrived. Shit, again!

Poofy entered the restaurant, taking off his overcoat as he walked. He stepped up to the bar and gave Shelby's butt a little pinch. "I still say you'd make one fine specimen of a man," he said.

She slipped the phone between her legs on the barstool, pushing it well up under her crotch so it wouldn't protrude from underneath her short dress. "Oh—it's you!" she said, acting surprised as if expecting someone else to walk up and pinch her ass. "How are you?" she asked as he cozied up next to her, looking directly down her plunging neckline at her ample bosom—he looked as if he might start drooling on her cleavage any minute. What was it with gay men?

"Hungry," said Poofy, eyes still fixed on her breasts. "Very hungry!" He put his hand on her thigh, which she quickly pushed away. "Where's Rexy, baby?"

"Well, let's eat then! Rex is in the men's room. He should be right out," she said, scooting back on the barstool. "Will you please ask the maitre'd to show us to our table?" He turned to flag the maitre'd and as he did Shelby slipped the phone into her panties, shoving it as far down as she could so it was resting directly between her legs against her slightly damp pudenda. She stood up and looked around, trying to plot an escape route. The maitre'd arrived to show them to their table. "Excuse me" she said to the maitre d'. "Can you direct me to the ladies room?"

"Of course," said the maitre' d. "It's down that hall there and to the left."

"Thanks. I'll be right back, Poofy," she told him.

"Don't be long!" he said with his silly, grin.

As soon as the maitre d' and Poofy turned to go to the table, Shelby waddled, as fast as she could with the portable phone slipping around in her panties, towards the rest rooms, praying she wouldn't run into Rex. Then, checking quickly to see if Poofy was watching, and relieved to see that he was chatting with the maitre d', she slipped into the kitchen. The rotund chef looked up from where he was sampling steaming vegetables from a large silver vat, the sous chefs stopped chopping their various vegetables.

"May I help you?" said the chef in a heavy, German accent.

Shelby looked around the kitchen, noticed a screen door past the refrigerators leading to a gravel parking lot. She pulled up her tight dress, reached in her panties and extracted the phone.

The chef dropped his ladle with a loud clang. "Ach du liebe!" he shouted.

Shelby put the phone on the cutting table and dashed past him out the back door, the screen door slamming shut. The chef and his assistants stood frozen, mouths agape.

She looked frantically round the back parking lot, trying to find a way around the building that would lead to Rex's car up front. She found a path between the restaurant and the motel, and, running in a crouch so she would not be noticed through the windows by any of the patrons, particularly Poofy, she slipped into the convertible, found the spare keys she'd spotted before when she and Rex were driving, started up the car and patched out of the lot.

Poofy, Rex, who had joined him, the maitre d' and the other patrons in the restaurant, mostly old, retired couples, all heard the chef's shout in the kitchen. The maitre 'd looked up, rather surprised, for the chef did not normally have outbursts of emotion on the job.

Poofy smiled and said, "Perhaps he dropped the pickled herring, no?"

The maitre d' smiled back and said, "Perhaps. I'll go have a look." He went to the kitchen. The chef and his assistants were looking out the back door, trying to spot the woman with the phone in her panties.

"Is there a problem, Chef Gunter?" he asked.

"Ach!" said the chef, turning around with a face as red as the tomatoes on the cutting table. "One of the customers has fled! A blonde frauline carrying a telephone in her underpants!" The maitre'd looked at the phone on the cutting board and soon they were all staring at it.

"This phone?" The maitre'd finally asked, pointing to it as if it were road kill. "The house phone?" The chef nodded. "In her panties?" asked the maitre'd. The chef nodded again. The maitre'd approached the phone and, without touching it, leaned over the cutting table and gave it a cautious sniff, wrinkling up his nose at Shelby's odor.

"Hmm" said the maitre'd. "I think perhaps we need a new phone."

Meanwhile, Rex noticed his car was no longer where he parked it. "Did you move my car, Poofy?" he asked.

Before Poofy could answer, the maitre'd returned to their table. "It appears your date changed her mind, Herr McFadden! I guess she was not hungry!" But the joke was lost on Poofy, who immediately ran for the front door, practically knocking over a silver-haired lady who was on her way to the rest room. He ripped open the front door, saw that the convertible was indeed gone, then ran back in.

"Which way did she go?" he asked the maitre'd.

"I don't know, Herr McFadden! I expect she went back to the freeway, since there is nothing in the other direction except China Camp. It also appears she made a phone call," answered the maitre'd, pointing to the tainted phone he had placed on their table.

"Goddamn it!" Poofy yelled, slamming his fist down on the table, causing the phone to rebound to the floor. He immediately reached down and attempted to pick it up, but it was so slippery it squirted across the floor, causing the maitre'd to jump out of the way as it skidded by.

"You should dry your hands before you use the phone!" yelled Poofy. Then he and Rex ran out the door.

The maitre d', chef, and sous chefs just looked at each other as they heard Poofy McFadden's Mercedes screech out of the lot. Finally, the maitre'd said in German: "She must have been a hot date in drag!"

Chapter 15

"Ready to gamble?" Antonio asked her a few hours later after drinking at Vince's bar with some of the other patrons and just enjoying conversation, watching people.

"Sure," she told him.

"Alright, c'mon, then." He got up and grabbed her hand. "Let's do it. I wanna see just how lucky you are."

"Ah no, I don't think I'm lucky." Her head rushed a bit when she stood up, thanks not only to the drinks she'd been consuming off and on all day, but also to the heat of his hand in hers.

"I am the lucky one, you know? Trust me, I know what I'm saying." He gave her a sideways glance to make sure she caught the meaning.

It was corny, but it also melted her heart. And all she could think was either this guy was fucking with her for sport, or he was a total freaking moron for not realizing how hot he was. And right on the heels of that thought, as she allowed him to lead her down into the casino, she was just utterly grateful and astonished at how good her life was. Not only in general, but specifically right now.

He stopped at a bank of slots, pulled a wad of bills out of his pocket and instructed her to pick the lucky one. "Alright. Let's see if Caesars is willing to share a little luck with us."

"I don't wanna play your money and lose it."

"Yo, no pressure, amiga, no pressure. Let's just take a chance, alright?"

So she stuck out her hand, he forked over a Jackson, and watched her slide it in a machine and press the button a few times until three sevens popped up, instantly making him 120 bucks richer.

"Well, if that ain't a way to start a night off right," he told her, lighting a smoke.

She piled silvery coins into a cup. Clutching the full container to her stomach, "Well, where now?"

Antonio pulled more green from his pocket, flagged down a waitress and ordered, then he passed another twenty her way and told her to try again at the machine in front of her.

"Not a good one."

He leaned his shoulder against the machine and crossed one foot over the other, relaxed and in control. "Yeah? You can tell, huh?"

"I can tell." She wasn't sure how come. She didn't remember being a pro at gambling.

"Well we gotta wait for these drinks, so find one that is."

She did. The machine didn't hit right away, and it didn't hit big, it just kept chipping up little by little, losing a few bucks, then winning a few more. By the time the waitress returned with their drinks, it was up to a hundred bucks. She clicked the cash out button and the cascade of heavy coins clinked and clacked into the tray beneath. As she scooped them into the plastic cup, Antonio asked, "How come you quit?"

She shrugged, "I think it was about done, no point in being greedy."

He laughed. "This is Vegas, baby, everybody's greedy out here."

He continued to smile, and it was clear she was a little buzzed because everything hummed around her, and he looked so charming, and he acted so charmed and it was all just so irresistible, so much freaking fun. She kissed him.

Not a big one, nothing salacious. Just a little more than a peck, mostly on the corner of his mouth. But his lips were soft and warm and when she pulled away, there was no doubt that she was going to want to do it again. Soon. She definitely wanted more of that.

"I'm having a good time," she told him.

"Yeah? Me too," he grinned.

"I'm glad you called and came over here."

"Yeah? Me, too."

"I kind of have a crush on you," she admitted.

"Yeah? Me, too."

"You have a crush on yourself?"

"You're fuckin with me again." He blushed.

How cute, she thought.

Eventually, they wound up at a roulette table, watching the action, so European, such blind luck.

Antonio pulled out his winnings and asked her to play them.

"Are you freaking gonzo?" she asked.

"Nah, go ahead. Go ahead. We're winnin an' shit."

"Dude, you're winning, that's your cash. YOU bet, I don't know what to pick."

"I don't know dick, man," he laughed. "I wanna see if you're like, as lucky as I think. 'Sides, you won all this, not me."

A little drunk and actually feeling lucky, she dropped the bills, slid the chips onto red.

"You sure?" Antonio asked. She nodded once. Reaching in his pocket, he pulled out a few more Bennys, changed them and placed those chips on red next to the ones she'd placed there.

"What the hell are you doing?" she asked and reached for them. Tense. She was feeling tense all of a sudden. Dry-mouth, stomach-tight, bubble-blooded tense. Gambling and losing her money was one thing. But losing someone else's money, someone she really sort of wanted to like her, was entirely another.

He pulled her hand back. "Relax, chica. I'm betting with you. On red."

"You sure you wanna do that?"

He only smiled. Then he watched as the dealer dropped and spun the ball. Tongue set on the corner of his mouth, while she nibbled her bottom lip. The white marble moved around the wheel.

18. Red.

She jumped. Hot DAMN, they really did have it going on tonight. He smiled some more and looked pretty damn impressed, too. It had to be HIS luck driving all this good fortune, which made her feel even luckier to be with him.

They cashed out and sat back down at Vince's bar where Antonio asked him for drinks and a couple shots of Cuervo.

She was relaxed. Looking over at him as he raised his beer, she raised hers to match his, really in awe of everything about him. Wasn't there a saying that said that we ended up liking someone because of how they made us feel about ourselves? Was that what was happening right now?

"Hey, you. Something urgent's come up and you need to come with me right now," Sherri whispered in her ear, making her jump because of her unexpected appearance.

She stared at 2Jacobs who stared right back at her with a very serious no-nonsense look. What the hell?

"Antonio?" Sherri asked. He nodded, a surprised look on his face. "Hi, I'm Sherri, her sister. Sorry, I gotta drag her away. Something's come up." 2Jacobs took her hand and pulled her off the barstool. "Now!" she instructed.

"I'll call you…," began Antonio.

"Later," Sherri called back.

When they rounded the wall separating the bar from one of the gambling areas, she suddenly was confronted by another duplicate image of herself dressed in a short, sexy dress. "Serina!" she cried out.

"Serina?" cried out the duplicate image, appearing confused.

What? She began to wobble, then everything went black.

Chapter 16

On the ride to airport, Shelby watched the strip recede and thought about Serina. After they got one of the hotel male staff members to carry her up to their suite, she had the house doctor come up and examine her. Other than delayed shock and some residual amnesia from her heavy duty car accident (God, she'd ended up thrown down the cliff side into the cold Pacific Ocean—it really was a miracle their sibling was still alive), he pronounced her healthy, but needing rest. The doctor hadn't been surprised Serina in her confusion and complete disorientation thought she was one of her triplets, Shelby, rather than her flaky self (after she explained that Serina was the "artsy" triplet while she was the boring "intellectual" triplet). Shelby represented success, which translated into security in her shocked mind and had latched on to that security for protection after the trauma.

Serina came around, but remained pretty groggy and tired. She'd finally figured out who she was and what had happened to her. Shelby and Serina had embraced and shed some tears, grateful they still had each other. Then, Serina, holding Shelby's hand as she tried to fight off sleep, told her about this special, hot, Latin hunk she thought she was falling in love with. Not that they'd had conventional sex yet, she reassured Shelby. Sherri and Shelby looked at each other, Sherri squeezing Shelby's hand, having been told about Shelby's sexual obsession for this apparently popular with her two sisters Latin lover.

Antonio! Shit! Shelby re-played their shared scenes in her head and tried to remind herself of the realistic things: That he was only bored and lonely and what guy wouldn't jump on board when some chick threw herself at him the way she had. That they ended up using one another to fight off the lonliness. That she was a fool. But she didn't really believe that. It was just...shit!!! Why couldn't he tell Serina wasn't her? Weren't they individualistic enough for him to be able to tell the difference between the two?

And she liked him so much. For sure. Right away. That un-definable quality that's just there between some people. That perfect *click* that snapped things into place and took it to another level.

And there's no explanation for it. It's just like a little piece of magic.

And then just like that, it was over. Or just like that, she had to fly home because of an emergency at her office. Or just like that, she actually needed to distance herself from this emotional problem to try to figure out what to do or not to do. Shit, what about Serina's death, her paintings selling suddenly for all that money, and Rex and Poofy McFadden.

Whatever. But for now, with Antonio, it had ended. POOF! The curtain falls, the magician takes his bow, and there's nothing left but the smoke hanging in the air to remind her it was all just a cheap distraction. Nothing was real, it wasn't magic, it was an illusion she'd let herself fall into. Sounded good, right?

The rest she'd deal with after dealing with her office emergency.

Hardly anyone at the airport and thank goodness she wasn't tagged for random security checks this time so she quickly checked in ready to board.

Later that morning after she arrived at work, she had to give an impassioned plea to some of her co-workers she supervised to help her divert the imminent disaster of the Anderton presentation, which was to occur that very afternoon, the reason for her hasty return. Most of them seem pretty gleeful at the idea of giving him enough rope to hang himself, until she cheerfully pointed out they could actually end up with a manager who knew what he was doing. The possibility of so many yanked chains didn't sit well and the required assistance she needed was finally wholeheartedly volunteerd.

They devised a very simple plan. One filled with subterfuge, diversion, and one outright attack.

For his part, Gary Anderton practically beamed as the day progressed, the silly fool. Salivating like Pavlov's dog who just got his bell rung for an audience with the bigwigs. He honestly believed this was his chance to break the surface and get a leg up. Clearly, he'd never dealt with their board of directors in any capacity before.

They stocked their ammunition during the lunch hour, and when they spotted Gary bounding to the elevator, demonstratively pushing the button to take him upstairs, they unleashed the first wave.

First Laura, Helen, and Brian were sent. They were merely delivery people. But their bounty was the key; the one thing that could do the trick. The thing that office workers the world 'round united over. It was the thing that could stop a five-year-old boy and a fifty-year-old man dead in their tracks. The thing that could greatly affect women and men alike. It knew no cultural biases nor social classes. Young, old, gay, straight, black, white, there were no boundaries. It was the universal weapon, one that could never be denied, turned away, or turned down. It could even make a stuffy room full of unseemly rich, cranky, old men turn their attentions away from the quarterly reports.

That's right, they were bringing in the big guns.

Krispy Kremes.

Minutes before Anderton made his appearance in the boardroom, Laura, Helen, and Brian arrived. Compliments of themselves and the entire 9th floor (no point in missing out on a little kiss-ass action), they dropped off three dozen (glazed and cream-filled) Krispy Kreme doughnuts. The delighted festivities began when Anderton arrived.

As he tried to establish a modicum of reserved professionalism and passed out his manual, a dozen stodgy men in suits suddenly bound to their feet, scurrying for coffee and doughnuts of their choice. Once the initial first round of enthusiasm had calmed, the men again took their seats. Content to munch and slurp away on the little sugar clouds, thoroughly distracted as they leafed sticky fingered, through the manuals, depositing gooey trails of glaze and the occasional splash of brown liquid upon the full color pages they pretended to understand.

Anderton cleared his throat, ready to begin.

Shelby knew this, because she'd squished up on a ladder in the adjoining lunch room, face at the grate of a small air duct that connected the rooms. She was with Charles, ready to release the second wave of the infantry.

"Now," she whispered.

"I can't," Charles answered.

"What? Why?"

"It's, they're…they're freaking me out."

Below, Anderton began, "Gentlemen, good afternoon. First, I would like to extend my most humble gratitude for this opportunity…"

Gruffly, "Skip the intros and cut the ball-licking, Anderson…"

"Uh, Anderton, sir."

"Whatever. Just get on with it, son. I have a 2:30 tee time. Hey, Johnson, you fatass old bastard, stop hogging the cream filled, pass one down here."

Shelby again, "Charles, do it now!"

"They're asleep!"

"Shit, man, hit the box, wake them up!"

"What if they don't go down there?"

"Gimme the box." She wrestled it from his hands and positioned it over the vent. Pulling the grate away from beneath it, she tapped it once, then again, wondering if they came out.

From below:

"…if you'll turn to page 38, you'll be able to see in writing my outline for…"

"HOLY SHIT, JOHNSON! DUCK!"

"What?"

Now, one word. The thing that could incite revulsion and fear in every living creature. It knew no cultural bias, it knew no social class.

"BATS! DUCK, YOU DUMBASS!"

A sudden cacophony of stricken shouts and wails.

"Oh my GOD!"

"BATS!"

"Call an exterminator!"

"Where did the bastards come from?"

"It touched me! IT TOUCHED ME! GET IT OFF ME!"

"Grab the doughnuts! Jesus Christ, someone grab the doughnuts. Don't let the little bastards shit on them!"

Shelby slid the grate back into position and re-attached it into place, getting a bird's eye view of the pandemonium that had escalated below.

The final tally:

1 mahogany table—ruined. 15 Corinthian leather swivel chairs—soaked. 4 dozen Krispy Kremes—eaten or otherwise salvaged. 1 sprinkler system—proven beyond a shadow of doubt to be in fine operating condition. 13 verbose and colorful manuals about how to more efficiently run our department—forgotten. 2 bats, ahem, let's just say that PETA would have a shitfit about them. And Anderton's job—for the time being at least—preserved.

Shelby's workday. A nice little diversion in a work day. But after, everything calmed down and returned to normal. For everyone else that is.

Chapter 17

Before Shelby had left, Serina reminded her of the small warehouse unit she'd rented for years because she stored an endless number of her paintings, unbeknownst to Rex Wilcox. She was no fool and there was no doubt in her mind he would want to make money off her so called death; and why not help him. She could use the money. And, since Serina more or less now remembered her own identity, she decided to explore the vast panoramas of fiery desert sunsets, long afternoon shadows of the desert mountains, pthalo blue streams lined with lime green cottonwoods, the golden high desert grasslands, the new artistic options were endless. Then there was Lake Tahoe with its luscious forests; yes, endless possibilities.

That very day, she rented a Jeep, using Shelby's credit card, of course, bought supplies at a local art supply store, a camera at another store, and drove northwest up into the mountains all the way to Tahoe City at the northern end of the lake, where their parents owned a family cabin. It was the perfect hideout for Serina when she needed it.

After dealing with taking in some basic supplies, she decided to navigate a dirt forest service road that lead to an old, rutted two track road, and it was there that she found some wild, magnificent scenery. The broad expanses, deep arroyos, rugged, rocky outcrops and dramatic differences in vegetation challenged Jacobs's painting sensibilities immediately: new colors, textures, light…all so different from the landscape she was familiar with in the Marin County area in Northern California—every turn of the two-track presented a new scene, a new vista, and new composition. Jacobs lost herself in the new landscape, moving quickly from scene to scene, frantically sketching out the basic compositions, capturing the colors and the light of the moment, hastily snapping photos and moving on. She felt powerful surges of energy like she had never felt before, as if she were a new, better Serina Jacobs, a true artist. An artist that, unfortunately, no one would ever know. She was dead, after all. Somehow, some way, another artist needed to be invented.

Later that evening upstairs in their suite at Caesars, Sherri was ready and waiting for her. She didn't have time to obsess and worry about what to wear, just grabbing some clothes in a hurry, taking only seconds to decide, and jumped in the shower.

"Where are we going?" she asked when she was ready.

"Dinner."

"Dinner? Ahh, man, I hate dinner," she whined. Tipping the scales at 120 pounds for her 5'7" height, naturally she hated dinner. "What are we going to do at dinner?"

"Drink," the only answer that would work.

"Oh, ok. Then I'll like it. Where are we going?"

"You pick," Serina offered, figuring that was the least she could do.

"No, you decide. I don't care, anywhere."

Hopefully, "Morton's?"

"No, that's too much to eat."

"Ok, ahh, California Pizza?" her next suggestion.

"No, if we're eating, I want a meal," she replied to that one.

"How about, um, how about Rock Lobster in Mandalay Bay. We can go to the shark exhibit after that."

"Can we drink in the shark thing?"

"I don't think so." She'd forgotten about that little issue.

"Then not there."

They finally decided to just walk over next door to the Mirage, and Serina fell in love all over again before they even got inside. It'd been a few years since she'd been in the Mirage. On the people mover outside, slowly going past the dolphin statues and mini-waterfalls and coin ponds with the tropical foliage, she sighed, taking it all in. It was a little different from what she first loved, the sound of Steve Wynn's voice was gone, but the water cascading around was the same. It still smelled like coconuts. Pennies and quarters shined up from the pools below—apparently people felt they didn't leave quite enough of their money inside, so they happily tossed even more to the place as they went in and out.

That was the magic Steve Wynn had the ability to create. No matter what, he could build a hotel/casino like nobody's business. The Mirage, Treasure Island, and Bellagio were all his creations.

He no longer owned them since he got forced out in a takeover by MGM Corporation. Now Kirk Kerkorian owned it all. But you could still feel the inspiration Steve Wynn dripped into these places. When he was here, it was as though he actually took pride in creating, showing off, and sharing his visions of paradise.

He'd owned the Golden Nugget downtown first. But he built the Mirage from scratch, striving for paradise in the middle of the desert. And he'd pulled it off. Waterfalls, a towering volcano, lush tropical plants, a rainforest—inside. Bamboo light fixtures, a hella fish tank in the lobby, and the smell of fresh flowers and coconut permeating everywhere. It was the first casino that didn't feel like a casino.

Mirage, an illusion. Even the house show was magical—Seigfried and Roy and their white tigers and disappearing elephant. Even more, it had the charm of the guy who created it though somewhat shattered now. But nothing that grand could utterly be destroyed. His dream still clung around certain areas, lingering like hope. Elusive like vapor.

Once Mirage was a success, he took over next door and built Treasure Island—again, exactly what its name evokes: Pirates and gold and swashbuckling. The free show there ran several times a day; pirates fighting the British in a sea battle. Explosions, high dives and rope-swinging; all very breathtaking and macho. And the pirates won every time.

Still wanting to outdo himself, Wynn then bought up the Bellagio, took an idea and just went to hell and back with it. Outside, a man-made lake that puts on water shows every fifteen minutes. Inside, a greenhouse that changes seasonally—the floral gardens. Then a fine art museum—no kidding. Vegas was well known for kitsch and cheese, but Wynn actually had the balls to bring in real culture to the place. Picasso and Van Gogh. The stunning blown-glass flower chandelier in the lobby, and the whole place just stank of class and luxury. Rumor had been it was a replica of where he and his wife honeymooned. She liked it so much he built it for her.

Romantic, wasn't it?

And the most bizarre part? It WORKED. It was romantic. Treasure Island WAS fun. And Mirage was—Mirage, still a crown jewel.

Serina had read up on the recent history of it all since Shelby visited Vegas so often.

They walked up the wooden steps, between the giant yellow plantains and up to the maitre'd. "Reservations for Jacobs," she told the woman, and they followed her into the back room and got seated amidst the trippy burgundy and purple colors in a red velvet wrap-around booth.

Serina ordered the Brazilian barbecue special, Sherri just ordered a side salad, but both ordered mojitos to drink. Sherri didn't like hers and ordered a beer, and instead of sipping at the remainder of the drink, she passed it on to Serina to finish off. She slammed it. She loved the things. They tasted like minty 7-up.

Good time, good food. She was having fun, but also couldn't stop anxiously fidgeting. She twisted her ring around, crossed her legs back and forth, back and forth. She chewed the ice in her drinks. She wound up having four mojitos and getting a little drunk.

After, Sherri was pretty well buzzed, too.

"Ok, what do you want to do?" Serina asked.

"I don't know."

"Ok, you want to gamble here?"

"I don't gamble. YOU gamble, excuse me, Shelby gambles," she answered.

"Where do you want me to gamble?"

So Serina gambled at the Mirage, just some slots. Sherri played some video poker at the sports bar. When Sherri became bored with the video poker, they went over to Treasure Island.

They watched the pirate show on the gangplank. The show was good, too. All those explosions so close, all those guys doing swashbuckling things; swinging from ropes and diving from high up on the masts. The pirates, the dashing good guys. Everyone cheered along. Inside, Sherri wanted to hang out at the Swashbuckler bar where she ordered another beer and talked about her boring fiancé, Don.

Shelby had told Serina all about boring, snobbish, much older than Sherri, Don. Gamely, she attempted to console her. "You know, I think that dude at the pool the other day sorta had a thing for you. You know, that hotel manager, real cute looking guy."

"Jarred?" she asked.

"Jarred! Whoo!" Serina whistled. "You must have noticed him, too, if you remember his name."

"Give it up, 1Jacobs. I can't go out with him. I don't cheat. You know, you and Shelby are exactly alike."

"Ok, and no, we're not." She tried to convince her to break up with Don and go out with Jarred, but Sherri just rolled her eyes, talked about Don until she ventilated the subject, and then had no other options. "I'm drunk. You have to take me back."

"Ok," she agreed.

"Will you stay in the room with me tonight?" she asked.

Brother! Shelby, get your ass back here and take care of our boring sister. Ok, ok. "Maybe for an hour until you fall asleep." God, this was too much!

Chapter 18

The summer in California had been characteristically mild, and Shelbys's frame of mind was such after the Vegas thing and the office madness success, that early that very same evening she shouldered her golf bag (she avoided golf carts—the whole point of the game, in her mind, was to get a good walk in, even if it was rife with cursing and frustration) and walked to the 4th tee at one of her favorite golf courses on the outskirts of Palo Alto. The fourth hole was a short, straight-away par 4 with OB left, bunkers right about 200 yards out, and the fifth fairway running parallel back the opposite direction.

Shelby noticed a solo golfer walking down the fifth fairway. After a few stretches and practice swings, Shelby teed up and ripped a wicked slice over the right hand bunkers into the hardpan between the fairways. The ball took a mighty hop, then another, and another right into the fifth fairway where the other golfer was bending over to fix a divot. Shelby could see now that it was a man, and the ball was headed directly for his uplifted ass.

"FORE!" Shelby shouted at the top of her lungs but, it was too late. The ball, which had slowed considerably, but was still hopping, bounced up and hit the man squarely on the butt. She could hear his loud yelp from 230 yards away.

"OW! Shit!" he screamed, jumping up and grabbing his ass.

Shelby dropped her driver, left her bag and broke off in a dead run down the fairway and across the hardpan to where the man had turned to see who had hit the errant shot.

"Holy shit!" she shouted as she ran up to him, out of breath. "Are you OK?"

"Jesus, that hurts like a son of a bitch!" he said, rubbing his ass, which, Shelby observed, was tightly packed into navy golf shorts under which stretched a pair of long, tan, muscular legs.

"Didn't you hear me yell fore?"

"Yeah I heard it," he said. "About a half a second before it hit me. Jesus that stings!" he repeated, still rubbing his right cheek.

"Well I am truly sorry. I never thought it would reach you!" Shelby explained, watching him rubbing with increasing interest.

"Don't worry about it. Who ever would of thought someone teeing off down there" he said, gesturing to the fourth tee, "could hit someone way over here? It's a hell of a long way, and a hell of a long way off course, too!" he laughed.

Shelby laughed, too, noticing his perfectly straight, if rather large, shiny white teeth, full tanned cheeks and a hint of blonde fuzz on his upper lip. His blonde hair, streaked by the sun, was evidently over shoulder length and was tied back in a ponytail. Talk about sexy. Yum! His eyes were shaded by wrap around sports sunglasses, bushy blonde eyebrows peeked over the top. His tan, muscular arms were covered by the same white hair, and she could see that his sports shirt could not conceal what appeared to be broad, strong shoulders. An athlete, she thought.

"Perhaps I should introduce myself," said Shelby, hand outstretched. He was about a head taller than her. "My name is Shelby Jacobs."

He smiled and dimples appeared. "Taylor Grant." His handshake was firm. They both laughed once again, a touch of shyness. He still rubbed his sore spot, but smiled just the same.

"Well," she said suddenly tongue-tied. "I hope you will forgive me. I promise to never again hit another slice!"

"I think I'll be fine," he said, walking around in little circles. "Probably have an attractive purple blotch on my butt, but besides that, I think I'll be ok. Let's see." He reached in his golf bag, pulled out a club and took a couple of powerful, manly practice swings. "Can't feel a thing when I swing. Let's try a shot."

There was no doubt this man had played a lot of golf. "What do you think it is to the pin—about 180? 185?"

She looked down the fairway to where the green was tucked behind a pond, bordered by a thick grove of mesquite on the right, casting long very late afternoon shadows across the green. Two giant cottonwoods framed a high grassy mound behind a green side bunker. She found the 150 marker and made a quick mental calculation.

"I would say you have to fly it 180 to clear the water," she replied, backing away from where his ball lay in the fairway as he walked around behind the ball and lined up the shot.

"Ok. 3-iron should do it, don't you think?" he said.

3-iron, she thought. Wow! That was only a club more than she would hit!

"Well," she answered, thinking there was no way this could reach it with a 3-iron. "A 3 is going to come into the green pretty low and hot, might scoot across into that back bunker. You might want to float a five wood in there." The golf lexicon flowed out of Jacobs. Slow down, stop showing off.

"You sound like you've played a lot of golf," said Taylor as he took a practice swing. He peered down the fairway to the green. "I do hit the five wood higher than the three iron—I might be able to put a little fade on it and hold the green. Hell—let's give it a try." He put the three back in the bag and took the cover off the five wood, which of course had a metal head—one of golf's many unsinkable anachronisms.

He addressed the ball, waggled the club a few times, then started it back slowly with his shoulders rotating, leading his arms back to the top of the swing, his upper body completely coiled and centered against the resistance of his solid stance, his back leg posted up in firing position. Then he began to uncoil, pushing off his back leg, releasing his hips towards the target, arms following the unfolding of his upper body, head almost completely still, eyes focused on the ball unwavering, as if he was a giant spring unraveling around a vertical pinion. The five wood came through the hitting area with a beautiful "swoosh", striking the ball with the familiar metal click (as opposed to the musical "thwok" made by a real wood), then following through toward the target, his torque released, watching the flight of the ball toward the green. It was a high, arching shot, starting out toward the left corner of the green, then fading gracefully towards the pin, then over the pin, and finally landing with a solid thud under the top lip of the rear bunker.

"Shit," Taylor muttered. "I knew I should have hit the three."

Shelby was blown away by the beauty and power of his graceful swing. "It's my fault. Maybe there's a little wind up there," she said, unwilling to admit to herself that this man could hit a five wood 200 yards—almost as far as she could hit it.

"Well, at least I know a bruised ass doesn't screw up your golf swing!" he announced, proud of how pure and straight he'd hit the shot. "So—where are your sticks, Shelby? I don't expect you *threw* this golf ball 230 yards into my butt."

"Oh—I left them on the tee!" she said, which was adjacent to the 5th green.

"Well why not pick 'em up when we get up to the green and play a few holes with me?" said Taylor, who appeared to be limping slightly.

"Oh you're very kind, but..." she started.

"No buts. You've done enough with butts today." He laughed at his own double entendre, and seemed kind of surprised when she laughed, too.

It was basically dark when Shelby and Taylor Grant holed their final putts on the ninth green. Shelby's golf was erratic compared to Taylor's steady, consistent straight-down-middle approach. He parred all of the remaining four holes except one, and almost birdied the par 3 eighth hole, lipping out an 18 footer. Shelby, on six, sliced her tee shot on onto the sandy hardpan, and struggled back to the green via the small mesquite trees and green side bunkers. By the eighth hole, she began to find a rhythm and hit a towering eight iron into the 157 yard par-3 eighth green that almost struck the flag stick. She also attributed her long, straight drive on nine to watching Taylor's slow, fluid swing and how he was forced into a solid, one-piece takeaway, led by his rotating shoulders.

Considering her sloppy play and accompanying epithets, like her masterful, creative if not impressive phrase, "you mother fucking dicklicker," used to describe her errant birdie putt on the eighth hole, Shelby was surprised when Taylor invited her to dinner at the clubhouse.

"Do you want to go freshen up?" Taylor asked as they walked off the ninth green.

"No, I think a shot of tequila will freshen me up just fine, thanks," she answered. Was she a little rough around the edges? There was something about him that made her feel like she needed to act more ladylike. Hmmm....

"Works for me," he agreed.

They made a beeline for the bar, leaving their clubs outside the entrance and not bothering to change out of their rubber-spiked golf shoes. After a couple of quick shots of Herradura Reposado, they decided to share an order of nachos and chicken mole enchiladas at the bar, where they could get much faster drink service than in the restaurant. But it was the "entertainment", which consisted of a rotund Mexican in a cowboy hat and white guayabera shirt, playing a Fender Squire along with a "music-minus-one" kareoke system, that kept them glued to their barstools, drinking shots and beers, long after they had polished off the food. When the singer launched into a stilted version, in his heavy Mexican accent of "Johnny B. Goode", which sounded more like a polka than Chuck

Berry's joyous rock n' roll romp, Shelby and Taylor just had to dance. It was just too absurd to pass up, particularly with a bellyful of Herradura Reposado and Carta Blanca. Shelby was impressed with Taylor's knowledge of various rock n' roll dance moves, and with the way he skillfully twirled her around without throwing her through the large arched window that looked out onto the 18th green.

After "Johnny B. Goode", the cantadoro launched into Margaritaville, which he had re-arranged on his kareoke machine to sound more like a bolero than tropical country. Taylor pulled Shelby close and sang drunkenly in her ear, changing one of Buffet's lines from "strummin' my six string" to "strummin' my g-string", at which point he reached down and gave her ass a squeeze. This was all she needed—she immediately sunk her face into the fuzz below his ear, sucking in his post-golf musk and giving his collarbone a wet lick. She then giggled with delight and stuck her tongue in his ear. What was up with her? This quickly she could return to her old habits, just dump Antonio from her mind?

Without thinking, Shelby reached down with both hands and grabbed his cheeks.

"Yow!" shouted Taylor, ripping her hands from his butt. "Fuckin' A!"

Shelby then remembered the huge, painful welt Taylor had on his ass, just where he squeezed. "Oh shit…Jesus. I'm really sorry, I forgot" she stammered. The drunker she got, the less she cared about anything, really.

"You'll pay for this!" slurred Taylor, smiling and grabbing Shelby's shirt just above the belt, pulling it up and out of her skirt. "I think you owe me some special treatment. Special fuckin' treatment…," he said, pulling her across the dance floor by her shirt towards the door.

Taylor pulled Shelby across the parking lot towards the practice green. A crescent moon shone through the mesquite trees at the bottom of a clear night sky crowded with stars. When they arrived on the green, Taylor turned and sank down onto the soft bent grass. Shelby quickly straddled him, her plaid skirt hiked up around her waist, her robin's egg blue panties almost fluorescent in the moonlight.

"Ok," she said, way too loud considering the country club was easily within hearing distance. "Let's see what you've to offer." She leaned over and smothered his mouth with her full lips, tongue immediately probing here and there, finding Taylor's and sucking it between her teeth, her arms pinning his to the putting surface, Taylor getting hard beneath her shining blue panties.

Suddenly she released her grip and quickly turned around, ripping down her panties as she shoved her hindquarters into Taylor's face.

"You check that out," she said in a ragged whisper, out of breath. Then Shelby shoved her crotch onto his mouth while fumbling with his belt buckle, then his zipper, then reaching in and pulling his erection out of his pants and taking it in her mouth.

Taylor gurgled under her wet, fragrant crotch, working the best he could with his head pinned to the grass. She was already swollen and came quickly with a shudder, and Taylor followed, arching his back off the damp grass and burying his nose in Shelby's crotch. His head fell back onto the green with a thump.

"My God," he grunted, gasping for air. Her butt was, thankfully, raised slightly. He could hear her breaths growing longer. She was quiet, still, gently stroking his still-hard member. Suddenly she stood up, her panties hooked around one ankle above her saddle-golf shoes, and looked at Taylor with his shirt pulled up and his splendid boner still pointed towards the stars.

"What the…," she muttured. Finally she stumbled back and looked at where Taylor was lying on the ground with his shirt pulled up. She closed her eyes, shook her head, then opened them again, swaying.

He pulled his shirt down and sat up, stuffing his softening wiener back in his pants. "You ok?" he asked.

She paused, wavering on her feet. He was a fine specimen. Almost a God. And God, did he turn her on. It was time to move on into the future. She couldn't look back. Fate was weird sometimes. She drew in a deep breath then stepped up, placed her spiked shoe, with the blue panties twirling on her ankle, on his chest, shoved him back to the ground, pulled his shirt up over his chest and sat squarely on his stomach, pinning his arms to the ground—she had not lost the playful look in her eye.

"I'm very fine,'" she finally answered, her slippery crotch sliding around on his belly.

"I would say so," smiled Taylor. He could smell the Herradura Reposado on her breath. "I want to know you, as they say, in the biblical sense."

She reached behind her and gave his pecker a squeeze, locking her lips onto his while she undid his pants and he fumbled with the clasp to her sports bra.

Ok, she was just drunk and horny, thought Shelby. Maybe she was drunk and horny to forget Antonio. Who cared. This was the here. This was the immediate now. A step forward into the future.

Chapter 19

Michelle Morgan, Harlin Radner and their valet, Karl, were among the first to arrive at the gallery on this fine Tuesday evening in downtown San Anselmo—a light breeze out of the west with the sun sinking behind the green and gold grasses of Bald Hill, affectionately known to the locals as "Baldy". It was the art show for some of the remaining known works of the deceased, the young, beautiful Serina Jacobs.

At first, Shelby watched from a pizza parlor across and down the street as Karl parked Morgan's black BMW limo in front of the gallery. Her thoughts were of Serina and Harlin and the brief reunion Serina had shared with her sister, and of her former life as the starving landscape painter who used to live in a rented hotel room less than half a block from where she sat now, eating Serina's favorite "Art & Tom" (artichoke and tomato) pizza and sipping Sierra Nevada Pale Ale from a pint glass.

Now, as Shelby saw Harlin emerge from the BMW, take Morgan's arm and, followed by Karl, enter the California Heritage Gallery, she contemplated how difficult it might be to win the heart of her twin's former love. And she knew her foggy idea was crazy, totally off the wall, for that matter. But, would it hurt anyone? No, just the opposite. Her plan might solve everyone's problems, or at least her broken heart. Besides, maybe Serina would even be grateful. Although it was obvious that Harlin had given up bikers and cowboys for women of a more distinguished sort, if that's what one could call Morgan—distinguished—really stretching it. As she finished the last bites of her "Art & Tom" pizza and swigged the dregs of her beer, Shelby decided that she could only take this adventure one step at a time. Like painting, it took many, many brush strokes before you had a work of art, right? Serina would know, but she wasn't about to share her plans with Serina just yet.

Rex Wilcox had arranged an elegant, candlelit table of various pates, French cheeses, English crackers, olives and assorted California red wines in the center of the gallery for his "sneak preview" of some of Serina Jacobs' paintings. Rex Wilcox, Poofy McFadden, and Shelby Jacobs had come to a contractual agreement of all monies earned from the sale of her paintings. Shelby had even divulged the information of a warehouse stash of paintings Wilcox could sell as long as he shared the profits with Shelby. She would manage and invest the finances for Serina who, according to Rex (he had no idea Serina was alive and kicking) from the sales of her paintings, Serina's estate would be worth millions.

"There is more paint on these than the one's before," announced Karl brusquely, pushing up the sleeves of his black turtleneck as if he was going to pick a fight. "No doubt this will make them even more ridiculously priced that the smaller paintings you have already obtained."

"Well, Karl, the larger the painting the more it costs—that's the general rule," said Morgan as he quickly glanced around the room. "But it doesn't have much to do with the actual amount of paint."

Wilcox took a moment to admire Morgan's black lady's Gucci loafers, especially the tassels, from a distance away.

Harlin Radner was immediately struck by some of the "discovered" work. "These are so much larger than Serina's other stuff!" he blurted, taking off his baseball cap, stuffing it in the pocket of his Levi jacket, and pulling his delicate fingers through his short, black hair.

"Yes, they certainly are," said Morgan suspiciously, peering over the rims of her tinted glasses. "And look at the style," she continued. "Seems our painter, Jacobs, was a might bit looser with the paint in her younger days. How do you explain that, Wilcox?" She pulled at her salt and pepper hair while peering at the paintings.

"I didn't know Serina…uh, I mean…Serina Jacobs…when she was living in Oregon," stammered Wilcox, one hand in the big pocket of his beige, wide wail corduroys, the other pulling at the pink tie over his oxford blue, button down shirt. "But I agree, it definitely appears that she had access to more paint…perhaps she was taking a workshop or something of that nature. But…unfortunately I'm afraid we'll never know. Unless her sister has some answers. She might make an appearance this evening."

"No I suppose not," mused Morgan, pulling her black sport coat down over her growing paunch.

"Poor girl," whispered Harlin under his breath.

"So how are you so sure these are genuine?" questioned Karl, approaching a 50"x 60" seascape and roughly rubbing his fingertips over the thick white texture of the breaking waves.

"I beg your pardon!" squealed Wilcox.

Harlin gently pulled Karl's arm away from the painting, whispering, "you're not supposed to touch the paintings, Karl."

"Nonsense!" shouted Karl, pulling away from Harlin. "How do we know this is the real thing then, eh?"

"Well excuuuuse me!" puffed Wilcox indignantly as Morgan sniggered quietly. "Are you accusing me of…of…plagiarism? Fakery? Fraud? Misrepresenting a work of art?" Wilcox felt as though he might burst with indignation, when suddenly, at the door to the California Heritage Gallery, there a appeared a tall, willowy, down to her buttocks blond hair, dressed in a long, black coat, touching the tips of her black boots. For a brief second, and for the second time, Rex was convinced he was staring at Serina Jacobs. He promptly got hold of himself and demurely walked over, placed her delicate white hand in his, and brushed it with his lips.

"Ms. Jacobs," he greeted.

Then he turned around: "Ladies and gentlemen, may I present Shelby Jacobs, one of the triplet sisters of our dear, departed painter, Serina Jacobs."

The entire gallery became deadly still. Some people were shocked at Shelby's appearance who'd known Serina personally, the few there who actually did. The balance of the stillness was due to the enlarged photographed, framed print of Serina Jacobs prominently displayed in the gallery for all to view, and now compared, to the living, breathing Shelby Jacobs, the mirror image of Serina. Even down to the long, black coat.

Wilcox, who had come under fire regarding the authenticity of Serina's paintings, now felt a form of vindication and returned to his habitual nut juggling without realizing it.

"What the hell is this?" grunted Morgan to no one in particular.

"That is Shelby, Serina's triplet sister," verified Harlin. "I haven't seen her in years. I forgot about their uncanny likeness." Many times during their schools he'd mixed the three up, causing some very embarrassing moments. Drawn because of the resemblance alone, he walked up to her and his fiancé, Michelle Morgan was close behind him.

"Harlin," she said shyly, putting down the wine glass Rex Wilcox had just given her and extending her hand. Harlin had certainly turned into a handsome man—not at all like she had envisioned in his gangly years. Serina did have good taste, she was surprised to learn. He took her hand, bowed dramatically, and gave it an overly long kiss, almost causing Wilcox to faint with disgust.

Morgan cleared her throat and stretched out her hand for a brief shake. "My pleasure." Harlin left the two of them alone and aimed for the bar.

"Ms. Morgan, it's my pleasure. I understand you are one of the buyers very taken by my sister's paintings," she used a husky tone of voice while addressing her. She did need to sound like she was subdued and in mourning, didn't she?

"Yes," said Morgan, nodding, sipping chardonnay. "Yes. These paintings are uncharacteristically strong for Serina Jacobs, I would say. Are you familiar with your sister's work?"

"Why, yes. We saw one another at least once a month," she replied, lowering her brilliant, blue-green eyes for several seconds. "Her work many times reflected her artistic mood swings," she explained.

"Precisely," said Wilcox stepping in, then gently steering Michelle Morgan away from Shelby, hoping to entice Morgan to spend mega bucks tonight.

Harlin reappeared, carrying two glasses. "I think the last time I drank tequila was in this gallery with Serina Jacobs herself," he gave as some sort of justification for this act. "Though this is much better than the rot gut she drank!"

Shelby winced at the slight but he was right. Herradura was liquid ambrosia compared to the lighter fluid experience of Jose Cuervo she knew Serina would drink. "So did you become sweethearts again?" she asked him gently.

"Oh no—though she was as beautiful as ever, if a little worse for wear." He blushed seeming to realize who he was talking to. "I don't think she ever knew how attracted I was to her. But she was so high most of the time I don't think she could have gotten her pants off, much less mine, even if she wanted to." Shelby smiled inside. Maybe her plan had a chance after all. And then she wept for her sibling little inner tear. Partly because she should have forced Serina to accept help from her financially. Instead, she'd been perceived as a fucking loser. That made her damn mad! Serina was by no means a loser. She was just as intelligent as she was, only artistically inclined. That actually made her more of a person than she herself was.

"But she was not that high when you saw her last, was she?" she quizzed him.

"Well, not really. But she had turned into kind of a bum, you know? I mean, a beautiful bum that made beautiful paintings, but a bum just the same, you know what I mean?" asked Harlin, not sure he was getting through to her.

"You mean she did not wash herself?" asked Shelby, pouring a little more tequila in her glass from the bottle Harlin had graciously brought along.

"Oh no! She just didn't have her shit together. No direction, living hand to mouth. That kind of thing," explained Harlin, popping a green olive in his mouth. Worse than that, she didn't seem to give a shit about it! She seemed perfectly content with her life when I saw her last. All twisted jokes, weird little observations, humming little tunes. Almost like a fucking nut case, I would say."

"Ah, perhaps she was just a little nervous to see you," explained Shelby, shrugging. Inside, she was getting pretty pissed. Stay calm. This guy liked Serina a lot, after all, she reminded herself.

"Not after 4 shots of tequila she wasn't!" laughed Harlin.

Just then their conversation was interrupted by Wilcox. "Well, Shelby, Serina Jacobs's portfolio has been purchased by several individuals in the past year. Michelle Morgan", said Wilcox, taking a sip from his glass of red wine, "purchased a painting at her last opening here in this very gallery and is interested in buying more of her work. However, since I recently discovered a number of Serina Jacobs's paintings have been stored in a warehouse," he winked at Shelby while scratching with his free remaining hand, "Ms. Morgan is also interested in purchasing some of them."

"That's right," interrupted Morgan. "Now let's see…I recently paid $20,000 for a 24" by 30", isn't that right, Karl?"

"Yes, unfortunately that is correct." said Karl coldly. "Highway robbery as they say in this country."

"And that was only a few days ago right after I was informed of Serina Jacobs's death. However, I don't believe that the late Ms. Jacobs has exactly caught fire in the art market just yet," mused Morgan, turning to watch the other patrons walking through the gallery, slowly studying each of the paintings.

Oh, but she's about to, thought Wilcox, grinning to himself.

Shelby picked up the grin and shot him a quick scowl.

"So let's do the math, shall we, Wilcox?"

"Shelby, the lady and the gentleman here have determined this painting—'Moon Rising over the Dunes" I believe it's called—to be worth $65,000, based almost entirely on it's size I might add."

Shelby turned to gaze at the painting, a serious tone pervading her demeanor as if she were about to perform a baptism, and nodded.

Wilcox blushed then quickly continued: "Well personally I feel that this particular painting would sell in the $80,000 range on the open market."

"Horse shit," said Karl, spitting on the floor.

"Now wait a minute," said Morgan. "I've got an idea. Rather than nickel and diming each other painting by painting, let's talk about a collection and the price for a collection! In which case I believe we would qualify for a volume discount, right Wilcox?"

"I think I could consider that, sure," said Wilcox.

"I'll give you a million cash, right now, for six of her paintings of my choosing," said Morgan, casually pouring herself another glass of wine.

Harlin gasped.

"Ach du lieber!" shouted Karl. "Are you mad?"

Harlin reached for the tequila bottle, opened it quickly, took a long swig and passed it to Wilcox who unwittingly took an equally hearty pull.

Wilcox was trying to think through the offer, but the burning tequila felt like it was caught in his esophagus and he began to cough and sputter violently. Shelby stepped over, grabbed the aging homo and began pounding him on the back, which only exacerbated the cough.

Harlin downed some more of his tequila.

Wilcox finally regained his breath. "Well," he began when Shelby interrupted.

"Ms. Morgan, we'll decline your present offer for six of Serina's paintings at a million cash. Be forewarned, when we bring in more of her collection from the warehouse, the price for *each* painting will be more than half a million. Tonight, you insulted her memory." With that she exited the gallery in a flourish, the long, black, now unbuttoned coat billowing behind her.

"Perhaps she's right," mused Morgan. "Wilcox, please have the paintings I choose boxed and shipped to my home. I will have my accountant call you tomorrow and arrange for the transfer of $3,000,000 to your account. Fair enough?"

"Yes Ms. Morgan!" said Wilcox. "I'm so pleased to know that you and your family and associates will be enjoying this fine work! Thank you! And I'll be sure to inform Ms. Jacobs of our transaction."

"You're quite welcome," said Morgan icily. "However, I would appreciate if you would do me the courtesy of calling before you broadcast the next Serina Jacobs art showing to the world so I can at least view the work privately beforehand.

"I'll do what I can," said Wilcox.

Morgan and Karl walked out the gallery door and then got into the BMW limousine parked at the curb while Harlin stuffed some olives in the pocket of his Levi jacket.

"These are good!" he said, and then joined them in the BMW and they were gone.

Wilcox turned and watched the milling crowd all there to see Serina's paintings. Wow, how things changed. And Shelby was one tough sister.

Chapter 20

Serina met Antonio in the main lobby of Caesars. "What do you want to do tonight?

"I got no agenda, baby, no agenda. It's on you."

"I hate having to pick," she told him.

"Want me to take you to the Peppermill?"

"Yes. Perfect."

"Want one o' them drinks at the Hilton? What's it called?"

"Warp Core Breech." Shelby'd told her about them. They sounded great.

"Right on. That was it," he said. "How's that for a start?"

"Perfect by me."

"You're easy."

"You didn't figure that out the first night, amigo?"

Laughing, "I thought that was just cause you couldn't resist me."

"Now that's the truth," she teased back.

"Can I tell you somethin?"

"Ahh, hell."

"I'm really glad I met you. And I think I might be falling in love with you."

"You are?" Uncanny. An they barely knew one another. "Me, too, you." This was all too weird and too fast. And what about that fortuneteller?

Before heading out to the Peppermill, she asked him for a quick favor and led him to a back corner of Caesars, to the entrance of the Magical Empire Show.

"Grab us drinks? While I find her?"

She looked around and it didn't take long. There was Sabina, walking around the room in her blue *I Dream of Jeannie* outfit with the beads and sparkles. Serina asked her if she'd do a reading for her, tipped her upfront, and began picking out cards when Antonio ambled over, sipping his beer and setting down a drink for her.

"I was here before," she reminded Sabina.

"Really? How'd I do?"

"Well, I don't think very well, I just want to check and see if things in the cards have changed. I mean, I know this isn't serious or anything, but it just sort of bugged me what you said."

Laying the cards out and glancing over them, she asked, "What'd I say?"

"Well, you told me that no one would ever love me, I'd never have a man."

"Ouch," she said. Her brows crinkled together and she started tapping the cards with her fingers. "Hmmm," her next comment.

"So has that changed? Look any different?"

"Well, actually, no," she admitted.

Serina sat up straight and stared at her, saying slowly, "Excuse me?"

"I see some interesting things here," she continued. "I see a whole lot of strength."

"Yeah, you said that before."

"I did?" She was a bit astonished. "You know, I'm still sort of new at this."

"Yeah, but like, you aren't actually claiming to be psychic or anything, right?" Serina asked. "This is just a job you do to entertain, right?"

"Well, sort of. I'm new to Tarot, but…"

"Ok, whatever"

Antonio cut in. Sharply, "Yo, wait a minute here. You're tellin her no one loves her? No one's ever gonna love her?"

"I just don't see anything like that. I really don't. I see some serious, sudden change right here," she pointed to a card. Sliding her fingers to another one, "And this, wow, it's like, violent or something. But I see you overcoming everything."

"Yeah, you said that before."

She beamed.

"This is bullshit!" Antonio said. "Yo, I'm her boyfriend. Understand? You're tellin me I don't exist? I don't matter?"

"No, no," she said quickly. "I just don't see you on the table here."

"Well who the fuck do you see?"

"Uh, no one, really. But look, like I said, I'm new, and this is just…"

"Look at her!" He said loudly, then said something really fast in Spanish that she didn't understand. "I mean it, man, look at her. She's fuckin gorgeous! An' she's smart, too. Know what else? She's nice. That's right. She's so sweet she'd never sit here tellin someone that no one's ever gonna love 'em. How could I NOT love her, huh?"

"Valdez," she interrupted softly, getting up. "It's ok, really. It's not her fault. It doesn't mean anything anyhow."

"Ahh, this is whacked!"

"It's fine." She took his hand, dragging him away. "She's just saying what's on the table. It doesn't mean anything, it's just dumb, I don't believe in it."

"Yeah but that's just bitchy o' her," he answered, reluctant to back off.

"It's ok," she insisted, tugging him away through the winding exit. "Doesn't matter. I just wanted to show you off to her. Her saying I'd never have anyone, and here I have YOU, I just thought that'd be cool. And I did that. So thank you for doing it."

"It's still shitty. I don't fuckin believe that shit, man, you know, pisses me off."

"Yeah, well, I don't believe it. Fate, whatever. Who cares?"

"You don't? What do you believe in?"

She squeezed his hand. "You. That's enough."

"Yo, fuck her," he said. "She's a fuckin hack, man. She's just fuckin with you. What did those cards say to you?"

"How the hell would I know? I can't read a tarot deck."

"You can't?" mocking astonishment. "Serious? Somethin you can't do. Here I was thinkin you knew everything."

She punched him in the arm, a little hard, and it made him laugh. They headed out into the fairly cool night air to catch a taxi to somewhere new.

The Peppermill turned out to be a cool place. Off strip, no gambling, not even any video-poker machines drilled into the bar. It was dark and bright at the same time, it was cozy. A fire pit at one end, exceptionally cool, the fire coming out of a neony white pond of water. The booths were comfy, extremely romantic in the most oddly Vegas way. Like a '70s fern bar. Plus lots of mirrors around.

Antonio slid next to her into a booth, and she snuggled up to him without hesitation.

He grinned, saying, "You know, people come here just to make out. It's known for it."

"Really? Is that why you brought me here?"

His only answer was a quick eskimo kiss before a waitress came to take their order.

They hung out, he drank a couple beers, she sucked down a couple vodka sodas, and when he tried to order shots, she asked him to hold up, that he ought to be in decent shape to handle the Warp Core. He looked at her like she was nuts and gave her a kiss.

When he pulled away, over his shoulder, her eyes caught a guy leering at her. He boldly wagged his tongue at her until she looked away.

The blond long hair, she figured. Some guys see all this hair on a chick and just gotta have her, some sort of massive male turn on. So she blew it off and returned to concentrating on Antonio.

"So you ready to go test those mega drinks?" she teased him.

"Ah, Statue Lips. Waitin' for that, huh?"

He left to go to the bathroom first, and he was barely out of sight when the leering tongue wagger approached. He indulged in a really long, deliberate look up and down her body, still leering. There was something vaguely familiar about him, but she couldn't place it.

He spoke, sliding into the booth next to her. "Buena," lasciviously licking his lips. "You looking pretty tonight."

Something seemed off. She wouldn't go so far as to call him sinister, not even menacing. But he sure wasn't friendly, the vibe was all fucked up.

But that wasn't unusual with some guys and how they hit on chicks. She'd had worse, that was for sure. They put off this attitude that was beyond macho, beyond B.D.S. even, bordering on psychotic. Maybe a protectionary mechanism so that if they get rejected they can call the girl a lesbian bitch and wag their tongue at the next one.

She attempted to blow him off gently. "Ok. Thanks," then turned the other way, slid away from him. As she was moving away, another guy with his head shaved bald slid in on the other side of the booth. He didn't push in as close, but she couldn't get up. He smiled nicely. His friend's finger ran along her forearm and she snapped back as she pulled her arm away.

She'd never been able to pull off this easy excuse before, but she decided to try it on for size. "My boyfriend's in the bathroom, he'll be right back."

"Fuck your boyfriend," he replied.

From the other side, "Yeah, fuck your boyfriend," the bald guy repeated.

Ok. So. It didn't exactly work out as well as she hoped it would.

"Yeah, I do fuck my boyfriend, he's the only guy I'm gonna be fucking."

"Don't be a cunt," the tongue wagging guy said.

She was shocked. Really shocked. Honestly. She'd been called a cunt before, but usually there was a little more that she'd done to earn it, or at least a little more animosity in the works.

She backed off, not wanting to get him all pissed off and have Antonio step back out here into a hornet's nest. "Look, I'm really sorry, I didn't mean to sound bitchy. I'm sure you're really cool, I'm just not interested. Nothing personal, ok?"

"Don't really care what you want. Buena crica, huh? Your boyfriend's a cabron."

Parroted over her other shoulder from the other guy, "Buena crica."

She didn't know what the first thing he said meant, but I understood what he just said about Antonio, and it really pissed her off. "You know him?" she asked.

"I know he left you here. Alone. With me."

"He'll be right back," she said, glancing around.

"I bet you're a sweet piece of pussy. He eat you out the way he should?"

Face flaming, she refused to back down from him. She just glared.

And he continued on. "I know he doesn't."

He grabbed her chin and forced her to look at him. She tried to turn away and back away from him.

"I'll do that for you."

"I don't know what you're talking about," she said, "but…"

"It's called cunnilingus, sweetheart. That's what I'm talking about."

Her skin crawled at the thought, but she didn't want to piss him off. He was aggressive enough already. "Look, no offense, really. But I'm not interested."

"We'll see," he answered, his eyes flitting for a second. then moving and twisting into her, really fast, very forceful. He pinned her against the back of the booth, pawing at her breast. Sticking out his tongue, he lurched his face near hers. His hand squeezed her breast hard, his tongue licking across her face. Yelping, she shoved him back as hard as she could. She didn't think that would be enough, so she prepared to kick, but there was a blur, and as quick as he was on her, he was off.

And there was Antonio standing between them, growling, "Back off."

He must have pulled him off while she was shoving against him. Straightening up, she peeled herself off the booth. But before she could stand up, Antonio put one arm out, motioning her to stay directly behind him as he pointed his finger menacingly in the gross guy's face. He said something in

Spanish she didn't get, followed up in English that she did understand, "Don't you ever fuckin touch her."

Then he clocked him. Hard. No warning. Just a sudden, sharp, powerful punch right in the face. Dropped the guy right to the floor with it.

Antonio cursed at him in Spanish again, spit on the guy's feet, turned and grabbed her hand, pulling her up, helping her step around the guy on the floor, and then pushed her in front of him, leading her out of the place. The guy sitting on the other side, never made a sound or moved a muscle as Antonio nailed his friend.

Antonio's got a whole new look on his face she'd never seen before. Maybe she'd witnessed shades of it like when he first jacked up his Jaguar. But this was an entirely different level. His forehead vein had popped out, his jaw was tightly clenched and eyes were gleaming, resolute.

Fierce.

She started to babble. "I'm so sorry, Antonio, I swear, I didn't, I didn't flirt with him or anything, he just came over and I tried to be nice, but, but…"

"I know," he replied, grabbing her hand and pulling her outside into the cool dark.

He kept pulling when he noticed there were no taxis around, leading them through the parking lot and toward the street. Behind them, she heard a door slam and glanced over her shoulder, seeing the guy's figure emerge, and another with him. It was dark out. They were in back of the place, off the strip, no other people around, no bright lights, no hum of activity. Safety wasn't a phone call or snap of the fingers away. And they're were walking fast, closing the small gap between them.

"He's coming," she told Antonio.

"Shit," he hissed, stopped in his tracks and turned around.

And there they were, directly in front of them. The crude fucker, ordinarily just another tired joker who crossed a line, but with his reinforcement with him, suddenly a serious threat.

She fought off a shiver, whether it was from the cold outside or vile feeling of danger creeping through the pit of her stomach, she wasn't sure.

Then Antonio took a half-step forward, his lips thinning, top one curled into a snarl, standing up straight to his full height, shoulders back, legs slightly spread. "Don't even fuckin think about it," he said, voice low, menacing.

Serina's eyes went back and forth between the two guys. Then his friend with the shaved head showed up, and an alarm went off when she sees the both of them. They seemed familiar to her.

Her dad always boasted of having a photographic memory with instant recall. Eidetic was the technical term for it. She remembered in pictures and Shelby remembered in numbers, but neither of them like he did. And all this booze, the lack of sleep had her kind of fucked up now. She began flipping through pictures like a page in a catalogue; craps tables, bars, restaurants, the pool, anywhere she might have seen these guys. Nothing fit, she couldn't zero in on it, couldn't get the pieces of this puzzle to come together.

Now, the action started happening. Feeling removed for a few seconds, like she was watching it on a screen. Maybe because it was too surreal, too bizarre to actually be happening right in front of her. The only sound was her own heartbeat in her ear, everything unnaturally lit by the heavy glow of a far off, high above, security lamp.

The tongue wagger spoke, pointing at Antonio. "It's called respect, asshole. And you need to learn it."

"Respect," his reinforcement reiterated.

"Respect huh?" Antonio mouthed back. "That's what you showed her back in there? Get the fuck away from us."

The bald guy punched Antonio in the face, and Antonio barely staggered. He cracked him with a serious right hand, closed fisted punch. A definite sound, the dead slap of skin on skin.

And then, while she watched, the tongue wagger suddenly was on her again. His hand snaked around her throat, and it jarred her back into the moment. No thought, reflex only, she kicked him, hard as she could. He shouted and doubled over with it, and his hand loosened on her throat. But before she could pull away, he was standing up again. Closed fisted, cat quick—

CRACK—right into her face.

Serina dropped. Instantly. But she didn't pass out.

It knocked her off her feet. Blunt, hard pain and exploding pressure in her eye. She was on the ground, blinking and rocked. Struggling to get up.

And then she spotted him going for Antonio, to double up on him. Antonio was still tangling with the bald guy. And this one went at him, too, lunging, taking him out with a hard tackle. They rolled to the ground, bald guy kicking at Antonio from above.

She was up. She tackled him, the bald one, flailing, kicking, *biting.* Screaming. Insane, just wailing on his ass. Somehow, he got on top of her. He sat up, reared back.

And there was Antonio. Utterly ferocious. Small trickle of blood from his mouth, face contorted with rage. He got his arm around the guy's throat, pulled him up. NO fucking around now. He slammed his face into the blacktop. She squirmed away, saw the other guy, tongue wagger, staggering up to Antonio again.

"Antonio!" she shouted.

He turned, not in time, and the guy whacked him in the face, making him reel. But before the guy could hit him again, Antonio gathered and unleashed a furious punch into the guy's chest. It rocked him, and Antonio dropped him with a few savage face hits.

He was a good boxer, for some reason popped into her head.

Antonio continued pounding on the guy, so she struggled to her feet again, got above him and started calling his name, trying to grab his arm to slow him down.

"Antonio!"she shouted, getting her arms wrapped around his shoulder, "Stop! STOP!"

He did. Panting, he knelt up and looked down at the guy, face bloodied, out cold. He glanced around, spotted the bald one, also knocked out, face down in the parking lot. Then he looked up at her above him, grabbed hold of her waist and pressed his forehead into her stomach, still catching his breath.

She held his head in her hands for a few seconds, knotted her fingers in his short hair, then said, "We have to go."

He nodded his head, pulled himself up. "You alright?" he asked.

"I'm fine, I'm fine. Are you? You're bleeding," she pointed to his mouth.

He blew that off, saying, "He knocked you good. I saw it. You alright?"

"I'm fine," she answered.

But he scrutinized her face, all viciousness gone from his expression, his eyes more full of sorrow.

She couldn't handle that. "We have to go," she repeated.

He nodded again, squatted down and tugged at the guy's jacket while she looked around nervously. No one was in sight, but that didn't mean no one saw them. Antonio was stuffing something in his pocket, ruffling around some more. Was he actually rolling the guy while he's out?

And, fuck it if he was.

He got a set of keys and stood up. Took her hand and started leading her away. "You're bleeding," she told him again. And this time, as they walked quickly, he licked at his mouth, swiped at it with the back of his hand.

"It's nothin'," he said when they get to Paradise Road and he steered them left, carelessly tossing the keys into a trash can.

"Where are we going?" she asked him. She was shaking, not from the cold, but from the adrenaline still coursing through her body. It was over, but the nervousness set in as though she was just getting ready to dive into it.

"I don't know, gonna look for a taxi, you know, whatever."

"I'm so sorry," she said, getting even more jittery. "I'm nothing but one disaster after another for you, this is all..."

"This ain't your fault," he said coldly. "You sure you're alright?"

"I could use a drink. And a smoke," she replied as he flagged down a taxi.

"Serious?" He opened the door and climbed in behind her.

"Uh, yeah," she said as she began wringing her hands, squeezing on her ring, getting more freaked as the images of what just happened kept replaying in her head.

That guy on her in the booth, licking her face. She swiped a hand across her cheek roughly, sending shocks of pain to herself. She pictured his tongue and wiped some more, ignoring the hot jolts with a shiver.

"Where to?" the driver asked, and Antonio said Caesars, but she shook her head.

"I don't want to go in there." *Not like this*, she left unspoken. "I need a drink," she repeated. "Are you ok?" she asked Antonio. He nodded, and she asked again, he nodded again. "Hilton," she finally told the guy, "back entrance, the Star Wars bar."

"Star Trek," he corrected her.

Whatever.

"Is that ok?" she asked Antonio and he nodded again, staring at her now. Mentally, she could see the guy over her, ready to unleash and her stomach did a flip. Squeezing her eyes shut, another picture appeared, the bald guy kicking Antonio in the ribs. Sour bile rose in her throat, and she snapped her eyes open. Just as that image faded, another popped like a camera flash, the tongue-guy over Antonio, smashing him across the jaw. She began to shake, all the fear suddenly exploding through her guts, exposing itself as nervous tremors.

She glanced at Antonio to center herself, reassure herself that he was ok. She grabbed onto him, asking him again, "Are you sure you're ok?"

"I'm fine," he seemed to laugh. "Calm down, it's alright," he soothed. He fumbled in his pocket, pulled out a smoke and lit it up, passed it to her as he exhaled roughly. He had blood on his hand, maybe his or maybe the other guy's.

Because of her. This was her fault. He could have been killed.

She accepted the cigarette and inhaled as deep as she could. From up front, "No smoking in my cab," and the window next to her lowered half way. She hit it again and tossed it out the window.

Chapter 21

By the time the taxi driver dropped them off, she'd managed to pull it back together, convinced herself that she was ok, Antonio was ok, and no, no one saw them, no one knew them, he wasn't going to get busted for this whole thing. And even if someone did see it and report it, she'd been there (shit, no, she had to pretend to be Shelby—correction, *Shelby'd* been there) as a witness to say that those crazy fucks started it. So it'd all be ok, it was all good. Antonio said he was fine and she just had to chalk this up to one more fuck up. Damn, she had to be careful not to fuck up Shelby's life.

Though she still couldn't exactly figure out what she did to provoke this whole thing. But she still felt like she somehow knew those guys. But how could she? She hadn't been in Vegas very long.

As soon as they were out of the car, she asked Antonio for another smoke. Somehow she must have dropped her pack on the ground at some point, or left them at the Peppermill when he pulled her out so quickly, didn't really know for sure. He lit up a couple, passed one to her. He seemed tense, coiled and ready. He wasn't shaking like she'd been in the cab, but he wasn't laughing yet either. He still seemed reticent, maybe even pissed. But he wasn't bitching her out or anything, and she was completely aware she hadn't returned to normal yet either, so she just rolled with it.

They went in, going past the game room, stopping at a restroom along the way. He told her he'd meet her in the hall, so he was gonna stop, too. Inside, she went directly to the sink and splashed some water on her face before looking in the mirror. Dumb-ass. She'd forgotten she was wearing makeup and when she stared into the mirror she had black streaks running down her face. She cleaned those up and washed off the licked area again, taking another look. Not that bad.

There was a mark, no doubt about it; a bit of a welt from where his fist thumped her, but it really wasn't all that bad. Combined with the fading marks on her neck, though, it could appear like she'd been into some serious shit. She stepped back and checked the rest of her clothes and body. She washed off a couple of small scrapes, one on her shoulder, one on her elbow, but they weren't bad either. She pulled her hair around, effectively covering up her neck, and hiding her shoulder, too. If she didn't tuck it behind her ear, it even covered the deepening red splotch on her face.

She exited the bathroom to meet Antonio; he was already out there and he looked fresher, too. She couldn't tell where his mouth had been bleeding from, it must have been inside his lip. He straightened his shirt. There were no visible marks on his jaw where he took at least a couple of hits.

But he was still tense, she was sure of that. "You sure this is ok with you?" she asked him.

"Anything you want, baby, anything you want."

So they went in and grabbed a booth in the back of the bar area, where it was darkest and where there was least likelihood of roaming Romulans coming up to them.

When the waiter came up, she ordered a Warp Core Breech and Antonio tried to get one, too, but she insisted they share one. Shelby had warned her about how huge these drinks were He looked at her strangely. When it was brought to their table, bigger than a goldfish bowl, purple and smoking all over the place, Antonio smirked and commented, "Now that is a fuckin drink. Trekkie fucks know how to party, huh?"

When they leaned in and started sucking away with their straws, she experienced some weird mental flash of the two of them as if someone else was watching them. Like they were some sort of distorted, grown-up, gen-X, sullied version of *The Lady and The Tramp* spaghetti scene.

Except that she was no Lady. Or lady. And she just nearly got Tramp skinned alive. They sucked on in silence for awhile. Finally, she said, "This is rum. That alright?"

He nodded and sucked. The alcohol began to warm her up, loosened the knots of dread still cramped up inside her. "Want some shots?" she asked him.

"They make you happy? Get 'em."

She waved over the waiter and tried to order the shots. She didn't know what they were called, and he started hassling her as he was supposed to do. They had everything in this bar named after Star Trek stuff, and part of the fun was that they made you talk the talk. But she only wanted the shots, so she tucked her hair behind her ear and said, "Please don't screw with me, just bring me a rack."

She didn't know if it was the tone of her voice, or the look on her face with the welt that was blazing away on it, but he softened and nodded. Before he got away, Antonio asked him for a glass of ice, too. He came back with a wire rack loaded with six shot glasses of milky green stuff and the glass of ice.

They each picked one up and shot it, the cool, minty smoothness of them a nice contrast to the warmth of the rum. Antonio handed her a cigarette. They both lit up, and that made it even better. She was unwinding, but she couldn't tell if he was. He seemed to be controlling himself rather than relaxing. He kept watching her then looking away if she tried to catch him in a long stare. Fingering the gold cross dangling around his neck, he quickly tucked it back inside his shirt. He wrapped some of the ice into a napkin. Handing it to her, he suggested she put it on her cheek.

"You're pissed at me," she said.

"No, I'm not."

She stared at his hand, knuckles puffy and banged up. "Your hand, it's…"

"It doesn't hurt, it's fine," he answered. "I've had worse from boxing."

"But aren't they gonna be pissed at work?"

"Nah, they know I box. It's happened before, you know, no big deal."

"Shit. I'm so sorry," she said.

"Don't say that. You didn't do nothin. I'm sorry," he replied.

"For what? For saving my ass?"

"I gotta tell you somethin," he said. "Those guys are assholes."

"Yeah, I figured that out," she said, taking a deep slurp.

"No, I mean…Like, I know them."

"You do?" As she asked that, there was another sudden flash in her head and then she had it. Leaving Vince's bar the other day, she'd passed a couple of guys who had leered at her. She'd been feeling plucky that day, didn't look away, and had smiled at them brazenly. Two big guys, one bald. It was them. She took a last drag on her smoke and crushed it out.

Snuffing his next to hers, he cleared his throat. "That was all my fault," he continued. "They know me, they were fuckin with me, and, and…"

"Fuck man," she said and took another sip, fiddling the cold ice against her face, another level of tension draining right out of her. "Thank GOD."

"What?"

"Valdez, do you have any idea how guilty I've been feeling? I thought I fucked up again and caused you all this trouble, that you got hurt cause of me. It was making me sick to my stomach."

He met her gaze, staring at her gravely. Quietly, "Then you know how I feel." His eyes were soft but pulled down with sadness. So much hurt radiating from him. Another new look. First the fierce one, then that raging one, now this. This one was awful, this sadness simmering to the surface. It was out there, everything she'd been feeling playing right across his face, reflecting in his dark, beautiful eyes. Only his sadness seemed more intense.

She reached up and stroked his face. "Antonio, I'm fine. And it's not your fault. That guy was just a total pig. You should have heard the shit he said to me." She kissed him lightly on the jaw. "And you kicked his ass for me," she smiled.

He seized her hand and pulled it down. "What did he say to you?"

"Um, well," she thought about it, recalling. "You wanna know? I'll tell you, but remember, you already kicked his ass, ok? It's already been taken care of."

"Just tell me," he insisted.

"Well, he pretty much ran the table on insults. First he called me a cunt…"

"He called you a cunt?" His teeth gritted together, eyes flashing.

"See, I'm not gonna tell you if you get all pissed off again."

"Why did he call you that?"

"I don't know! Because he's an asshole! I swear, I didn't do anything," she pleaded.

"I know you didn't. I know it, I told you, this is my thing. My fault." He so sweetly kissed her hand, though his brows knitted together in deep worry and he wouldn't look at her.

"Antonio, please," she begged him. "Don't do this." She dropped the ice and stroked the back of his neck. Played with the edges of his hair. "I'm ok, Valdez. You didn't do this. They're the assholes, you said it yourself. And I'm fine. In fact, the more I think about it, the more I realize how bad you kicked their ass, the funnier it gets."

He sighed heavily, but she swore she could detect him lightening up a little, so she continued. "Can you imagine it? Can you? If someone busts them out there before they wake up? What would they say? One guy and a chick beat them senseless?" bursting out in laughter as the humor began to dawn on her. "We are so badass," she told him.

"You are a badass," he admitted, starting to grin. "I saw you, you know. I was keepin an eye out. You, you fuckin rushed that guy and went postal on his ass."

"I know! Holy shit, I was freaking out. I bit him! I bit him pretty hard, too, the goofy bald fucker. I don't know who he thinks he is. Vin Diesel can go bald, not his lame ass though. You know him, right? Can I ask you something?"

"Yeah, shoot."

"That bald guy? Is he a little retarded or something?"

"Huh? No, why?"

"Fucking echo, man. All he does is repeat what Senor Tongue wagger says. He was like JarJar Binks with that gross tongue."

Antonio laughed at that. So she said, "Come on, man, do a shot with me, Mr. Badass. Nobody calls your woman a cunt and walks away from it. Shit, I'm just glad that bitch card reader didn't insult me more, you'd have put the hurt on her, beads and all."

So they did a shot, slurped some more at the giant drink as the smoke emanating from it slowly began to subside.

Again he asked, "So what else did he say?"

"Oh, shit, who cares?"

"I care." He made her put the ice back on her face.

"Alright. Um, let's see, I saw him when you were still there, he was behind you a ways, and he stuck his tongue out at me."

"Why didn't you tell me?"

"Cause I didn't know! I thought it was just some crude, random idiot. I blew it off. I thought if I told you it would start some whole big scene and I didn't want that."

"Guess that didn't work out so good then, huh? What else?"

"Then you left and he came over. He was hitting on me and it was disgusting, and I blew him off. Oh, I know, this is cool. Usually when guys hit on me and I want to blow them off, I have to just do it on my own, but this time I actually got to say, 'my boyfriend will be right back'. So that was very cool," she beamed at him. "I can call you my boyfriend, right?"

"Sure you can, but I guess that didn't work out so good either, huh?"

"No, that's when he called me a cunt. So I tried to be nice, and he said something in Spanish, I didn't know what it meant though, 'good' something."

"You remember the word?"

"Um, yeah. Crika, I think?"

"Crica," he corrected her, sounding a little pissed off.

"What's it mean?"

"Never mind," he replied.

Then she remembered something else, how he called Antonio a cabron. She remembered that cause she knew what it meant, but she wasn't sure she should mention it to him. She glazed right over it, went to the tongue part, how he licked her face and grabbed her.

"Anything else?" Antonio asked.

She left out him talking about eating her out, saying how Antonio didn't. Primarily because, well, Antonio hadn't, yet. In fact, other than the car scene, they hadn't done any sex yet though sometimes he acted like they had which kind of confused her. It didn't bother her, and she didn't *expect* him to and she was positive he *wanted* to, but with Sherri here and all, and Shelby expected back any minute from San Fran, the deal with everyone thinking she was dead from her car accident, she'd been delaying it, wanting it to be something special, that first big event, at least with him. But the other type of sex, well, she knew it was a macho thing with a lot of guys, they just wouldn't do it. And since he managed to completely turn her on anyhow, without even trying, she really didn't care. She wasn't about to make an issue out of it, especially concerning some tongue-wagging dickhead.

She made him do another shot with her after repeating all that stuff. She was getting a little lit up. It felt good to be unwinding, especially after all that. It was the best way to get him to come down, too. She lit another smoke, and he did the same. She flagged down the waiter and ordered another rack of shots and a mini-Warp Core.

"So....," she paused for a few seconds. "I told you my side, now you tell me yours. How do you know them?"

He scratched his thumb across his forehead and thought. Finally, "We used to be tight," he said.

"You? And them? Were they assholes even then?"

"Yeah, guess so. I don't know, it didn't bother me, you know. Didn't bother me, or I didn't notice it."

"So I take it Echo was the brains of your group and JarJar was the sexy one."

"Fuckin Echo, I like that," he said.

"You're sure there's nothing wrong with him?"

"Jacobs, I'm sure."

He stopped with that, so she pressed him. "Well, when did things turn to shit?"

"Awhile ago," he sighed.

It seemed like he didn't know what to say, not so much that he was unwilling to discuss it. So she tried another angle. "Did they ever fuck with Mindy like this?" She was real curious about his former girlfriend.

"No, she fucked them," he answered and stared directly at her this time.

Cabron.

"Where the fuck are those shots?" She craned her neck to search for the waiter. That explained a hell of a lot. *Cabron. Now she knew he didn't eat the girl out. Had a girlfriend ever cheated on him?—Yes.* Mindy. "Mindy told them stuff about him and fucked them behind his back. I want to fuckin kill her. To just grab her and rip her hair out for hurting him like this." Did she just say that out loud?

"'Salright," he said. "I'm over it. She ain't worth it."

Yes, she did say that out loud. "I'm so sorry, Antonio. You have to know I'd never do something like that, right? I wouldn't cheat on you. You know that, right?"

He nodded and she pulled him down close, wrapped her hands around his neck and kissed him. "I'd never do that. I'd never do that to you. I wouldn't want to."

"Even if you was pissed at me?"

"Never. I won't ever do that," she said right in his ear. "I don't think I could anyhow. You've wrecked me Valdez, you've wrecked me for other men."

He was laughing against her cheek, his eyelashes fluttering when he blinked. She pulled back when she noticed the waiter coming with their next round. "You need a shot after all that," she said.

"There's more," he replied.

"Shoot."

"I don't really feel like talkin about it, though," he said and slouched down a little.

"Ok." She'd seen enough hurt from him for one night. If he wanted to take his time with this, she could wait. She could understand that.

"But I'm gonna have to tell you. Sometime. Soon."

"Ok."

"It's not good," he said.

She swallowed hard. "Ok."

"Yo, let's do these shots now."

And they were great. And then they sucked on the fresh smoking drink. They just sat and drank and smoked, getting pretty drunk.

After the last of the shots, he reached over and tucked her hair behind her ear, caressed her cheek, lightly running his fingertips over the injured area. He looked sad as he did it, gazing at that instead of her eyes. "Snap out of it, Valdez," she said, knocking his hand away. "I'm fuckin' fine, alright. Shit. I'm ready for round two. Let's go scrape them off the parking lot and kick their ass all over again."

"Yo, I believe you," he said, laughing.

"Yeah, I'm not fuckin' around. I'm not afraid of them. Not if you're on my side. You were a good boxer, weren't you?"

"You weren't afraid of them, were you?"

She snorted. "I don't know. I was more scared after. I don't know what I was then, though. I think I was pissed."

"You looked pissed," still laughing. "I'll never forget how you looked, man."

"YOU looked pissed," she told him.

"Yeah, I was, man, I was. But you, shit. I swear, I scare you more than they do."

"You don't scare me at all," she answered.

"Yeah, I see you. I can see when you're scared. Don't ever try an' play poker, Jacobs. Stick with the card counting. Cause you show everything you're feeling before you remember to hide it."

"Oh, that's bullshit, that's *you*." Card counting? What was he talking about? That was Shelby's thing, numbers; remembering them, but she couldn't help it. It wasn't her fault she had the knack. Like her, she inherited it.

"Nah, huh uh. I let you see things in me. But I've seen you get scared with me an' shit. But you didn't give an inch with them. You just attacked, man."

"Told you, I'm badass. They pissed me off, fuckin' with my man

He grinned. "I won't let them hurt you again. I promise."

"Valdez," she said, "I wasn't worried about me."

He put his hand over her face and shoved her away, mock disgusted. And she let it go. Because she knew he meant it. He'd do anything to keep her from getting hurt. But she was more worried about him. But she wouldn't insult him by pushing the point. He proved he was a big boy. He could take care of her, he could take care of himself.

Chapter 22

TWO WEEKS LATER

Like Serina, Shelby enjoyed periodic field trips to the Oakland Art Museum where she would sit for hours in front of turn-of-the-century classics by William Wendt, Guy Rose, Percy Gray, Gottardo Piazzoni and a new acquisition by Edgar Payne that replaced the E. Charlton Fortune that had been so rudely absconded by Michelle Morgan. On this day she took the old route from when she and Serina had lived as kids in Marin County, driving past the Larkspur ferry terminal and San Quentin over the Richmond-San Rafael bridge.

The Marin County locals liked to tell folks that the Richmond-San Rafael Bridge was the longest bridge in the world, an obvious untruth. "Oh yes, it's true," the locals would explain. "It connects California's most exclusive community—Marin—to deepest, darkest Africa—Richmond!" Shelby Jacobs, as a teen, believed this observation to be true, having had the opportunity to witness the difference many times on the drive up to Lake Tahoe, which went through an area she, her friends, and more often their parents, simply referred to as "deepest darkest". On the west side of the bridge, rich, white folks built shopping malls with elaborate sculptures in parking lots graced with Mercedes, BMWs, Porsche's and an occasional Bentley. On the east side of the bridge, once past the Chevron oil refinery, the streets fell into disrepair, the shops had bars on the windows, and jobless blacks gathered on the street corners to drink Schlitz Bull out of brown paper bags.

The favorite landmark on Canning Blvd, which at the time was the fastest connection from Marin to Interstate 80, was B&K Liquors, where the Marin folks rolled up the windows and locked the doors of their station wagons and drove slowly past, hoping to witness a drug deal or knife fight in the crowded parking lot in front of the besieged liquor store. Shelby did not know a single white soul who had the balls to stop at B&K, even in dire emergency. And it was only a few miles, and just across the bay from their own comfortable upper class homes.

Leaving Marin, headed towards the East Bay, there was an ominous hint that you were indeed headed into another world: the imposing edifice of San Quentin State Prison jutting out into the bay just before the bridge. San Quentin occupied perhaps some of the most valuable real estate in the world, within rifle shot of four-star restaurants, famous investment banking firms, and the Golden Gate Ferry Terminal at Larkspur Landing, once the home of the Hutchinson Rock Quarry, where Dirty Harry chased the Zodiac killer up and down the conveyor belts before he finally plugged the "punk" on the dock of a sludge pond. As a student at Redwood High School (which was lovingly called "San Quentin West") Shelby, Sherri and Serina could see the big prison from the second story classrooms and often pondered what Charlie Manson and Sirhan Sirhan were up to at any given time, imagining them pounding out license plates in between gang rapes.

After she arrived at the Oakland Art Museum, she eventually sat down in front of her favorite, William Wendt. The docent of the museum who had seen the picture of Serina Jacobs in the newspaper about her tragic death, and now directly before her sat a duplicate image of the deceased painter, began to wonder if the idea of reincarnation perhaps held some merit after all. Now curiosity got the better of her and she could not resist interrupting her reverie.

"Excuse me," she said quietly, approaching the bench where she sat transfixed by the William Wendt. "I was wondering if you were familiar with an artist by the name of Serina Jacobs? You have a striking resemblance to her, you know."

Shelby broke out of her trance and looked unnervingly into the eyes of the docent for several seconds before she spoke. "Ah, but I thought Serina Jacobs is dead, no? Are you saying I look like a dead woman?" Shelby answered with a teasing smile, her eyes flashing mischief.

The docent giggled. "Oh so you do…I mean did…know her?" she asked.

"Yes, I met her and I am familiar with her work—it is very much like the paintings here, no? Now that the artist is dead, when will you be adding Serina Jacobs to your collection?" asked Shelby in a more serious tone, though she already knew the answer. An artist had to be dead for some time, usually, before their work was added to a museum collection. Unless you were Russell Chatham and started your own museum, or Andy Warhol who probably blew every curator in New York.

"Oh that's up to the curators, you know," she whispered, as if one of them were perhaps nearby. "Oddly enough I have never seen any of Serina Jacobs's work, though I can imagine it's quite similar to what we have here. Like you, Ms. Jacobs spent hours in this part of the museum soaking up these paintings."

"Yes," said Shelby, looking around the room. "I would say Jacobs's style tries to be somewhere between William Wendt and Edgar Payne, though you don't see the confidence in her strokes that you see in this work."

"Well, I'll let you get back to your…uh…viewing I guess it is. Nice talking to you. Just let me know if you have any questions."

As the docent ambled back to her information station, Shelby noticed a man in the same vicinity, dressed in tight Levi's, black cowboy boots, a short, black, leather jacket, and San Francisco Giants baseball cap, on backwards. She couldn't help but notice his perfect butt that simply took her breath away. He turned around and then, looking further up, she realized: Harlin Radner! "Damn!" muttered Shelby, turning quickly back to the Wendt and hunching over as if to shrink into herself and disappear. Suddenly she felt like she was sixteen again, and in the presence of an awesome, inscrutable power that could instantly vaporize all vestiges of reason and turn her into a drooling puppy dog begging for a scratch behind the ears. But then she reminded herself: Pull yourself together. You're not that spineless wimp—that helpless slave to a man's organ—that 'gets so easily led when emotions overtake the thinking'. Besides, what about your 'plan'?. And with that Shelby rose from the bench and sauntered over to where Harlin was looking at some modern sculpture—a piece that appeared to be a man and a woman locked in an intimate embrace, made of 10 penny galvanized nails. She carefully positioned herself behind him and backed up slowly, ultimately bumping her ass into his body.

"What the…?" Harlin began to say, turning around.

"Oh, pardon me!" Shelby murmured. My apologies!"

"Holy shit!" said Harlin a little too loud, causing the docent to get back up from her chair at the information station. "It's you! Shelby! Or is it Sherr?"

"Oh, I'm sorry," he said, catching the steely gaze of the docent and lowering his voice. She gently touched his arm. "No problem. I'm Shelby. But what are you doing here this fine day?

"Well—I like to go to museums now and then! Did you take me for the uncultured type?" Harlin said teasingly.

"No, of course not…it's just that I…," she stammered.

"Tell you the truth," Harlin interrupted. "Michelle…my fiancé…asked me to come take a look at the Edgar Payne the museum just picked up. I suppose that's why you're here, too?" he asked.

"So where is the Payne?" Harlin asked.

"The Payne? Ah, the new acquisition!" She gestured to where Edgar Payne's "Sierra Divide", a 24" by 28" oil of a granite peak towering above a sapphire blue alpine lake, painted in Payne's signature geometric blocky strokes, hung alone in a corner of the museum.

"My—it's gorgeous!" gasped Harlin when he saw the work of art. "So much more powerful than a picture in a book, don't you think?"

"Well of course. But the books are good. Not everyone can afford to have such priceless paintings hanging in their homes," she answered.

"Yeah, I guess you're right. Guess the po' folk have to go to museums or look at the books. Unlike you and me, of course," Harlin said, half-joking.

Shelby smiled. Serina must have told him she was well off.

"Well, Michelle sent me over here to have a look at it in person…see if we should buy it. What do you think, Shelby? Would you buy it?" Harlin asked earnestly, looking for another opinion.

"Well of course! If it were for sale! But how can it be? It is the property of the museum," said Shelby, gesturing to the rooms full of artwork around her.

"Bullshit!" said Harlin matter-of-factly. "You're a rich woman. You should know better. Everything has a price. At least that's what Michelle tells me."

"Yes, but some things are meant to be shared by all," was her passionate comeback.

"You mean to tell me you're not here to purchase the Payne?" asked Harlin. "Or are you bluffing like you did at the Gallery a few weeks ago?"

"Bluffing?" asked Shelby.

"You know what I'm talking about! The way you and Wilcox worked Michelle—you think I don't know a shill when I see one?" Harlin said, raising his voice and causing the docent to get up from her information station once again.

"What!" protested Shelby quietly, feigning concern.

"Hey…," said Harlin, lowering his voice again. "Don't worry about it. I thought it was beautiful, the way you and Wilcox duped Michelle into paying three million bucks for those paintings. She may be a big shot movie woman, but she can be a gullible son-of-a-bitch, too—sometimes she can't tell where the script ends and the real world begins, know what I mean? And she doesn't know jack about art. She's just a poser."

Shelby internally danced a little jig while she listened to Harlin lay into Morgan. This sounded to be more of a engagement of convenience than she ever imagined.

"But you're talking about your fiancé…with such disrespect!" teased Shelby gently.

"Arrogant little bitch that she is," Harlin laughed. "Do you want to know how I met Michelle Morgan? It's really kind of funny and it happened after my father died.

Shelby shook her head, no, and he related the events:

Ever since the murder of his father during a bungled robbery of his San Francisco apartment, Harlin Radner had ceased to be an active participant in the world around him. Where he once rode dirt bikes in motocross races, felled giant Douglas Firs with screaming chain saws, partied with bikers at stock car races around the country, and eventually settled in to dig post holes and brand cattle with a born-again heroin addict in the deserts of eastern Oregon, he now simply sought protection.

His father was an ordinary salesman who had risen to the executive ranks of an international company. Once his younger sisters had all finally moved out of the family home in Ross, California (Harlin had moved out just as soon as he turned eighteen), his father summarily divorced his wife of 32 years and married his secretary, Noriko, a Japanese immigrant. Stephen Radner's apartment was a veritable Geisha house: visitors were required to remove their shoes and don Japanese sandals upon entering, meals were served in a sunken dining room where Harlin's various girlfriends and wives, generally tall women, fidgeted uncomfortably on their pillows and made inappropriate comments about Pearl Harbor.

Then on one night, a rainy January night—the night after Harlin's 24th birthday—a gourmet sushi feast that Harlin's cattle-ranching wife had barely touched, forcing them to make a late night trip to MacDonald's on the way back to their hotel on Union Square, Stephen Radner was shot twice in the abdomen as he got out of his steamy shower. Apparently the burglar assumed the Radners would be out, as they were almost every Thursday, at the San Francisco Symphony across town at Davies Hall. But Stephen Radner had come home from the office late, and had planned to meet Noriko during the first intermission. Noriko found him around midnight—naked, still, quiet—in a pool of blood almost a half- inch deep on the tile floor of his Japanese-styled bathroom.

Harlin Radner, unlike his now-dead father, had always lived a consciously rumpled life, eschewing the looks and ways of modern men of means: expensive clothes, fancy foreign cars, designer purses, and perfumes or makeup of any kind. His lifestyle once worried his parents, who believed such a sloppy demeanor might indicate the dreaded "blue collar" tendencies. Yes, Harlin liked women, especially hairy, crude, tough, even smelly women. This was not the son Stephen Radner had dutifully climbed the corporate ladder to raise in style, and, even though Harlin would at least wear clean, pressed jeans and perhaps a fitted black cashmere jacket to family gatherings, Mr. Radner considered him an embarrassment.

While it bothered Harlin to know that he was disappointing his father, it never bothered him enough to change his lifestyle. Sometimes he considered changing: jumping into the mainstream of San Francisco life, marrying some proper independent female who was perhaps an investment banker, taking up golf, joining the Junior League, and generally making an effort to "give back" to the parents that had so patiently put up with his eccentric, wild and often dangerous lifestyle. His father, of course, loved his son unconditionally just exactly as he was, as all good fathers eventually do, and despite his frequent complaints about his appearance, he would not have changed a single hair on his head.

Now that his father was gone, Harlin realized that he would never have the opportunity to be the son he thought Stephen Radner had always wanted. Nonetheless, in preparing for his funeral, Harlin Radner decided that he owed it to him to at least try. "Better late than never," he said out loud as he set out from the St. Francis Hotel in his high plains slicker, work boots and "O.K. Feed Barn" tractor's cap. His common-law wife, Willamina MacMillan (usually just Willie Mac) had taken a six AM limo to SFO.

"Your father never gave a damn about me. I might as well do him a favor and head back to the ranch," Willie Mac told Harlin early that morning.

"That's fine, Willie Mac, but don't be surprised if I don't come back myself any time soon," Harlin answered back.

"You'll come when it suits you, I reckon," said Willie Mac.

It was the last time he spoke to Willie Mac.

By the time Harlin got to I. Magnin, he was drenched, even though it was just a short walk across Union Square to the famous department store. El Nino had been soaking the Northern California coast incessantly since the beginning of November with darker-than-usual clouds and relentless downpours. Expensive apartments on Nob Hill were starting to slip down onto Battery Street and tropical Moonfish had been caught in the unusually warm waters just outside the Golden Gate. Since Harlin had depended on rain as part of his livelihood for the past few years, he could not sympathize with the complaints of the San Franciscans who had not seen the sun for the entire month of January. "What's so unusual about that?" he wondered aloud. "The sun doesn't shine in this city all summer long!"

As Harlin wandered aimlessly through the cologne department of I. Magnin, rainwater dripping off the bill of his cap, he was greeted by a woman that, Harlin thought, should have retired twenty years ago. "Hello," said the tiny, frail woman. "Is there something I can help you with?"

The woman was smiling through a bright white set of shiny dentures that were too big for her thin, cracked, red lips. Lipstick clung to the tops of her teeth and her eyelashes appeared so heavy with liner that Harlin thought they might fall off at any moment. He could tell from the lines on the saleswoman's heavily powdered forehead that she was probably thinking, what has the cat dragged in this time? Miss Violet, as she was affectionately known by the staff, was used to all sorts of unkempt men coming into I. Magnin, but she had never encountered what appeared to be a real cowboy.

"Well," said Harlin slowly, "let's see. I need something for a funeral."

"Oh dear, I'm sorry." Miss Violet had a drawl—Texas, thought Harlin. Or maybe Louisiana. He could tell by the way she had said "deeeuh".

"Are you an acquaintance of the deceased or was it…family?"

This caught Harlin off guard—does it make a difference, he wondered. Black is black, right? Black is black, I want my father back. The tune jumped into his head and Harlin thought he might finally cry, but quickly caught himself by focusing on the diamond chain that held Miss Violet's glasses to her wrinkled cleavage.

"Well," said Miss Violet, "I suppose it doesn't matter, really."

Harlin was transfixed by the light flashing off the diamonds. "He was shot. Shot in his bathroom," he answered.

"Oh, yes," whispered Miss Violet, moving closer to Harlin. "You mean Mr. Radner! My, that was horrible!" Harlin thought he might gag on Miss Violet's overpowering perfume. She was now practically whispering in Harlin's ear. "Did you…know him?"

Well I suppose so, thought Harlin, I'm going to his funeral. "Yeah, I knew him." Just then his attention turned from the diamonds to a sound—a snapping noise—that seemed to be coming from behind Miss Violet. It was much too sharp to be a fart, unless Miss Violet's flaccid butt cheeks could mimic a hand clap. And it was unlikely that any fart, no matter how viscous, would cut through Miss Violet's perfume. But the noise was coming from *further* behind Miss Violet. Harlin looked over Miss Violet's shoulder to a circular clothing rack packed full with colorful silk pajamas.

"Um, if you don't mind, would it be ok if I just browsed around a bit?" Harlin backed away from Miss Violet and then carefully moved around her toward the circular pajama rack.

"Sure, dear…you take your time." Miss Violet turned slowly to watch Harlin as she approached the rack. He's an odd one—going to a funeral and thinking about silk pajamas, thought Miss Violet.

Harlin followed the snapping noise—it was coming from the inside of the circular pajama rack, so he parted the clothing and looked inside. There was girl, around seventeen, sitting on the floor with a pile of clothes, a shopping bag, a pair of pliers and bits of broken plastic everywhere. The girl quickly stuffed the pliers in the shopping bag when she saw Harlin. Before saying anything, Harlin looked up to see if Miss Violet was still watching—she was, via the mirror above the makeup counter. Rather than talking (which might make Miss Violet suspicious) Harlin gave the girl in the clothing rack a curious 'what are you doing' look, which was enhanced by his natural half smile and his ability to raise one eyebrow while lowering the other. The girl in the pajama rack looked up at him—she had black lips against a china-white-complexion, heavy purple, false eyelashes, jet black hair streaked with red, and a number of painful-looking face and ear-piercings. The girl was expensively dressed, Harlin imagined—in various leather items. She did not appear to be in need of free clothing.

They stared at each other for a long moment before the girl lifted her middle finger to her lips, shooshing him and telling him to fuck off at the same time. Harlin, who had been known to nick a few items when he was a teenager (although never caught), was not inclined to report the shoplifting incident to

Miss Violet, who still hovered near the makeup counter, watching Harlin's curious activities in the mirror. In a way he wished the girl luck, although she clearly wasn't shoplifting out of necessity, a successful illegal experience or two could build character. At least Harlin looked at it that way.

Harlin hailed Miss Violet and they embarked on finding an appropriate outfit for Stephen Radner's funeral—or at least that's what he was expecting. "Did you find any pajamas that you like?" Miss Violet asked. She was leading him back towards the pajama rack, although the snapping noises did not continue.

"Pajamas? I don't wear pajamas," he replied.

"A tee-shirt perhaps?" Miss Violet was now wondering what he slept in.

"Nope—a tee-shirt sometimes if it's cold."

"Well, we do have a fine selection of sleep ware—even nightshirts for men—if you would like me to show you something." The idea of sleeping in the nude was something Miss Violet seemed morally obligated to rectify, though Harlin did not appear to be as malleable as many of her customers.

"So—where's the funeral section?" he asked, steering Miss Violet away from the pajama rack.

"Oh—we don't have a funeral *section*, honey. It's not like a wedding. But we do have some *very* tasteful outfits that would be *very* appropriate at a funeral." Miss Violet drawled all over when she said "very".

Soon, Harlin was *very* appropriately equipped with a black suit (he couldn't remember the last time he wore an actual suit) and *very* eager to get the hell out of I. Magnin. While Miss Violet was tolerable—slightly charming, certainly comical—Harlin had not figured out a way to tell the earnest, senior saleswoman that he preferred to dress in more casual clothing, without coming right out an saying it. "Something less fitted, perhaps," he would comment, but Miss Violet had a mind to reform Mr. Radner. After an hour of trying on suits, Harlin felt like throwing up, so he gave in and settled for something a little more conservative than he preferred, but still worked with his black cowboy boots. He paid ($800 in crumpled bills), and headed for the door, but not without a brief detour to the silk pajama rack. He quickly peered into the shoplifter's dark hiding place—only a pile of broken plastic sensors remained. As he headed for the door, Harlin noticed Miss Violet, watching his every move from the mirrors in the cosmetics department. It wasn't the first time he felt like a sore thumb in genteel society, and it certainly wouldn't be the last.

Meanwhile, unbeknownst to him, just outside the department store, continued Harlin:

Michelle Morgan should've had tinted windows in the back seat of her custom black BMW limo. The famous movie producer was easily recognizable: her almost notorious streaked hair, squat body, and trademark Vuarnet tinted cat-eye sunglasses were all over the national tabloids and entertainment rags, but Morgan had such an aloof air of superiority that, in a crowd, it appeared she was surrounded by a bubble of liquid nitrogen. Rather than ask for autographs, people were generally in a hurry to get out of her way. The presence of Karl, Morgan's 250 lb., 6'6" Aryan bodyguard, did not exactly invite casual contact, either.

In many ways, Michelle Morgan was viewed as a local hero. A renegade film producer that chose to snub the Hollywood establishment. Morgan's second independent film "Cruising the Back Roads", became a huge sleeper hit when a licensing deal was struck for the "Back Roads" name and logo with a huge restaurant chain that featured fifties rock n' roll music, roller skating waitresses with beehive hairdos, huge posters of James Dean, Marilyn Monroe, and other fifties cultural icons—nearly five years after the original film was released. Morgan, whose production company was nearly bankrupt and had taken to writing science fiction novels to pay the bills, was saved by the licensing deal. The film was re-released, additional merchandising deals for Tee-shirts, dolls, CDs, video games, coffee mugs and mouse pads were cut, and Morgan had the cash flow she needed to make more movies without having to suck up to Hollywood.

Even though Morgan now employed thousands in various entertainment-oriented businesses throughout the San Francisco Bay Area, her hero status was tainted by her cold, condescending personality and her habit of parading around the city with a retinue of what looked like, to the casual observer, street thugs. So, as Michelle Morgan sat in the back seat of her custom BMW limo, waiting for her current boyfriend to return a certain piece of rayon lingerie at I. Magnin for real silk, not a soul stopped to solicit an autograph. Instead, the lunchtime passersby stole a furtive glance towards the limo, then moved down the sidewalk as quickly as the crowds would allow.

Morgan was generally oblivious to what was happening around her most of the time, and this time was no exception. Although she looked out the car window and saw the people flowing in and out of the I. Magnin entry, her mind was on her new hobby: art collecting. Suddenly Morgan was distracted by a commotion in the entry to I. Magnin. She could hear the store alarms going off and now she saw a young woman, made up like a Geisha, dressed in leather and adorned with body piercings—pushing her way through the crowd, shouting and shoving people aside. One of the shoppers, who Morgan thought to be a misplaced goat-roper, almost fell on his face as the punky looking girl gave him a particularly hard shove. Then, it appeared to Morgan, that the punk dropped something into the goat-roper's bag. Then the young girl broke free of the crowd and disappeared into the stream of lunch hour downtown workers.

Morgan was entertained. A shoplifter had obviously made a successful heist. Morgan saw the girl dodge the traffic on Geary Street and sneak into the parking garage a block away—the security guards were still nowhere in sight. Then Morgan turned her attention back to the store entrance where a security guard had finally shown up—he had his big brown hands on the wrong person! When the decrepit saleslady, who Morgan was surprised was still walking much less working, reached into the man's bag and pulled out a pair of pink silk PJs with the sensor clearly attached, Morgan grimaced. As creepy as Morgan appeared to the public, she could be righteously indignant when confronted with injustice. And this…this cowboy…could not have possibly been a shoplifter, at least in the eyes of Michelle Morgan, a woman who had spent most of her life creating simple stereotypical characters for the movie-going masses.

Morgan did not like the way the plot was unfolding before her eyes on the sidewalk in front of i. Magnin. The story line was wrong—the cowboy had been framed. As the security guard started to steer the man back towards the store, Morgan felt compelled to act. She slowly, deliberately opened the back door of her BMW custom limo, picked her way through the lunch time passersby (immediately shadowed by Karl, her bodyguard, who was asking "what is it, boss? Want me to go find Carminda?") and put her hand on the shoulder of the security guard, who, still holding the man by the shoulders, quickly turned the both of them around to face the interloper. The crowd in the street slowed when they noticed the famous film producer.

"Excuse me," said Morgan, in her soft, boyish voice "But I believe you have the wrong person."

Miss Violet, who had been leading Harlin and the guard back into the store, was taken aback.

"Well I beg your pardon," she said with as much poison in her drawl as she could muster. " Mistah Radner here was caught shoplifting. We found this pair of PJs in his bag." She held up the PJs so that Morgan could see the attached sensor. "Clearly, he is the perpetratuh."

"Well," disagreed Morgan, "had you been watching the entire scene unfold, as I was from the back seat of my limo here...," Morgan gestured the BMW, still idling quietly, "you would have observed the young woman with the various body piercings push her way through the crowd and run off down the street with two bags full of your fine clothing, obtained I presume, at a five finger discount. Undoubtedly she planted these pajamas in Mister...Mister...," Morgan stumbled.

"Harlin."

"Mister Harlin's bag." Morgan's statement was complete.

"No...Radner. The name is Harlin Radner." Harlin was mildly entertained by the whole experience.

Miss Violet wouldn't hear of it. "Pardon me," she said, addressing Morgan in a stern grand motherly drawl. "I have been...observing this man for the past hour and, in my many years of providing service to distinguished shoppers in this fine establishment, I have learned to identify those types that are prone to shoplifting. And this man here is one of them. May I ask who are you to question my judgment in this manner?"

But Morgan was not paying attention. Instead, she motioned to Karl, signaling to him with a brush of her hand against her open palm. Karl nodded and approached the Filipino security guard, whispering in his ear. The bodyguard nodded, released his hold on Harlin Radner and walked a few steps down the sidewalk with Karl at his side.

Meanwhile, Miss Violet continued her tirade with Morgan, who now had her hand on Harlin's shoulder and was nodding gently, periodically glancing up the street to where Karl and the security guard were conducting their business.

Suddenly, the security guard shouted, "That's her!" and bolted into the traffic on Geary Street, dodging cars and then sprinting down the driveway of the Union Square garage shouting, "Stop, thief, stop, thief!" which, in his thick Filipino accent sounded like "Stapdee!" echoing into the bowels of the underground parking facility.

Miss Violet stood aghast. "Well what in the world do you suppose...," she was muttering when Karl interrupted in his own thick Schwarzenegger accent.

"The guard has seen the real thief, the punk rocker. He has gone to apprehend her."

"What do you mean? This is the thief!" shouted Miss Violet, shoving Harlin. "Here is the nightie he stole!"

"Just a minute," interrupted Morgan, taking the nightie out of Miss Violet's hands. "This is the nightie? Ma'am—could you do me a favor? Could you please read the size on the nightie?"

"Why sure," said Miss Violet, yanking the nightie away from Morgan and fetching her rhinestone studded glasses from between her powdered cleavage. "Let's see now…it's a petite!" Miss Violet dropped her glasses and looked slowly up to Hadley. "Why, young man," she said. "You done stole the wrong size!"

Shelby and Harlin burst out laughing, and continued to laugh uncontrollably, causing the docent to get back up and stare at them. That only caused them to laugh even harder. Finally, still shaking with sporadic laughter, they walked out of the museum as Harlin explained to Shelby how Michelle Morgan *asked him* to marry her not a week later and how he agreed to the marriage as long as it remained platonic. He became engaged to Morgan for the security, which he lost after the death of his father not the money. Truth be told, his father had left him filthy rich, something he managed to keep secret.

Things can't be more perfect, thought Shelby.

Chapter 23

Hordes of families from the foggy coasts and sizzling valleys come for summer vacation to the splendid Lake Tahoe region. Gambling on the Nevada side was an added enticement for many. It was here that young Serina Jacobs Shelby Jacobs spent the majority of their summer months with their family in a simple, plank style, summer cabin overlooking the lake from a lakefront two acre piece of property. And it was in this cabin, accessible by boat, or by walking a mile on rocky and wooded trail around the lake, or by car that Serina Jacobs had spent the last ten days after leaving Las Vegas.

The cabin hadn't been used regularly since the death of their father and the subsequent exit of their mother almost 10 years ago to the east coast, though Serina and her ex, Stefan, had spent a number of chemically charged long summer weekends there over the course of their marriage, and Serina, on occasion, used it as a base camp for escape/backpacking/fishing expeditions.

When Serina Jacobs had first arrived, some of the old timers around the lake's marina had indeed read about her demise while she was at the small market to get food, and drink and had offered their condolences. It had been kind of eerie people thinking she was dead. On that occasion, people at the marina had helped her with her grocery bags piled high and they loaded them into the small cabin cruiser.

After that, it had taken about 5 trips going up and down 70 stone steps to get all the groceries from the dock to the cabin, and by the time she finally plopped down onto the blown-out sofa, she was both panting and soaked-through with sweat. The sun had dipped behind the tall pines mountain tops on the west side of the lake and the steady afternoon breeze had relaxed.

Soon it would be dark. So Jacobs had gotten up, grabbed a Bud off the counter, she had yet to put the groceries away, and decided to go under the house to turn on the water and electricity. Afterwards, before she'd been able to put away the groceries, she'd discover a long dead mouse in the clutches of a rusty trap, had grimaced, then had looked around for the fresh bottle of Cuervo Gold she had bought in the little market for double the normal price, unscrewed the cap and had taken a long pull, followed by a healthy slug of Bud.

She had decided the cupboards would need a good cleaning before they received any food. She looked around for a dishtowel, and began to notice the rustic interior of the cabin. An unusual pair of antlers hung above the fireplace, painted with Day-Glo swirls of chartreuse and neon orange and decorated with shiny gold fishing hooks. There was a stack of CDs next to a big black boom box, but besides that, the cabin looked as if it hadn't changed from the day Dave Jacobs bought it years ago. The east and west wall of the single room, which included kitchen, dining area, and living area, was covered with old faded photographs, some simply tacked on, of relatives proudly holding up fish or hiking amongst alpine wildflowers. Below a single, small latch window on the east wall stood a rough hewn table on which sat a wicker basket full of plastic knives, forks, spoons and paper napkins, as if someone was getting ready for a picnic. Next to the modest, stone fireplace on the west wall were two small portraits, charcoal on paper, of a man and women—the twin's parents. She'd proceeded to wipe down the cupboards.

1Jacobs sat down again in front of her easel and dabbed a mixture of yellow ochre and permanent green deep into her one-dimensional forest, trying to simulate the waxy sheen of the madrone leaves, Bobby Weir singing of his "Sugar Magnolia", the fresh scent of pine needles wafting into the room from the open window.

She thought about their father and younger brother, both long dead, victims of violent, freak accidents. Their younger brother, Timothy, by far the more talented artist, died after a game of three-on-three outside of his dorm at the University of Oregon, when he jumped into the McKenzie River and didn't get coughed up until two days later. Their father, Dave Jacobs, found his young son twisting in an eddy between the granite boulders downriver- blue, stiff and bloated.

Less than a year later, their loud, magnanimous father had taken a duck-hooked Titliest 2 dead center in the forehead as he wandered into a parallel fairway in search of his own errant drive, and died instantly.

Serina paused, stood up and slowly backed away from the painting, wondering if perhaps she was trying to get too detailed, to cutesy, with the madrone leaves. She picked up a turp soaked rag and worked the filbert into it. Then he put down the filbert and picked up a small, bright flat, dipped it in the oil/turp mix, then into the permanent green light, just the tip, to add highlight to the edges of the leaves. After a few tentative dabs, she stopped again, contemplating. She knitted her brow, felt a pang of static anxiety, and stood up suddenly as if an uninvited guest had just entered the room. She looked around, noticed the air had become chill in the early evening, shut the windows, and felt an overpowering urge for a cold beer.

1Jacobs, popping open a can of Bud, realized that on the canvas there wasn't enough differentiation between the intensity of the color in the foreground and those trees that were nearer the horizon. This was a problem she could handle.

She tried to refocus on the painting, but her mind would not shut up. Suddenly she decided to take a break, surfing the world wide web on her newly installed Internet service on her new notebook computer (thank you, Shelby). Serina decided on a Yahoo search for Art and stumbled across the Arts & Antiques.com site. There, on the home page, was an advertisement for an art show displaying newly discovered works of the late landscape painter, Serina Jacobs. "Wow," she mumbled aloud. "That's me." Then a great idea niggled at her brain. Why not attend the art show herself? Yeah, why not? Shelby wouldn't care if she went as Shelby, would she?

Chapter 24

Shelby was sick of thinking and worrying and counting and thinking. Always keeping her brain on overload to analyze the shit out of things, everything worked out when she just laid back and let it roll anyhow.

And she did know what she wanted. She wanted to eat, and smoke, and drink. And she wanted to sleep, peacefully. On soft beds, after getting drunk or stoned or whatever and eating good food and gambling for a long time.

And then, mostly, she just wanted to fuck. Exactly like she'd been doing with Antonio before Serina's accident. She just wanted to fuck and forget about that long time when she didn't fuck—when no one wanted her, when she didn't want anyone. Specifically, she wanted to continue fucking Antonio. Cause he was good. And as much as she liked fucking, she liked the way he liked to fuck—the way he called out her last name, the way he was *not* indifferent to her, the way he just wiggled and grunted and loved it so much and allowed her to turn him out right along with her. She couldn't get enough of that. She became lost in it.

And along comes Serina. Kind of like 'along comes a spider', only Valdez can't tell one spider from the other.

So that was it, everything else could come and go. Eat, drink, sleep. She could fuck her mind into nothing in Las Vegas. Lost and fucking in Las-fucking-Vegas with Antonio fucking Valdez. Aces by her.

She found herself slipping back into her insecurities, not only festering about what this thing with Antonio and Serina was doing to her, but worrying about why she couldn't let go. If this would last like this. She knew Serina was holed up at the Lake Tahoe cabin. She'd just talked to her and Serina was going to attend her own art show in her place. It was the perfect time to risk seeing Antonio Valdez one more time. See if he was already fading out on her or not.

Because over the past few weeks, he hadn't faded out on her in the least. How she'd prayed, begged he would.

Out of sight, out of mind didn't work for her. Absence made her heart grow fonder.

But maybe when he saw her, she saw him, the spark wouldn't be there.

From what Serina's shared, she and Antonio still hadn't done the normal sex thing; no penetration. God, that sounded so sick. Just the thought made her cringe with jealousy. Shit!

She looked in the mirror too often. Still failing to see what he saw, but now seeing all the flaws again. Funny how they'd sort of receded for a little while there.

All this time she hadn't seen him at all: 137 hours of work at The Company, 17 packs of cigarettes, 3 utterly banal conversations about rear view mirrors, 7 conversations about wedding chapels, now 52 fidgets with her ring on the plane (she'd gone ahead and boarded the plane to Las Vegas—she had to know, was hoping for closure one way or another)—coinciding with 52 stupid, insecure thoughts of "what is this going to be like?", and 1 very tiny bag of peanuts later.

She grabbed her luggage and walked outside into the warm, mid-afternoon air.

And there he was (she'd called him in advance—needed him to be standing exactly where he was). Leaning against the wall, one foot over the other, top one tapping away a mile a minute with anticipation as he looked over, saw her, and said, "Yo!"

And there was that spark.

She had no doubt. Not about herself, not about him.

She was so happy to see him. And he was so happy to see her that he picked her up and squeezed her, laughing in her ear.

And for the life of her, she could not figure out how all this started, how it snowballed.

Her heart was beating harder, every nerve wired, flooded with relief to see him in one (fine, very fine) piece. There was no worry, there was no doubt, there was no loneliness, just nothing bad at all.

It was all good. All good.

When he put her down, he gave her kisses. When he pulled back, she looked at his face and didn't see a single trace of dark or sad or bad or lonely. When she thanked him for picking her up, he playfully pushed her face away and picked up her suitcase and started walking, nodding for her to follow.

"I'm glad you weren't late," he said. "I gotta work soon. One more shift then I'm off for a few days."

They walked pretty fast to get to his car. He drove pretty fast to get to his place. He hit the elevator button repeatedly to take them up to his apartment. When he stopped, she hit it a few times more, adrenaline surging with every push.

Turning the lock, opening the door, him being polite, asking, "You hungry? Thirsty? You wanna eat or somethin 'fore I go to work?"

"Are you retarded, Valdez? Come *here*!"

And then, finally, he was all over her, mouth and hands, fumbling as they removed their clothes. All of them, every last stitch, just getting naked and rubbing all over, getting used to and reacquainted with bodies that they'd gotten to know pretty well. And for her, being delighted and surprised all over again.

She remembered it. She remembered him.

But, Serina, she'd tasted him. Forget it. Enjoy the here and now.

But that hadn't been *this*. *This* was real. *This* was tangible—licking and kissing and feeling and being felt all over. Not a memory, not a dream, not a desire. Not one-sided sex. It was tasting and hearing and smelling and seeing him—inundating her senses with him, knowing they would go all the way, as far as they could.

It was being wound so tight, so hot, being completely overwhelmed by him. And even better, it was having enough cognition to realize that he was the same. He was fighting, he was gritting his teeth and fighting it off but he was overwhelmed by her; her, Shelby, *not* Serina. But they were out of synch. She was with him, but lagging behind, and he couldn't hold on and wait for her. He wound up shaking and hissing and collapsing down onto her once he was spent.

"Shit," he sighed. "Uhhhh. Sorry. It's been a long time, you know?"

"It's fine, don't worry about it," she answered, locking down her own itchy restlessness.

"Yo, I was savin that one for you, too."

"Shhh," she hushed him. "That was for me, Valdez. That was awesome. Rest awhile now."

"Shit," he drawled. "I ain't bustin a nut an' leavin you all hot. Been savin up just for you. Went too fast instead. Shit, I gotta go to work soon, too."

She came back down, still hot and itchy, but not quite seething anymore.

He kissed her cheek. "It was so fuckin hard, too, especially seein you all those times, and nothin. What was up with that, by the way? Like, I don't know 'bout you, but I like sex, man. I like to get off. I like a lot of it."

She laughed, trying to ignore he just referred to being with Serina. Trying to avoid answering his question. "Yeah, I've figured that out."

"Aw, man. No, like, it was more, it is more, you know, with you. Can't get enough with you."

That was sweet of him to say, though she wasn't sure she believed him, but it was nice of him to say.

He went on. "Serious. But like, when I got no one, I'll jerk off, pretty much every day, you know? But thinkin 'bout you, then waitin for you, I was goin nuts an' shit. Fuck, I nearly lost it as soon as I saw you at the airport. Held off, held off. Couldn't no more. An' you're still holdin." He laughed a little, kissed her on the mouth. "Was it hard for you, waiting all this time?"

Shit, now she had to lie because of the golf course thing. "Yeah. And I never was like you. I didn't really like sex that much. And you've made a freaking nympho of me now. Just thinking about you at night was the worst." All that was true.

"Me? Or Vin Diesel?"

"Mostly all you. Seriously. Hey, who's your Vin Diesel?"

"You."

"Be honest," she goaded him.

He sighed. "J Lo."

That really cracked her up. "You wanna nail J Lo? I can't decide which is funnier, that you want her or that you actually called her J Lo!"

"Doggie style. No doubt."

"I can live with that. She's not blonde, I like that. Tell you what," she said. "If you ever get a chance to do her, go for it."

"Shut up," he answered.

"I'm serious. You can. As long as it is doggie style only. And you can't do her the courtesy of a reach around like you do for me."

He laughed. "That how you show jealousy, huh? I can fuck her, so long as I don't try an' get her off?"

"I'm just permitting your fantasies. That's all. Would you let me fuck Vin?"

He looked into her eyes, saying it simply, "No."

"Oooh, is that how you show jealousy?"

"I ain't jealous. I'm just possessive of you."

"I've noticed that. It ought to piss me off, but I actually like it."

"I'll let you think about him. Sometimes. When I ain't around."

"Generous. You think of J Lo when I wasn't around last couple of weeks?"

He smiled shyly and blushed. "Couple times. Mostly you, though."

"So even between thoughts of me and J Lo, you held off. I'm impressed."

"Shit," he said and finally wiggled around, got off of her. "An' you beat me. You're still holdin off."

"Oh, yeah, I really won this contest," she mocked.

"Ouch," he said. "You're mean when you're horny."

"Ahh, Valdez, I'm just fuckin' with you." She sat up, preparing to get up.

Antonio snaked his hand up her leg, right to the top of her thigh, buried it in her crotch. She jolted with it, so fluid and bold a movement, still tender and revved up down there. "Alright, just, relax," she told him, attempting to will herself to keep getting up.

"Ahh, lemme make it up to you," he purred.

"Valdez," she tried to say, but it came out as a sigh instead. "We, you…You have to go, you said that, you gotta go to work."

"In a minute, baby, relax, just a few more minutes," he soothed with his voice, coaxing with his hand. "Lemme make it up to you."

And he did.

And when it was over, he murmured softly in her ear, cuddling her under his full weight, saying, "Te amo, Jacobs."

"Me, too, you," she answered back. She let him doze off for awhile like that, and she swam in and out herself. Then, worried he'd be late for work and starting to suffocate under his weight, she nudged him to wake him up.

"Baby, you have to go to work," she said and gently pushed his hips to the side as he blinked and stretched a little.

He moved off and she sat up feeling the sudden draft of cool air on her body. Antonio yawned deeply, stretched some more, shaking his head. Then, as if suddenly getting it, he leaped up, saying, "Shit!"

He showered quickly while she just tossed on a T-shirt and underwear for now. Getting dressed in his bedroom, he shouted out, "You gonna be alright here while I'm gone? You can have whatever you want, you know, to eat an' shit. I got you a couple bottles o' Absolut."

"I'll probably get a cab and go check in at the hotel anyhow. Maybe swim for awhile, gamble…" Like old times….

Chapter 25

A very hot heat wave in Northern California had broken, and it looked like rain was on the horizon within the very dark, brooding, fast moving clouds. Wilcox's California Heritage Gallery was appropriately dressed for the gloominess, bright with white Christmas lights against the darkening sky. And, unlike the days when Serina Jacobs was alive and her paintings were selling for $400 bucks a pop, (on a good day) the buffet was now scrumptious: baked goat cheese on toasted baguette, an assortment of pate, authentic jalapeno poppers, a collection of designer sausages, stuffed artichoke hearts, chicken satay, grilled vegetables, pot stickers, plus a variety of expensive California and French wines. There was even a bottle of Herradura Reposado and a tub of Sierra Nevada Pale Ale—for the locals.

The gallery itself had not changed much—like any gallery it was just a big room with bare white walls, and free standing white wall partitions throughout (all encircled in white Christmas lights), covered with Serina Jacobs's paintings pulled from the warehouse with Shelby Jacobs's permission. However, Wilcox had a little cosmetic work done, and had even installed a free standing kiva-style fireplace in one corner, which, on this rare, cool, late summer evening, was blazing in anticipation of arriving guests. Wilcox stoked the logs as he sipped on a glass of chilled Mont St. Helena Chardonnay, then stood back to survey the newly discovered work of the late Serina Jacobs. It was by far the best work she had done—placed her in an entirely different league of artists, really. Clearly Jacobs had been seriously inspired by the Lake Tahoe landscape and the high desert region of Reno, Nevada, more so than she had ever been while working landscapes in Marin County of northern California. Or maybe she had just learned how to apply that inspiration to the canvas more effectively when she escaped to get away from home. He couldn't help but wonder why she'd chosen to store these lovely pieces and not show any of them to him. Whatever it was,

Wilcox was confident that these paintings would command top prices in the landscape market.

Michelle Morgan, Karl and Harlin were, of course, first to arrive. Wilcox had promised, after some coercing from Karl, to give them a half hour to preview the work before the other dealers and guests showed up. Karl and Morgan had wanted a private showing, but Wilcox insisted that he could not be ready any sooner than the designated opening time, and Morgan finally acquiesced, particularly after Karl reminded her that this was supposed to be more of a selling excursion than a buying one. Upon viewing the paintings, Morgan was decisively noncommittal, but Harlin was ebullient.

"I can't believe Serina painted these!" he cried, pouring himself a shot of the Herradura and cracking open a bottle of Sierra Nevada. It was the first time Wilcox ever noticed the big diamond rock on his right finger.

"Maybe she didn't!" suggested Karl, popping chunks of designer sausage in his mouth, occasionally dripping sauce on his black turtleneck. On the fourth chunk, he grimaced and spit it out on the floor. "Bleeeeccch! Give me some water! What is this shit?"

"Ah," said Wilcox, bending over and retrieving the partially chewed sausage piece with a napkin. "You must have had a bit of the Jalapeno chorizo!"

"That's what you get when you eat like a fucking pig, Karl" laughed Harlin. "Here, try this," he added, handing him his open Sierra Nevada.

Karl took a long sip, grimaced, but did not spit it out. "You call this beer?" he cried, handing the bottle back to Harlin who immediately dumped it in the trash and opened another.

Michelle Morgan shook her head. "You made an interesting point before you poisoned yourself, Karl," said Morgan. "Perhaps these aren't authentic? How can we tell?"

"Well, Ms. Morgan," said Wilcox with an air of authority. "If you can't tell an original from a fake, perhaps you shouldn't be dealing in fine art!"

"No shit," muttered Harlin under his breath to himself.

Karl shot him a cold stare—lately he had become suspicious of Harlin. He wasn't as docile or cooperative as he used to be.

"You're absolutely right, Wilcox!" Morgan said, apparently unharmed by the slight. "Besides, if the paintings were ever determined to be fakes, I would have your balls on a platter!"

Karl and Morgan erupted into loud laughter while Wilcox tentatively reached for his scrotum, then thought better of it.

Harlin just shook his head and thought, how much longer can I put up with this shit?

More guests started to arrive, none of whom Wilcox recognized. They each introduced themselves as dealers or art collectors from various art centers around the world: New York, Chicago, Santa Fe, Scottsdale, even Paris.

Wilcox was especially attracted to the small Parisian man, who wore a beautiful, red silk scarf over a finely crafted, purple velour smoking jacket, and held an ivory cigarette holder between his teeth. "Do not worry, Monsieur," he said after introducing himself only as Jean-Marc. "I will not smoke in the gallery—it harms the fine paintings, no?"

"Oui," answered Wilcox, smiling, but he could tell from the way the French art dealer eyed the woman from Scottsdale who was festooned with heavy turquoise jewelry under a brightly colored serape, that that the Frenchman was straight.

It wasn't long before the gathering, now about 50 people, was interrupted by the sudden, unexpected appearance of a woman dressed in an emerald green, long, tapered, cashmere coat, shimmering, flaxen hair down to her buttocks, entered the gallery. Almost as if on cue, everyone turned to stare. Harlin weaved through the crowd and reached for her velvet gloved hand, proffering a gentlemanly kiss on its backside.

Harlin turned and announced, "Ladies and gentlemen, may I present Shelby Jacobs, one of the triplet sisters of Serina Jacobs, the fine artist whose beautiful paintings we have been privileged to be invited to view today." Under his breath and slightly over his right shoulder, Harlin hissed, "Get lost, Karl!" Karl smiled as he drifted backward into the crowd.

Wilcox surveyed the crowd, who, seeing that the stunning, elegant beauty was not a reincarnated Serina Jacobs, returned to their conversations and critiques of Jacobs's work. Most of them had never seen a Serina Jacobs, except for the ad in Art & Antiques, but when they saw the prices listed for the work, they figured the dead artist must have become a real player in the last year or so. $75,000 for an 18" by 12" oil on board was right up there with William Wendt.

Jacobs couldn't take her eyes off Harlin, the full memory of how she had put him up on a pedestal all these years came flooding back full force. Curious that she did so without even knowing what he was really like, what he might have become. How he had always come to her in her dreams as her savior, her angel waiting to take her to a place of warmth, light and love.

But as she watched right at this immediate moment with Harlin believing she was Shelby (this was kind of fun, actually—not being herself, but posing as Shelby), she sensed that he had grown cold, hard, indifferent; that perhaps his life with Michelle Morgan was just a way to experience and fund his freedom, his escape. Shelby had briefly mentioned to her about the death of Harlin's father (Serina didn't remember them being particularly close) and the fact that he had plenty of his own money. The real question was, what was he escaping from or did he even know—but it came to her that, despite his bright eyes, sweet smile, sharp humor and quick laughter, he, too, was perhaps struggling with his place in life. Most all, her mind raced with the possibilities of her life with Antornio. Had her meeting him been fate, God's sign to point her in an entirely different direction for a new life? Was she finally over her bizarre obsession of Harlin?

"How is your fiancé this evening? I hope she's enjoying herself," she asked Harlin.

"Are you kidding?" whispered Harlin. "That wimp?" They looked over to where Michelle Morgan was standing, holding a glass of Cabernet in both hands and conversing with the man from Santa Fe, who was a good head shorter than Morgan—the man appeared to be talking to Michelle's rather floppy tits.

"She's hangin' loose," Jacobs couldn't help commenting.

A fine spray of beer spewed out as Harlin burst out laughing. Attempting to stop, he asked, "You like tequila? Wilcox has got a fine bottle of Herradura here—I think he must have been expecting you," laughed Harlin, pulling her to the hors d'oeuvre table.

"Can't say no to that offer," she grinned. Wilcox had indeed bought the Herradura and the Sierra Nevada for her, meaning Shelby Jacobs, of course. She caught Wilcox's eye from across the room. Wilcox gave her a quick wink, which Harlin caught, then his expression turned sour. He gestured with his head toward the door, indicating she should take a look. There, arm-in-arm, were her ex-husband, Stefan, clearly plastered, and a small Asian man, about as tall as Michelle Morgan, though more petite in body structure, in a charcoal gray 3-piece suit, white shirt and bright red tie. She immediately turned back to where Wilcox stood, whom he expected to have a firm grip on his testicles at the sight of these two, but he was gone. Serina could hear Stefan's voice from behind.

"Excuse me!" he shouted above the crowd. "Does anybody know where we can find Rex Wilcox?"

"Right here!" said Wilcox, emerging from the back room with an envelope in his hand. Stefan took the arm of the little Asian man and they weaved their way through the crowd of art dealers and guests. "Stefan—so nice to see you! It's been a long time!" said Wilcox, giving each a light peck on the cheek.

Stefan giggled. "Jeez, Wilcox, what happened to your hair? I would think an old fag like you would want to get a rug or something—cover up that chrome dome of yours!" He let out a loud guffaw.

The oriental guy gave Stefan a little playful drunken shove "Stefan, honey, now you be nice!" He, too, proceeded to laugh.

Pathetic, thought Wilcox.

"This, Wilcox, is my lawyer," Stefan then announced, pulling the little Asian man forward. "Lee Ho Fook!"

The man took a little bow, then produced an envelope from inside his suit coat pocket, which he gave to Wilcox. "For you, Mr. Wilcox."

"Well thank you, Mr. Fook!" said Wilcox, opening the envelope. "And what have we here?"

Jacobs, obviously curious, had moved to within earshot of the conversation while she tried to keep up a conversation with Harlin.

Karl had also taken an interest in the proceedings, seeing that Mr. Fook appeared to have some business dealings with Wilcox.

Wilcox opened the envelope and read the letter, smiling, while Stefan and the Asian man rocked unsteadily back and forth.

"Who are those men?" Harlin asked her.

Just then Stefan looked over, caught her eye, smiled, and whispered something in the Asian man's ear, who turned and smiled at her, too.

"Excuse us, Rex," said Stefan. "We'll just let you conduct your business in private for a moment." They turned, approaching Jacobs and Harlin.

"Well, hello there, Jacobs!" Stefan shouted. "Well I'll be damned if you don't look like the spitting image of my dead wife! Which sister are you?" Jacobs held out her slightly shaky hand, and Stefan took it, giving it a feaux kiss in the old English tradition as he bowed low, almost losing his balance.

"Stefan," she murmured, amused and saddened at the same time. "I'm Shelby."

"Well shit, you could of fooled me!" the Asian lawyer said, transfixed by her face."

"This is Harlin Radner. He is the fiancé of Michelle Morgan," said Jacobs, gesturing to where loose breasted Morgan continued to chat with the man from

Santa Fe. It looked as if he might take a bite out of one of her melons at any moment, or perhaps pick up the chunk of uncut emerald at the end of her necklace and use it as a microphone.

"*The* Michelle Morgan?" asked Stefan, turning to look. "Well shit, if we ain't in fast company, honey!"

The Asian lawyer reached in his pocket for a cigarette while Stefan started to sing the theme to "Battle Planet". Then, as he went to light his cigarette, Jacobs reached out and gently lowered his hand from his mouth.

"No smoking," she reminded him with a kind smile.

"What the fuck?" he answered. He stared at her for several seconds, trying to absorb her words.

"You can't smoke in here. It's not good for the paint," said Jacobs.

"Well fuck that!" he finally declared, seeming slightly bewildered, then turning on his heel and shoving his way through the crowd to the hors d'oeuvre table where he grabbed a full bottle of Zaca Mesa Chardonney and made his way to the street.

"I think he might have had a little too much wine at Aeriola's tonight," explained Stefan. "My name is Stefan, by the way," he added, extending his hand to Harlin. I was married to Serina for a couple of years"

Harlin's jaw dropped open and he looked Stefan up and down.

"Married to Serina!" he exclaimed. "I never knew she was married!"

Jacobs looked at Harlin, then at Stefan. Uh, oh.

"Sure," said Stefan, steadying himself on Harlin's arm. "But I'm beginning to believe in reincarnation. I guess I never saw you around much when Serina was alive," this to Jacobs.

"Amazing!" cried Harlin. "I knew Serina in high school!" Stefan stood back, eyed Harlin, mouth agape. "Ohmigod!" he finally exclaimed. "You're *that* Harlin Radner?" He stumbled forward and locked Harlin in an awkward embrace. "We finally meet after all these years! Serina said she had dreams about you!"

"I know," said Harlin, trying to disconnect from clinging Stefan, who smelled like stale Chablis and patchouli oil. "I saw her again, shortly before her fatal accident, and she told me all about it. And you, though she didn't say you were officially married. "

"Uh oh," said Stefan. "Well...I loved her, no matter what she thought. I just couldn't stand being with just one woman...or man for that matter!" Stefan laughed and tried to get a read on Harlin to see if he swung both ways or treaded the straight and narrow, but Harlin looked away.

"Yes. I loved her, too, though I don't think she ever knew it," said Harlin. Stefan reached out and touched his hand.

"Well, she's in a better place now."

Stefan's standard schlock whenever he talked about the deceased. Jacobs moved her head back and forth very slightly. This was too much!

Jacobs excused herself to mingle with the crowd, and immediately went to the hors d'oeuvre table, poured herself a healthy amount of Herradura, then noticed a discussion between Wilcox and Mr. Fook that did not appear to be going well. Apparently the Asian lawyer had finished his smoke outside and now this ding-a-ling he-man, Karl seemed to be involved.

Serina moved to within earshot and struck up a conversation with a short, dumpy woman with a huge, hairy mole on her neck who was from New York. "I don't generally deal in landscapes—New Yorkers don't go in for this kinda stuff too much. But they like it for the country homes and such, ya know. They tend to go for those fox hunt prints from the English countryside—makes 'em look like royalty, ya know."

Serina Jacobs nodded. The one time she went to New York during college, she traveled half way across the country in a Toyota economy car, crashed in her friend's sister's apartment, then spent an entire day traipsing around the city, scared out of her wits that she might get mugged at any moment. And, though the Monet's in the museum of modern art were impressive, she was too jacked up on cheap coke to really appreciate it. And, she remembered, one of the reason's she took the trip was to get over the latest heartbreak wrought on by Stefan, who had taken up with a dancer, but she hadn't been able to stop thinking about him.

Now, in the California Heritage Gallery, she still felt the same animalistic attraction to him, go figure. She was looking over the New Yorker's shoulder at Stefan's somewhat larger but still shapely ass underneath his worn designer jeans, noticing that, as usual, he wasn't wearing any undies, when she heard Karl shouting at Mr. Fook.

"There will be no further discussion of this matter!" Karl shouted, his big hands on Lee Ho Fook's scrawny shoulders. "The will is authentic, do you understand?" he continued, shaking Mr. Fook.

Wilcox stood by looking smug. He probably figured Morgan and Karl would side with him, since Serina Jacobs's will could only benefit their existing business relationship.

Then Mr. Fook, whose face had turned a bright shade of red, let out a blood curdling "aaaayyyy yaaaaa" and slammed his right knee into Karl's crotch. Stefan screamed as Karl released Mr. Fook and doubled over. The crowd hushed, and Morgan pushed her way through to where Karl lay in fetal position on the floor, breathing heavily. Mr. Fook stood over Karl, calmly brushing off his shoulders.

"What the hell is going on here?" demanded Michelle Morgan.

"Mr. Fook here has a problem with Jacobs's will," answered Wilcox

"What will?" asked Morgan

"Jacobs's will. You know, the one Jacobs wrote that bequeaths her paintings to her sister, Shelby Jacobs and Shelby has graciously allowed my gallery to continue selling Serina's paintings exclusively," said Wilcox, giving Morgan a wink.

"Oh *that* will," said Morgan, smiling. "Now, Mr. Fook, we have had this will looked over by many attorneys and it's entirely authentic. We even had a handwriting analyst confirm it."

"This man here," shouted Mr. Fook, shaking with anger, "he should know better than to grab a China man!" And with that Lee Ho Fook took the letter from Wilcox, stuffed it in his suit coat pocket, turned on his heel and strode through the crowd out the door once again.

"Well!" began Wilcox, speaking over the hushed crowd. "I hope you're all enjoying yourselves! Nothing like a little action at an art show, I always say!" Everybody laughed. Stefan hurriedly stepped outside to join his Asian friend.

Harlin, who had no affection for Karl, took it upon himself to play nurse anyway, and was kneeling where Karl still lay curled in fetal position near the entrance to the back room, making certain his breathing was getting back to normal. Morgan stood over them, mildly amused at Karl's condition. The other art dealers and guests went back to their conversations except the man from Santa Fe, who stood with Morgan surveying the damage.

"Nice work, Karl," Morgan said, half joking. "So what was it got your dander up?"

"I don't think Karl is quite ready to talk," said Harlin.

"I can talk," Karl croaked, and started to get up slowly, Harlin assisting. Karl shoved him away. "The Chinese had a letter claiming that the paintings belonged to that man—the one who smells like shit."

"That would be Stefan," said Harlin. "Jacobs's ex-husband. Did you know she was married, Michelle?"

"No," Morgan replied. "But what is even more amazing is that she was married to him. I think he plays for the other team, as they say."

"He plays with whomever will play with him," corrected Wilcox with disdain.

"Who are you to say, you little faggot?" said Karl.

"Ok, Karl, calm down," Michelle Morgan instructed. "Let's get back to business. I believe that is what we are here for, is it not?"

Karl nodded.

"Now, Wilcox...," Morgan continued. "Has anyone expressed any interest in this latest *find* of yours?"

"I believe everyone is quite impressed with the work," Wilcox replied.

"Impressed enough to write a check?" Morgan asked.

"Well, it's not considered good form to make offers at the show," said Wilcox. "Besides, the prices are on the paintings. I expect the dealers will let me know tonight if they're interested, and then we will negotiate."

"I'm interested in the desert landscapes!" said the man from Santa Fe. "Desert landscapes sell very well down in Santa Fe. People from all over the world come there to purchase art just like this!" he gestured to some of the paintings on the wall.

"I'm definitely interested in some of the forest landscapes," piped up the lady from New York.

"I was under the impression that most of Jacobs's work was Northern California," someone else commented.

"That's true," answered Wilcox. "This is the only work she did in the desert, the high desert around Reno. And as you can see, she also painted forest and lake landscapes. Most of them were started during a college spring break. Then she returned after graduation to complete it, in almost utter secrecy, in about an eight month period time, we believe, while living in a family getaway cabin around Lake Tahoe. Her sister discovered when going through Serina Jacobs's paperwork that she'd been paying for warehouse storage for quite some time, which is where these paintings were found."

"I take it your not interested in the Northern California work?" asked Morgan.

"Not yet," said the man, smiling. "But I will call you tomorrow to talk about these particular paintings, Rex," he added, gently touching his forearm.

"Just out of curiosity," said Morgan, taking a grip on the man's shoulder, "What do you think you'll pay for this work—asking price?"

He smiled and covered her hand with his own. "Well, I don't know. What do you think, Michelle?" he asked with a coy look in his eyes.

"I am a great believer in the volume discount!" said Morgan, laughing.

The man from Santa Fe laughed, too. The man from Santa Fe took note of the hearty jiggle of her magnificent breasts when she laughed—he could hardly ignore it, since they were staring him in the face.

Poofy McFadden couldn't remember the last time he had been to an art opening, and he attended this one with little interest in the artwork. It was really Shelby Jacobs he had come to see, since he had, to date, little opportunity to see her since the identity confusion and her escape from the restaurant. He still had concerns about Serina's death, her paintings that were apparently selling for an ungodly amount of money, and the fact that Shelby just happened to be her triplet sister. The third sister, thank goodness, didn't want to get involved with Serina Jacobs' art estate. But, something did feel off about all this and he couldn't quite put his finger on it as to why. On the other hand, the few people who had known Serina personally had verified the existence of a triplets.

Poofy looked regal in his double-breasted, brass-buttoned. navy sport coat, matching ascot, and decorative cane: a regular English fop. "Where's our girl, Rexy?" he asked loudly as he approached Wilcox, Morgan, Karl and the man from Santa Fe. Wilcox gave him a stern stare while Karl fumed at the thought of these two gay men having 'a girl'. Morgan and company fell silent, eager to hear what possible response Wilcox might have to this obvious suggestion of pedophilia.

"Ms. Morgan, Lyle, Karl—this is Poofy McFadden, an old, dear friend of mine from Scotland who has made quite a name for himself as a plastic surgeon in San Francisco."

"A plastic surgeon?" asked Michelle Morgan. "Maybe you and I should talk when you have a moment?"

"I would be honored," said McFadden. He didn't let on that he was completely aware he was talking to a major movie mogul.

"Excellent!" said Morgan. "You can call Karl here to set up on appointment and we'll figure out when we can meet." Karl reluctantly handed Poofy a business card—he had finally come to accept that many professional males were gay, especially around the San Francisco Bay area, and although he didn't like all that limp-wristed banter, he had learned to put up with it, although he was still worried about McFadden's 'girl'.

Poofy looked around the room and spied Jacobs, surrounded by her sister's ex-husband and her childhood sweetheart, and figured if they were convinced Shelby Jacobs was indeed who she said she was, then who was he to question her. Still…He scanned the crowd of art dealers, took special notice of the little Frenchman and nodded to Wilcox, who shook his head to say "not one of us", noticed the giant flobbing hooters this time on Michelle Morgan and thought 'how uncomfortable'! Then he saw a tall, tanned, muscular, blonde man come through the door, dressed in dark, well cut trousers and a pale blue cashmere sweater. Nice!

Suddenly Stefan shouted from across the room, "Taylor! What the hell are *you* doing here"?

"Hello, Stefan! You seem so surprised to see me!" he said, giving Stefan the obligatory embrace. "I read about this art show in the newspaper and thought I should extend my respects and maybe buy one of her paintings." It was clear that Taylor had a pretty good heater going, too—his face glowed like an overripe mango, contrasting with the soft white fuzz on his cheeks. His teeth were practically blinding when he smiled, though it wasn't the artificial whitener look, and his blue eyes sparkled under his bushy blonde eyebrows. "Well, Stefan, you gonna introduce me to your pals, or not?"

Stefan and Lee Ho Fook had just popped a handful of Vicodin outside to take the edge off their letdown. Lee Ho was just plain nasty fucked-up and he didn't really care to let his friend, Taylor Grant, who he knew through some business associates (Stefan did have a normal corporate job in good old San Francisco) and had gone golfing with on several occasions, see this side of him. "Sure," he finally said. "This here is Lee Ho Fook, an attorney and a friend." Taylor gave the Asian Fook a firm handshake. And this is Harlin, my ex wife's childhood sweetheart." Taylor gave Harlin's hand a firm squeeze, which Harlin returned, smiling broadly.

"And this," said Stefan, Jacobs had her back towards them, talking to one of the guests. Stefan grabbed Jacob's coat causing her to turn to face Taylor Grant. "Is Shelby Jacobs, one of Serina's sisters and my former sister-in-law. Shelby, this is my friend from the city, Taylor Grant."

Taylor hesitated for several seconds, staring at the beautiful Jacobs sibling. Serina Jacobs's picture had been included in the newspaper article he'd read about for this art show. At the time, he couldn't understand how he could have had golf course sex with a ghost. She was the reason he'd come tonight. The sister, not a ghost; the sibling he couldn't forget. Finally, he took her outstretched hand, and she gave him a delicate squeeze.

"So pleased to meet you, Mr. Grant," she said.

Taylor smiled, still staring into Jacob's blue green eyes, such an unusual shade. It was her, he was absolutely certain of it. His sex partner from the golf course. "It's very nice to see you again—as in my ass still hurts a lot." He laughed slightly, then turned to survey the paintings.

Jacobs didn't know what to make of his strange comment and frowned. Nice to see her again? She'd never seen him in her life! She knew she hadn't. He was hot. She'd remember him. His ass hurt a lot? What the heck? Shelby…!

Harlin watched the interchange and had a sneaking suspicion that these two had met before, though Shelby remained detached. She was always detached. The more he saw her, the more he craved her. Maybe it was some sort of substitution obsession in his mind because Serina was gone, as in forever.

"So, Stefan, this is the work of your late ex-wife? Very impressive!" The paintings in the gallery were quite haunting, arresting. Real talent.

"Yes," admitted Stefan, "these are Serina's paintings, though I must admit, I didn't know she spent that much time in Tahoe or in the high desert."

"I am Karl," the big Serbian thug announced, coming up from behind, extending his hand to Taylor, who was a bit taken aback by his big hand and strong grip. He squeezed extra hard, causing Karl to squeeze harder, so he squeezed with all his might and he kept squeezing back, harder and harder until he whimpered with pain.

"Well…It's…very…nice to meet you…Karl!" he gasped, loosening his grip until he finally let go. His hand was white from loss of circulation. Good God. Karl's biceps were bigger than his thighs!

"My pleasure, especially since you are a fellow German," said Karl.

"Oh…I know I might look German, but I'm actually Norwegian," corrected Taylor, watching the tension in his neck muscles above the collar of his black turtleneck.

"Even better!" said Karl, baring his stumpy front teeth in a pinched smile.

Jacobs stole a glance at the package bundled tightly in the crotch of Karl's jeans. She couldn't help but wonder what he was really like, all that 'bigness', then turned back to Stefan.

"So you were married to Serina Jacobs?" asked Taylor again.

"I was, for a couple of years, back when I was into women," answered Stefan, giving Taylor one of his secret gay society smiles, but completely aware he walked the straight and narrow.

"Well from what I can tell, she must have been quite a woman!" said Taylor, glancing sideways at Shelby, who stood quietly observing the conversation along with Harlin.

"And you were her childhood sweetheart! How special!" said Taylor, turning to Harlin.

"Well, we were steadies in junior high, and we hung out together a little in high school. After that, we went our separate ways, but I was always thinking about her. She was one of a kind. A very sweet and special girl. But,boy…what a fuck up!" Harlin said.

Jacobs gave him a quizzical glance. Well, yeah, she had been, she had to admit. But it still kinda hurt to hear the brutal words coming from Harlin's mouth.

"How's that?" asked Taylor.

"Oh, she was a very talented artist, as you can see," said Harlin, gesturing to the paintings, his eyes darting around the room. "And she played a mean guitar, too. But I'm afraid her obsession with recreational chemicals kept her from really accomplishing anything. At least while she was alive."

Taylor reached out and touched Harlin's hand. "It sounds like you really cared about her," he said with all the sensitivity he could muster.

"More than she will ever know, I'm afraid," admitted Harlin. Sheepishly, he smiled at Jacobs, lightly stroking the top of her gloved hand hanging at her side.

Jacobs wondered what that was all about. She shuddered. Shit, was he interested in her as Shelby? But, wait, maybe that was ok. Didn't she, Serina, love Anthonio, or at least think she did? Antonio didn't know the real Shelby, right?

Chapter 26

"Wanna go to your place? Will those guys come over, the fuckheads from that night?" Shelby had the full scoop of the 'fight' from Serina. In fact, she had every intention of getting more details about those guys from Antonio directly.

"I won't open the door if they do."

"So you knew them pretty well," she said it as a chum, hoping he'd bite and she'd get more information.

He bit. "Yeah, I knew them pretty good. I used to deal with him. Both of 'em."

"Blow. Drugs. Not dice, right?"

"Yeah," he admitted, rubbing his chin against her shoulder, squeezing her waist.

"That's what started the trouble?" she prodded.

"Yeah. I wanted out. They didn't want me out. Don't work that way, you know?"

She just moved her head up and down, giving him silence in the hopes he would fill it.

"See, me and Brent, he's the bald one, we was tight. Real tight. Yo, we moved out here together from New York, man. We been pals since we were kids."

She wanted to ask him if Brent really was as thick as Serina said he seemed. But that might derail him, and she had noticed that if she interrupted when he talked, he would get sidetracked and clam up.

"An' like, he ain't a total fuckwad, you know? Not like the other one."

"The tongue wagger," she threw in. She'd died laughing when Serina described him.

"Yeah. Castillo. He's a fuck. We were never tight."

She wanted to ask him if he was the one who fucked his former girlfriend, Mindy, but decided to wait for a better opening.

"When me an' Brent moved here, we brought some shit out with us, started moving it right away an' it was easy as shit. All these tourists. Everybody wants something, man. Everybody. And lots of 'em want some blow or some reefer or whatever. But once we sold our shit, we had to look for a new supply."

"An' that's how we hooked up with Ramon. Ramon Castillo, the tongue guy. So we started working with him, an' for his boss, El Honcho. It's good to be hooked up with a crew like that, gives you more protection an' all. Shit was cool, we did good, you know? Like, we moved a lotta shit, and I didn't have to do nothing else. I got that car, I got my place. All I had to do was go out and party and move shit around and then I'd half fuck around with boxin."

"Then I started fuckin up a little. Fuckin up a lot. I was partying too much an' shit, started fuckin up my boxin gig, fucked up with chicks. Things got bad, really pretty bad. An' I knew I had to get out. I guess part of me still cared or something. I knew my mom would shit if she knew the shit I was pulling. She'd be real disappointed in me. It'd break her heart. I mean, she didn't raise me like that. I told you 'bout that, how hard it was for her when my pops left…"

His voice trailed off. He had told her a little about his dad and how he left them when Antonio was only six. Apparently it bothered him to talk about it even now.

"Anyhow, I just wanted away from all that shit, that's when I went to dealer school, for the dice. An' fucked up as it was, I was like, pretty good at it an' shit. I don't know how, but I just seemed to pick up dealing the dice really easy. Some guys'd have trouble with the math and shit, memorizing it all, but it just clicked for me. I thought I was getting my shit together, gonna be able to dig myself out. School sucked, an' working at the Cortez sucked, but still. I knew dealers could end up making mad cash. Plus, I was getting all this pussy…" he halted and tensed immediately after he said it.

"Uh huh," she said calmly to let him know it was ok. He could have crossed a serious line there, but she didn't want to throw him off course. Besides, there was the Serina thing, now that was a heavy duty line.

He stumbled to recover, "Sorry, just you know, I mean, all the cocktail waitresses and showgirls were 'round and shit. And they like the nose candy, which I still always had, an' they all hook up with dealers, just cause they're around all the time."

"Valdez, it's cool. It's fine. I understand. You were having fun."

"Then there was this one chick who I banged a couple times, wasn't nothing too serious, but I took her out one night, an' she ended up with Ramon. Pissed me off. Seriously pissed me off, and he really rode my shit 'bout it too. Then I hooked up with Mindy, and she, I don't know," he shrugged.

"You really liked her," she filled in.

"Nah, it ain't that, man. I wanted to, though. I just was feeling like it was time to cool the shit. So I tried for awhile, but then I started fuckin around again, an' I knew she was fuckin around. And it just went back and forth all the time, I don't know. She knew 'bout Ramon, and when she was good an' pissed at me, she went an' fucked him. I guess it was to spite me, I don't know.

"Shit." He stopped talking for a minute. "When I found out, I sorta flipped. An' for what? Why? She ain't worth it. I guess it's good though. I mean, things got bad. Really bad. But that's how I ended up getting out, so I guess it's sorta good, you know?"

"So you don't deal anymore? Not at all?"

"No. That's sorta why things are tense with those guys."

"But you're out of it. You promise?"

"Jacobs, I swear. I ain't into that shit no more."

"Ok." She faced him squarely.

"I'm serious. I got…I nearly got sucked down cause o' all that. My life was shit. Just shit. I wouldn't go back to that."

"I believe you. It's just…I can't, I don't want to part of something like that."

"You wouldn't be," he stared her dead in the eye. "I mean it, things are still sorta fucked, but it's getting better. You're making my life better. I won't fuck up like that."

He stopped offering information. And she stopped pressing. Did it matter anyhow? Probably not. She sighed, feeling better with him next to her. That realization sent a new bolt of fear straight through. What would she do if he was no longer part of her life? Without thinking, she said aloud, "Shit, I don't know what to do. I think I'm really scared, Antonio."

"Jacobs, I'm sorry…"

"I'm not scared of them. That's not what I meant." Shut up, Jacobs, just shut up, realizing she sounded like the dreaded insecure female. But, she had reason and he could never find out that reason.

"Oh." Recognition dawned, "Ooh."

"Aren't you scared?"

"Yeah," he sighed. "Yeah."

"You are? Really?" For whatever reason, that really made her feel better. She kissed him on the cheek. Darkness passed for the moment. "I feel so much better now."

He looked incredulous for a few seconds. Blinked. Laughed and shoved her away, pushing her to the floor. "Asshole," he teased.

Maybe he did know her.

His phone rang while he was in the shower, and an answering machine picked it up instead of voice mail.

"Hey, M to the R O, Mista Dawg," the deep voice drawled. "I'm gonna kick it at the VooDoo tonight, bring your lady, the biznitch who's the shiznit, I'll bring mine. Well, shit, I'll bring a few just to be sure. Peace."

Antonio finished up. She jumped in after him and he talked to her while he shaved.

"Who called?" he asked.

"A friend called. "Marion? I think that's his name? He said he'd be at the VooDoo tonight and wants you to come there."

"Yeah? Wanna go?"

"Really? You want me to meet your friends?"

"Yo, he's gonna hit on you."

"You're kidding, right? Is he going to piss me off like that other guy did?" She was referring to the guy who hit on Serina, then wound up in a fist fight with them.

Antonio laughed, getting it. "Nah, don't think so. You'll see."

"Does he deal drugs?"

"Nah, I know him from boxing."

"He's a boxer? Was he good?"

"With a name like Marion, you think he had something to prove?"

"He…uh, he mentioned me," she told him. He didn't bite. "That is, unless you've got some other girl he was talking about. The biznitch in your life."

In a teasing voice, "I told him 'bout you. Couple days ago."

She loved it that he was out there talking about her to his friends. But she stuck it to him about it anyhow. "So you told him I'm the biznitch with the shiznit, huh? Or did he just come up with that on his own?"

"His words. My general opinion, though."

So they went to meet the mysterious Marion at the VooDoo Lounge.

Luckily, she'd brought some spare clothes to Antonio's condo, so she took her time getting ready, putting on the nicest clothes she had there, including a tall pair of platform sandals. Antonio looked hot, and when they got off on the 51st floor at the Rio, they stepped into the VooDoo. It was a cool place, decorated to look like its name, lots of purple and dark colors, trying to evoke thoughts of the darker, sensual and mysterious side of Carnival. It was super cool when it first opened, but it was already date-stamped, but in the best way possible. The Rio and VooDoo were newer than the old school places, but it had already passed the glitzy, top-of-line, brand new exciting feeling and hurtled straight into pure Vegas cheese. The most striking thing about it was the view. The Rio was off the strip, situated behind Caesars. Out on the 51st floor balcony, the view was not only across the whole city, but also the whole strip flashing brightly below.

They picked up their drinks inside, then, holding on tightly to Antonio's arm to keep her balance in the shoes, they ambled outside to check out the view. His eyes flitted at something behind her and he stopped moving, nodded and gently coaxed her to turn around and look.

She knew immediately it was Marion walking towards them, not because the guy was grinning at Antonio and nodding, but because he was exactly like Antonio made him sound, exactly like his voice on the phone sounded. He was big alright. He had to be about 6'4", skin a dark burnished umber, shaved head, silky shirt flowing gracefully and tucked into tailored dress pants. Not only tall, but big. Not fat. Big. Linebacker big. Heavyweight big. How come she was meeting all these big people suddenly? Only this guy wasn't like big Karl in Marin County. This guy flowed as he walked, as smooth and velvety as his voice on the phone.

He ignored Antonio and walked straight up to Jacobs, instead. Shaking his head from side to side a of couple times, he said, "Mmm. Mmm. Mmm. The mysterious woman who is exactly as hauntingly beautiful as I imagined she would be." Bowing slightly, he offered his hand. Somewhat shyly, she gave him hers, and he bent deeply to kiss the back of it, eventually releasing it by sliding his fingers down her palm and across her fingers instead of just dropping it.

Her face broke into a smile. "Hello, Marion," she said and pressed back into Antonio. Not because she felt threatened. Only to reassure Antonio that she wasn't interested. Antonio released her briefly to knock knuckles with him, but slipped his arm back around her waist as Marion gave him some good-natured heat for not being around much lately.

She sipped her drink while they riffed a few minutes, remaining pressed against Antonio the whole time. When they hit a lull, Marion's eyes fell back on Jacobs and he just stared for a few seconds. "So you're a boxer?" she asked to break the silence.

"That's right, lovely lady. Do you like boxers?"

"I like *this* boxer," she indicated Antonio. "Is that how you guys met?"

"Valdez! You haven't told her, have you?" Antonio shook his head and adjusted his weight, remaining silent. Marion went with it. "I knew who he was from the gym. We knew who the other was, but we weren't down, dig? No bad blood, hey, shit, no. Just indifferent to each other. Then, make a long story short here, the Puerto Rican playa done played too much on his bitch, and she found out, you see. So to school him, she done did some playin' on her own, and that playin' was done with Marion."

"And you're friends now, because?"

"Because your man here, after he done got dogged by me, he showed his colors then. I don't know how things went down between him and the woman exactly, other than that she was out of the picture. But with me? Oh, he was, shall we say, rankled. Now you look at your boy there, and look at me. I got a good six inches on him, in more than one place, I'll have you note," he winked when he said it. "And also at least forty pounds. But he didn't flinch, rankled as he was, and challenged Marion. I respected that, and I apologized for my less than noble behavior. Explained to him that I'm not really the party he should be uh, taking umbrage with."

"So you talked him down then?"

"Oh, no no. Hell, no. Hey, shit, it wasn't that easy. He climbed in the ring anyhow, wanting to get his anger worked out on old Marion. Now, like I said, I have the height, I have the weight, but this boy has the moves, has the skill. He earned my respect."

"So he beat you?"

"Oh, no no. Hell no. Hey, shit, you ever see Cool Hand Luke?"

She laughed. "Yeah, when Kennedy punched out Newman over and over, but Newman keeps getting up."

"No, darlin', I'm talking about the eating eggs part. Sonofabitch ate fifty eggs! Don't you see?"

"Oh. Um. No, actually."

He laughed really hard. "You don't? That's good, I'm just fuckin' with ya anyhow. No, eggs are not relevant to this story, but he wasn't going down like Newman. His spic ass actually did put some hurt on this boy. I thought he had a chance to school me, so I failed his ass in the seventh round of this most unofficial contest. KO'ed cold, you hear. When he got up again, I don't think he ever knew he was out. Just shook his head as he climbed to his feet and said, 'That all you got?'" He laughed deeply again. "Then we went out for beers and to hound some fresh new pussy."

Jacobs laughed and then checked Antonio's reaction. He was nodding his head, but his jaw remained clenched shut. His eyes lacked any fierceness or animosity, though, and he seemed amused in a dogged sort of way. "Was this Mindy?" she couldn't help but ask.

"Mindy?" Marion recoiled. "Mindy? Hell, no, I never banged that bitch. Told him from the start she wasn't worth the drama." He softened, looked her up and down again and said, "But I can tell right off that you are worth any drama that shall ensue."

"She don't give me no drama, bro," Antonio interrupted flatly.

"Exactly, hermano," he answered back.

"Thank you," she inserted. "Nice to meet you, too."

"Oh, nice now. Be better once you leave this boy and come play with Marion."

She laughed again. "You're funny."

"I'm not kidding," he winked at her.

Jacobs glanced at Antonio and he just cocked a brow, saying, "He ain't kidding. Told you he was gonna make a play for you."

"Ok. That's very flattering, thanks."

"Girl like you deserves all sorts of flattery. Any time you want, baby girl. Any time; day, night, rain, shine, you give Marion a call and I'll flood you in flattery."

"Ok, when is he going to stop?" she asked Antonio, subtly tightening her arm around him.

"Not till you give in," he answered.

"Marion, let me ask you something? Do you really want to hook up with me? Or do you just want to flirt with me to annoy Valdez, here? Or do you just want to flirt with me to flatter me and Valdez?"

He smiled a big toothy grin, looked back and forth between Jacobs and Antonio a few times before saying, "Ho, shit, eh? Let me ask you something, lady. Are you really curious about motive or are you just trying to put Marion back on his heels? 'Cause Marion doesn't sweat the motive, he's just interested in the crime."

"Marion's a cop, Jacobs," Antonio reminded her.

Laughing, she said, "Yeah, but Marion, you should know then, suspects can be acquitted based on motive."

"Good gosh, beautiful lady," he whistled. "And the road to hell is paved with good intentions."

"Well, Marion, I like you and all, but you and me? We won't be going to hell together no matter what the motive was." she winked at him.

He laughed. A big hearty laugh, then winked at Valdez, throwing in the comment, "Crizzo to the frizzo. I see you finally settled on a girl's got some blood flowing above her cleavage there, hombre. I like you, lady. Now I know you got it all going on I'm gonna have to really put the moves on you."

Marion hung with them for awhile, never really relenting on Jacobs, but she didn't mind, and Valdez didn't seem pissed about it either. He acted playful about it, and she was fairly certain if she ever did make a move like she was actually interested in him, he'd be appalled instead of pleased. Or maybe he would actually fuck her, but then he'd tell Valdez what a whore she was. Something like that. But she laughed him off. He attempted to get her to at least dance with him, but she refused. Then Antonio tried to coax her to the dance floor with him, and she turned him down, too. They simply relaxed, soaked up the night and had a few drinks, until Marion eventually caught the eye of a couple of sweet things just like he'd predicted, so they gave him space to do his thing and took off.

In the car, Antonio asked, "How come you wouldn't dance with me, huh?"

"I could barely stand in these shoes, how was I supposed to dance?"

"Yo, you started getting your footing, that ain't it."

They parked at his building, but instead of going upstairs, they walked around outside. She clutched her shoes while he swung her other arm around.

With an impish grin, he asked, "Dance with me now?"

"Valdez…," she answered. Honestly. But he held her hand tightly, whirled her around once, making her giggle.

"C'mon," he teased. "We never danced together."

"There's no music, Valdez."

"So fuckin what? I'll sing." He did. He started by humming as he spun her around again. Then he dance/walked her until they were out by the lighted pool.

Dropping his jacket on the ground, he swiftly pulled her in against him. "You got them shoes off now, dance."

"Antonio…"

"Que?"

"This is silly. I never danced with anyone before."

"You never danced with anyone before?" he asked and moved her around, humming again. He guided for a moment, then turned her around a few more times.

She stepped on his feet. Feeling foolish, Jacobs back away. "My feet hurt from these damn shoes," she insisted and sat down at the edge of the pool, dangling her feet into the water. "I want to dunk them."

"'K," he gave in, pulling off his socks and shoes. Sitting behind her, he scissored his legs on each side of Jacobs, dipping his feet in, too.

They kicked like that for awhile, his arm romantically around her waist, breaking the silence by asking, "So, you like Marion?"

"I like him fine. Not as much as I like *you*."

"'Course not."

"Asshole."

"He's a good guy, you know? He's helped me a lot, Jacobs. Like, with…I don't know."

He stopped, obviously a heavy moment, and very apparent the wheels were turning in his head. He was trying to spit something out, but she wasn't sure how to prod him. So she waited for it. Finally, "Can I tell you something?"

She nodded. It wasn't cold, but she snuggled up to him closer, leaning her head back, placing her hands on his knees.

"Remember the shit I was telling' you? 'Bout Brent an' Castillo an' all that?"

She moved her head up and down not wanting to break his concentration with words.

"Yeah, well, like, Marion, he talked all sorts o' sense to me. He's the one helped convince me I could get out o' that shit. I mean, he's a cop an' all, know what I'm saying? He knew about me, he prob'ly coulda busted me, but instead, he helped me."

"And this was after you tried to punch him out?"

He laughed. "Yeah, yeah it was. Even that, you know, he took all the shit so well. We just got to be buds afterwards. That's what helped me, it really did. Like, I started training with him, got really serious, stopped partying altogether. At that time, I was still dealing, though. Marion, he ain't no fool, he knew what I was into. He never busted me or nothin, but he told me I had to cool it. He freaked me out, told me how I could get screwed with my car and my condominium and all, how dumb it was for me to have this shit with no way to prove how I paid for it. You know all that shit, right?"

"Kingpin laws and all."

"Yeah. So that's when I went to dealer school. Figured I'd start sorting things out. I got hooked up with Mindy. I told you how that shit went. I knew she fucked around. Pissed me off, but we'd just break up, get back together, then I'd fuck around, like that.

"So I was getting ready to get out o' this whole game anyhow. Marion, he was really cool with me, 'stead o' busting me, he was always talking sense to me, and my mom was so proud o' me, moving up. So I knew I wanted out, just didn't know how to do it. Ain't like you can just walk away, you know? Don't work like that, not when you're in a crew.

"I don't know, I was stubborn, too. I'll be honest. I didn't wanna give up the cash. I figured just cause I'd stopped usin', that was the biggest part. Even though I knew it wasn't." He gave her a squeeze. Sighing, "Ah, shit."

"What?"

"Just. This is hard. I hate telling you all this shit."

"It's ok. I'd rather know it."

"Yeah. I know I gotta tell you, I wanna tell you, it's just…shit. It's not good. I don't want you thinking, I don't know, I don't want you thinking and worrying 'bout it." He placed his chin on her shoulder. "I don't want you thinking all this bad stuff about me. But I know it's bad."

"Antonio, it's cool. Just tell me. I mean, you don't hold my past against me."

He snorted. "Yeah, you ain't got a past."

"You don't get pissed that I slept with a hundred guys before you."

"Thought you said it was fifty."

"Oh. Yeah. Whatever. That didn't freak you out though, did it?"

"I wasn't freaked when I thought it was fifty. I don't know 'bout this hundred shit."

"Stop!"

"Hey, I'm just fuckin with you. I don't care who was before me. I don't mind not being the first. Just so long as I'm the last."

She couldn't really comment on that right now. Serina was like a dark cloud between them and he had no clue. None. Totally in the dark. She laughed instead. "But you're the first, too. You were my first love, Antonio."

"Mmmm. Good," he replied, giving her a longer stare than necessary.

"So tell me about Marion."

"Alright. So I was still dealin. I wanted out, but, well, you know. You know how they say people gotta hit rock bottom before they really change? I guess that was it. I'd gotten low, but not low enough. Then, this one day, I made a run, picked up our shit, three kilos o' coke. After I picked it up, I had to stop in an' see the boss, El Honcho. He checked it all out, gave the all good and sent me off to finish shit up.

"Then I went to Brent's place. I dropped off his kilo. Had to go over an' give Ramon his then. So I went to his place. I go over there, guess who answers the door?"

"Mindy," she answered. That was a given.

"Yeah. Fuckin Mindy. Starts mouthing off to me, telling me what a shit I am, she's done with me, she's with Ramon now, on an' on, man."

There wasn't a whole lot she could say so she pressed back against him. She wanted to turn around and face him, kiss him, tell him he didn't deserve that. But she decided not to. She had no idea if he earned that treatment or not. But more importantly, she did not want to interrupt his flow right now. They'd get all into it and he would stop talking and it'd be worse when she tried to pry it from him later.

"Felt like a fuckin cabron. Castillo, he was cracking up, bustin my balls, so fuckin high on himself. I just dropped his shit an' left. I went out, got all fucked, even dipped into the blow I had for sale. Picked up this chick an' was coming back here, an' she just started mouthing off, too. Reminded me so much of Mindy, man, so much. I'd given her all this blow and she was wired an' worked up, started raggin on my driving, telling me slow down, an' it was pissing me off so I just went faster. And she's bitchin more, an' I'm thinking more o' Mindy and her fuckin smart-ass mouth and so I'm going faster and she starts really freakin and then I start freakin and then there's a fuckin *cop* behind us. I had a fuckin kilo o' coke in my car, pro'bly drank nearly a bottle o' tequila, and this crazy bitch is *screaming* an' I did a shitload o' the blow so I'm paranoid and now there's a *fuckin cop on my ass*!"

"So next thing I know, bam, he flicks on his lights, and I know I'm cooked if he pulls me over with this shit in the car. I'm only a couple blocks from the strip, so I pretend I don't see him, you know. Like, he don't have his sirens on yet, so I just fuckin *go*! I get on the strip an' he follows an' I see I catch a break cause the next light is ready to change. He can't follow if I turn cause there's a shitload o' traffic coming in the cross direction, plus I can park an' get lost, whereas if he's serious 'bout following me an' I go straight, he can call other cops and tell 'em I'm on the strip. So I turn into the Mirage, fuck it. He flicks his siren once as I turn but he can't follow cause the other traffic's coming now, right? You know, you seen it, you *know* how these cab drivers are. They ain't moving aside for no one, they'll ice your ass. I mean, fuck, he's five-0, but shit, this is Vegas and people fuckin *go* man.

"So I pull up an' slam it in park at the valet station. This bitch is still screaming an' shit but I just blow her off, reach under the seat, get my shit out an' cut it open wide just in case. Sure 'nough, here comes the fuckin black an' white, lights still goin, coming up the driveway. She's freakin, I'm freaked, and here comes the cop."

"Jesus!" she couldn't help but remark. "What'd you do?"

"Yo, man, I got out as he's drivin up, all sorts o' people crossing in front o' him, so he's goin slow. I grab my shit, get out, go right to the railing o' the volcano pool."

"You did *not*," said Jacobs.

"Fuck yeah, pitched the whole rest o' the fuckin kilo into it. 'Plop'. 'Bout sixty fuckin grand uncut dissolved right there. But shit, man, I wasn't getting busted with it. Fuck that. Fuck that."

"What'd the cop do?"

"Cop? Yeah. Wasn't no cop. It was Marion. MARION! He spotted me an' was finishin his shift, was checking to see if I wanted to go out for awhile. That's all. He thought I was pulling over to talk to him. Knew shit was up once he saw me there and looked down, saw the plastic floating an' the brick breaking up."

"What'd you do?"

"What'd I do? I was fuckin strung out, Jacobs! I'd been snortin the shit all day, this bitch was still screaming, my girl was tagging one o' my amigos, and I just tossed a kilo into a fountain, cause this jack-off wanted to have a drink!"

"You punched him."

"Fuck, yeah, I punched him! Wanted to kill the fucker."

"You sort of like to punch Marion, don't you?"

He shrugged against her body.

"So. Did he take you in for that?"

"Marion? Fuck *no.* He told me straight up, though, you know, shit has to stop. Next day it sunk in. Like a light switch, you know, 'click'. I'd thought I had already quit fuckin up, but I really hadn't, you know? An' I had to get the fuck out, I wasn't going out like that. My mom? My mom would kill me if she knew all this shit. She'd blame herself and she deserves better 'n that. I had a chance, you know, I had a job going with MGM, I was raking in the cash as a casino dealer now 'stead o' drugs. So, fuck it."

"So that's when you quit?"

"Yep. If it wasn't for Marion, I'd prob'ly be in jail right now. Or worse."

"And that's when things turned to shit with these other two guys? The assholes from the other night?"

"Yeah, well. Sorta…"

Before he finished answering, they heard someone calling his name loudly from nearby. They both turned towards the direction of the voice, now hearing a few squeals and peals of laughter then seeing Marion charging toward the pool with a woman slung over his shoulders.

As she laughed and screamed in protest, he jumped, fully clothed, still holding her, into the pool.

"Did I mention Marion lives here?"

Laughing, "No. But I see that now."

"Yeah, two floors below me. When the place was opening up I helped him snag it. Figured it was the least I could do an' all. Watch it!"

As he said that, she tried to scramble and back up, but it was too late. Marion reached up out of the water, grabbed hold of her arm and pulled her in, laughing in his deep tenor the whole time.

So it was one very thorough dunking in the pool in Shelby's best clothes, four extremely drippy walks upstairs (Marion and his lady, Shelby and Antonio), a nice long sleep in Antonio's big comfy bed and one car ride to the airport later.

They were saying bye-bye. Heck almighty, did it ever suck!

They smooched a lot. They professed love for one another. It took every ounce of control within her to not burst out crying.

"Just, fuckin…Stay. Stay," he insisted.

"I can't," she answered. And she couldn't. She needed to get away from him. She needed to breathe and see what that was like again. She needed to get perspective and figure it all out. Besides, she did have to work every now and again. "I'll miss you."

"You're still scared," he confronted head on.

"Even more, now," Jacobs answered.

"I'm scared you ain't comin back."

"I'll be back, Valdez, one way or another." She couldn't help but wonder how Serina's appearance at the art show had gone.

Now he flashed his big puppy eyes. Smiling and happy, fading off quickly, darkness filling them. A slow blink, his long lashes closing and opening gently. Heavy lidded when they rose. Forsaken. Sad.

Shit.

"I'll see you soon," she said and stretched up to kiss him. She didn't meet his gaze when she pulled back. She wanted the kiss as her last memory, the sweetness of that instead of the haunting of his longing eyes. His hands slipped away as she backed away and picked up her suitcase. Her heart tightened and she blinked back tears as she walked away. Finally she turned around long enough to flash him the peace sign. She took one last look.

Shitty. That's what it was.

Just shitty. Shitty leaving.

Chapter 27

Harlin Radner was scared. More scared than he had ever been. More scared than when his Bultaco dirt bike got stuck in 3rd gear at the Washington State Men's Championships and, unable to control his speed, hit a jump at 50 mph and went flying over his fellow racers like Evil Knieval, landing in a bog just off the track, breaking both his legs. He was more scared than when his girlfriend overdosed on PCP and went staggering around their apartment with an axe, imitating Jack Nicholson in "The Shining" and asking him if he would like to be chopped to pieces, 'just for the experience'. He was even more scared than when his father's wife called to tell him of his father's violent death, and about the bathroom full of blood.

Michelle Morgan had asked him to have a seat in her personal library, amidst towering walnut shelves of ancient volumes and reels of film accessible only by ladder, before a roaring fire, as if she was preparing to romance him. A thick June fog had set into the valley, condensing on the window and swirling around the outdoor lights. Morgan had brought a bottle of Courvosier, and she smiled at Harlin as she poured his snifter almost full. "How have you been, darling? It feels like we haven't talked for such a long time!" said Michelle, taking a seat in her big leather recliner, rather than cozying up to him on the couch.

Talked, thought Harlin. They never talked! Morgan sat in the recliner swirling the brandy in her snifter, waiting for Harlin's response.

"I'm fine!" he finally said. "Finer than frog's fur! I went for an excellent horseback ride in the morning, then took my bike out to Nicasio, played a little pool at the Rancho, took a nice walk through the redwoods. It was an excellent day!" He didn't mention that he'd stopped in to see his attorney to finalize the paperwork to purchase some commercial rental property. He'd decided to also start looking around for his own home to purchase. He wanted to end his engagement. It was time. Had she found out? God, it wasn't good if she did. He had hoped to have more time to silently escape when Michelle left for a business trip scheduled the next day. Now Michelle Morgan just nodded her head and smiled. "How was yours?" Harlin asked.

Morgan did not answer directly. "You happen to run into town?" she asked.

Shit, thought Harlin, becoming even more nervous.

"No," he lied.

"Hmmmm," Morgan took a long pull on the brandy, then held the snifter up before the fire, swirling it gently, watching the flames refract off the golden liquid.

Harlin felt he was suddenly on a very slippery slope.

Morgan was watching him closely over the rim of the snifter.

Harlin took his glass from the table and nearly chugged it in long gulps, as if he were drinking beer out of a bottle. He slammed the glass back onto to table and wiped his lips with his shirtsleeve.

"Well," smiled Michelle, leaning back into her recliner, "my day was going pretty well, getting prepared for my trip, you know. And I certainly had no cause to think anything strange was going to happen today until my attorney happened to call me out of the blue on my cell." She paused to take a gulp of the brandy. "So I was certainly surprised when I discovered something I had no knowledge about!"

Harlin reached over, took up the bottle, and poured himself another full snifter. Remain extra cool, he thought as he poured. But his coolness was shattered when Karl stepped out of the shadows from behind the curtain and handed him some paperwork. Harlin couldn't help but gasp when he realized his was looking at the closing papers his attorney had drawn up for escrow on the commercial properties. He placed them on the table, drained his brandy glass, and reached for the bottle.

"Surprised?" asked Morgan, leaning back in the big leather recliner and swirling the amber liquid.

"I guess. How did you find out?" asked Harlin,

"You realize, of course, what this means?" Morgan said, not answering Harlin's question, raising her eyebrows, flickering flames reflecting off the snifter she twirled in her hand.

Harlin attempted to gauge her seriousness, trying to decipher where she was going. The evidence and the way she was acting meant she knew more, and he had to be careful not to upset her any more than necessary. For the past several years, Michelle Morgan had become very accustomed to control and getting precisely what she wanted. But Harlin suddenly felt cool, collected, centered. He had been in a psychological battle with this woman from the day they met, each trying to outsmart the other. It was this mutual mistrust that in turn provided the mutual respect they built their relationship on. It was twisted, he knew, but in a way it was fun. Like sport, a motorcycle race, perhaps. At the same time, he was tired of this game. He wanted to experience love again. Love he'd missed out on with Serina. Love he hoped to experience with Shelby Jacobs, if she would allow him to.

"No Michelle," he replied after another healthy swig of brandy. "Why don't you explain it to me?" Michelle hated it when he took this patronizing tone.

"It means you are a dead man!" answered Karl, leaning over to look him in the eyes.

Harlin shoved Karl away and leaned back on the sofa. "Back off, you creep!" he snarled. Then he turned to Morgan. "So, Michelle—you plan to add murder to your list of many talents? Is that what I'm hearing?" Harlin asked, crossing his legs and sinking deeper into the sofa. Karl fumed silently by the fireplace, his neck veins starting their familiar throb.

Morgan leaned forward in her recliner. "Well, Harlin, you do enjoy your motorcycle, your horses, your unlimited access to literally anything that your heart desires, no?"

Harlin's mind spun in ultra fast circles. Michelle didn't know the extent of Harlin's wealth, something his attorney and accountant had managed to keep well hidden with the various off-shore accounts. As much as he wanted to cry out, "I'm a free agent, motherfucker!" he felt he had to go along, at least for now. Tonight. In the library. "Of course I do. Michelle—and I've always supported our relationship, your little projects, even your art collecting endeavors!" he said with an insincere smile.

"Good," said Michelle. "Because I need you."

"You need me? How so?" Harlin asked, sitting up on the edge of the couch, curious as to what his role might be in Michelle Morgan's odd, twisted mind.

"We need you to sit tight and hold off on ending our engagement until I finish this new business venture. It's huge and I can't have anything in my life rocking the boat right now," explained Michelle, even looking downright sincere.

"Otherwise, I'll be happy to apply some force," Karl added, leaning over him.

"Shut up, you fucking ape!" shouted Harlin, sick and tired of having to listen to his threats.

"You're a conniving bastard and you know it!" Karl shouted back.

"Harlin, Karl. We're going to have to work together on this," said Morgan calmly. "So may I please suggest that you each bury your respective hatchets and cooperate."

Harlin and Karl just glared at each other, then Karl reached over and took a swig right out of the brandy bottle, just to spite Harlin.

"Well shit, Michelle, how the hell long am I supposed to wait, for God's sake!" complained Harlin.

"I would never ask you to do anything that wasn't reasonable now, would I darling?" said Morgan, calmly opening her chair side humidifier and pulling out a long Cordoba, so still in vogue with the female gender. Harlin watched as she opened the silver tube and slid out the cigar. Karl reached over with the snipper as Morgan continued: I simply have no intention of pissing away over a few million dollars just so you can get a quicky elsewhere—right now appearances and not rocking the boat are everything to me. I can't allow this announcement, ending our engagement to happen just yet…I'm sure you understand that, don't you, sweetheart?"

Harlin's bullshit alarm sounded loudly in his head. She only used words like "darling" and "sweetheart" when she was lying, making excuses, or when she wanted something. This situation appeared to be a combination of all three. Morgan paused while Karl lit the cigar. Harlin decided to keep his mouth shut; he wanted to get a clear understanding of what his she had in mind.

Harlin, who had a bad feeling about where this conversation was going, became downright scared again. Both Morgan and Karl grinned, leering at him. Harlin looked from one to the other, back and forth, took a swig of brandy and coughed.

Finally Morgan said: "So you're with us then, eh, my dear?"

"Shit, Michelle, it doesn't sound like I have much of choice, does it? I'm either with you or I'm pushin' up daisies as far as I can see, and I'm not quite ready for my solemn reward just yet."

"Very well," said Morgan, standing up and tossing the half-smoked Cordoba into the fire. "Let's sleep on this little situation and regroup in the morning. Karl will you please keep an eye on my handsome fiancé tonight? We just want to make sure he doesn't get cold feet about all of this. He might be tempted to take a little midnight ride."

"What the…," Harlin started to complain.

Karl grabbed his arm.

"Hey!" he shouted.

"Be gentle, Karl!" said Morgan, smiling as she walked up the stairs to the bedroom they normally shared.

"You asshole!" Harlin shouted after her.

Morgan chuckled. "No, my dear, actually you are the asshole for wanting to bale out on me. I gave you everything and this is the thanks I get?"

"Come with me," ordered Karl.

The young waiter, like most of Michelle Morgan's staff, was actually an aspiring actor that sought to break his way into the movie business from the bottom up, like a mailroom flunky that ends up as CEO of a major corporation. And, though he was quite handsome in sort of a small, slight Tom Cruise sort of way, Harlin sensed that he was probably dumb as a post.

"Mr. Morgan," he said after he had set out the food. "I have orders not to allow you out of these quarters or to use any phones."

"Well excuuuuuse me, soldier!" Harlin laughed. "But my last name is Radner, not Morgan!"

"Either way, orders are orders, sir," said the waiter. "Now, I must ask you to give me the cell phone I just saw you sneak off my pants!" he insisted.

"Of course I will return your cell phone. But first I must ask you to take off your clothes. The young waiter stood there dumbstruck. "Remove my clothes? What for?" he asked.

Harlin pulled his own T-shirt over his head.

"Because I want you," he said, grabbing him by the lapels of his short-waisted, red waiter's coat and pulling him toward him. "I've wanted you from the moment I saw you."

The waiter blushed. "But Mr. Mor…"

He planted his lips on his, forcing his mouth open with his tongue, nibbling on his lip. Yuck, he thought, not believing what his life had turned into for the moment. The waiter pulled the waiter coat off, and reached for his belt buckle. His pants fell to the floor and he fumbled with his young hard-on poking through his briefs when Harlin pushed him into the bathroom behind him, then quickly stuffed a wash rag into the waiter's mouth before he could shout out. He then took a towel and wrapped it tightly around the waiter's head. Then Harlin tied his hands behind his back with a dinner napkin. He sat him on the toilet and tied his ankles with another towel, then stood up to survey the terrified, half naked, young man. These towels won't last long, he thought. He had to hurry. He bolted the bathroom door then put on the waiter's white shirt, black bow tie, and red jacket, then pulled on his black slacks. He picked up the cell phone, shut the door and ran down the hall.

Karl thought the waiter was taking an awfully long time and finally decided to sprint up the stairs to the guest quarters. Michelle Morgan sat down in one of the rockers in the sitting room, dipping her spoon in the vial, taking a large snort, then following it up with a healthy gulp of Absolut. Soon Karl returned with the waiter, gagged and bound with towels and stripped to his briefs. Morgan sunk her head in her hands and muttered, "Jesus," as Karl unbound the unfortunate would-be actor.

"Where is he?" Karl asked as soon as he had untied the waiter.

"I don't know where he went, sir," quaked the shivering young man in a shaky voice. "I don't know what happened after he tied me to the…to the…commode."

"And how did you happen to end up in that unfortunate state?" asked Morgan, head bowed, looking at the deck.

The waiter hugged himself, shuffled his feet, stammered. "I was…attacked," he finally said.

"By whom?" asked Morgan.

"He…he…tried to rape me," said the waiter on the verge of tears. "Then…he grabbed me."

"My fiancé tried to rape you?" asked Morgan, looking up, humiliated.

"Mam'm," Karl interrupted. "If you will excuse me, I must go find him."

"Certainly, Karl, go find him. Bring him back, kicking and screaming," Michelle Morgan said, feeling as if she was an actor in one of her own movies, powerless, following the script. Then she said to the waiter, "Son, go get some clothes on and bring me another vodka. Better yet, just bring the bottle, and a fresh glass and some ice.

Harlin, in the meantime, had made it to a dimly lit lot full of white-paneled trucks of all shapes and sizes next to the movie studio buildings. Suddenly, he stopped and crouched behind a truck. Across the lot, Karl was emerging from the sound stage, then he entered the main commercial building, and Harlin stood up. He needed one of the vehicles parked in a 5 car garage adjoining the house. So he snuck around the back of the house where he encountered another one of the house boys having a smoke on the back step.

"Hey there," he called out. The entire staff knew he was engaged to Michelle Morgan.

Quickly, he continued moving toward the garage.

"Have a good one," the lone house boy answered back and turned, stomped out his cigarette, and went up the back steps into the house.

Harlin broke into a run for the back door of the garage. He found his Harley in the dark, the key in the ignition, and rolled it out the back door. The bike roared when he started it up, and, Harlin steered it down the curvy drive toward the front gate.

Morgan, upon hearing the roar of the Harley, stood up and ran to the railing to see him drive by. She turned to the waiter, who was watching as well, and said "Where's Karl?" The young man shrugged, Morgan ran to the front door and shouted for Karl.

Then the waiter said, "Mr. Morgan, I think that's him!" And she ran back to the railing to see the black BMW emerge from the garage and tear down the drive with a squeal into the dark.

Karl saw the motorcycle's headlight nearing the front gate and bore down on the accelerator, catching up with her just as the automatic gate began to swing open. He passed them and brought the BMW to a screeching fishtailing stop in front of the gate, swinging around perpendicular to the road to block his exit. Harlin slammed on the brakes and attempted to turn the bike around but Karl was already out of the car running towards him, yelling. Harlin jumped off and stumbled backwards to the pavement.

Karl jumped on Harlin, pinning him. "You think you are so smart!" he hissed.

Harlin raised Karl slightly away from him, pulled up his leg and kneed Karl in the groin, hard; very hard. Karl screamed out in pain, rolling off Harlin.

Harlin scambled back up, ran to the BMW, got in, revved the running engine, speeding away.

Karl managed to get up when he heard the engine roar and attempted to run after the car, only to get sprayed with dust as it screeched through the open gate, out onto the dark country road and into the night.

Chapter 28

SEVERAL WEEKS LATER

Serina had been back at the Lake Tahoe cabin for weeks, painting, thinking, re-examining, and looking for someone or something to blame for her current miserable state. 1Jacobs felt as if her life had been hijacked by art. After Stefan had finally walked out the door for good, she imploded, lost contact with the outside world of humanity, lost herself in nature, paint, canvas, and her ever present music. Now, she realized that, even though she hoped her paintings brought something—pleasure, pain, whatever—to the usually anonymous owners, she had no one to please. And it was her need to please somebody, in some way, that was the source of all her motivation. Unfortunately she had chosen Harlin Radner as the person she wanted to please most only a short few months ago—a figment of her imagination, placing him up on this fantasy pedestal—not even bothering to check if the man was even remotely available.

Then, out of the blue, when her brain wasn't functioning in a rational manner after her cold swim in the Pacific Ocean in the middle of the night, she meets Antonio. Should she pursue the relationship? Or, was she just plain jinxed when it came to men. And what about her future; she was considered dead, as in no more, gone forever, shark meat.

Confused and dejected, she got up, went to the fridge, surveyed the contents and, seeing there was nothing to eat, settled on a glass of merlot. Then turning to the cupboards she found a can of tuna and a box of Triscuits…and realized that, though her bank account was quite healthy (another separate bank account set up in Shelby's name—the money from the sales of her paintings at Rex Wilcox's gallery), she had in reality come full circle and was more alone than ever. She took a big sip of her wine and reached for the can opener.

It's just too hard. All of it. Just. Too. Hard.

Not just life, or being dead, but this thing with Antonio. It's just too hard. She couldn't win no matter how hard she tried.

She got used to being alone. Got scared sometimes of ending up lonely. But knew that was better than the alternative—hooked up with someone she didn't really want to be around anyhow. Better to be all alone. Forever. Even if she hated it. Hated being alone. Hated having no one to talk to, no one to look at, no one to look at her. No one to touch. Nothing but her own thoughts.

And then somehow along the way with Antonio, she stopped adding it all up and just gave in. Gave in because it felt good. Gave in because he was so good. Everyone was special. But to Serina, he was a miracle.

Magic.

And she couldn't figure out what she did to earn his affection. But now she may have made a deal and had to hold up her end. Before it was easier. No one expected shit from her. Not even her mere presence. Not her body. Not happiness.

Him and those big dark eyes. Imploring, exploring hers. It was almost a curse that he was born with those eyes, the way they reveaedl everything. All his happiness, all his pain.

And now she'd taken it upon herself mentally to look at them; suffer if he suffered; take away every trace of pain. And she was convinced he counted on her to do exactly that. To make him happy. Serina loved him and gave in to him and fought for him and trusted him and she got hurt for him and went right back for more. She gave him that hope.

How could she follow through now? There was no handbook for this. No training seminar. There were no posted odds to know if this was wise or not. Would she or could she succeed?

All she really wanted was less. Less stress. Less sadness.

Didn't everyone? And the way to have that was to separate from society. But aloneness devoured. Isolation devoured. People felt less, searched for less.

But somewhere deep inside, people still *wanted* more. They craved.

And finally she figured it out and had no clue what to do with the knowledge. Worse, she was terrified of having it ripped away. She'd wanted less, and had experienced less. And then when she got more, she greedily sucked it up and now she was so scared of having it taken away that part of her wished she never had it in the first place.

Poof! Just like that, it could all disappear as though it never was.

But all he really wanted was her. And she didn't know what that was. Who that was. She had no idea what he saw and how to keep giving it to him. What he liked was what she was, and what she was, was *dead, the live her was named Shelby.* Shit! And alone.

Before, she figured she was more or less always happy. Until suddenly she was *really* happy. Then she realized she had been really sad. And now she was sad because she was happy. Because happiness could fade, and then she'd be sad again. And she would have to go back to fake being happy. And the saddest part was that maybe she would forget how it felt to be really happy.

Poof!

More importantly, she hoped he was happy. That'd be more than enough.

She rubbed her eyes and munched on the tuna on crackers.

The cell phone rang. It was Antonio returning her call.

Chapter 29

That afternoon, the phone rang in Shelby's office and it was Sherri.

"Don's an asshole," were her first words.

Silence.

"I mean it. We had a fight. I was driving, and he was telling me what a shitty job I was doing driving. He kept yelling at me about not looking out of the right mirror to see behind me."

"Right. Because you were using a cosmetic mirror instead of the rear view as you traditionally do."

"I'm serious, Jacobs. He really was freaking out on me about it. He screamed at me to pull over and insisted on driving. Then he yelled at me some more, saying he couldn't get any rest and had to do everything because I can't do anything, I can't even drive."

"Because it's so taxing for him to drive to the store to pick up a carton of eggs."

"He says he's under all this pressure, and I don't understand pressure and the kind he's under."

"Ok, is he a person or a lump of coal being squished into a diamond?"

"This new job, me being here, he just says he's under pressure all the time and he's on the verge of blowing."

"Ooooh, that's good. So he's more like a volcano."

"This is serious. I don't know what to do."

"What do you suppose he'd spew when he blows? You know, like instead of lava and ash would he just erupt by shouting a bunch of incomplete sentences and dangled participles?"

"Please."

"Ok. So. He begged you to come live with him, and now he's telling you that it's putting him under pressure. He is an asshole. Just leave and go home to your place. Take some of the pressure off him. We'll go to Vegas. Maybe that PR guy will take you out."

"Jarred? Serina told you about Jarred?"

"Whooo! Listen to you, remembering his name."

"No, I'm staying right here. I'm going to make this work. I'm staying."

This continued for a few more rounds. She bitched about him, the fact that he was an asshole, and clearly she was unhappy. But, by God, she was staying with her man.

So finally, Shelby said, "You want to get away for awhile? You could come with me to Vegas for a few days anyhow."

"I'm not going out with that other guy." She waited a beat. "When are you going?"

"Sunday. I planned on leaving here on Sunday."

"How long?" she asked.

"A week."

"You're going to see Antonio?" she asked.

"I don't know, yet. Serina and all, you know?"

"I know," she said. "Don's home now, I have to go."

Two hours later, she called back.

"Don has off starting Sunday. We're coming out to Vegas to meet you. And get married."

"Great!"

Chapter 30

Here was the deal. Serina asked Antonio to meet her at Caesars in Tahoe. Asked him to drive up her way from Las Vegas. Not that he knew she lived in Lake Tahoe. He thought she was Shelby. Shelby who lived and worked in San Francisco

And Lake Tahoe was quite breathtaking. Antonio had never been there before.

The water of the lake sparkled around the palaces and resorts. The mountains were snow-capped. Less manic. More balanced in Tahoe. Like nature and commerce had reached an amicable détente.

Caesars was on the south side of the lake, right on the California border, rustic and serene. The buildings in Tahoe weren't squashed right on top of each other like in Vegas. And instead of the cascading lights bouncing off hard, worn pavement with concrete sucking up every square inch, there was grass and trees and water filling in the blanks. Not the manufactured lake like at Bellagio, but real water. It somehow came across as a harmonic dichotomy of natural and manufactured. Whereas in Vegas, there wasn't much nature other than sand, so it just got built to the hilt until it became the thriving, gaudy display it was today. In Lake Tahoe, man's hand was evident; it just wasn't as greedy looking.

Serina loved it.

At the same time, she wasn't sure if it was quite as honest as Vegas. Or maybe because the gambling in Tahoe wasn't the main focus, maybe it wasn't actually as corrupt as Vegas.

Nah. They were just more subtle with the illusions out here. Maybe even *more* deceptive. Maybe it wasn't all about gambling in Tahoe, but it was still all about money; money ruled the world, after all. Out here they just used the soft sell. Padded it all in lush scenes that would make Thoreau's heart swell at the serenity and majesty. Careful not to destroy that ambience, made it seem all so natural, like the money was just a passing distraction. It didn't entertain with bright lights and big booms to get you to empty your pockets out with hollers and yelps. Instead, it just sort of lulled and swaddled you in peacefulness so the money just floated out of your wallet with an easy sigh and gentle wink.

Serina met Antonio in the Caesars main lobby and they checked in then headed to their room to drop off their luggage. They started kissing in the elevator on the way up. They were making out as soon as he got the door open; she pulled his shirt over his head, kicked off her sandals; he tugged at the zipper of her pants, dragging her inside.

Heading towards the bed, stumbling, clothes falling—his shirt, her shorts. Fumbling in the doorway with his belt. She unbuckling it, and always more kissing. Hard, wet kisses. Kisses with teeth, touches with nail. He picked her up. Tossed her. Her heart beating even harder when she landed on the bed, him jumping on top of her, panting.

He was panting, kissing, rubbing all over her, pulling at her clothes. They got her underwear off, they manage to get his pants unzipped, peeled back. Her shirt still on, his shoes still on, he attempted to pull away to finish stripping, but she couldn't wait. She pulled him down.

Cooing to him, "I'm yours, fuck me," reaching for him, stroking him and guiding him closer.

He crushed her mouth with another kiss, full tongue, the bite of teeth, as she wrapped her legs around his waist, trying to press up and make him enter her. God, she wanted him, needed him, desired him, right at this very instant.

Breathless, he groaned, "I'm gonna come too quick. We gotta slow down or I'm gonna come."

"So am I," she panted, crazy with desire.

He pushed in. Swift, hard, he entered with a grunt, forcing one out of her with the impact. Shameless, she moved against him, gripping him tight as he began thrusting away—no tamed control, no working into a groove, just grinding into each other.

"Mine," he growled as he pumped away. "Mine, uh, *mine*, you're MINE!"

She didn't know if it was his words, his voice, because she hadn't seen him in awhile, but she loved it.

"Te quiero, so fuckin bad. You, too, you get off, get off on me," he ordered. He plunged deep and stayed buried inside, stopping his movements. Sliding a hand down, Antonio massaged demandingly at her hot spot, pulling even more feeling out of her. Rubbing hungrily, he moved his hips, picking up the same frenetic pace he'd just interrupted. She groaned at the power of it, shivered with the goodness of it, and he groaned right back in answer.

She could feel it starting to build, everything getting too intense, rushing too hard, feeling too insanely good. Then he resorted to panting out single words, Spanish and English mixed together as his chest heaved up. Growling, "You, mine…caliente, vienes…ahora, come…ahora. I'm…uh…uh…I'm YOURS!"

That did it, and she came instantly. It swept through her as he sucked her tongue and it was like a clap of thunder hitting. His hand outside rubbing, his dick deep inside pumping, those words, "I'm yours," all colliding together and—CRACK!

She wailed, simply couldn't choke it back. Couldn't talk, couldn't tell him she was experiencing an orgasm, but he had to know; she no longer grinded against him, just shuddered—hard. Grabbing his wrist, she pulled his hand away, unable to withstand it any more, but he continued pumping inside, even harder, forcing more breath, more shudders, more shocks out of her. She bit his shoulder and that apparently did it for him, something did, because he started shuddering, groaning loud, gave a couple last involuntary thrusts deep inside. He hissed and shivered, but didn't pull out, just collapsed down into her.

Neither of them moved for awhile. She wasn't sure she could move. He was heavy on top of her, moist breath exhaling onto her neck. She stroked her hand up and down his back as he softened and slipped out. What was only a few minutes ago an overwhelming animal desire was softened, morphing back down into something less wild, but altogether more dangerous and just as powerful.

She knew she felt the other. She wondered if he felt this, too. If he felt the same toward her. This, whatever it was. Closeness. Gratitude and wonder. Affection, perfection; affinity, divinity—

Love.

Antonio checked her out before proceeding downstairs to get in some gambling just for fun. "Wow!" he whistled.

That was all she needed. It refreshed her, one little three letter word.

As soon as they sat down, she fell into the gambling groove, kind of unusual since this was more Shelby's thing, counting the cards. But it was Shelby who taught her the art years before. Serina had never been able to get it down to perfection.

Something strange happened in the middle of the third shoe. She was rolling just fine, but Antonio got up and left the table. She guessed he was going to do his own thing so she played the shoe out, watched the shuffle and waited to see if he came back. Ten hands into the next shoe, when the count went pretty bad and he hadn't returned, she got up to leave.

She found him at a nearby bar. "You left me," she said, sliding up next to him.

"Yeah, figured I'd leave 'stead o' losing my winnings for a change."

"You did that good?"

"You bet," he said, tossing several chips in her direction. "Wanna cash them in?"

They were thousand dollar chips, eight of them. "You got all these?"

"Huh uh. That's only half." His eyes were twinkling.

"Stop!"

"Shhhh," he laughed. "They don't blink as much here, people playing and winning big money, but still."

"Let's go somewhere else and try to win more!" How come when she was drop dead poor, she never won? Wasn't that always the way; now that she was filthy rich, she was winning money like it was going out of style. But it was fun! It explained Shelby's gambling fever.

It was a great day. Instead, he used the gym, then joined her for a swim afterward at the indoor pool, a really nice one. All decked out with waterfalls and lagoons. They had it almost all to themselves. They splashed and they dunked and they slipped against each other, dove around each other; all good, wet, brainless fun.

It was strange, being out of Antonio's town and in this different setting, just blowing off and goofing around. And it was relaxed and cool. They weren't in a frenetic rush to do it all and do too much and fearing they weren't doing enough. There were no decisions to make; where to go, whether or not to stay, what to do. It had somehow all been decided and taken care of. There was no fretting about the past or worrying about what was to come.

It was a brainless period of time, and she was loving it.

And she knew she was going to tune up and pour it on really soon, but that wasn't a problem either. Because she could do it and knew exactly how to do it. All she had to do was let herself do it. And he would pull her along and fuck her until everything melted away and she would be oblivious and brainless all over again.

Upstairs they ordered room service as they get showered and dressed and the day slipped into evening.

Time to gamble.

It was an excellent evening.

Everything clicked. At least eventually. They hit a couple of rough spots. They were at Harvey's, where they just passed a rough spot; bad count, bad cards, bad luck, losing hands. But a new shoe was being shuffled and she had them tracked; there were two spots with a nice big lump of faces to be played. And her mind was humming along perfectly.

Empty. Brainless. She was just gobbling up the cards and notching the numbers higher or lower without any effort, like it was second nature. Almost like the constant numbers popping in her head were a mantra. A meditative chant that removed her from the moment and delved her deeper into it at the same time. Making her *part* of it.

True count +3, the deck was due to bleed out face cards and a couple aces according to where she marked them in the shuffle. She played two hands with doubled bets. As the dealer started sliding out the hands she notices that Valdez is in the action, too. He had three hands spread before him. Such a good, smart boy.

He got dealt double aces and split them, blackjacking one. She blackjacked one of her hands. He also pulled a nine on top of his other ace, had a pair of faces, and a junk hand totaling 14. He hit his 14, got a 4 and stood pat. Jacobs's other hand was 12 facing the dealer 8, so she hit it. She drew a queen and busted that one. But the dealer flipped her hole card to show a 7 and took her hit, getting a ten. Five out of six hands of theirs win, including a bona fide 3:2 paying blackjack for Jacobs.

The thrill and excitement bubbled to her head, a pure rush of winning adrenaline unleashed as the tension faded.

She hadn't looked at Antonio's bets. But now she saw him slide the dealer a nice fat tip, and as she follows suit, the pit boss came over to watch them play. Her heart fluttered under his intense scrutiny, but she kept the count going anyhow. She didn't watch Rodriguez's bets and made some deliberately bad increases, senseless drop offs. Instead of betting the way the count said she should, she bet according to wins. Since she'd just won, she increased her bet even though a wad of faces just splashed in front of her. She won the hand anyhow, even more faces splashing across the table in the right places. She should drop back, but didn't. Jacobs added even more to her ante and caught the pit boss' eyes flickering on her probably thinking with that dubious glance—*lucky dumb bitch.*

Because Jacobs knew what he knew. He knew how to play, and he knew how to count. Even if he couldn't keep up a count as well as she could, he knew that after that many faces any real player would drop off. But she increased her bet anyhow because she was high and winning. He probably thought she knew a little about the game, and she was riding a lucky wave. He didn't seem to begrudge her the winning streak; rather he seemed amused. But then he went back to hawkeyeing Antonio. Because *he* had the big money, and he just made the big score.

The guy had to be wondering exactly what the fuck was going on. Were they really that lucky? That maybe his instinct was to underestimate her, but that he also knew better. This was his job.

So even though that instinctual thought of *lucky dumb bitch* flitted through his head, it was immediately followed up by a more learned and reasoned response to keep hawkeyeing and re-evaluating the situation. Right now, maybe he was thinking that Antonio was the counter because of how he backed off. Or maybe it was Jacobs and they were screwing off intentionally to avoid his wrath.

Or maybe they really were just a couple of lucky dumb fucks who stumbled on his table tonight. That was why he had to stay cool and be diplomatic. He couldn't just spark up, mouth off, let loose, and hustle them out of there quite yet. Because other appearances might be deceiving. The mere fact that they were here meant they had to consider their wallets more seriously than if they just saw them walking down the street. And a person just never quite knew when some rich folks might be slumming.

Whatever.

The point was, this guy, the pit boss, he wouldn't just toss them out or hassle them while there was the possibility they were dumbfucks with fat wallets the casino could claw into. And he wouldn't take the chance that they weren't dumbfucks; that they were indeed systematically lowering the profit margin of the casino. So he would do the only thing he could do right now.

Watch.

And Jacobs and Valdez did the only reasonable thing they could do.

Cut the shit.

But not to the point of backsliding and losing money. They could also just get up and leave if it got to that point.

Jacobs decided to increase her bet even though she shouldn't, then played out the hand and pulled out a win based on sheer luck alone. This amused her and she couldn't conceal a grin. She managed to clamp down a couple of giggles.

Because that's how it went sometimes. It was in the cards, all in the cards. Even though she read them and it should all be going wrong, things just clicked and out they came to make her a winner. And she was by no means a seasoned pro like Shelby.

It was a very good night.

There were no auxiliary thoughts or desperate pangs. No looming deadlines to finish paintings for an art show, no one breaking balls and no one with semi-broken balls chewing into her psyche. It was exactly what it should be—a game.

And Jacobs was concentrating, and therefore brainless, and it was fun.

The pit boss never did say anything, no other floor personnel hovered around them either, so they must have fooled them. Or, probably they didn't, but they stopped and left before the casino decided to ask them to leave. They both cashed out approximately six grand each and they weren't carded while doing so. Better yet, they had more chips they chose not to cash. Lots of them.

They were up; way up.

They decided to go to Harrah's to try their luck there. Jacobs played her hands, watched the count, sidetracked the aces, and kept an eye on the discard pile. Fell right into the rhythm of the game over there, too. Deep in concentration, lucid of her surroundings, relaxed and comfortable.

Antonio pushed back his chair and walked away. She could tell by his saunter that he was done for the night. Was she getting to know him, or what? Time to hang out, he'd update her on the money situation, maybe they would have some drinks and then he'd fuck her brains out again. And maybe if they fell into a pretty good groove, she'd be able to fuck him semi-conscious and oblivious, too. They could get lost in one another.

Lost and fucking in Lake fucking Tahoe.

She was right. He took them back to Caesars and ordered a couple drinks. Filled her in on where they stood.

Leaning conspiratually close, "I got over twelve grand in cash on me."

She nodded, lit a cigarette, and started flipping it around her fingers as she sipped at her drink.

"'Jacobs, we got lots o' chips. Figure I'll leave 'em that way 'stead o' sweatin out the tax man."

"Will that work?"

"Shit yeah. Just told you, got twelve large cash. That'll pay our room here, be our bankroll. The rest can stay in plastic, won't have to worry 'bout losing it in a bad streak then."

"Yeah, but, I know you said they'll take chips, but that's Vegas ones. We're a long ways from Vegas. Won't they be pissed about coming all the way out here?"

"Listen to me. I got a lot o' chips. They won't think twice about driving out here to cash in on seventy-two thousand dollars."

She choked and her cigarette burned her ring finger as she hit a dead stop. She dropped it and shook her hand, still coughing up her vodka. She retrieved the smoke and hit it hard, then crushed it out. Pulled an ice cube from the drink and soothed it across the tiny burn on her finger. She took another drink and asked the question. "You want to repeat that to me?"

"You heard me."

"I couldn't have heard you right."

"You did. Why you think that boss came an' eyefucked us so hard? Then we added s'more over at Harrah's, too."

"Holy shit, Antonio. I, I don't know what to say."

He leaned back in his chair, squinted at her. "Yeah? I do. Thank you, that's what I gotta say."

"My pleasure. Wasn't just me, though."

"Yeah, was mostly you. You know, we do make a good team, though."

"Yes, we really do. Apparently. We're like Cruise and Hoffman, man."

"Dude," he said and lit a smoke, "nah."

"We are, though," she insisted. "We're like Cruise and Hoffman. Only with tattoos."

Him grinning, "And sex."

"And without the cool room at Caesars."

"And them seizures."

"They weren't seizures," she corrected. "They were fits."

"What-EVER," he said with a laugh. "Course, you do sorta have your own kinda freak outs I guess."

"Oh, fuck off, Valdez."

"I mean it, though. I mean about us. We're a good couple, you know. We're cool together, don't you think?"

She smiled in agreement.

"'Jacobs, can I ask you something?"

Aww, shit. That was just never any fucking good. She nodded gamely, taking a big gulp from her drink.

He squinted at her again. "You catchin a buzz?"

She chewed on an ice cube. "No, this is my first drink. Could use another if we're done for the night, though." She knew that wasn't the actual question. He had something else he was working up to. She glanced around, avoiding his eyes, momentarily delaying the imminent query. Then she softened and met his gaze, giving him the opening.

Then it came. She was expecting something to come out of left field, something somewhat odd or unexpected lobbed in her general vicinity. Instead it was a 92 MPH fastball straight from the pitcher's mound and it beaned her right in the melon before she even had a chance to flinch, let alone duck.

"Ready to marry me, Shelby?"

Serina Jacobs spit ice chips everywhere and knocked over her glass. Then she leaped to her feet to avoid the cubes and the remaining liquid that was pouring all over the small table between them. Heart pounding, she began shaking as she vainly tried to pick up the slippery ice cubes. Shelby, he proposed to "Shelby". Oh my God! Did Antonio know Shelby? Oh my God; it never occurred to her that he might actually know the real Shelby. Did he? Shit! When he first met her, did he think she was Shelby then? She couldn't remember if she ever told him her first name. Had he ever seen any of her I.D.?

Antonio helped her scoop them back into the glass, then got up, and went to the bar to ask for a towel to mop up the mess.

"Sorry," she said as she smoothed her hair back and sat back down again. Desperately, she attempted to hide her shaking hands.

He grinned when he took his seat, saying, "Shocked you, huh?"

"Yeah." Her laugh was shaky. Maybe this was some sort of weird joke.

He rested his arms on the table, leaned forward and nervously licked his lips. "I uh, I wasn't kidding."

Wishful thinking wasn't working. God, who the hell was he proposing to? The real Shelby, or Serina, the fake Shelby?

His eyebrows raised, his eyes wide; that innocent, earnest look. "I'm in love with you, Shelby Jacobs. I never thought, you know, that I'd be like this. An' it ain't gonna change…"

She gulped and twisted her ring around on her finger under the table. As he continued talking, her skin suddenly felt very hot and her head hummed. She could laugh right now. She could cry. She didn't know what the fuck to do.

She stared at him while he talked. Thinking: *Oh, Jesus. What have I done?* He was calm and cool, professing his undying love for "Shelby". And he was oblivious. *I've really gone and done it. This is my fault. MY fault. I've gone and fucked his brains out. I wanted to do it. I said I wanted to do it, and now I have. In one short week I've gone and fucked him senseless. Shelby! Shit, why didn't she say anything? Damn. Didn't she, Serina, think she love this man?*

And he was *still* talking. "…want everyone to know. I know it's soon, it's really quick, but I'm sure o' this, baby…"

Her hands were clamped together under the table, shaking. Here's what she was going to do; look at him, but she'd stop listening now. She had to stop listening or else her head was going to explode. He still talked, telling her how he needed her. That's why she couldn't let this happen, her head exploding, that is. Because if her head exploded, she'd lose control of her mind, her speech, everything. And worse yet, as she looked at him, brainless or not, as appalling and scary as this was right now, she really could climb all over him and give it a winning try to fuck him. That's how much he turned her on. Harlin? Where was Harlin in her mind? He needed to save her from this mess right now.

Oh my GOD!

He was getting off his chair but he wasn't getting *up*. He's getting *down*. Holy *shit*, he was down on one knee and he was taking her hand! OH. OH. GAH. She can't look away. Riveted. As though watching a crash in slow motion. She should stop him, say something. Why couldn't she think of something to *say*? It was, it was too late. He was talking, he was going to say it. He was…

"Shelby, please? Will you marry me?"

Frozen.

Deer in the headlights, knife to her throat, unwanted marriage proposal. *Frozen.*

He was watching her. Expectantly. Hopefully.

Wide eyed, kid on Christmas morning, down on one knee proposing. *Hopeful.*

She…She couldn't hurt him. She could NOT hurt him. She couldn't say *no.*

Looking at him. She was looking at him. She couldn't hurt him and tell him no.

But…

She couldn't DO this. She couldn't do THIS. She COULDN'T do this. It wasn't his fault, was it? Serina wasn't Shelby; how could he know?

Why? WHY was this happening? Why was he doing this? She thought he knew her.

He DID know her, until he lost the last vestiges of his fucked senseless mind and became confused between sisters; two of three identical sisters.

He was so sweet and he was so handsome and he was so smart and he was so strong and mostly he was just so good. And she couldn't do this. She couldn't hurt him. She couldn't make him feel foolish.

"I love you, Antonio. I love you so much." He looked up at her, but his eyes wavered, they were losing their sureness. "Please, I love you, get up, though. Get up, not like that, not like this."

"I, I..." he stuttered a couple of times as she pleaded and nudged him up, back into his chair.

She could only think of one thing to say. And as she sat there looking at him she knew it wasn't the right thing. She couldn't just *reject* him outright. And she couldn't say yes. How could this happen like this? One minute cruising along, and the next spinning out of control. Like a powerful freight train that suddenly, inexplicably jerked and derailed. Things were taking a giant leap into the proverbial shitter here. And she knew it, knew before she said it, even though it was the only thing she could think of to say—the only one option, so she uttered it:

"I have to go to the bathroom."

Before she even started to stand up, she knew it, knew what happened to them:

Antonio and Shelby (the Serina Shelby).

They just jumped the shark.

She staggered awkwardly to the closest public bathroom, clutching her purse, feeling as lightheaded as if she'd just downed a pint of vodka and taken back-to-back hits from a water bong. Totally unsteady. Heavy-hearted as though she'd just run over a puppy on the highway.

How did this happen? Things were humming and running along fine, and now, suddenly, *bam!* Like a C-4 rigged piñata exploding worm-infested candy. I didn't know what or who to blame here. It had all been just so freaking PERFECT.

Shit. Holy Shit.

How the fuck were they going to fix this? How was she going to fix this? There were no reasonable, palatable options here. My God, she had *sex* with him. Oh God, did Shelby have *sex* with him?

This wasn't even supposed to happen.

Under the sallow lights, she stared grimly at her reflection and fought off the hyperventilation that threatened to overtake her. She didn't know what to do. She couldn't say yes, she couldn't say no.

Walking out of the bathroom, she saw him from afar. Sitting there waiting for her. He was fidgeting. One leg, bouncing up and down. Slumped down in his chair, his fist against his temple, supporting his heavy head. Even from this distance, she saw him swallow, his eyebrows wrinkled together with downcast eyes.

There was no doubt how his eyes were going to look when she went back over there. They'd be dark and opaque, possibly picking up some reflections from the lights above. Certainly reflecting the disappointment and pain.

She couldn't see that.

She couldn't DO this.

She did the only thing she could.

She bolted.

Chapter 31

"Well obviously I've got to get my sorry ass out of town," said Harlin to Shelby Jacobs.

"Jeez, Harlin," answered Shelby, laughing. "I'm leaving here shortly for Vegas. My sister, Sherri, is marrying this jerk, Don, and I promised to come." Harlin had called her out of the blue at her office to tell her about his escape from his soon to be ex-fiancé.

"A marriage?" he asked. "Are Rex Wilcox and that McFadden surgeon going to the wedding?"

"No, uh, uh. Rex and McFadden said they were taking off for a six month vacation to Europe, didn't you know? After making all that money from the sales of Serina's paintings, they decided to have some fun for awhile."

"You're kidding? Rex Wilcox has flown the coop?" said Harlin, surprised. Then a thought dawned on him. "Hey, could you handle some company, and maybe an escort to the wedding. It'd be a great way for me to lay low until things calm down with Michelle a bit if I come along."

"Come along?" asked Jacobs, confused.

"Yeah, come along. You're the one who kind of got me into this mess with your wicked beauty and charm, so it's only right you help get me out of it!" Harlin said, suddenly sounding quite serious. "You made me realize I did not, no way, no how, want to remain engaged to Michelle, let alone marry her. I guess Serina made me begin to think along that line before she died"

Shelby paused, took a swig of her cold coffee that was still sitting on her desk, wiped her lips with her shirtsleeve when she tasted that god awful stuff, then did the same across her forehead, where beads of perspiration had begun to form. As far as she knew, Serina was at the Tahoe cabin. Antonio. She'd risk it. If he didn't know she was coming and Serina wasn't in town, what was the harm. She still had to figure this all out after the wedding. She and Serina had to talk. Like, Serina needed her own separate life—like a legal life! That would be good.

"Listen, Shelby Jacobs," Harlin continued, now almost in a teasing whisper on the other end of the line. "I have a rich, sleazy fiancé—dangerous as well. So if you've got even the tiniest little smidgen of integrity…"

She let out a long, loud sigh. "Ok, ok…enough Harlin," she interrupted. "You can come if you can get a flight out." She quickly gave him her flight information.

"All right, then!" said Harlin. "Catch you at the airport."

Sherri and Don arrived in Las Vegas to get married about the same time Shelby and Harlin did. Shelby quickly introduced Harlin Radner, then rented a car and they all went out to dinner together at Morton's, finally, one of Shelby's favorite restaurants.

Don was saying, "So then I looked at her and said, 'Let's just do it. We're going to get married anyhow, let's do it out there.' And Sherri agreed. She doesn't always do the smartest things, but I think this was a good decision."

Sherri flinched at his last comment, but didn't say anything.

Shelby and Harlin remained pretty quiet, content to just listen to them. When they ordered, Shelby decided on the 48 oz. porterhouse, and Don called her on it. "Why would you get that? You'll never be able to finish it with everything else; that just doesn't make sense. It's too much."

Harlin laughed, "I don't think she knows the meaning of 'too much'."

She retorted, "I get it cause it tastes the best. The smaller one doesn't taste the same. Who cares if I eat it all?" Then she ordered the Godiva chocolate cake for dessert.

Don turned his attention to Harlin. "So what do you do, Harlin?"

Harlin took a swig of his beer, and answered, "I'm into horses; riding, breeding, traveling."

They talked about that as Sherri told Shelby that they had to get dresses tomorrow. "Or tonight, if we're buzzed up and it sounds like a fun thing to do."

Harlin was mid-sentence, telling Don about his training, but Don cut him off, put his attention back on Sherri, saying, "You aren't going out shopping tonight all drunk. That's stupid. You'll get them tomorrow."

"But it'll be fun tonight," she said. "We both hate shopping, especially for dresses. We'll want to get sun at the pool tomorrow."

"I'm getting the license tomorrow, you can get dresses. You don't need sun. You can do something for this wedding, put some effort into it. I don't want to watch you shop tonight."

She watched Sherri slump and look dejected. "You know, Don," she started, "I'd rather do it tonight…"

"It's ok, Shelby," she cut in. "Tomorrow is fine." She put on a big, bright, fake smile.

Harlin just slugged his beer and bumped his knee into hers under the table.

Don said, "These girls, you know? Nothing but trouble, don't you think, Harlin?"

"Nope. Sometimes, they can be kinda fun."

Don began to prod him. "So what did you notice first about Shelby other than that she's Serina and Sherri's duplicate image? You know, when you saw her again after all these years?"

Harlin smirked. "Her tits."

She slapped him hard across the arm as he ducked and laughed. "Pig!" she said, laughing. "Hey, I gotta be honest. It was your tits I noticed first."

"I do have nice tits," she said.

"Humph. You never flash them when it's necessary," Sherri chided.

"The first thing I noticed about Sherri was her smile. *First* thing," Don emphasized.

"What does your dad do?" he asked, completely changing track.

"Sales," he answered as the salads are served. "But he died."

"What did he die of?" Don pressed.

Shelby decided this was going into sensitive areas and tried to end the inquisition. "Don," she said. "Stop prying and eat your salad."

"I'm not prying. I just wonder what happened to his dad.

Harlin looked him dead in the eye, "'My dad was murdered in his penthouse in San Francisco 'cause of a burglary gone bad and I don't fuckin care to talk about it."

"Oh," was all Don said as he stuck a fork in his salad. "So how did you two get together?"

"I sorta met her again at the art show for Serina," answered Harlin. "An' me and her been friends since then."

"She and I," Don corrected.

Jacobs took the napkin off her knees and tossed it on the table.

Harlin just said, "Excuse me?"

"You said 'me and her', but it should be 'she and I', that's proper grammar."

"Oh. Whatever," answered Harlin.

Don dug in some more, getting excited. "No, no. It's not whatever. It's important. Language, you see, is a method of communicating. And when you speak, it's important you do it well, because you're communicating things about yourself. And if you speak poorly or improperly, you're conveying that to other people. You don't want them to think less of you because of how you speak, so..."

"Communicate this, Don," Shelby Jacobs interrupted. "Fuck you, ok?"

He blinked at her and looked ready to start into his speech again.

She did not even let him get in a word. "You're right," she continued. "Language is to communicate. And Harlin here communicated something to you. Now either you're too stupid to understand what he was saying or you're too uptight to bother listening. Take your pick. I don't really care. He communicates just fine. You're the one with the problem, you're just so wrapped up in lording your superiority over people that you don't listen to what they're saying. You just look for flaws so you can correct them. That communicates a hell of a lot more than 'she and I' or 'me and her' does any day. So don't you ever deign to communicate to him by being condescending to him. Are you understanding what I'm *communicating* to you, Shakespeare? I take your mouth all the time to keep the peace, and Sherri takes it for whatever reason. But he," Shelby wagged her fork in Harlin's direction, "doesn't ever have to take it."

Under the table, Harlin squeezed her knee and she knew he was fighting really hard to not bust out laughing.

Sherri looked stunned, but it seemed like she was fighting off a smirk, too.

For his part, Don took it amazingly well. He blinked a few times, probably deciding which way to roll with it. Maybe he could tell that no one was on his side. Or maybe he knew he was being an asshole and was willing to admit he got called out on it. He simply dived his fork into his salad and said, "So I presume you like him, then?"

"Yes," she answered. "I like him." Then she continued to eat her salad.

After dinner they went for drinks at the bar in the Polo Towers. She'd never been there before, didn't even know about it. It had an absolutely stunning view of the Bellagio, New York New York, Alladin, and MGM. Not to mention some damn good drinks and a quiet ambience, too. Shelby's heartbeat quickened a little whenever she stared at the Bellagio—Antonio.... Sherri was beat by eleven, so she drove them to their hotel; they were staying at Treasure Island.

The bellman took Shelby and Sherri up to their suite. It was magnificent. The regular rooms and suites at Caesars were something to see in the nice sections—they had hot tubs and stand up showers and mirrors in cool places and they were all plush and spacious. But this—this was really something to see. It had a foyer and living room and huge high definition TV, a great view of the strip and two full bathrooms with frosted glass doors and multi-nozzled showers and marble everywhere. A giant Jacuzzi in one of them, another hot tub in the bedroom, fully stocked bar, mini-fridge. Very swank, very high-roller. Harlin had insisted on paying since he'd invited himself to tag along with Shelby.

She looked around, whistled. "Yeah, alright, man, we can stay here."

By the time they settled into their suite, there was a message from Sherri. Her voice was tight. She said she'd see Shelby tomorrow at the pool; she would call to wake Shelby up. She wondered when they were going to get the dresses.

Chapter 32

When Sherri called the next day at 8 a.m., Shelby told her they were still sleeping and that she would call her back in a couple of hours. She bitched that it would be really crowded at the pool by then, so Shelby told her to go down and save her a lounge chair. She didn't want to do that, and wasn't happy, but Shelby hung up, thereby forcing Sherri to accept that proposal, like it or not.

Later that morning Shelby joined Sherri and they ordered drinks; alcoholic drinks. They were really supposed to be looking at dresses within the hour. They laid out in the sun and drank instead.

She'd set up the wedding for late that night. Booked the pirate ship at Treasure Island. That cost a nice penny more than just getting hitched in a chapel, but she figured it'd be fun. More memorable. Shelby told her she would pay for the ceremony as her wedding present. So they had time in the evening to go shopping. Don was off doing his own stuff for the day; Shelby convinced him they should be traditional and not see each other until the wedding. Harlin was off doing his thing somewhere. So the two of them set up at the pool to waste the afternoon.

Four hours, six beers, minimal conversation and an entire pack of cigarettes later, she said: "I can't get married tonight."

"Ok," Shelby answered. "Then don't."

"No, I mean it, Shelby. I can't do this. I'm not ready."

"You don't have to. You really shouldn't be getting married without your Serina around anyhow. She'll be pissed if she misses it."

"You have to help me," she said.

"What the hell do you want me to do about it?"

"I can't just blow off the wedding. Don would kill me. I don't want him pissed at me. You have to do something to delay it."

Shelby laughed. "How the hell am I going to do that?"

"When they say, 'Does anyone here have any objections', you object."

"Are you insane? Don will *kill* me."

"He won't kill you. He'll be pissed off."

"Really pissed off."

"So what if he's pissed off? You have to help me. If you don't want to do that, maybe you cab flash your tits."

She sighed and sad, "Look, Sherri. You don't want to get married? Then don't. But don't make me do it. This is your thing."

When she sighed, a large figure cut in front of them, and stood looming over Shelby, blocking her sun. Flipping up her shades to get a clear view, she caught his toothy grin.

"Hi, Marion," she said to Antonio's cop friend. Seeing him immediately made her feel guilty about Antonio. Another issue to talk about with Serina.

He smiled and whistled. "How long you been out here, darlin'? And why haven't you called me yet?"

She laughed. "Marion, this is my triplet sister, Sherri."

He whistled and nodded approvingly at Sherri. Kissed the back of her hand same as he had done with Shelby. "Where do you live, foxy doll?"

Sherri smiled back. "California."

"Oh, California, huh? Hey, shit, I never been there, but lookin' at you two makes me want to go. If you're any indication, they sure do grow 'em lovely on the west coast. You two ladies watch yourself here, though. You stay in this sun much longer you'll end up dark as me. So why haven't you called me yet?" he asked Shelby again.

She laughed some more. "Marion. Please. I mean…."

"Oh hey shit, come on now. You get that Ricky Ricardo man of yours ass in gear, we gots to all get together, that's what I'm talking about. Bring this sweet, charming sister along." He gave Sherri another wink. "Maybe later tonight?"

"I can't," Sherri answered him. "She can't either. I'm getting married tonight."

"Married?" Marion recoiled. "Oh my GOD, darling, WHY?"

Sherri looked as though she was ready to cry, and Marion stumbled to backpedal. "Oh, my bad, my bad, there, Sherri. No offense, darlin'. None at all. I was just overcome with a feeling of deep personal loss, a gorgeous honey like you being taken off the market. It'll be great, though, great."

"But, I don't *want* to get married!" Sherri nearly yelled.

Marion knelt down next to her, nodding his head in understanding. "MmHm. What's going on? Pregnant? Are you pregnant? Is that what we're talking about here?"

"No!"

"Oh. Is he rich? Is that it? You're marrying for money?"

"NO!"

"Oh. Well, hey shit. Then. You don't want to do it, don't do it. That's all Marion can tell you," he rose up to his full height again. "Listen. I've got to get into work, but you, Jacobs, either you or your man give me a call. He knows my digits, we gots to get together. And you, *Miss* Sherri Jacobs, good luck tonight. Hey, shit, don't do anything I wouldn't do." He bowed and walked away.

Sherri blurted out, "Let's go shopping now. We have to get something to wear."

So they went to the mall to shop at Neiman Marcus (Needless Markups) for dresses. She found hers quickly. "I'm not actually getting married in this anyhow. Fuck it. It's good enough. Don't you think it's good enough?"

"It's not white," Jacobs answered. It wasn't. It was a grey color. "You should at least fake it. Get something white."

"Alright!" She bitched and searched around awhile. "You can't let this happen," she reminded Shelby as she tried on another one. Came out looking stunning in it. With her blond hair and blue green eyes, and a nice dark tan, the white looked fantastic on her.

"You look drop-dead beautiful," said Shelby. It was not a traditional wedding dress. A white dress with some sparkly beads along it. A cocktail dress. Short, showing off her legs, skin tight, very low cut, no back. Extremely slinky.

"You can't let this happen," she said again. "I don't want to marry him."

"Sherry, you have to tell him that then. Save everyone the trouble of this whole thing. Just tell him, he'll understand."

"No he won't." She searched in her purse, brought out a smoke, and went to light it up.

"Ok, Lucky Strike," Shelby took it from her. "You can't smoke in a clothing store."

"This is Vegas," she retorted.

"Nevertheless."

Huffing out, she picked out a dress for Shelby. It looked great on the hanger, shitty on the body, at least Shelby's body. From inside the dressing room, "This sucks. It makes my boobs look bad."

"Impossible," she answered back.

"No, really. It squishes them down." She stepped out and showed her.

"Take that off," she said. "It's not good. And it won't work if you need to flash your tits."

They found one for her finally. It was the black version that matched hers. They purchased them and headed to the shoe section to check it out. While they we're looking at shoes, she pleaded again, "Please. I'll owe you one. You have to do something."

Shelby sighed as she looked at a really cool pair of Manolo Blahnik silver mules. "I really like these shoes," was her response.

"If I buy you those shoes will you promise to wreck my wedding?"

"They're nine hundred bones," she pointed out.

"How about if I buy you a few shots instead?"

"Listen, do you think so many women have a shoe hang up because of Cinderella? Or do women just like buying and wearing shoes?"

"Since when do you have a shoe hang up?"

"I don't think I do. But I like these. I've never had a nice pair of shoes. I've never worn anything this dressed up before. These are like Cinderella shoes, check it out. These are *actually* silver, dude! See that, on the heel? It's not silver colored, it is *real* silver. I like silver."

"Shelby, forget the shoes for a minute. We have to figure this out. How am I going to get out of this wedding?"

"Manolo Blahnik is what those *Sex and the City* chicks wear. I always wanted a pair of Jimmy Choo shoes, though. It's fun to say isn't it? Jimmy Choo shoes. Jimmy Choo shoes. Jimmy Choo shoes."

"Will you please pay attention to me?"

"Come on, say it once, Jimmy Choo shoes."

"Jimmy Choo shoes," she said, exasperated.

"There you go. Now use that as your mantra. Concentrate on that, keep saying 'Jimmy Choo shoes' and the answer will come to you."

"Are you going to help me or not? Are you really going to let this happen when you know it's a mistake?"

"I don't know how to walk in heels, but I think I could manage it for a little while. I don't know, though. It's a lot of money. Doesn't it seem sort of, I don't know, frivolous? Grossly selfish, even? To spend that kind of money on a pair of shoes just for me?"

A deep sigh. "If I encourage you to buy the shoes, will you help me get out of this wedding?"

"Am I ever going to wear them again? I mean, here's the thing. If I buy these shoes FOR your wedding, and then I help you to NOT get married, weren't the shoes really not only frivolous, but also futile?"

"Life is futile and frivolous, Shelby. I think you're allowed to buy yourself a pair of expensive shoes if you want them."

"So you think I should buy them then? Even though you won't actually be getting married tonight? I mean, the dresses were one thing, but…" She bent down and set the left shoe next to her foot, lining up to see if it looked like it would fit properly.

"You want to know what I think? I think those shoes were absolutely made for you. You need to have those shoes. You deserve to have those shoes…No, you know what? You've earned those shoes. You will earn those shoes by helping me get out of this mess."

Shelby slipped it on, saying, "They aren't Jimmy Choo. It's not as fun to say Manolo Blahnik shoes. Manolo Blahnik mules have a nice sound though. Still…that's so much money. Manolo mules. Manolo mules."

"3Jacobs. That shoe looks stunning on you. You have to get it. I insist on it. "

"I don't know. I'm a little short on cash, you know? After spending all that money on a wedding present for you guys. For a wedding you don't want to have now."

"I'll buy one of them."

"I mean, geez, this'll be the what? Fifth wedding present I've gotten you now. And the fifth wedding you are *not* having. That's a lot of presents, isn't it?" Shelby was referring to all the weddings Sherri planned, five different guys, and each time she cancelled the wedding.

"3Jacobs," she pleaded. "I'm begging you! Please…!"

It was really serious with Sherri when she started pleading. She believed it emphasized the bond between them. Shelby felt it was manipulative.

"You never returned any of those presents, 2Jacobs. Oh yeah, and I gave you the cash for renting the boat tonight. You think you'll be getting that money back? If I had that money back I could afford these shoes. Oh yeah, that's right, if you would get the money back *now* I wouldn't need shoes, now would I?"

Quietly, she reached in her purse and dug out a credit card, passing it over to her. "I'll buy you the shoes. Are you happy now? I just quit my job and moved away from home and I can't afford them either. But if it's the only way you'll help me, I'll do it."

Shelby kicked them off, picked it up and headed to the register to get its mate. "So, do you want to go get dressed in your room for this wedding that I'm going to wreck? Or do you want to come to our suite with me?"

She breathed in deeply with relief. Shelby knew all day that she would help her. Quite frankly, she could care less if Don was pissed at her or not. She just wanted Sherri to sweat it out and at least consider fixing her own mess.

She started babbling again. "Ok, um, I'll go to my room, everything is there. But we have to talk about this. You should come with me. What are you going to do exactly?"

"2Jacobs, relax," she replied. "And put your plastic away. I'll buy my own shoes. I was just fucking with you."

"No, really. We have to figure out how this will go so there are no mistakes. What if he blows you off? Or what if I panic? What are you going to do as a backup plan?"

"Don't you fucking push me right now, Sherri. You will buy these things if you piss me off."

She stayed off her back as they finished up. In fact, she ran outside to grab a smoke as Shelby tried on and paid for the Cinderella slippers. She tried to get her to come up to her room to stay with her while they get dressed for the wedding, but Shelby blew her off, telling her all her stuff was in her suite. She tried to get her to come in for drink, but she blew that off, too.

"No, I don't want to drink when I'm driving a rental car, that wouldn't be cool. Besides, it's about time for me to pick Harlin up."

"What if Don comes up to the room?"

"Well, Sher, then just act all lovey dovey. Or tell him. Tell him it's off."

"3Jacobs!"

"Fine, then just act normal. Whatever."

"I still don't know what you're going to do to stop this," she pushed again.

"Stop! Just, relax, ok? I don't know what I'm going to do either. What do you care? Huh? What does it matter? I'm telling you, I'll take care of it and you will not be married tomorrow? Isn't that enough? Don't you prefer that?"

She nodded and went inside, and Shelby pulled out of the hotel parking lot. 8 hours, 53 laps in the pool, $12.54 in gasoline and $900 worth of shoes since she'd dropped him off, Shelby picked up Harlin from Bellagio's, hoping

Antonio wasn't around to see her, staying in the car in the main turn around, then taking off quickly once Harlin was settled in the car.

The wedding was set for midnight, a little less than four hours away, but they were supposed to be there early to go over details or whatever. Even earlier to have drinks. It couldn't be too confusing, she got the scaled back package without pirates flying all over and explosions going off. Just Sherri, Don, Shelby, Harlin and the official performing the ceremony. Don didn't even have a friend to be the best man; which didn't surprise Shelby in the least.

"She doesn't want to get married," she told Harlin after he slid in the car on the passenger side and they were driving.

"Cool," he said. "We can just meet her then go somewhere like 54 or something."

"No, she's going to the ceremony. She refuses to tell Don she doesn't want to get married. She wants me to do it."

"Whoa, that's bullshit," he replied.

"I don't know what to do," said Shelby. "She won't let me tell him that she doesn't want to marry him. She just wants me to stop the ceremony."

"What are you gonna do, huh?"

"I don't know! I don't know what to do!"

"Want me to do it? I'll tell him."

She laughed. "You'd sort of enjoy it, wouldn't you?"

Grinning, "A little."

Chapter 33

Serina Jacobs had retrieved her voice mail messages. Shelby was back in Vegas with Sherri for Sherri's wedding. So, Serina did the only sane thing she could after bolting from Antonio in Tahoe. She ran to her sister. Caesars had no problem giving 'Shelby' another card key. In the suite, she found Shelby's room, helped herself to one of her swimsuits, tossed her dirty clothes in a pile on the floor, threw on some casual clothes over her swimsuit, then stopped downstairs at the bar. It was too early for Vince, Shelby's buddy, to be on. She sucked down a couple of vodkas and smoked two cigarettes. She weaved through the hallways, found the pool and went for an evening swim.

Not to clear her head, but to think more sharply.

As she kicked and splashed through the water, all she wanted to do was escape her confusion. Escape from herself. Essentially, she had done precisely that when she made the conscious decision to remain dead and walk in Shelby's world as Shelby.

But now she was confused about everything; more confused than when she lived her crazy, useless life as Serina. Jangled, tangled, twisted and contorted thoughts. And on top of everything else, she wasn't sure why she ran exactly. Even if Antonio knew Shelby, the real Shelby, she'd spent enough time with him to realize he loved her, meaning her, Serina, right? Truth be told, she was still perplexed about how a guy like Antonio could fall so hard for her.

Skimming through the water, only one thing shined as clearly as the setting sun. A thought, a knowledge of inescapable truth:

She was a bitch. And she was wrong. She hated what she'd done. She hated herself.

She kicked harder, cutting the water harshly with her arms. Nothing made sense, nothing clicked except that one basic fact—she was insipid.

What the fuck had she done?

It was to be expected. She could have seen this coming. Antonio, he was a dumbfuck, he should have seen this coming. He knew how insecure she was. He was so fucking simple, he thought by making her look in a mirror, she would suddenly see a lovely, beautiful creature staring back at her just because he said it was so. *He* made her try to believe. He pushed her and pushed her and got her to trust him to the point she trusted herself and told him to trust her in return.

He really thought he could undo years worth of mirrors? He thought just because he accepted her it would wash away the cloying layers of rejection and indifference? She was supposed to trust a few weeks of cooing and cuddling over innumerable dismissals and rejections, especial when it came to artistic talent? Talent he knew absolutely nothing about because he had no clue who she really was. She'd been living a lie from the moment she'd laid eyes on him. Of course back then, she honestly believed she was Shelby.

Infuriated, she thrashed through the water. Why shouldn't she have believed him? She was revolting. Blaming HIM now? That's how sick she was? Of course she trusted him. She wanted to. He was not blame. Just like he wasn't to blame for laying it all out and offering to make her happy. She craved happiness. She wanted to believe him.

No, Antonio was not to blame. Her fucking inescapable self-doubt was to blame along with her false identity.

Panting, she flipped and kicked even harder. Loathing herself for what she'd done, for succumbing to fear and letting that hurt him. And then it suddenly crystallizes.

She only had these insecurities and fears because other people put them there. It was incomprehensible to blame Antonio for treating her right just because other people treated her shitty. Fuck *them!* They were to blame for this. She was to blame, she did this. But she had a shitload of help over the years.

Goddamn right she was going to Jerry Springer this bullshit and turn it externally. Wasn't that the right way to handle this mess? She was the guilty party but fuck it, this was the twenty-first century now, and everyone knew that every convict was also a victim. Fuckin'-A right. She was a victim here. She was not taking this rap alone.

She huffed out of the pool, setting her sights, knowing exactly who she needed to confront. As she stormed across the pavement, she passed a man and he lightly grabbed her arm.

"What?" she whirled on him and snapped.

"Sorry, I didn't mean to startle you, I just wanted to say hello."

It was Jarred, the PR director of the hotel. The guy who obviously had the hots for Sherri. "Oh. Hello. I'm Shelby, not Sherri."

They exchanged pleasantries and he glanced around the area, finally asking, "Your sister, Sherri. Is she here with you?"

Oh the poor bastard. "Sorry, no."

"Will you tell her I asked about her? She's quite saucy, isn't she?"

"Listen, Jarred. Do you like women who drink constantly?"

Him shrugging. "I'm Irish, so…"

"I'll tell her you said hello." Hey, what the hell, she wasn't married yet.

She dried off, cleaned up and tucked back into clothes, but didn't cool off in the least.

She stood in line to pay to get in, hellbent on having her say here. As they were running her card to print up her ticket, she dragged on a cigarette and the smoke must carry some miniscule amount of rationality with it. Because another wave of clarity hit and she stopped and thought for the first time about what she was doing. And this clearly was not the most judicious thing she could do. It probably didn't come close to the sordid cowardice of running from Tahoe, but she knew it was wrong.

The girl behind the cage passed her plastic back to her along with a ticket as she snuffed her butt. Telling herself to keep calm, keep this grasp on reality. The ticket was already paid for, so she might as well go in, just for entertainment. She wouldn't even bother going over to her. Serina would just go down there and have a few drinks in the dark by the fire pit. Because she was sane, and she was logical, and she was mature. She alone held the shovel that dug this hole. She was responsible for her actions, and it was Serina who was wrong. She was not a victim here, she was the offender.

Antonio was the victim. She did this to him, and she had to find a way to atone. Briefly, she considered ditching out and going to find him. Calling him, going to his place, anything.

But she still didn't know what to say. Worse, she didn't know if she could handle it. Whatever option he chose, be it anger, blame, pleading or just despair, all the options were too much for her to handle right at the moment. She couldn't handle any of it right now. Not only was she a bitch, she was a craven, spineless bitch. So, she allowed the guilt to wash over her, pushed her way past the wizard at the door to go drown the waves of self-contempt in vodka, reminding herself to at least stop this streak. She'd been cruel enough to Antonio, she couldn't lash out at someone else now, too. Just be human. Be nice.

But when she came out of the darkened hallway and into the rotund hall, Serina saw her leaning against the bar, talking to another couple. A hot flash of anger bolted through her guts at seeing them together, wondering what she was saying to them. Probably wishing them a happy life, no, promising them a happy life together—after all, it was in the cards. Her in those blue beads and slutty, gauzy outfit.

She played it cool, sauntering up to the bar behind her and ordering a drink, eavesdropping on their conversation.

Her nectared voice dolled out goodwill, "…extreme prosperity in the near future."

Rationality flew right out the proverbial window when she heard that.

"You Goddamn tarty, smarmy, bead-wearing, dream-crushing, prognosticating, tarot reading, come-hither, cloying, heartless, insufferable, snotty, saccharine BITCH!" She knocked her deck of cards off the bar, sending them fluttering to the floor.

So much for being nice.

She stared at Serina, glittered lashes seemingly glued open in shock. The other couple backed away slowly, as if any sudden movement on their part could draw Serina's attention to them.

Too late. She focused on them like a laser.

"What'd she say to you? Huh? What'd she say? She tell you that you'll be happy? Or did she tell you that you're condemned to a life of silent, solitary desperation?"

The man backed away in horror, leaving his woman to reach out for him and find nothing but thin air before she stumbled away, too. *Valdez would have never done that. He'd have pulled close or pushed her behind him. He'd have protected her from a shrieking, shrewish bitch on a rampage.* Screw them anyhow. They didn't matter. Serina turned back to her, picked a remaining card off the bar and threw it in her face as someone seized her arm gently, and started asking her to calm down. She shouted after them, "Oh, go ahead, run away, everybody runs away."

The fortuneteller stuttered, "I, I don't know what you're talking about…"

"You don't remember me? You don't remember what you told me? Liar."

Suddenly contrite, sweet, "I don't! I'm sorry if I gave you bad news, I didn't mean anything, I was just…I don't remember, I see a lot of people in here."

The intruder tried to defuse the situation, asking Serina to be calm, to lower her voice. Asking if he could help her. Serina blew him off entirely, already blazing at full throttle, all her self-loathing suddenly finding an external object upon which to focus and vent her frustration.

"You," Serina hissed. "You told me I'd be alone, I'd never have love. FUCK YOU!" There was a tug on her arm, a voice speaking to her, calling her Ma'am. Ignoring it, she stuck her finger in the woman's face. "I *had* a man. I had the perfect man, and I left him. I left him because of YOU. Because YOU told me it wouldn't be real. You're nothing, you're nothing but a sham, this is just entertainment, and you had to say something that vicious to me? Why would you do that? Why would you be so cruel?"

Incensed, she ripped her arm free from the person holding it, shouting louder as suddenly more bodies appeared to restrain her. A fake wizard placed his body between them, but she struggled to get around him, to get free of the holds. Screaming now, "I should SUE your ass, I should KICK your ass. I want an answer, dammit! Why would you say those things to me? WHY?!"

She stared dumbly. Not the dumb-fucker look exactly. The terrified, shocked, dumb fucker look as the arms around Serina started dragging her farther from her.

"Is it entertaining for YOU? Is that it? You go home and giggle over telling some people they're in for trouble? You made it a self-fulfilling prophecy for me, you bitch! Do you hear me? I LEFT him because of that doubt and he was PERFECT."

She wrenched and strained, clawing out for her. But they were too strong. They had her off her feet and were carrying her away in an upright position. "PHONY!" she shouted at her, physically relenting to them. "You're a PHONY and you know it!"

Her mouth curved with a sadistic, smug grin as she stared back at Serina. "Then why'd you listen to me if I'm a phony?"

Serina lunged, actually breaking most of the holds on her and made a dash. Only got two steps ahead before they had her again, but it was far enough to make her cringe and retreat a few steps. Once Serina was back in their grip, being hustled out, she became bold. There were two guys on her, one holding each arm, pulling her away. The bitch batted her sparkling lashes and tossed her veil over one shoulder, walking, still out of Serina's reach, but walking with them. She continued, "If you know it's only entertainment, why would you believe me?"

"I didn't believe you. I don't believe you, it just…you're a dumb BITCH for saying that to me."

"I'm a dumb bitch? I'm not the one who left her boyfriend because of something an entertainer told her. Check yourself out, get under control. Then come back and see me, I'll read you for free a third time."

"I KNEW you remembered me." Serina sprang at her again but couldn't break free from her restraints.

Giggling, "If you ever see him again, send your boyfriend back, too. He was cute. I'd do more than read his cards."

"SLUT!"

And then Serina was hustled out as a guy in a suit tries to placate her, $78.60 worth of anger hurled within what was probably less than a total of seven minutes. The suit ended up giving her a voucher for a free buffet after she told him what that suave charlatan bitch said to her. And, well, thus ended that ugly little episode, so she shrugged and looked around. Mission completed, that was a lovely little diversionary ploy to temporarily get her mind off the more pressing and unpalatable matters.

"Shelby?"

Serina turned around. It was that guy from the art gallery showing. Taylor somebody. She smiled, attempting to look normal once again.

"I'm been looking for you. They told me at the front desk you'd either be down here somewhere or at a wedding at Treasure Island. I'm so glad I found you!"

Hmmm…Had to be some guy Shelby knew personally. What the hell! It was time for her secret to come out. Serina was on a role! There was only one way. "You want to come over to Treasure Island with me to the wedding?" She aimed for an alluring smile and batting of the eyelashes. He fell for it hook, line, and sinker.

"I'd love to!"

An off they went.

Chapter 34

Meanwhile, Shelby was now up in the hotel suite getting ready when there was a knock at the door. Maybe it was the Vodka she'd ordered. She opened the door.

Leaning on the doorframe, dark eyes searing into her, "Yo, you fuckin kiddin me?"

Fucking Vince or fucking Marion. Sold her up the river and told Antonio she was in town. Damn!

Her heart dropped to her feet as she stood there, numb. Dumbly.

"Well?" Antonio straightened up, cocked a brow expectantly. Antagonistically. "Huh? Cat got your tongue? 'Zat why you left, ran out o' shit to say? That it?"

Shallow breath and sweating palms, she had no choice but to step aside as he moved past her, walking into the room.

"Uh…"

"Uh? UH?! That's all you got to say to me?"

"I really love you? I'm really sorry?"

"SHUT UP!"

"Right," she nodded and turned away, started closing the door when the room service waiter appeared, so she stepped back again and let him through as Antonio began pacing around in the living room. He stopped to look at the cart and snorted derisively. Points at the bottle of vodka, "Nice. Really fuckin nice, Jacobs. Glad you're havin fun."

She pursed her lips and nodded at the waiter as he handed her the bill. "Everything look all right, Ms. Jacobs?"

"Yes, fine, thank you," she signed on his tip and passed the pen and paper back to him.

He hovered momentarily. "Can I get you anything else then?"

"No. No thanks."

"Well…have a good evening?"

"Thank you." She showed him to the door, nodding again, giving him a wink to let him know he didn't have to worry.

At least she hoped not.

Hovering by the cart, unable to look directly at Antonio. "Do you want a drink?" she offered.

"Fuck you."

"Right." With a shaking hand, she picked up a glass, started filling it with ice.

"What the FUCK you doin?"

"Yes. I'm fixing a drink. You sure you don't want one? Got plenty."

Accusing, "You really wanna drink right now?"

"No, but I think I'm going to need one before long."

"Put. The glass. Down. NOW."

She obeyed. He stalked over, lifted her chin roughly, searched her eyes. "You drunk already?"

"No." He was beginning to piss her off.

He turned away. Hands up in the air. One word. "Why?"

Silence.

"WHY?" Spinning around, Antonio pinned her in his glare. Cat quick, he threw her glass of ice against the wall over her head, yelling as it shattered, "WHY, GODDAMNIT?"

Mouselike, barely a whisper, "I don't know." She knew she should of told him she was in town. Damn!

"You don't KNOW?"

"Scared. I was scared."

"So you fuckin LEAVE? You leave me in TAHOE?"

What the fuck was he talking about? Tahoe. Serina. Shit, what the hell happened?

He got in her face and Shelby dropped her eyes. "You bein funny now? Is this a joke? Or you just don't have a conscience, is that it?"

"No, I'm not being funny." She squirmed and he grabbed hold of her arms, shaking her once. God, she didn't know what to say. If only she had a clue of what went down with Serina.

Shaking her again, "I should fuckin hate you. You LEFT me. You know how long I sat there waiting? Huh? Do you?"

"No."

"A long fuckin time, Shelby! Cause I didn't believe it. I wouldn't fuckin believe it. You made an asshole outta me."

"You're not an asshole."

"Well you must think I'm something to leave like that. The fuck you do? Drove straight down here? I didn't know for sure until Marion called me, telling me you were here for Sherri's wedding." He shoved her away.

She winced. "No. I, I…, well, yeah. I'm here because Sherri's getting married. I forgot and had to leave. I wouldn't hurt you by leaving for no good reason." What happened up there?

"Oh you wouldn't? You wouldn't. Yeah, I never woulda thought you'd ditch me like that neither."

"I'm sorry."

"You're sorry?"

"I'm sorry I hurt you. I'm sorry I did that. I'm sorry I came here and left without telling you."

"Better be fuckin sorry."

"I am. I just didn't know what else to do. Sherri was counting on me…"

"So you didn't care how much you hurt me? So you LEFT me? That makes sense? What sorta fuckin asshole are you?"

It felt like the room was moving under her feet. Like it was expanding and contracting around her with his breathing. Quietly, "I really am sorry." She became aware of crocodile tears leaking out of her eyes. Unfortunately, so did he.

"Oh, fuckin cry, Jacobs. Ain't gonna work." He hardened more, lunged at her, grabbing her and shoving her back until she cracked into the wall. Shouting, "I wanna know WHY!"

"STOP PUSHING ME!" she screamed, finally looking him in the face. He didn't back off or release her. Instead, he gripped tighter, and she caught a surreal look to him. Feral. Aimed at her. It was nearly unfathomable, bending her brain as the room spun around her. Like he wasn't Antonio anymore; he'd morphed into some cloneish being and all the contemptible jealousy and shadowy violence was bubbling to the surface. Threatening, a dangerous specter of something she knew and loved. And both Shelby and Serina had done this to him. It wasn't right. It needed to be fixed, if it even was fixable.

And then, poof, it was gone, and became Antonio. Enraged, but Antonio. In her face, demanding an answer.

Shaking her, "GodDAMNIT, WHY?"

"Because you don't understand. I need to explain, everything, but after the wedding."

"WHY? Why can't you explain now?"

"Because I have to do this for Sherri first!"

His grip slackened and he backed off. Angrily shoving the room service cart out of his way as he paced around. "You don't know what the fuck you want, Jacobs."

"Bullshit."

"Bullshit? Think you me happy by running away when I ask you to spend the rest of your life with me?"

"You asked me to MARRY you, Antonio?" Oh….my….GOD!

"What? You don't remember my proposing to you? And running away. Running all the way down here to Vegas?"

"That's…that's not right."

"Oh it ain't? You know why you're fuckin did it? Cause you WANNA marry me." He pointed at her, moved back in, stuck his finger in her chest, then up to her chin, forcing her to look up at him again. "You fuckin know if you don't jump on this you'll never fuckin have anything like it again. And you're so scared o' losin it that you're willing to throw it away. And you'll try an' get it back and you never fuckin will, not with anyone else, Jacobs. Only me."

She slapped his hand away and took a step back. Infuriated. "Is that some sort of threat? No one else could ever love me? I'm so lucky to have you because no one else ever could? If I'm that unworthy then why the fuck do YOU want me?"

He shook his head with grim laughter. "Dumbfuck. That ain't what I'm sayin. You could walk outta here right now, get a hundred guys to fall in love with you by morning. But it won't matter, cause I'm the only guy YOU love. I'm the only guy you ever loved."

The sting and pressure of tears threatened behind her eyes again as the whole room lurched. She held her head in her hands to get it all to stop, too much confusion, too much conflict. Antonio reached out to hold her shoulders, gently this time. Shelby searched his face and all she knew for certain was that part of what he said was true. "I do love you, Antonio." The problem was, who did he actually love? Serina or her? Maybe he loved the combination of their two personalities. God, she did not have time for this right now.

"Then don't make this so fuckin hard, Shelby. I love you, too. Ain't that enough?"

"Yes."

"Then you will?"

She started reeling again, her knees getting weak. "Will what?"

"Marry me."

"Antonio," her stomach turned, "I can't give you an answer right now. I told you, I have to deal with Sherri's problems first."

"Fuck!" He shoved her away. "WHY?"

"Because I have to go back there, they need me. Sherri wants me to stop the wedding, but *during* the wedding."

"They don't fuckin need you. They don't want you. They want you and need you to do stuff for them. I just want YOU, don't you fuckin get that?"

"You're…you're pushing me. Please stop. We can talk later. Just not right now!"

He spun and paced again, looking out the window. He sighed. "It's about the money, ain't it? Admit it."

"It's NOT. That's NOTHING." She was really working into a high pitched angry scream.

"So it's just ME then, that it? You just don't really wanna be with me."

"Jesus, you fucking idiot, NO. That's not IT.

"Then why the FUCK did you LEAVE ME?"

Exasperated, taking in a slow, long, deep breath, "Probably so I wouldn't have to go through THIS! Look, I know you don't understand, but I need to explain some things to you later"

"What? You're just a whore that wants to fuck all the time?"

Her face burned with the sting of that. She acted on impulse, and her hand flew up and slapped him across the face. "Fuck you!" she snarled, shaking herself, watching him recoil, seeing the red mark across his face. And then she went too far. "Is this about the money, Antonio? You tell me. Is it?"

"The fuck you talkin' about? That ain't why I want you, that's not it, you know that's not it," he shook his head but he suddenly calmed.

"When did you make me as a card counter?" she decided to throw out there. She knew Serina'd also been gambling with him.

"Huh?"

"When? Was it that first day? You just didn't say anything? IS this about the money, Antonio? Is that why you came after me so hard? The money from my job and the money from my gambling?"

"You want the fuckin truth? Do you?"

"YEAH! I want the truth!"

He came in close, his breath creeping across her face. "I came after you cause I wanted to fuck you. That's all. Yeah, I knew you card counted. Shit, everybody in Vegas knows you card count. Yeah, I'm an undercover cop, working with Marion. They told me to keep an eye on you. I told them you were only counting for recreation. I saved your butt. You know why? Because I fell in love with you."

She sat down, those tears finally winning. She tried to talk. Let the tears flow for a minute, tried again. "Antonio, I'm beggin you, please come to Sherri's wedding with me. Then, after, we can straighten this all out. I swear to you, it'll all make sense."

It was time. She needed Serina. The truth had to come out.

Twenty minutes later, she and Antonio agreed to get ready for the wedding. Yeah, tears did still work with the guys.

Chapter 35

So now that they knocked that out of the way, they got ready for the night. "So I should look good tonight?" he called out from her bedroom in the suite while she finished showering.

"You always look good." Where was Harlin? He was supposed to be Don's best man.

Hopefully he was just going to meet them at Treasure Island. Yeah, that had to be it. Harlin wouldn't let her down.

"You know what I mean. I gotta be stylin for this non-wedding."

He nearly knocked her out when she saw him all spiffed and shined up. She'd explained about Harlin, Serina's ex-boyfriend sharing the suite. He hadn't been thrilled about it, but they both discovered they wore the same size and decided to borrow some of Harlin's clothes. Now he was in black as he almost always was. But this was something else.

"You look hot!" She couldn't help but wonder what he might look like in a cop's uniform. The very thought made her feel all tingly. Then, still in a towel, she showed him her new shoes as she attempted her first few hesitant steps in them. She was wobbly. Really wobbly. She got the dress pulled on and went into the bathroom for a few minutes to put on makeup and pull up her hair.

She dug through the small leather makeup case and her fingers stumbled over a few chips thrown in haphazardly with the seldom used mascara and eyeliners. She picked one up, it's from the Hard Rock, a thousand bucks. She'd nearly forgotten about them, from several trips ago, the extra chips she didn't want to cash in. It heartened her. Like found money. She flipped one through her fingers, then put it back away. It covered the wedding and the shoes, though. That was pretty cool. Time to get her ass in gear and play a little devious game on good old Don. She was going to enjoy this. She'd already left a message for Serina to get her ass down here. Antonio deserved to know the truth.

He just whistled and stared when Shelby came back into the bedroom. She faltered when she looked up instead of watching her own precarious footsteps. Her heel slid sideways and she stumbled. Immediately, she became engrossed in a nervous flashback concerning Dr. Scholl's. Their mom had bought her and her sisters a pair to wear one summer. Serina would flip flop around nonchalantly in hers as would Sherri, but Shelby's were always sliding forward so that she would catch that hard wood edge of the heel right in her soft instep. Standing back up and adjusting the shoe, she realized that now for some inexplicable reason, she had just spent 900 bucks on a similar, higher, pointy-heeled version of designer hell.

"Holy shit, Jacobs," said Antonio.

"I know, I'm a dumbass. I don't know if I can wear these now and I don't have anything else."

"Not that, chica. Yo, that ain't what I mean."

"Huh?" She started grabbing all her stuff, smokes, lighter, ID, money, lip stuff. Shoving it into a little sparkly purse she had. Faltered again as she stepped to the doorway of the living room. "Shiznit!"

"Tu eres tan lindo, Shelby," he said. "Mi Dios. I can't believe…tu estas el mio."

"Huh? Antonio, we don't have time again," she said, still worried about her balance.

"No, not that. It's just, holy shit. You look amazing."

"Yeah? Grazie, baby. So do you."

"No, I mean, really. You look different like that."

"These shoes are making me taller," she stood next to him. "At least a few inches."

He chuckled and looked down. "Estoy en amor con tu." He kissed her forehead.

"Can I hold on to you as I walk, Antonio? Try to keep my balance 'til I'm used to these things?" And as she hung on to his arm, it really did steady her and make it easier.

They both met Sherri at Treasure Island's Gold Bar, mainly because she refused to go back to Swashbuckler's again. She looked stunning all done up in her dress and Shelby told her so. It made her tan look really dark, her eyes sparkle brightly. But her face was contorted with anxiety. "You need to chill out," Shelby reminded her.

"I can't. I can't stand this."

"Well, how about this? Once Don gets down here, I'll just talk to him and tell him it's not going to happen tonight."

"NO! No, you can't. He'll kill me! He'll kill me, 3Jacobs. I told you, you have to DO something. Flash your tits if you have to."

"Alright," she sighed.

"What then? What are you going to do?"

"When they ask for objections I'll throw a hissy fit."

"Over what? What are you going to say?"

"I'll just say that you shouldn't be getting married without all your other friends around. And then if Don gets pissed at me, I'll go off on him. It'll make a big scene and you won't have any choice but to call it off."

"Are you sure you can handle that?"

"Not a problem," she answered and waved to the bartender. "I just need a few toddies before I do this."

"Yo, what if they don't have that part, asking for objections?"

"They have to, they always do."

"Nah, huh uh, I don't think so. 'Specially in these shorter ones."

"Antonio, you're trippin. It's standard. They'll ask that."

"I'm just sayin, maybe you know, you should think of somethin else just in case."

Shelby glanced over at Sherri, who was watching this exchange and getting noticeably more jittery as it continued. "Don't worry about it. They'll ask for objections."

Three vodka sodas (Shelby's), five shots of tequila (four Antonio's, one Sherri's), five beers (one his, four Sherris's), one half pack of cigarettes (split between Shelby and Sherri) and exactly 93 minutes later:

Don met them outside the door to board the boat. He marveled over Sherri for a couple minutes, and Shelby didn't blame him one bit. For his part, he looked crisp and clean, very neatly pressed and dapper in a light grey suit with monochrome tie.

"Shit, Don," said Shelby, "that hotel iron did a really good job. Looks as good as the Rowenta."

"Oh, this is the Rowenta," he nodded and checked out his own creases.

"You brought it out here with you?"

"This was an important occasion."

"You lugged an IRON to Vegas?"

"How often does someone get married? I wanted to look my best."

And—Well, I didn't know how often some people get married, but I knew that Sherri did NOT get married pretty often. The number five wedding cancellation. Gee, would Sherri ever really get married? And as she looked at Don and how he was looking at Sherri and Shelby began thinking about how he lugged that iron all the way out here, she really couldn't help but feel sorry for the guy. Because, yes, he was annoying and Shelby didn't think he treated Sherri very well, but she still didn't like seeing anyone get their heart broken.

And as they made their way out onto the permanently docked boat where pirates dove off amid explosions, Shelby stumbled up the stairs leading onto the deck, and Antonio caught her with a laugh and prevented her from reeling and knocking into Don.

It was a stunning night. Enough coolness even though it was a dry desert summer, with just the slightest breeze blowing. Harlin was there waiting for them. Shelby pried away from Antonio and arranged herself next to Sherri as Harlin stood next to Don on the other side. Suddenly, a whole lot of voices could be heard behind them in the salon. Shelby turned around to see what all the commotion was about and to ask them to shush it.

But, before she could open her mouth, Harlin's voice called out, "Serina?" Shelby looked at Harlin and Sherri, Harlin looked at Shelby Sherri, then back out behind them.

Shelby turned around all the way. Not ten feet away was Serina, standing next to Taylor, Shelby's golf course sex partner. "Shit!' she mumbled aloud, not because Serina was there, but because of Taylor.

From Harlin, "Oh, my God!" He was looking at the two people coming up the boat stairs; Michelle Morgan and Karl, Karl with a menacing look on his face, Michelle smiling at her caught victim, her fiancé.

Then Michelle Morgan realized there were three Jacobs on the boat with her, not just two. "Serina Jacobs?" she screamed out.

Antonio turned around to see what Harlin and Shelby were staring at and also opened his mouth in shock. He looked at Shelby. He looked at Sherri He looked at Serina. Then back at Shelby. Damn! There were THREE of them. All kinds of thoughts began fleeing across his mind. Oh, NO! The full implication began to dawn on him. OH, NO!

And just then the guy came out to recite the words and take the vows and make this all official, causing Shelby, Harlin, Sherri and Don to turn around and face him when the boat lulled beneath their feet. Shelby caught her footing and got a feel for the slight rock of it on the water as she focused her eyes on Sherri.

She looked terrified with her thousand-watt fake smile plastered across her face. She had a small bouquet shoved in her hands as the boat continued to slightly rock and her diamond glistened on her finger as she gripped the flowers and her back was rigid as she cunningly avoided eye contact with Don.

Shelby took a step back and quickly adjusted her footing again so that she could glance past Don and check out Harlin standing next to him, also a hot looking guy. She became lost. Would her sister, Serina, maybe focus on him once more? Yeah, it was selfish, but she wanted Antonio for herself; wanted him badly. She let the minister's words drown in the thick air, just feeling her brain buzz as the vodka pumped through her. Just thinking about Antonio in his dark suit, his dark hair, those liquidy, opaque, dark eyes blinking slowly and looking back at her, a little smile playing on his lips. Now he knew the truth. Serina. Shit, and he was a cop. *Shit!* And hadn't that been Michelle Morgan she just heard; the Michelle Morgan who spent a lot of money on Serina's paintings. The *dead* Serina. Michelle Morgan who was Harlin Radner's fiancé. Damn, it was getting crowded on this boat! She tried to keep a small part of her consciousness attentive to the proceedings at hand, ears searching for her cue.

She never heard them. Instead, within a couple minutes, she heard the man's voice asking, "Sherri, do you take Don to be your lawfully wedded…"

Antonio coughed, working her name into the hoarse rasp. "Uh-JACOBS-HUH."

Panicked, Shelby looked at Sherri, whose face was still a mask of petrified phony happiness. Her eyes flitted in Shelby's direction, but she didn't turn her head as the minister finished his question, "…until death do you part?"

OHMYOHSHITWHATDOIDONOW? Did she SERIOUSLY have no choice but to FLASH HER TITS??

Shelby took a quick step forward to get by Sherri's side, neurons firing to search for something to say, lurching with the rock of the boat as she stepped, one heel sliding sideways and reeling her, struggling for balance, recklessly lunging into Sherri as Shelby toppled.

Sherri steadied her, and dropped her flowers in the process. Glancing over at the men, Shelby saw that Don appeared mortified, made a move to pick up her flowers while Harlin stood by biting his cheek and one cocked brow. Handing Sherri's bouquet back to her, Don shot Shelby a look that said, "Get a hold of yourself," and shook Shelby's shoulder as he gave her a nudge back to her own spot.

Taking a brief glance behind her, seeing Serina with Taylor, Michelle Morgan with Karl, Antonio, Shelby saw her opening and went for it. She purposely stumbled back again, reaching and pulling Don's necktie for support. As she faked the stagger, the boat rocked again as if it were now on cue, her left tiny pointy heel slipped from beneath Shelby and she lurched for real, completely lost her balance and reeled back, tugging Don for support.

Got none.

Instead of steadying Shelby, he staggered forward into her as she pulled on him. Shelby fell back, he fell forward. Flying back. Not hitting the deck. Falling—

Falling OVER—

Shelby shouting, "SHIIIIT!"

Don shouting, "SHIIIIIIIII…"

SPLASH.

Serina rushed up in a vain attempt to help her sister, Shelby. The boat lurched some more and Michelle Morgan and Karl who were directly behind her, bumped into Serina and she was falling.

SPLASH.

Karl tried to grab Michelle Morgan, but she followed OVER and INTO the water behind Serina, and Karl SPLASHED in behind Michelle.

Off the boat, into the drink. All of them all the way down into the pirate waters, Don landing on Shelby, water breaking the fall so she didn't get crushed. Struggling up, him still above her, she pushed him aside and kicked for the surface. Gulping for air, Shelby saw him do the same. Heard him shouting, "GODDAMNIT!" Then an instant gurgling of water.

Wave after wave of water splashing as more bodies hit the water.

And all Shelby could think of was, "MY SHOES!"

She only felt one on one of her feet, reached down and pulled it off as Don continued cursing and flapping in the water once he came back up for air. Then more bodies hit the surface, cussing, spraying more water all around.

Shelby tossed the remaining shoe up onto the deck above, and saw the minister, Harlin, Antonio, Taylor and Sherri all looking down at all of them splashing around. The minister looked concerned. Antonio and Taylor were cracking up, Harlin couldn't stop laughing, and Sherri was beaming a real smile, saying, "Shelby Jacobs, you're an asshole!"

"My shoe!" Shelby shouted back up to her. "My Manolo mule!" She dove back under but couldn't see a thing, the water was warm but unlit. Feeling her way down, it was at least 8 feet deep, so she couldn't cruise along the bottom too long. Shelby felt with her hands but didn't come across anything so she shot back up to the surface to catch her breath.

Back on the surface, Don was no longer flapping around, he was trying to climb back onto the boat, but the only entry he found was a thick rope net and when he attempted the climb he fell back down, swearing again.

Harlin was shouting down to Serina, "Serina, you're alive! I love you! Will you marry me?"

Serina screamed up to Harlin, "Yes, Harlin!" That was why she ran away from Antonio. Not only because of Shelby. She did still love Harlin. "Yes, yes, yes!" she shouted up to him.

Serina looked over at Shelby. "Shelby, Antonio wants to marry you. I think you should."

Shelby, "I love you, Serina."

Serina, "I love you, Shelby."

Michelle Morgan, "I'll sue your ass, Serina Jacobs, for pretending to be dead."

Harlin to Michelle Morgan, "Oh, give it a rest, Michelle! I've got more money than I know what to do with. I'll pay you and everyone who bought Serina's paintings double what they paid for them." Money always got through to Michelle.

"Did you find it?" Sherri shouted to Shelby.

"No! Is it up there?"

"I got the one you threw up here, I don't see another."

In the water again, Don screamed, "Fuck your shoe!"

"I don't think that's proper grammar, Don."

"You wrecked my wedding!"

"You pushed me!" Shelby shouted back.

For perhaps the first time, he was non-plussed. He just shouted and splashed water at Shelby.

From above, Antonio's voice, "Hey! Don't you fuckin splash her!"

Then Sherri, "Yeah, Don, don't be an asshole, you threw my sister in the water!"

Don screamed and kicked toward the boardwalk behind Karl, Michelle, and Serina, where they found the pirates' exit and crawled out. There were already four hotel guys waiting there for them, and then one came down the ramp toward the water, shouting to Shelby, "Come on, this way, get out of there."

"My SHOE! It's a Manolo mule!" she shouted, as if that explained it all.

"You can't be in there," he shouted back.

From above, Antonio again, "Jacobs, forget the shoe, just get out of there."

"Valdez! It's SILVER," she answered back and dove under again, searching the bottom frantically. She came up empty. "Dammit!"

"C'mon baby, get outta there, you're gonna get in trouble soon. It's just a shoe." She blew him off and dove under the water, holding her breath as long as she could before surfacing empty-handed. Heard him shout her name again. "Jacobs!"

"What?"

"Forget the shoe!" he yelled.

"Valdez!"

"What?"

"That shoe cost nine hundred dollars!" she yelled up to him.

"Jacobs!"

"What?"

"Find that fuckin shoe!"

So Shelby dove under again—nothing. Panting to catch her breath, she went again. Nothing. She heard him shout her name, looked up to see him with his jacket and shoes off, standing on the ledge of the boat. There were other hotel people up there now, ordering him to get down. Sherri took his tie from him and waved down at Shelby, mouthing, "thank you. I love you."

"Valdez, what are you doing?" Shelby shouted to him.

"I'm gonna rescue your shoe," he laughed, and stepped onto the railing, looking ready to dive in as the hotel guys started going bananas and shouting at him.

"Valdez, wait! Don't!" she shouted and saw him hesitate. "Don't jump in here."

"Is it cold?"

"No, it's nice. I mean, don't just jump in here. Use that rope," she pointed to it tied up next to his head. "Swing into the water."

And, well, he did. Serina, Harlin, Taylor who had joined them, Michelle, and yes, even Karl, cheered and clapped. More than anything, it cracked Shelby up. He didn't do a one-handed glide as he confidently winked at the crowd when he swung in. He more or less just grabbed on, shoved off, then let go with an unceremonious PLUNK down into the water.

That really brought the house down up on deck, where some gonzo was yelling at them to get out. "That shoe cost NINE HUNDRED DOLLARS!" Shelby screamed up to them, and they backed off with that. Shelby could already tell this would be the story of how she got kicked out of Treasure Island, but she could also tell that none of them wanted to be responsible or liable for paying for her $900. shoe, and since they didn't actually know at this point what happened to get Shelby in the water, they weren't going to fuck with her too much.

Shelby and Antonio took turns diving under the water to search, he dunked her a couple of times on his way up. While he was underwater one time, Shelby heard Sherri on the deck talking to a guy in a suit. "I was getting married and my fiancé and the minister accidentally pushed her in the water and she lost her shoe. It cost nine hundred dollars, and if she doesn't find it she's going to make me pay for it. I know she will."

"Well, miss, I'm sorry about your wedding..."

"Oh, that's ok. Noooo problem."

"Can we reschedule it for you?"

"No, not right now. Thank you."

"What sort of shoe costs nine hundred dollars?"

Shelby shouted up to him, "It's a Manolo Blahnik!"

"Oh, well then," he said. "Have you retrieved it yet?"

"No."

"Shall I send in some divers?"

So it was 24 exhausting dives under (Antonio finally came up with the shoe), two very drippy walks up the plank to get out of the water, one very stern lecture from a man in a suit, two apologies from other guys in suits, two big hugs from Sherri (one for Shelby and one for Antonio), countless promises of drinks forever on her, seven minutes of righteous ranting from Don (he chilled when

Sherri stuck it to him by saying, "Relax, I'm sure the Rowenta can iron out your wet suit), 78 minutes spent in their room as management laundered and dried their clothes (they insisted), two showers and 16 (comped) room service drinks later.

Shelby kicked off her shoes in the cab and could tell Antonio was in a pretty merry mood as he slung his arm around her shoulders and tapped his fingers in time to the music against her arm.

"So, is this the real Shelby Jacobs, and if so, will you marry me, chica," he said.

"Si."

Printed in the United States
61695LVS00006B/68

9 781424 158096